ALSO BY JOHN SANDFORD

Winter Prey
Mind Prey
Sudden Prey
The Night Crew
Secret Prey
Certain Prey
Easy Prey
Chosen Prey
Mortal Prey
Naked Prey
Hidden Prey
Broken Prey
Dead Watch

KIDD NOVELS

The Fool's Run
The Empress File
The Devil's Code
The Hanged Man's Song

X000 000 026 7293
ABERDEEN CITY LIBRARIES

INVISIBLE PREY

INVISIBLE PREY

John Sandford

SIMON &
SCHUSTER

London · New York · Sydney · Toronto

A CBS COMPANY

First published in Great Britain by Simon & Schuster UK Ltd, 2007
A CBS COMPANY

Copyright © John Sandford, 2007

This book is copyright under the Berne Convention.
No reproduction without permission.
® and © 1997 Simon & Schuster Inc. All rights reserved.

The right of John Sandford to be identified as the author of this work
has been asserted by him in accordance with sections 77 and 78 of the
Copyright, Designs and Patents Act, 1988.

1 3 5 7 9 10 8 6 4 2

Simon & Schuster UK Ltd
Africa House
64–78 Kingsway
London WC2B 6AH

www.simonsays.co.uk

Simon & Schuster Australia
Sydney

A CIP catalogue for this book is
available from the British Library.

Trade Paperback ISBN-13: 978-0-7432-7625-2
ISBN-10: 0-7432-7625-6
Hardback ISBN-13: 978-0-7432-7624-5
ISBN-10: 0-7432-7624-8

This book is a work of fiction. Names, characters, places and
incidents are either a product of the author's imagination or
are used fictitiously. Any resemblance to actual people living or
dead, events or locales is entirely coincidental.

Book design by Nicole Laroche

Printed and bound in Great Britain by
Bath Press, Bath

INVISIBLE PREY

1

AN ANONYMOUS VAN, some-kind-of-pale, cruised Summit Avenue, windows dark with the coming night. The killers inside watched three teenagers, two boys and a girl, hurrying along the sidewalk like windblown leaves. The kids were getting somewhere quick, finding shelter before the storm.

The killers trailed them, saw them off, then turned their faces toward Oak Walk.

The mansion was an architectural remnant of the nineteenth century, red brick with green trim, gloomy and looming in the dying light. Along the wrought-iron fence, well-tended beds of blue and yellow iris, and clumps of pink peonies, were going gray to the eye.

Oak Walk was perched on a bluff. The back of the house looked across the lights of St. Paul, down into the valley of the Mississippi, where the groove of the river had already gone dark. The front faced Summit Avenue; Oak Walk was the second-richest house on the richest street in town.

Six aging burr oaks covered the side yard. In sunlight, their canopies created a leafy glade, with sundials and flagstone walks, charming with moss and violets; but moon shadows gave the yard a menacing aura, now heightened by the lightning that flickered through the incoming clouds.

"Like the Munsters should live there," the bigger of the killers said.

"Like a graveyard," the little one agreed.

The Weather Channel had warned of *tornadic events*, and the killers could feel a twister in the oppressive heat, the smell of ozone thick in the air.

The summer was just getting started. The last snow slipped into town on May 2, and was gone a day later. The rest of the month had been sunny and warm, and by the end of it, even the ubiquitous paper-pale blondes were showing tan lines.

Now the first of the big summer winds. Refreshing, if it didn't knock your house down.

ON THE FOURTH PASS, the van turned into the driveway, eased up under the portico, and the killers waited there for a porch light. No light came on. That was good.

They got out of the van, one Big, one Little, stood there for a moment, listening, obscure in the shadows, facing the huge front doors. They were wearing coveralls, of the kind worn by automotive mechanics, and hairnets, and nylon stockings over their faces. Behind them, the van's engine ticked as it cooled. A Wisconsin license plate, stolen from a similar vehicle in a 3M parking lot, was stuck on the back of the van.

Big said, "Let's do it."

Little led the way up the porch steps. After a last quick look around, Big nodded again, and Little pushed the doorbell.

They'd done this before. They were good at it.

THEY COULD FEEL the footsteps on the wooden floors inside the house. "Ready," said Big.

A moment later, one of the doors opened. A shaft of light cracked across the porch, flashing on Little's burgundy jacket. Little said a few words—"Miz Peebles? Is this where the party is?"

A slender black woman, sixtyish, Peebles said, "Why no . . ." Her jaw continued to work wordlessly, searching for a scream, as she took in the distorted faces.

Little was looking past her at an empty hallway. The groundskeeper and the cook were home, snug in bed. This polite inquiry at the door was a last-minute check to make sure that there were no unexpected guests. Seeing no one, Little stepped back and snapped, "Go."

Big went through the door, fast, one arm flashing in the interior light. Big was carrying a two-foot-long steel gas pipe, with gaffer tape wrapped around the handle-end. Peebles didn't scream, because she didn't have time. Her eyes widened, her mouth dropped open, one hand started up, and then Big hit her on the crown of her head, crushing her skull.

The old woman dropped like a sack of bones. Big hit her again, as insurance, and then a third time, as insurance on the insurance: three heavy floor-shaking impacts, *whack! whack! whack!*

THEN A VOICE from up the stairs, tentative, shaky. "Sugar? Who was it, Sugar?"

Big's head turned toward the stairs and Little could hear him breathing. Big slipped out of his loafers and hurried up the stairs in his stocking feet, a man on the hunt. Little stepped up the hall, grabbed a corner of a seven-foot-long Persian carpet and dragged it back to the black woman's body.

And from upstairs, three more impacts: a gasping, thready scream, and *whack! whack! whack!*

Little smiled. Murder—and the insurance.

Little stooped, caught the sleeve of Peebles's housecoat, and rolled her onto the carpet. Breathing a little harder, Little began dragging the carpet toward an interior hallway that ran down to the kitchen, where it'd be out of sight of any of the windows. A pencil-thin line of blood, like a slug's trail, tracked the rug across the hardwood floor.

Peebles's face had gone slack. Her eyes were still open, the eyeballs rolled up, white against her black face. Too bad about the rug, Little thought. Chinese, the original dark blue gone pale, maybe 1890. Not a great rug, but a good one. Of course, it'd need a good cleaning now, with the blood-puddle under Peebles's head.

OUTSIDE, there'd been no sound of murder. No screams or gunshots audible on the street. A window lit up on Oak Walk's second floor. Then another on the third floor, and yet another, on the first floor, in the back, in the butler's pantry: Big and Little, checking out the house, making sure that they were the only living creatures inside.

WHEN THEY KNEW that the house was clear, Big and Little met at the bottom of the staircase. Big's mouth under the nylon was a bloody O. He'd chewed into his bottom lip while killing the old woman upstairs, something he did when the frenzy was on him. He was carrying a jewelry box and one hand was closed in a fist.

"You won't believe this," he said. "She had it around her neck." He opened his fist—his hands were covered with latex kitchen gloves—to show off a diamond the size of a quail's egg.

"Is it real?"

"It's real and it's blue. We're not talking Boxsters anymore. We're talking SLs." Big opened the box. "There's more: earrings, a neck-lace. There could be a half million, right here."

"Can Fleckstein handle it?"

Big snorted. "Fleckstein's so dirty that he wouldn't recognize the *Mona Lisa.* He'll handle it."

He pushed the jewelry at Little, started to turn, caught sight of Peebles lying on the rug. "Bitch," he said, the word grating through his teeth. "Bitch." In a second, in three long steps, he was on her again, beating the dead woman with the pipe, heavy impacts shak-ing the floor. Little went after him, catching him after the first three impacts, pulling him away, voice hard, "She's gone, for Christ's sakes, she's gone, she's gone . . ."

"Fucker," Big said. "Piece of shit."

Little thought, sometimes, that Big should have a bolt through his neck.

Big stopped, and straightened, looked down at Peebles, muttered, "She's gone." He shuddered, and said, "Gone." Then he turned to Little, blood in his eye, hefting the pipe.

Little's hands came up: "No, no—it's me. It's me. For God's sake."

Big shuddered again. "Yeah, yeah. I know. It's you."

Little took a step back, still uncertain, and said, "Let's get to work. Are you okay? Let's get to work."

Twenty minutes after they went in, the front door opened again. Big came out, looked both ways, climbed into the van, and eased it around the corner of the house and down the side to the deliveries entrance. Because of the pitch of the slope at the back of the house, the van was no longer visible from the street.

The last light was gone, the night now as dark as a coal sack, the lightning flashes closer, the wind coming like a cold open palm, push-ing against Big's face as he got out of the van. A raindrop, fat and round as a marble, hit the toe of his shoe. Then another, then more, cold, going pat-pat . . . pat . . . pat-pat-pat on the blacktop and con-crete and brick.

He hustled up to the back door; Little opened it from the inside.

"Another surprise," Little said, holding up a painting, turning it over in the thin light. Big squinted at it, then looked at Little: "We agreed we wouldn't take anything off the walls."

"Wasn't on the walls," Little said. "It was stuffed away in the storage room. It's not on the insurance list."

"Amazing. Maybe we ought to quit now, while we're ahead."

"No." Little's voice was husky with greed. "This time . . . this time, we can cash out. We'll never have to do this again."

"I don't mind," Big said.

"You don't mind the killing, but how about thirty years in a cage? Think you'd mind *that*?"

Big seemed to ponder that for a moment, then said, "All right."

Little nodded. "Think about the SLs. Chocolate for you, silver for me. Apartments: New York and Los Angeles. Something right on the Park, in New York. Something where you can lean out the window, and see the Met."

"We could buy . . ." Big thought about it for a few more seconds. "Maybe . . . a Picasso?"

"A Picasso . . . " Little thought about it, nodded. "But first—I'm going back upstairs. And you . . ."

Big grinned under the mask. "I trash the place. God, I love this job."

OUTSIDE, across the back lawn, down the bluff, over the top of the United Hospital buildings and Seventh Street and the houses below, down three-quarters of a mile away, a towboat pushed a line of barges toward the moorings at Pig's Eye. Not hurrying. Tows never hurried. All around, the lights of St. Paul sparkled like diamonds, on the first line of bluffs, on the second line below the cathedral, on the bridges fore and aft, on the High Bridge coming up.

The pilot in the wheelhouse was looking up the hill at the lights of Oak Walk, Dove Hill, and the Hill House, happened to be looking when the lights dimmed, all at once.

The rain-front had topped the bluff and was coming down on the river.

Hard rain coming, the pilot thought. *Hard* rain.

2

SLOAN CARRIED a couple of Diet Cokes over to the booth where Lucas Davenport waited, sitting sideways, his feet up on the booth seat. The bar was modern, but with an old-timey decor: creaking wooden floors, high-topped booths, a small dance floor at one end.

Sloan was the proprietor, and he dressed like it. He was wearing a brown summer suit, a tan shirt with a long pointed collar, a white tie with woven gold diamonds, and a genuine straw Panama hat. He was a slat-built man, narrow through the face, shoulders, and hips. Not gaunt, but narrow; might have been a clarinet player in a fading jazz band, Lucas thought, or the cover character on a piece of 1930s pulp fiction.

"Damn Diet Coke, it fizzes like crazy. I thought there was something wrong with the pump, but it's just the Coke. Don't know why," Sloan said, as he dropped the glasses on the table.

At the far end of the bar, the bartender was reading a *Wall Street Journal* by the light from a peanut-sized reading lamp clamped to the cash register. Norah Jones burbled in the background; the place smelled pleasantly of fresh beer and peanuts.

Lucas said, "Two guys in the bar and they're both drinking Cokes. You're gonna go broke."

Sloan smiled comfortably, leaned across the table, his voice pitched down so the bartender couldn't hear him, "I put ten grand in my pocket last month. I never had so much money in my life."

"Probably because you don't spend any money on lights," Lucas said. "It's so dark in here, I can't see my hands."

"Cops like the dark. You can fool around with strange women," Sloan said. He hit on the Diet Coke.

"Got the cops, huh?" The cops had been crucial to Sloan's business plan.

"Cops and schoolteachers," Sloan said with satisfaction. "A cop and schoolteacher bar. The teachers drink like fish. The cops hit on the schoolteachers. One big happy family."

The bartender laughed at something in the *Journal*, a nasty laugh, and he said, to no one in particular, "Gold's going to a thousand, you betcha. *Now* we'll see what's what."

They looked at him for a moment, then Sloan shrugged, said, "He's got a B.S. in economics. And I do mean a B.S."

"Not bad for a bartender . . . So what's the old lady think about the place?"

"She's gotten into it," Sloan said. He was happy that an old pal could see him doing well. "She took a course in bookkeeping, she handles all the cash, running these QuickBook things on the computer. She's talking about taking a couple weeks in Cancun or Palm Springs next winter. Hawaii."

"That's terrific," Lucas said. And he *was* pleased by all of it.

S O   T H E Y   T A L K E D about wives and kids for a while, Sloan's retirement check, and the price of a new sign for the place, which formerly had been named after a tree, and which Sloan had changed to Shooters.

Even from a distance, it was clear that the two men were good friends: they listened to each other with a certain narrow-eyed intensity, and with a cop-quick skepticism. They were close, but physically they were a study in contrasts.

Sloan was slight, beige and brown, tentative.

Lucas was none of those. Tall, dark haired, with the thin white line of a scar draped across his tanned forehead, down into an eyebrow, he might have been a thug of the leading-man sort. He had intense blue eyes, a hawk nose, and large hands and square shoulders; an athlete, a onetime University of Minnesota hockey player.

Sloan knew nothing about fashion, and never cared; Lucas went for Italian suits, French ties, and English shoes. He read the men's fashion magazines, of the serious kind, and spent some time every spring and fall looking at suits. When he and his wife traveled to Manhattan, she went to the Museum of Modern Art, he went to Versace.

Today he wore a French-blue shirt under a linen summer jacket, lightweight woolen slacks, and loafers; and a compact .45 in a Bianchi shoulder rig.

Lucas's smile came and went, flashing in his face. He had crow's-feet at the corners of his eyes, and silver hair threaded through the black. In the morning, when shaving, he worried about getting old. He had a way to go before that happened, but he imagined he could see it, just over the hill.

WHEN THEY FINISHED the Diet Cokes, Sloan went and got two more and then said, "What about Burt Kline?"

"You know him, right?" Lucas asked.

"I went to school with him, thirteen years," Sloan said. "I still see him around, when there's a campaign."

"Good guy, bad guy?" Lucas asked.

"He was our class representative in first grade and every grade after that," Sloan said. "He's a politician. He's always been a politician. He's always fat, greasy, jolly, easy with the money, happy to see you. Like that. First time I ever got in trouble in school, was when I pushed him into a snowbank. He reported me."

"Squealer."

Sloan nodded.

"But what's even more interesting, is that you were a school bully. I never saw that in you," Lucas said. He scratched the side of his nose, a light in his eye.

Sloan made a rude noise. "I weighed about a hundred and ten pounds when I graduated. I didn't bully anybody."

"You bullied Kline. You just said so."

"Fuck you." After a moment of silence, Sloan asked, "What'd he do?"

Lucas looked around, then said, quietly, "This is between you and me."

"Of course."

Lucas nodded. Sloan could keep his mouth shut. "He apparently had a sexual relationship with a sixteen-year-old. And maybe a fifteen-year-old—same girl, he just might've been nailing her a year ago."

"Hmm." Sloan pulled a face, then said, "I can see that. But it wouldn't have been rape. I mean, rape-rape, jumping out of the bushes. He's not the most physical guy."

"No, she went along with it," Lucas said. "But it's about forty years of statutory."

Sloan looked into himself for a minute, then said, "Not forty. Thirty-six."

"Enough."

Another moment of silence, then Sloan sighed and asked, "Why don't you bust him? Don't tell me it's because he's a politician."

Lucas said to Sloan, "It's more complicated than that." When Sloan looked skeptical, he said, "C'mon, Sloan, I wouldn't bullshit you. It really *is* more complicated."

"I'm listening," Sloan said.

"All right. The whole BCA is a bunch of Democrats, run by a Democrat appointee of a Democratic governor, all right?"

"And God is in his heaven."

"If we say, 'The girl says he did it,' and bust him, his career's over. Whether he did it or not. Big pederast stamp on his forehead. If it turns out he *didn't* do it, if he's acquitted, every Republican in the state will be blaming us for a political dirty trick—a really dirty trick. Five months to the election. I mean, he's the president of the state senate."

"Does the kid have any evidence?" Sloan asked. "Any witnesses?"

"Yes. Semen on a dress," Lucas said. "She also told the investigator that Kline has moles or freckles on his balls, and she said they look like semicolons. One semicolon on each nut."

An amused look crept over Sloan's face: "She's lying."

"What?"

"In this day and age," he asked, "how many sixteen-year-olds know what a semicolon is?"

Lucas rolled his eyes and said, "Try to concentrate, okay? This is serious."

"Doesn't sound serious," Sloan said. "Investigating the family jewels."

"Well, it is serious," Lucas said. "She tells the initial investigator . . ."

"Who's that?"

"Virgil Flowers."

"That fuckin' Flowers," Sloan said, and he laughed. "Might've known."

"Yeah. Anyway, she tells Virgil that he's got semicolons on his balls. And quite a bit of other detail, including the size of what she calls 'his thing.' She also provides us with a dress and there's a semen stain on it. So Virgil gets a search warrant . . ."

Sloan giggled, an unattractive sound from a man of his age.

". . . gets a search warrant, and a doctor, and they take a DNA scraping and examine Kline's testicles," Lucas said. "Sure enough, it's like they came out of Microsoft Word: one semicolon on each nut. We got the pictures."

"I bet they're all over the Internet by now," Sloan said.

"You'd bet wrong. These are not attractive pictures—and everybody involved knows that their jobs are on the line," Lucas said. "You don't mess with Burt Kline unless you can kill him."

"Yeah, but the description, the semen . . . sounds like a big indict to me," Sloan said.

"However," Lucas said.

"Uh-oh." Sloan had been a cop for twenty years; he was familiar with howevers.

"Burt says he never had sex with the daughter, but he did sleep with her mom," Lucas said. "See, the state pays for an apartment in St. Paul. Kline rents a place from Mom, who owns a duplex on Grand Avenue, what's left from a divorce settlement. Kline tells Virgil that he's staying there, doing the people's work, when Mom starts puttin' it on him."

"Him being such a looker," Sloan said.

"Kline resists, but he's only human. And, she's got, Virgil believes, certain skills. In fact, Virgil said she's been around the block so often it looks like a NASCAR track. Anyway, pretty soon Burt is sleeping with Mom every Monday, Wednesday, and Friday."

"How old's Mom?" Sloan asked.

"Thirty-four," Lucas said.

"With a sixteen-year-old daughter?"

"Yeah. Mom started young," Lucas said. "Anyway, Burt says Mom got the idea to blackmail him, because she's always hurting for money. He says she put the daughter up to it, making the accusation. Burt said that she would have all the necessary grammatical information."

"And Mom says . . . ."

"She said that they had a hasty affair, but that Burt really wanted the daughter, and she was horrified when she found out he'd gotten to her," Lucas said. "She says no way would she have done what she would have had to do to see the semicolons, or get semen on the neckline of the dress. That's something that her daughter had to be forced into."

"Mom was horrified."

"Absolutely," Lucas said. "So Virgil asks her if she'd gained any weight lately."

"She was heavy?"

"No, not especially. I'd say . . . solid. Plays broomball in the winter. Blades in the summer. Or, more to the point, about a size ten-twelve. She said no, she hadn't gained any weight since she had the kid, sixteen years ago. So Virgil points out that the dress with the semen stain is a size ten and the girl herself is about a size four. The kid looks like that fashion model who puts all the cocaine up her nose."

"Oooo." Sloan thought about it for a moment, then asked, "What's Mom say?"

"She says that they trade clothes all the time," Lucas said. "If you want to believe that a size-four fashion-aware teenager is going to drag around in a size ten."

"That's a . . . problem," Sloan agreed.

"Another problem," Lucas said. "Virgil put the screws on a neighbor boy who seemed to be sniffing around. The neighbor kid says the girl's been sexually active since she was twelve. That Mom knew it. Maybe encouraged it."

"Huh."

"So what do you think?" Lucas asked.

"Mom's on record saying she doesn't do oral?" Sloan asked.

"Yeah."

"Jury's not gonna believe that," Sloan said. "Sounds like there's a lot of sex in the family. She can't get away with playing the Virgin Mary. If they think she's lying about that, they'll think she's lying about the whole thing."

"Yup."

Sloan thought it over for a while, then asked, "What's the point of this investigation?"

"Ah, jeez," Lucas said. He rubbed his eyes with his knuckles. "That's another problem. I don't know what the point is. Maybe the whole point is to push Burt Kline out of his job. The original tip was anonymous. It came into child protection in St. Paul. St. Paul passed it on to us because there were out-state aspects—the biggest so-called overt act might've been that Kline took the girl up to Mille Lacs for a naked weekend. Anyway, the tip was anonymous. Maybe Kline said something to a Democrat. Or maybe . . . Virgil suspects the tip might've come from Mom. As part of a blackmail hustle."

"Flowers is smart," Sloan admitted.

"Yeah."

"And Mom's cooperating now?"

"She runs hot and cold," Lucas said. "What she doesn't believe is, that she can't cut off the investigation. She thought we'd be working for her. Or at least, that's what she thought until Virgil set her straight."

"Hmph. Well, if the point is to push Burt out of his job . . . I mean, that's not good," Sloan said. He shook a finger at Lucas. "Not good for you. You don't want to get a rep as a political hit man. If the point is to stop a pederast . . ."

"If he is one."

Silence.

15

"Better get that straight," Sloan said. "Here's what I think: I think you ask whether it was rape. Do you believe he did it? If you do, screw him—indict him. Forget all the politics, let the chips fall."

"Yeah," Lucas said. He fiddled with his Coke glass. "Easy to say."

MORE SILENCE, looking out the window at a freshly striped parking lot. A battered Chevy, a repainted Highway Patrol pursuit car, with rust holes in the back fender, pulled in. They were both looking at it when Del Capslock climbed out.

"Del," Lucas said. "Is he hangin' out here?"

"No," Sloan said. "He's been in maybe twice since opening night. Where'd he get that nasty car?"

"He's got an undercover gig going," Lucas said.

Capslock scuffed across the parking lot, and a moment later, pushed inside. Lucas saw the bartender do a check and a recheck, and put down the paper.

Del was a gaunt, pasty-faced man with a perpetual four-day beard and eyes that looked too white. He was wearing a jeans jacket out at the elbows, a black T-shirt, and dusty boot-cut jeans. The T-shirt said, in large letters, *I found Jesus!* and beneath that, in smaller letters, *He was behind the couch.*

Lucas called, "Del." Del looked around in the gloom, saw them in the booth, and walked over.

Sloan said, "My tone just got lowered."

"Jenkins said you might be here," Del said to Lucas. "I was in the neighborhood . . ." He waved at the bartender. "'Nother Coke. On the house." To Sloan, he said, "Whyn't you turn on some goddamn lights?" And to Lucas, "People have been trying to call you. Your cell phone is turned off."

"I feel like such a fool," Lucas said, groping for the phone. He turned it on and waited for it to come up.

"That's what they thought you'd feel like," Del said. "Anyway, the governor's calling."

Lucas's eyebrows went up. "What happened?" His phone came up and showed a list of missed calls. Six of them.

"You know Constance Bucher?" Del asked. "Lived up on Summit?"

"Sure . . ." Lucas said. The hair prickled on the back of his neck as he picked up the past tense in *lived*. "Know *of* her, never met her."

"Somebody beat her to death," Del said. He frowned, picked at a nit on his jeans jacket, flicked it on the floor. "Her and her maid, both."

"Oh, boy." Lucas slid out of the booth. "When?"

"Two or three days, is what they're saying. Most of St. Paul is up there, and the governor called, he wants your young white ass on the scene."

Lucas said to Sloan, "It's been wonderful."

"Who is she?" Sloan asked. He wasn't a St. Paul guy.

"Constance Bucher—Bucher Natural Resources," Lucas said. "Lumber, paper mills, land. Remember the Rembrandt that went to the Art Institute?"

"I remember something about a Rembrandt," Sloan said doubtfully.

"Bucher Boulevard?" Del suggested.

"*That* Bucher," Sloan said. To Lucas: "Good luck. With both cases."

"Yeah. You get any ideas about your pal, give me a call. I'm hurtin'," Lucas said. "And don't tell Del about it."

"You mean about Burt Kline?" Del asked, his eyebrows working.

"That fuckin' Flowers," Lucas said, and he went out the door.

3

LUCAS WAS DRIVING the Porsche. Once behind the wheel and moving, he punched up the list of missed calls on his telephone. Three of them came from the personal cell phone of Rose Marie Roux, director of the Department of Public Safety, and his real boss; one came from the superintendent of the Bureau of Criminal Apprehension, his nominal boss; the other two came from one of the governor's squids. He tapped the phone, and Rose Marie answered after the first ring.

"Where are you?" she asked without preamble. He was listed in her cell-phone directory.

"In Minneapolis," Lucas said. "I'm on my way. She's what, four doors down from the cathedral?"

"About that. I'm coming up on it now. About a million St. Paul cops scattered all . . . Ah! Jesus!"

"What?"

She laughed. "Almost hit a TV guy . . . nothing serious."

"I HEAR the governor's calling," Lucas said.

"He is. He said, quote, I want Davenport on this like brass on a doorknob, unquote."

"He's been working on his metaphors again," Lucas said.

"Yeah. He thinks it gives him the common touch," she said.

"Listen, Lucas, she was really, *really* rich. A lot of money is about to go somewhere, and there's the election coming."

"I'll see you in ten minutes," Lucas said. "You got an attitude from St. Paul?"

"Not yet. Harrington is here somewhere, I'll talk to him," Rose Marie said. "I gotta put the phone down and park . . . He'll be happy to see us—he's trying to get more overtime money from the state." Harrington was the St. Paul chief.

"Ten minutes," Lucas said.

He was on the west side of Minneapolis. He took Highway 100 north, got on I-394, aimed the nose of the car at the IDS building in the distance, and stepped on the accelerator, flashing past minivans, SUVs, pickups, and fat-assed sedans, down to I-94.

Feeling all right, whistling a little.

He'd had a past problem with depression. The depression, he believed, was probably genetic, and he'd shared it with his father and grandfather; a matter of brain chemicals. And though depression was always off the coast, like a fog bank, it had nothing to do with the work. He actually *liked* the hunt, liked chasing assholes. He'd killed a few of them, and had never felt particularly bad about it. He'd been dinged up along the way, as well, and never thought much about that, either. No post-traumatic stress.

As for rich old ladies getting killed, well, hell, they were gonna die sooner or later. Sometimes, depending on who it was, a murder would make him angry, or make him sad, and he wouldn't have wished for it. But if it was going to happen, he'd be pleased to chase whoever had done it.

He didn't have a mission; he had an *interest*.

EMMYLOU HARRIS came up on the satellite radio, singing "Leaving Louisiana in the Broad Daylight," and he sang along in a crackling baritone, heading for bloody murder through city traffic at ninety miles per hour; wondered why Catholics didn't have something like a St. Christopher's medal that would ward off the Highway Patrol. He'd have to talk to his parish priest about it, if he ever saw the guy again.

Gretchen Wilson came up, with Kris Kristofferson's "Sunday Mornin' Comin' Down," and he sang along with her, too.

THE DAY WAS gorgeous, puffy clouds with a breeze, just enough to unfold the flags on buildings along the interstate. Eighty degrees, maybe. Lucas took I-94 to Marion Street, around a couple of corners onto John Ireland, up the hill past the hulking cathedral, and motored onto Summit.

Summit Avenue was aptly named. Beginning atop a second-line bluff above the Mississippi, it looked out over St. Paul, not only from a geographical high point, but also an economic one. The richest men in the history of the city had built mansions along Summit, and some of them still lived there.

OAK WALK WAS a three-story red-brick mansion with a white-pillared portico out front, set back a bit farther from the street than its gargantuan neighbors. He'd literally passed it a thousand times, on his way downtown, almost without noticing it. When he got close, the traffic began coagulating in front of him, and then he saw the TV trucks and the foot traffic on the sidewalks, and then the wooden barricades—Summit had been closed and cops were routing traffic away from the murder house, back around the cathedral.

Lucas held his ID out the window, nosed up to the barricades, called "BCA" to the cop directing traffic, and was pointed around the end of a barricade and down the street.

Oak Walk's driveway was jammed with cop cars. Lucas left the Porsche in the street, walked past a uniformed K-9 cop with his German shepherd. The cop said, "Hey, hot dog." Lucas nodded, said, "George," and climbed the front steps and walked through the open door.

JUST INSIDE the door was a vestibule, where arriving or departing guests could gather up their coats, or sit on a bench and wait for the limo. The vestibule, in turn, opened into a grand hallway that ran the length of the house, and just inside the vestibule door, two six-foot bronze figures, torchieres, held aloft six-bulb lamps.

Straight ahead, two separate stairways, one on each side of the hall, curled up to a second floor, with a crystal chandelier hanging maybe twenty feet above the hall, between the stairs.

The hallway, with its pinkish wallpaper, would normally have been lined with paintings, mostly portraits, but including rural agricultural scenes, some from the American West, others apparently French; and on the herringboned hardwood floors, a series of Persian carpets would have marched toward the far back door in perfectly aligned diminishing perspective.

The hall was no longer lined with paintings, but Lucas knew that it had been, because the paintings were lying on the floor, most faceup, some facedown, helter-skelter. The rugs had been pulled askew, as though somebody had been looking beneath them. For what, Lucas couldn't guess. The glass doors on an enormous china cabinet had been broken; there were a dozen collector-style pots still sitting on the shelves inside, and the shattered remains of more on the floor, as if the vandals had been looking for something hidden in the pots. What would that be?

A dozen pieces of furniture had been dumped. Drawers lay on the floor, along with candles and candlesticks, knickknacks, linen, photo albums, and shoe boxes that had once contained photos. The photos were now scattered around like leaves; a good number of them black-and-white. There was silverware, and three or four gold-colored athletic trophies, a dozen or so plaques. One of the plaques, lying faceup at Lucas's feet, said, "For Meritorious Service to the City, This Key Given March 1, 1899, Opening All the Doors of St. Paul."

Cops were scattered along the hall, like clerks, being busy, looking at papers, chatting. Two were climbing the stairs to the second floor, hauling with them a bright-yellow plastic equipment chest.

LIEUTENANT JOHN T. SMITH was in what Lucas thought must have been the music room, since it contained two grand pianos and an organ. Smith was sitting backward on a piano bench, in front of a mahogany-finished Steinway grand, talking on a cell phone. He was looking at the feet and legs of a dead black woman who was lying facedown on a Persian carpet in a hallway off the music room. All around him, furniture had been dumped, and there must have been a thousand pieces of sheet music lying around. "Beautiful Brown Eyes." "Camping Tonight." "Itsy Bitsy Teenie Weenie Yellow Polka Dot Bikini." "Tammy."

An amazing amount of shit that rich people had, Lucas thought.

SMITH SAW LUCAS, raised a hand. Lucas nodded, stuck his head into the hallway, where a St. Paul crime-scene crew, and two men from the medical examiner's office, were working over the body.

Not much to see. From Lucas's angle, the woman was just a lump of clothing. One of the ME's investigators, a man named Ted, looked up, said, "Hey, Lucas."

"What happened?"

"Somebody beat the shit out of her with a pipe. Maybe a piece of re-rod. Not a hammer, nothing with an edge. Crushed her skull, that's what killed her. Might have some postmortem crushing, we've got lacerations but not much bleeding. Same with Mrs. Bucher, upstairs. Fast, quick, and nasty."

"When?"

Ted looked up, and eased back on his heels. "Johnny says they were seen late Friday afternoon, alive, by a researcher from the Historical Society who's doing a book on Summit Avenue homes. He left at four-thirty. Neither one of them went to church on Sunday. Sometimes Mrs. Bucher didn't, but Mrs. Peebles always did. So Johnny thinks it was after four-thirty Friday and before Sunday morning, and that looks good to me. We'll rush the lab work . . ."

"That's Peebles there," Lucas said.

"Yo. This is Peebles."

SMITH GOT OFF the cell phone and Lucas stepped over, grinned: "You'll be rolling in glory on this one," he said. "Tom Cruise will probably play your character. Nothing but watercress sandwiches and crème brûlée from now on."

"I'm gonna be rolling in something," Smith said. "You getting involved?"

"If there's anything for me to do," Lucas said.

"You're more'n welcome, man."

"Thanks. Ted says sometime between Friday night and Sunday morning?"

Smith stood up and stretched and yawned. "Probably Friday night. I got guys all over the neighborhood and we can't find anybody who saw them Saturday, and they were usually out in the garden on

Saturday afternoon. Beheading roses, somebody said. Do you de-capitate roses?"

"I don't know," Lucas said. "I don't, personally."

"Anyway, they got four phone calls Saturday and three more Sunday, all of them kicked through to the answering service," Smith said. "I think they were dead before the phone calls came in."

"Big storm Friday night," Lucas said.

"I was thinking about that—there were a couple of power out-ages, darker'n a bitch. Somebody could have climbed the hill and come in through the back, you wouldn't see them come or go."

Lucas looked back at Peebles's legs. Couldn't be seen from outside the house. "Alarm system?"

"Yeah, but it was old and it was turned off. They had a series of fire alarms a couple of years ago, a problem with the system. The trucks came out, nothing happening. They finally turned it off, and were going to get it fixed, but didn't."

"Huh. Who found them?"

"Employees. Bucher had a married couple who worked for them, did the housekeeping, the yard work, maintenance," Smith said. "They're seven-thirty to three, Monday through Friday, but they were off at a nursery this morning, down by Hastings, buying some plants, and didn't get back here until one o'clock. Found them first thing, called nine-one-one. We checked, the story seems good. They were freaked out. In the right way."

"Anything stolen?"

"Yeah, for sure. They got jewelry, don't know how much, but there's a jewelry box missing from the old lady's bedroom and an-other one dumped. Talked to Bucher's niece, out in L.A., she said Mrs. Bucher kept her important jewelry in a safe-deposit box at Wells Fargo. Anything big she had here she'd keep in a wall safe behind a panel in the dining room . . ." He pointed down a hall to his right, past a chest of drawers that had held children's clothing, pajamas with cowboys and Indians on them, and what looked like a coonskin cap; all been dumped on the floor. "The dining room's down that way. Whoever did it, didn't find the panel. The safe wasn't touched. Anyway, the jewelry's probably small stuff, earrings, and so on. And they took electronics. A DVD player definitely, a CD player, a radio, maybe, there might be a computer missing . . . We're getting most of this from Mrs. Bucher's friends, but not many really knew the house that well."

"So it's local."

"Seems to be local," Smith said. "But I don't know. Don't have a good feel for it yet."

"Looking at anybody?"

Smith turned his head, checking for eavesdroppers, then said, "Two different places. Keep it under your hat?"

"Sure."

"Peebles had a nephew," Smith said. "He's in tenth grade over at Cretin. His mother's a nurse, and right now she's working three to eleven at Regions. When she's on that shift, he'll come here after school. Peebles'd feed him dinner, and keep an eye on him until his mom picked him up. Sometimes he stayed over. Name is Ronnie Lash. He'd do odd jobs for the old ladies, edge trimming, garden cleanup, go to the store. Pick up laundry."

"Bad kid?"

Smith shook his head. "Don't have a thing on him. Good in school. Well liked. Wasn't here Friday night, he was out dancing with kids from school. But his neighborhood . . . there are some bad dudes on his street. If he's been hanging out, he could've provided a key. But it's really sensitive."

"Yeah." A black kid with a good school record, well liked, pushed on a brutal double murder. All they had to do was ask a question and there'd be accusations of racism. "Gotta talk to him, though," Lucas said. "Get a line going, make him one of many. You know."

Smith nodded, but looked worried anyway. The whole thing was going to be enough of a circus, without a civil-rights pie fight at the same time.

"You said two things," Lucas prompted.

"There's a halfway house across the street, down a block. Drugs, alcohol. People coming and going. You could sit up in one of those windows and watch Bucher's house all night long, thinking about how easy it would be."

"Huh. Unless you got something else, that sounds as good as the nephew," Lucas said.

"Yeah, we're trying to get a list out of corrections."

"Was there . . . did the women fight back? Anything that might show some DNA?"

Smith looked over his shoulder toward Peebles. "Doesn't look like it. It looks like the assholes came in, killed them, took what they wanted, and left. The women didn't run, didn't hide, didn't struggle as far as we can tell. Came in and killed them. Peebles was probably killed at the front door and dragged back there on the rug. We think the rug should be right in front of the door."

They thought about it for a minute, then Smith's cell phone rang, and Lucas asked quickly, "Can I look around?"

"Sure. Go ahead." Smith flipped open the phone and added, "Your boss was out in the backyard talking to the chief, ten minutes ago . . . Hello?"

LUCAS TOOK the stairs up to the bedroom level, where another team was working over Bucher's body. The bedroom was actually a suite of four rooms: a sitting room, a dressing room, a bathroom, and the main room. The main room had a big king-sized bed covered with a log-cabin quilt, two lounge chairs, and a wood-burning fire-place. All four rooms had been dumped: drawers pulled out of chests, a jewelry box upside down on the carpet.

A half-dozen paintings hung crookedly on the walls and two lay on the floor. Another quilt, this one apparently a wall hanging, had been pulled off the wall and left lying on the floor. Looking for a safe? The bath opened off to the right side and behind the bed. The medicine cabinet stood open, and squeeze bottles of lotion, tubes of antiseptic and toothpaste littered the countertop beneath it. No prescription medicine bottles.

Junkies. They'd take everything, then throw away what they couldn't use; or, try it and see what happened.

A St. Paul investigator was squatting next to a wallet that was lying on a tile by the fireplace.

"Anything?" Lucas asked.

"Look at this," the investigator said. "Not a dollar in the wallet. But they didn't take the credit cards or the ATM cards or the ID."

"Couldn't get the PINs if Bucher and Peebles were already dead," Lucas said.

The cop scratched his head. "Guess not. Just, you don't see this every day. The cards not stolen."

LUCAS BROWSED THROUGH the second floor, nodding at cops, taking it in. One of the cops pointed him down the hall at Peebles's apartment, a bedroom, a small living room with an older television, a bathroom with a shower and a cast-iron tub. Again, the medicine cabinet was open, with some of the contents knocked out; another quilt had been pulled off the wall.

The other bedrooms showed paintings knocked to the floor, bed-covers disturbed.

A door to a third floor stood open and Lucas took the stairs.

Hotter up here; the air-conditioning was either turned off, or didn't reach this far. Old-time servants' quarters, storage rooms. One room was full of luggage, dozens of pieces dating back to the early part of the twentieth century, Lucas thought. Steamer trunks. A patina of dust covered the floor, and people had walked across it: Lucas found multiple footprints came and went, some in athletic shoes, others in plain-bottomed shoes.

He browsed through the other rooms, and found a few more footprints, as well as stacks of old furniture, racks of clothing, rolls of carpet, shelves full of glassware, a few old typewriters, an antique TV with a screen that was nearly oval, cardboard boxes full of puzzles and children's toys. A room full of framed paintings. A cork bulletin board with dozens of promotional pins and medallions from the St. Paul Winter Carnival. The dumbshits should have taken them, he thought; some of the pins were worth several hundred dollars.

He was alone in the dust motes and silence and heat, wondered about the footprints, turned around, went back downstairs, and started hunting for his boss.

ON THE first floor, he walked around the crime scene in the hallway and past another empty room, stopped, went back. This was the TV room, with a sixty-inch high-definition television set into one wall.

Below it was a shelf for electronics, showing nothing but a bunch of gold cable ends. He was about to step out, when he saw a bright blue plastic square behind the half-open door of a closet. He stepped over, nudged the door farther open, found a bookcase set into the closet, the top shelves full of DVD movies, the bottom shelves holding a dozen video games. He recognized the latest version of Halo, an Xbox game. There was no Xbox near the TV, so it must have been taken with the rest of the electronics.

Were the old ladies playing Halo? Or did this belong to the Lash kid?

Smith went by, and Lucas called, "Hey, Johnny . . . have you been up on the third floor?"

"No. I was told there wasn't much there," Smith said.

"Who went up?" Lucas asked.

"Clark Wain. You know Clark? Big pink bald guy?"

"Yeah, thanks," Lucas said. "When're you talking to Peebles's nephew?"

"Soon. You want to sit in?"

"Maybe. I noticed that all the electronics were taken, but there were a bunch of games and DVDs there that weren't," Lucas said. "That's a little odd, if it's just local assholes."

Smith rubbed his lip, then said, "Yeah, I know. I saw that. Maybe in a hurry?"

"They had time to trash the place," Lucas said. "Must have been in here for half an hour."

"So . . ."

"Maybe somebody asked them not to," Lucas said.

"You think?" They were talking about the Lash kid.

"I don't know," Lucas said. "They stole the game console, but not the games? I don't know. Maybe check and see if Lash has another console at home."

LUCAS FOUND Rose Marie in the small kitchen talking with the state representative for the district, an orange-haired woman with a black mustache who was leaking real tears, brushing them away with a Kleenex. Lucas came up and Rose Marie said, "You know Kathy. She and Mrs. Bucher were pretty close."

"I-ba-I-ba-I-ba . . ." Kathy said.

"She identified the bodies," Rose Marie said. "She lives two doors up the street."

"I-ba-I-ba . . ."

Lucas would have felt sorrier for her if she hadn't been such a vicious political wolverine, married to a vicious plaintiffs' attorney. And he couldn't help feeling a *little* sorry for her anyway. "You oughta sit down," he said. "You look tippy."

"Come on," Rose Marie said, taking the other woman's arm. "I'll get you a couch." To Lucas: "Back in a minute."

THE KITCHEN had been tossed like the rest of house, all the cabinet drawers pulled out, the freezer trays lying on the floor, a flour jar dumped along with several other ceramic containers. Flour was everywhere, mixed with crap from the refrigerator. Dried pickles were scattered around, like olive-drab weenies, and he could smell ketchup and relish, rotting in the sunshine, like the remnants of a three-day-old picnic, or a food tent at the end of the state fair.

To get out of the mess, Lucas walked through the dining room and stepped out on the back porch, a semicircle of warm yellow stone thirty feet across. Below it, the lawn slipped away to the edge of the bluff, and below that, out of sight, I-35, then United Hospital, then the old jumble of West Seventh, and farther down, the Mississippi. Cops were standing around on the lawn, talking, clusters and groups of two and three, a little cigarette and cigar smoke drifting around, pleasantly acrid. One of the cops was Clark Wain, the guy who'd explored the third floor. Lucas stepped over, said, "Clark," and Wain said, "Yeah, Lucas, what's going on?"

"You went up to the third floor?"

"Me and a couple of other guys," Wain said. "Making sure there wasn't anybody else."

"Were there footprints going up? In the dust?"

"Yeah. We had them photographed but there wasn't anything to see, really—too many of them," Wain said. "Looked like people were up there a lot."

"Nothing seemed out of place?"

Wain's eyes drifted away as he thought it over, then came back to Lucas: "Nothing that hit me at the time. They didn't trash the place like they did some of the other rooms. Maybe they took a peek and then came back down—if it was even their footprints. Could have been anyone."

"All right . . ." Rose Marie came out on the porch looking for him, and Lucas raised a hand to her. To Wain he said, "Gotta talk to the boss."

They stepped back into the dining room. Rose Marie asked, "What do you have going besides Kline?"

"The Heny killing down in Rochester, that's still pooping along, and we've got a girl's body down by Jackson, we don't know what happened there. The feds are pushing for more cooperation on illegal aliens, they want us to put somebody in the packing plants down in Austin . . . But Kline is the big one. And this."

"Did Burt do it?" Rose Marie asked. She and Kline were old political adversaries.

"Yeah. I don't know if we can prove it," Lucas said.

He told her about the DNA and the size-ten dress, and the girl's sexual history. She already knew about the semicolons and that Kline had admitted an affair with Mom.

"The newest thing is, Kline wants to do something like a consent agreement," Lucas said. "Everybody agrees that nobody did anything wrong and that nobody will ever do it again. He, in return, pays them another year's rent on the room and a car-storage fee for her garage, like twenty thousand bucks total."

"That's bullshit. You can't sign a consent agreement that gets you out of a statutory-rape charge," Rose Marie said. "Especially not if you're a state senator."

"So I'll send Virgil around and you tell him what you want him to do," Lucas said.

She made a rude noise, shook her head. "That fuckin' Flowers . . ."

"C'mon, Rose Marie."

She sighed. "All right. Send him up. Tell him to bring the file, make a presentation. Three or four people will be there, he doesn't have to be introduced to them, or look them up later. Tell him to wear a jacket, slacks, and to get rid of those goddamn cowboy boots for one day. Tell him we don't need an attitude. Tell him if we get attitude, I'll donate his ass to the Fulda City Council as the town cop."

"I'll tell him . . ." He looked around. Several panels in the wall of the dining room had been pulled open. One showed a safe door; another, rows of liquor bottles; a third, crockery serving dishes with molded vegetables as decoration.

"Listen. This is a sideshow," she said, waving a hand at the trashed room. "The governor wants a presence here, because she's big political and social money. But you need to focus on Kline." She popped a piece of Nicorette gum, started chewing rapidly, rolling it with her tongue. "I don't care who fixes it, but it's gotta be fixed."

"Why don't we just go the grand jury route? You know, 'We presented it to the grand jury and in their wisdom, they decided to indict'? Or not indict?"

"Because we're playing with the legislature, and the Republicans still own it, and they *know* that's bullshit. Radioactive bullshit. We need to be in position before this girl shows up on Channel Three."

LUCAS WALKED HER out to her car; when she'd gotten out of her spot in a neighboring driveway, he started back to the house. On the way, thinking more about Kline than about the Bucher murder, he spotted a red-haired reporter from the *Star Tribune* on the other side of the police tape. The reporter lifted a hand and Lucas stepped over.

"How'd she get it?" Ruffe Ignace asked. He was smiling, simple chitchat with a friend.

"There are two of them," Lucas said quietly. "A maid named Sugar-Rayette Peebles and Constance Bucher. Peebles was killed downstairs, near the front door. Her body was wrapped in a Persian carpet in a hallway. The old lady was killed in her bedroom. They were beaten to death, maybe with a pipe. Skulls crushed. House is ransacked, bedrooms tossed. Probably Friday night."

"Any leads?" Ignace was taking no notes, just standing on the neighbor's lawn with his hands in his jacket pockets. He didn't want to attract the attention of other reporters. Lucas had found that Ignace had an exceptional memory for conversation, for however long it took him to go somewhere and write it down.

"Not yet," Lucas said. "We'll be talking to people who knew the women . . ."

"How about that place down the street?" Ignace asked. "The halfway house? Full of junkies."

"St. Paul is looking into that," Lucas said.

"Did it look like junkies?" Ignace asked.

"Something like that, but not exactly," Lucas said.

"How not exactly?"

"I don't know—but *not exactly*," Lucas said. "I'll get back to you when I figure it out."

"You running it?"

"No. St. Paul. I'll be consulting," Lucas said.

"Okay. I owe you," Ignace said.

"You already owed me."

"Bullshit. We were dead even," Ignace said. "But now I owe you one."

A **WOMAN** called him. "Lucas! Hey, Lucas!" He turned and saw Shelley Miller in the crowd along the sidewalk. She lived down the street in a house as big as Oak Walk.

"I gotta talk to this lady," Lucas said to Ignace.

"Call me," Ignace said. He drifted away, fishing in his pocket for a cell phone.

Miller came up. She was a thin woman; thin by sheer willpower. "Is she . . . ?" Miller was a cross between fascinated and appalled.

"Yeah. She and her maid," Lucas said. "How well did you know her?"

"I talked to her whenever she was outside," Miller said. "We used to visit back and forth. How did they kill her?"

"With a pipe, I think," Lucas said. "The ME'll figure it out."

Miller shivered: "And they're still running around the neighborhood."

Lucas's forehead wrinkled: "I'm not sure. I mean, if they're from the neighborhood. Do you know Bucher's place well enough to see whether anything was taken? I mean, the safe was untouched and we know one jewelry box was dumped and another might have been taken, and some electronics . . . but other stuff?"

She nodded. "I know it pretty well. Dan and I are redoing another house, down the street. We talked about buying some old St. Paul paintings from her and maybe some furniture and memorabilia. We thought it would be better to keep her things together, instead of having them dispersed when she died . . . I guess they'll be dispersed, now. We never did anything about it."

"Would you be willing to take a look inside?" Lucas asked. "See if you notice anything missing?"

"Sure. Now?"

"Not now," Lucas said. "The crime-scene guys are still working over the place, they'll want to move the bodies out. But I'll talk to the lead investigator here, get you into the house later today. His name is John Smith."

"I'll do it," she said.

LUCAS WENT back inside, told Smith about Shelley Miller, then drifted around the house, taking it in, looking for something, not knowing what it was, watching the crime-scene techs work, asking a question now and then. He was astonished at the size of the place: A library the size of a high school library. A ballroom the size of a basketball court, with four crystal chandeliers.

John Smith was doing the same thing. They bumped into each other a few times:

"Anything?"

"Not much," Lucas said.

"See all the silverware behind that dining room panel?" Smith asked.

"Yeah. Sterling."

"Looks like it's all there."

Lucas scratched his forehead. "Maybe they figured it'd be hard to fence?"

"Throw it in a car, drive down to Miami, sayonara."

"It's got names and monograms . . ." Lucas suggested.

"Polish it off. Melt it down," Smith said. "Wouldn't take a rocket scientist."

"Maybe it was too heavy?"

"Dunno . . ."

Lucas wandered on, thinking about it. A hundred pounds of solid silver? Surely, not that much. He went back to the dining room, looked inside the built-in cabinet. Three or four sets of silverware, some bowls, some platters. He turned one of the platters over, thinking it might be gilded pewter or something; saw the sterling mark. Hefted it, hefted a dinner set, calculated . . . maybe forty pounds total? Still, worth a fortune.

A uniformed cop walked by, head bent back, looking at the ceiling.

"What?" Lucas asked.

"Look at the ceiling. Look at the crown molding." Lucas looked. The ceiling was molded plaster, the crown molding was a frieze of running horses. "The crown molding is worth more than my house."

"So if it turns up missing, we should look in your garage," Lucas said.

The cop nodded. "You got that right."

A COUPLE of people from the ME's office wheeled a gurney through the dining room and out a side door; a black plastic body bag sat on top of it. Peebles.

LUCAS WENT BACK to the silver. Where was he? Oh yeah— must be worth a fortune. Then a stray thought: Was it really?

Say, forty pounds of solid silver; 640 ounces . . . but silver was weighed in troy ounces, which, if he remembered correctly, were about ten percent heavier than regular ounces. Sterling wasn't pure, only about 90 percent, so you'd have some more loss. Call it roughly 550 troy ounces of pure silver at . . . he didn't know how much. Ten bucks? Fifteen? Not a fortune. After fencing it off, reworking it and refining it, getting it to the end user, the guys who carried it out of the house would be lucky to take out a grand.

In the meantime, they'd be humping around a lot of silver that had the dead woman's initials all over it. Maybe, he thought, they didn't take it because it wasn't worth the effort or risk. Maybe smarter than your average cokehead.

Another gurney went by in the hall, another body bag: Bucher. Then a cop stuck his head in the dining room door: "The Lash kid is here. They've taken him into the front parlor."

LUCAS WENT that way, thinking about the silver, about the video games, about the way the place was trashed, the credit cards not stolen . . . Superficially, it looked local, but under that, he thought, it looked like something else. Smith was getting the same bad feeling about it: something was going on, and they didn't know what it was.

RONNIE LASH was tall and thin, nervous—scared—a sheen of perspiration on his coffee-brown forehead, tear tracks on his cheeks. He was neatly dressed in a red short-sleeved golf shirt, tan slacks, and athletic shoes; his hands were in his lap, and he twisted and untwisted them. His mother, a thin woman in a nurse's uniform, clutched a black handbag the size of a grocery sack, stood with him, talking to John Smith.

"They always say, get a lawyer," Mrs. Lash said. "Ronnie didn't do anything, to anybody, he loved Sugar, but they always say, get a lawyer."

"We, uh, Mrs. Lash, you've got to do what you think is right," Smith said. "We could get a lawyer here to sit with Ronnie, we could have somebody here in an hour from the public defender, won't cost you a cent." Which was the last thing Smith wanted. He wanted the kid alone, where he could lie to him.

Mrs. Lash was saying, ". . . don't have a lot of money for lawyers, but I can pay my share."

Ronnie was shaking his head, looking up at his mother: "I want to get this over with, Ma. I want to talk to these guys. I don't want a lawyer."

She put a hand on his shoulder. "They always say get a lawyer, Ronnie."

"If you need one, Ma," the Lash kid said. "I don't need one. Jesus will take care of me. I'll just tell the truth."

She shook a finger at him: "You talk to them then, but if they start saying stuff to you, you holler for me and we'll get a lawyer up here." To John Smith: "I still don't understand why I can't come in. He's a juvenile."

"Because we need to talk to Ronnie—not to the two of you. We need to talk to you, too, separately."

"But I didn't . . ." she protested.

"We don't think you did, Mrs. Lash, but we've got to talk to everybody," Smith said. His voice had lost its edge, now that he knew he'd be able to sweat Ronnie, without a lawyer stepping on his act.

LUCAS LEANED AGAINST the hallway wall, listening to the exchange, mother and son going back and forth. The Lashes finally decided that Ronnie could go ahead and talk, but if the cops started saying stuff to him . . .

"I'll call you, Ma."

At that point, Lucas was eighty-three percent certain that Ronnie Lash hadn't killed anyone, and hadn't helped kill anyone.

THEY PUT Mrs. Lash on a settee in the music room and took Ronnie into the parlor, John Smith, a fat detective named Sy Schuber, and Lucas, and shut the door. They put Ronnie on a couch and scattered around the room, dragging up chairs, and Smith opened by outlining what had happened, and then said, "So we've got to ask you, where were you this weekend? Starting at four-thirty Friday afternoon?"

"Me'n some other guys took a bus over to Minneapolis, right after school on Friday," Lash said. "We were going over to BenBo's on Hennepin. They were having an underage night."

BenBo's was a hip-hop place. Ronnie and four male friends from school spent the next five hours dancing, hanging out with a group of girls who'd gone over separately: so nine other people had been hanging with Ronnie most of the evening. He listed their names, and Schuber wrote them down. At ten o'clock, the mother of one of the kids picked up the boys in her station wagon and hauled them all back to St. Paul.

"What kind of car?" Lucas asked.

"A Cadillac SUV—I don't know exactly what they're called," Lash said. "It was a couple of years old."

Coming back to St. Paul, Ronnie had been dropped third, so he thought it was shortly before eleven o'clock when he got home. His mother was still up. She'd bought a roasted chicken at the Cub supermarket, and they ate chicken sandwiches in the kitchen, talked, and went to bed.

On weekends, Lash worked at a food shelf run by his church, which wasn't a Catholic church, though he went to a Catholic school. He started at nine in the morning, worked until three o'clock.

"They don't pay, but, you know, it goes on your record for college," he said. "It's also good for your soul."

Schuber asked, "If you're such a religious guy, how come you were out at some hip-hop club all night?"

"Jesus had no problem with a good time," Ronnie said. "He turned water into wine, not the other way around."

"Yeah, yeah." Smith was rubbing his eyeballs with his fingertips. "Ronnie, you got a guy down the block from you named Weldon Godfrey. You know Weldon?"

"Know who he is," Ronnie said, nodding. He said it so casually that Lucas knew that he'd seen the question coming.

"You hang out?" Smith asked.

"Nope. Not since I started at Catholic school," Lash said. "I knew him most when I went to public school, but he was two grades ahead of me, so we didn't hang out then, either."

"He's had a lot of trouble," Schuber said.

"He's a jerk," Ronnie said, and Lucas laughed in spite of himself. The kid sounded like a middle-aged golfer.

Smith persisted: "But you don't hang with Weldon or any of his friends?"

"No. My ma would kill me if I did," Ronnie said. He twisted and untwisted his bony fingers, and leaned forward. "Ever since I heard Aunt Sugar was murdered, I knew you'd want to talk to me about it. It'd be easy to say, 'Here's this black kid, he's a gang kid, he set this up.' Well, I didn't."

"Ronnie, we don't . . ."

"Don't lie to me, sir," Ronnie said. "This is too serious."

Smith nodded: "Okay."

"You were saying . . ." Lucas prompted.

"I was saying, I really loved Aunt Sugar and I really liked Mrs. Bucher." A tear started down one cheek, and he let it go. "Aunt Sugar brought me up, just like my ma. When Ma was going to school, Aunt Sugar was my full-time babysitter. When Aunt Sugar got a job with Mrs. B, and I started going to Catholic school, I started coming over here, and Mrs. B gave me money for doing odd jobs. Gave me more money than she had to and she told me that if she lived long enough, she'd help me with college. No way I want those people to get hurt. I wouldn't put the finger on them for anybody, no matter how much they stole."

Lucas bought it. If the kid was lying, and could consciously generate those tears, then he was a natural little psychopath. Which, of course, was possible.

Lucas felt John Smith sign off, Schuber shrugged, and Lucas jumped in: "So what'd they steal, kid?"

"I don't know. Nobody would let me look," Lash said.

Lucas to Smith: "Can I drag him around the house one time?"

Smith nodded. "Go ahead. Get back to me."

"We all done?" Ronnie asked.

"For now," Smith said, showing a first smile. "Don't book any trips to South America."

Ronnie's face was dead serious. "No sir."

OUT IN the hallway, Mrs. Lash was standing with her back to the wall, staring at the door. As soon as Lucas stepped through, she asked, "What?"

Lucas shrugged. "Ronnie's offered to show me around the house."

She asked Ronnie, "They say anything to you?"

"No. They don't think I did it," Lash said.

To Lucas: "Is that right?"

Lucas said, "We never really did. But we have to check. Is it all right if he shows me around?"

She eyed him for a moment, an always present skepticism that Lucas saw when he dealt with blacks, as a white cop. Her eyes shifted to her son, and she said, "I've got to talk to the police about Sugar. About the funeral arrangements. You help this man, and if he starts putting anything on you, you shut up and we'll get a lawyer."

"WHAT I WANT to know, is what these people took," Lucas told Lash. "We know they took some electronics . . . a game machine, probably a DVD. What else?"

They started with the TV room. "Took a DVD and an Xbox and a CD player—Mrs. B liked to sit in here and listen to her albums and she figured out how to run the CD player with the remote, and also, it was off here, to the side, so she didn't have to bend over to put a CD in. The DVD was on the shelf below the TV and she couldn't get up if she bent over that far, Aunt Sugar had to do that," Lash said. He looked in the closet: "Huh. Didn't take the games." He seemed to look inward, to some other Ronnie Lash, who knew about the streets, and muttered to himself, "Games is same as cash."

"Your games?" Lucas asked.

"Yes. But why didn't they take them?"

Lucas scratched his nose. "What else?"

"There was a money jar in the butler's pantry." Lash led the way to the small kitchen where Lucas had run into Rose Marie and the weeping politician.

"This is a butler's pantry?" Lucas asked, looking around. "What the hell is that?"

"The real kitchen is down the basement. When you had a big dinner, the food would get done down there, and then it'd come on this little elevator—it's called a dumbwaiter." Lash opened a panel to show off an open shaft going down. "The servants would get it here and take it to the table. But for just every day, Mrs. B had the pantry remodeled into a kitchen."

"Okay."

An orange ceramic jar, molded to look like a pumpkin, with the word "Cookies" on the side, sat against a wall on the kitchen counter. Lash reached for it but Lucas caught his arm. "Don't touch," he said.

He got a paper towel from a rack, put his hand behind the jar, and pushed it toward the edge of the countertop. When it was close enough to look into, he took the lid off, gripping the lid by its edges. "Fingerprints."

Lash peered inside. "Nope. Cleaned it out. There was usually a couple of hundred bucks in here. Sometimes more and sometimes less."

"Slush fund."

"Yes. For errands and when deliverymen came," Lash said. "Mostly twenties, and some smaller bills and change. Though . . . I wonder what happened to the change barrel?"

"What's that?" Lucas asked.

"It's upstairs. I'll show you."

Lucas called a crime-scene tech, who'd stretch warning tape around the kitchen counter. Then they walked through the house, and Lash mentioned a half-dozen items: a laptop computer was missing, mostly used by the housekeeping couple, but also by Lash for his schoolwork. A Dell, Lash said, and he pointed to a file drawer with the warranty papers.

Lucas copied down the relevant information and the serial number. Also missing: a computer printer, binoculars, an old Nikon spotting scope that Bucher had once used for birding, two older film cameras, a compact stereo. "Stamps," Lash said. "There was a big roll of stamps in the desk drawer . . ."

The drawer had been dumped.

"How big was the printer?" Lucas asked.

"An HP LaserJet, about so big," Lash said, gesturing with his hands, indicating a two-foot square.

"Heavy?"

"I don't know. I didn't put it in. But pretty heavy, I think," Lash said. "It looked heavy. It was more like a business machine, than like a home printer."

"Huh."

"What means 'huh'?" Lash asked.

Lucas said, "You think they put all this stuff in a bag and went running down the street?"

Lash looked at him for a minute, then said, "They had a car." He looked toward the back of the house, his fingers tapping his lower lip. "But Detective Smith said they probably came in through the back, up the hill."

"Well?"

Lash shrugged: "He was wrong."

IN THE upstairs hallway, a brass vase—or something like a vase, but four feet tall—lay on its side. Lucas had noticed it among the other litter on his first trip through the house, but had just seen it as another random piece of vandalism.

Lash lifted it by the lip: "Got it," he said. To Lucas: "Every night, Mrs. B put the change she got in here. Everything but pennies. She said someday, she was going to call the Salvation Army at Christmas, and have them send a bell ringer around, and she'd give, like, the whole vase full of coins."

"How much was in there?"

Lash shook his head: "Who knows? It was too heavy to move. I couldn't even tip it."

"So hundreds of dollars."

"I don't know. It was all nickels, dimes, and quarters, so, quite a bit," Lash said. "Maybe thousands, when you think about it."

On the rest of the floor, Lash couldn't pick out anything that Lucas didn't already suspect: the jewelry, the drugs. Maybe something hidden in the dressers, but Lash had never looked inside of them, he said, so he didn't know what might be missing.

On the third floor, they had a moment: Lash had spent some time on the third floor, sorting and straightening under Bucher's direction. "Sugar said Mrs. B was getting ready to die," Lash said.

They'd looked into a half-dozen rooms, when Lash said, suddenly, "Wait a minute." He walked back to the room they'd just left, which had been stacked with furniture and a number of cardboard boxes; a broken lamp stuck out of one of them. Lash said, "Where're the chairs?"

"The chairs?"

"Yeah. There were two old chairs in here. One was turned upside down on the other one, like in a restaurant when it's closing. At least . . ." He touched his chin. "Maybe they were in the next one."

They stepped down to the next room. Several chairs, but not, Lash said, the two he was thinking of. They went back to the first room. "They were right here."

"When did you last see them?"

Lash put a finger in his ear, rolled it for a moment, thinking, then said, "Well, it's been a while. I was cleaning this room out . . . gosh, Christmas vacation. Six months."

"Two old chairs," Lucas said.

"Yeah."

"Maybe Mrs. Bucher got rid of them?"

Lash shrugged. "I suppose. She never said anything. I don't think she thought about them."

"Really old, like French antiques or something?" Lucas asked.

"No, no," Lash said. "More like my mom's age. Or maybe your age."

"How do you know?"

"Because they were like . . . swoopy. Like one big swoop was the back and the other swoop was the seat. They were like, you know, what'd you see on old TV—*Star Trek*, like that. Or maybe chairs at the Goodwill store."

"Huh. So you couldn't mistake them," Lucas said.

"No. They're not here."

AS THEY WENT through the last few rooms, Lash said, finally, "You know, I'm not sure, but it seems like somebody's been poking around up here. Things are not quite like it was. It seems like stuff has been moved."

"Like what?"

Lash pointed across the room, to a battered wooden rocking chair with a torn soft seat. Behind the rocker, four framed paintings were stacked against the wall. "Like somebody moved that rocker. When the old lady wanted something moved, she usually got me to do it."

"Was there something back there?"

Lash had to think about it for a moment, then went and looked in another room, and came back and looked at the old rocker and said, "There might have been more pictures than that. Behind the rocker."

"How many?" Lucas asked.

"I don't know, but the stack was thicker. Maybe six? Maybe five. Or maybe seven. But the stack was thicker. One of the frames was gold colored, but all covered with dust. I don't see that one. Let me see, one said 'reckless' on the back . . ."

"Reckless?"

"Yeah, somebody had painted 'reckless' on it," Lash said. "Just that one word. On the back of the painting, not the picture side. In dark gray paint. Big letters."

"Portrait, landscape . . . ?"

"I don't know. I didn't look at the front, I just remember that word on the back. There are a couple of paintings gone. At least two."

"There were some pictures down the hall in that third room, the one with the ironing boards," Lucas said.

"No, no, I know about those," Lash said. "These up here had frames that were, like, carved with flowers and grapes and stuff. And the gold one. Those other ones are just plain."

"Chairs that weren't very old, and maybe some paintings," Lucas said.

"Yeah." They stood in silence for a moment, then Lash added, "I'll tell you what, Mr. Davenport, Weldon Godfrey didn't steal any chairs and paintings. Or maybe he'd take the chairs, because his house never had much furniture. But Weldon wouldn't give you a dollar for any painting I can think of. Unless it was like a blond woman with big boobs."

They tramped back through the house, and on the way, Lash's pocket started to play a rock version of "The Battle Hymn of the Republic." He took a cell phone out of his pocket, looked at it, pushed a button, and stuck it back in his pocket.

"You've got a cell phone," Lucas said.

"Everybody's got a cell phone. Mom'n me, we don't have a regular phone anymore."

BACK ON the first floor, they ran into Smith again. Smith's left eyebrow went up, a question.

"Maybe something," Lucas said. "Ronnie thinks a few things may have been taken. Can't nail it down, but stuff looks like it's been moved on the third floor. Couple of chairs may be missing, maybe a painting or two."

"Tell him about the car," Lash said.

"Oh yeah," Lucas said. "They used a car to move the stuff. Or a van or a truck."

Lucas explained and Smith said, "The Hill House has a security

system with cameras looking out at the street. Maybe we'll see something on the tapes."

"If they took those chairs, it'd have to be pretty good-sized," Lash
said. "Not a car. A truck."

"Maybe they'll turn up on *Antiques Roadshow?*" Smith said.

"Maybe. But we're not sure what's missing," Lucas said. "Ronnie's
not even sure that Bucher didn't get rid of the chairs herself."

Mrs. Lash was sitting in the foyer, waiting for her son. When Lucas
brought him back, she asked Ronnie, "Are you okay?"

"I'm fine. But just wait here for one minute, I want to look at
something. I noticed it when the police brought us in . . ." He went
back down the hall and into the music room, his feet cracking
through bits and pieces of broken glass.

"He's been a big help," Lucas said to Mrs. Lash. "We appreciate it."

"I'm sure," she said. Then, "I've seen you at Hennepin General. I
used to work over there."

"My wife's a surgeon, she's on staff at Hennepin," Lucas said. "I'd
hang out sometimes."

"What's her name?" Lash asked.

"Weather Karkinnen."

Lash brightened: "Oh, I know Dr. Karkinnen. She's really good."

"Yeah, I know." He touched a scar at his throat, made by Weather
with a jackknife. Ronnie came back, gestured toward the music room
with his thumb.

"There's a cabinet in there with a glass front. It used to be full of
old vases and dishes and bowls. One of them had Chinese coins in
it. I'm not sure, because some of it's broken, but I don't think there
are as many pieces as there used to be. It looks too . . . loose."

"Could you identify any of it? If we came up with some stuff?"

Lash shook his head doubtfully. "I don't know anything about it.
I never really looked at it, except, one time when Mrs. Bucher
showed me the coins. It just looks too loose. It used to be jammed

with vases and bowls. Coins are all over the floor now, so they didn't take those."

"Okay . . . Any other last thoughts?"

Ronnie said to Lucas, " 'The love of money is the root of all evils.' Timothy, six-ten."

The little asshole was getting on top of him.

Lucas said, " 'Money is better than poverty, if only for financial reasons.' Woody Allen."

His mother cracked a smile, but Ronnie said, "I'll go with Timothy."

4

AS THE LASHES LEFT, Smith and another cop came rolling down the hall, picking up their feet, in a jacket-flapping, gun-flashing hurry.

"Got a break," Smith said, coming up to Lucas. "Let's go."

Lucas started walking. "What happened?"

"Guy showed up at Rhodes's with some jewelry in a jewelry box. Jewelry was cheap but the box was terrific. Our guys turned it over, it's inscribed 'Bucher' on the back."

Rhodes's was a pawnshop. Lucas asked, "Do they know who brought it in?"

"That's the weird thing," Smith said. "They *do.*"

"Where're we going?" Lucas asked.

"Six-twelve Hay. It's off Payne, nine blocks north of Seventh. SWAT is setting up in the parking lot behind the Minnesota Music Café."

"See you there."

PAYNE AVENUE WAS one of the signature drags across St. Paul's east side, once the Archie Bunker bastion of the city's white working class. The neighborhood had been in transition for decades, reliable old employers leaving, a new mix of Southeast Asians and blacks moving in. Lucas dropped past the cathedral, onto I-94 in a minute or so, up the hill to Mounds Boulevard, left and left again.

The café was an old hangout of his, at the corner of East Seventh and Payne, with a graveled parking lot in back, and inside, the best music in town. A dozen cars were in the lot, cops pulling on body armor. A half-dozen civilians were watching from the street. Smith arrived ten seconds after Lucas, and they walked over to Andy Landis, the SWAT squad commander.

"What you got?" Smith asked.

"We're in the house behind him and on both sides," Landis said. "Name is Nathan Brown. Don't have anything local on him, but the people in the house behind him say he moved here from Chicago four or five years ago. There're about fifty Nathan and Nate Browns with files down in Chicago, so we don't know who he is."

"Got the warrant?" Smith asked.

"On the way. Two minutes," Landis said.

"Love this shit," Smith said to Lucas.

"You ever been on the SWAT squad?"

"Ten years, until the old lady nagged me out of it," Smith said. "Turned my crank."

"Wasn't it called something else? They called you the 'breath mint'?"

"CIRT," Smith said. "Critical Incident Response Team."

"SWAT's better," Lucas said.

THE WARRANT ARRIVED and the SWAT squad moved out in three groups. Lucas and Smith tagged behind.

"The couple who found the bodies . . . did they notice anything missing around the house?" Lucas asked.

Smith shook his head. "Not that they mentioned. But they weren't housekeepers—the wife does the cooking, the husband did maintenance and gardening and the lawn. And with shit thrown all over the place like it was . . . The niece is on the way from California. She'll probably know something."

THE SWAT TEAM came in three groups: a blocking group at the back door, and two at the front of the house, one from each side. They came across the neighboring lawns, armored, face shields, carrying long arms. Moved diagonally across the lawn of the target house, quietly swarming the porch, doing a peek at the window, then kicking the front door in.

Nathan Brown, as it happened, was asleep in a downstairs bedroom. His girlfriend was feeding her kids grilled-cheese sandwiches in the kitchen, and began screaming when the cops came through, had the phone in her hand screaming "Nine-one-one, nine-one-one," and the kids were screaming, and then the cops were in the bedroom on top of Brown.

Brown was yelling, "Hey . . . hey . . . hey," like a stuck record.

Lucas came in as they rolled him and cuffed him; his room smelled of old wallpaper, sweat, and booze. Brown was shirtless, dazed, wearing boxer shorts. He'd left a damp sweat stain on the sheet of the queen-sized bed.

After some thrashing around, the freaked-out girlfriend sat in a corner sobbing, her two children crying with her. The cops found a plastic baggie with an assortment of earrings on the floor by Brown's pants. Asked where he got them, Brown roused himself to semicoherence, and said, "I shoulda known, there ain't no fuckin' toot' fairy."

"Where'd you get them?

He shook his head, not in refusal, but knowing the reaction he'd get: "I got them off a bus bench."

That was stupid enough that it stopped everybody. "Off a bus bench?" Smith said.

"Off a bus bunch. Up at . . . up at Dale. Dale and Grand," Brown said. His eyes tended to wander in his head. "Friday night. Midnight. Lookin' for a bus so I don't got to walk downtown. The box was sittin' right there, like the toot' fairy left it."

"Full of jewelry," said one of the cops.

"Not full. Only a little in there." He craned his neck toward the door. He could hear the children, still screaming, and their mother now trying to calm them down. Cops were starting to prop themselves in the doorway, to listen to what Brown was saying. "Did you knock the door down?" Brown asked. "Why the kids crying? Are the kids okay?"

"The kids are okay . . ." The air was going out of the SWAT guys.

"Is the house hurt?" There was a pleading note in Brown's voice.

Smith stepped away, put a radio to his face. Lucas asked, "Anybody see you pick this box up?"

Brown said, "Not that I seen. I just seen the box, thought somebody left it, opened it up, didn't see no name."

"There was a name on the bottom of the box."

"Didn't look on the bottom of the box," Brown said helplessly.

Lucas didn't take long to make up his mind. Smith was uncertain, but after talking to Brown, and then to Brown's girlfriend, Lucas was pretty sure that Brown was telling the truth about the jewelry box.

Smith served the search warrant on the woman, who owned the house, and the cops started tearing it apart.

LUCAS WENT BACK to his car alone, rolled down Payne to the café, got a notebook from behind the car seat, took a table on the sidewalk out in front of the place, bought a beer, and started doodling his way through the killings.

The murders of Bucher and Peebles looked like a gang-related home invasion. Two or three assholes would bust a house, tape up the occupants—most often older people, scouted in advance—and then take their time cleaning the house out. Easier, safer, and often more lucrative than going into liquor or convenience stores, which had hardened themselves with cameras, safes, and even bullet-proof screens.

But with Bucher and Peebles, the robbers had not taken credit cards or ATM cards. In most house invasions, those would be the first targets, because they'd yield cash. Bucher and Peebles appeared to have been killed quickly, before they could resist. Most home invaders, even if they were planning to kill the victims, would keep them alive long enough to squeeze out the PIN numbers for the ATM cards.

ATMs had cameras, but it was easy enough to put a rag over your face. They might not have intended to kill. Say they came onto Peebles, somebody got excited and swatted her with a pipe. Then they'd have to kill Bucher just to clean up.

But there was no sign that Peebles resisted . . .

The halfway house was becoming more interesting. Lucas made up a scenario and played it through his head: suppose you had a couple of real hard guys in the halfway house, looking out the second-floor windows, watching the housekeepers come and go, the two old ladies in the garden during the day, the one or two bedroom lights at night, one light going out, then the other.

They'd be in a perfect spot to watch, sitting in a bedroom all evening, nothing to do, making notes, counting heads, thinking about what must be inside.

Get a car, roll down there during a storm. Real hard guys, knowing in advance what they were doing, knowing they were going to kill, maybe drinking a little bit, but wearing gloves, knowing about DNA . . .

But why would they take a bunch of junk? Stereos and game machines? The stuff they'd taken, as far as Lucas knew of it, wouldn't be worth more than several hundred dollars on the street, not counting the cash, stamps, the vase full of change, and any jewelry they might have gotten. If they'd kept the old ladies alive long enough to get PINs, they could have probably taken down a thousand dollars a day, Friday through Sunday, all cash, *then* killed them and run with a car full of stuff.

Maybe, though, there was something else in the house. What happened to those chairs? The paintings? Were those figments of Ronnie Lash's imagination? How much could a couple of swoopy chairs be worth, anyway?

HE TOOK OUT his cell phone and called home: the housekeeper answered. "Could you get the address book off Weather's desk, and bring it to the phone?" The housekeeper put down the phone, and was back a minute later. "There should be a listing for a cell phone for a Shelley Miller."

Lucas jotted the number in the palm of his hand, rang off, and dialed Miller, the woman he'd talked to at Oak Walk. The cops had been taking her inside when Lucas and Smith left for the raid.

She came up on the phone: "This is Shelley . . ."

"Shelley, this is Lucas. Anything?"

"Lucas, I'm not sure. There's just too much stuff lying around. God, it makes me want to cry. You know, my great-uncle is in one of the portraits with Connie's husband's father . . ." She sniffed. "But . . . Connie always liked to wear nice earrings and I think she probably kept those at her bedside. She had diamonds, emeralds, rubies, sapphires, pearls . . . uh, probably a couple of more things. They weren't small. For the single-stone earrings, I'd say two or three carats each. Then she had some dangly ones, with smaller stones; and she always wore them. I'd see her out working on the lawn, grubbing around in the dirt, and she'd have very nice earrings on. She also had a blue singleton diamond, a wedding gift from her husband, that she always wore around her neck on a platinum chain, probably eight or ten carats, and her engagement ring, also blue, a fragment of the neck stone, I think, probably another five carats. I really doubt that she locked them up every night."

After digesting it for a moment, Lucas asked, "How much?"

"Oh, I don't know. I really don't. It would depend so much on quality—but the Buchers wouldn't get cheap stones. I wouldn't be surprised if, huh. I don't know. A half million?"

"Holy shit."

"I thought you should know."

THE CAFÉ'S OWNER, Karen Palm, came by, patted him on the shoulder. She was a nice-looking woman, big smile and dark hair on her shoulders, an old pal; as many St. Paul cops hung out at the café as Minneapolis cops hung out at Sloan's place on the other side of the river.

"Were you with the SWAT team?" she asked.

"Yeah. You heard about the Bucher thing."

"Terrible. Did you get the guy?" she asked.

"I don't think so," Lucas said. "He was just in the wrong place at the wrong time . . ."

"Well, shoot . . ."

They chatted for a minute, catching up, then Carol called and Palm went back to work. Carol said, "I'm switching you over to McMahon."

McMahon was a BCA investigator. He came on and said, "I looked at the people from the halfway house. I've run them all against the feds and our own records, and it's, uh, difficult."

"What's difficult?" Lucas asked.

"These guys were cherry-picked for their good behavior. That's the most famous halfway house in the Cities. If that place flies, nobody can complain about one in their neighborhood. So, what you've got is a bunch of third-time DUI arrests and low-weight pot dealers from the university. No heavy hitters."

"There can't be *nobody* . . ."

"Yes, there can," McMahon said. "There's not a single violent crime or sex crime against any of them. There's not even a hit-and-run with the DUIs."

"Not a lot of help," Lucas said.

McMahon said, "The guy who runs the place is named Dan Westchester. He's there every night until six. You could talk to him in person. I'll run a few more levels on the records checks, but it doesn't look like there'll be much."

LUCAS DROPPED a five-dollar bill on the table, stretched, thought about it, then drove back to Brown's house. Brown was in the back of a squad, his girlfriend and her daughter sitting on a glider on the front porch, the girlfriend looking glumly at the busted door.

Smith was standing in the kitchen doorway and Lucas took him aside.

"I've got a friend who knew Bucher. She says Bucher used to wear some diamonds, big ones . . ." Lucas said. He explained about Miller, and her thoughts about the jewelry. Smith said, "A half million? If it's a half million, no wonder they didn't take the ATM cards. A half million could be pros."

"Unless it was just a couple of dopers who got lucky," Lucas said. "There could be some little dolly dancing on Hennepin Avenue with a ten-carat stone around her neck, thinking it's glass."

"So . . ."

"These guys take the game box, but not the games. They take diamonds and swoopy chairs and a painting, but they also take a roll of stamps and a DVD player and a printer and a laptop. It's not adding up, John."

"Brown's not adding up, either," Smith said. "He's an alcoholic, he's on the bottle, really bad, and there's a liquor cabinet full of the best stuff in the world back there, and it's not touched." Smith looked down to the squad where Brown was sitting. "Jesus. Why couldn't it be easy?"

LUCAS LEFT the raid site, headed back to the Bucher house and the halfway house. The crowd outside had gotten thinner—dinnertime, he thought—and what was left was coalescing around four TV trucks, where reporters were doing stand-ups for the evening news.

Inside, the crime-scene people were expanding their search, but had nothing new to report. He walked through the place one last time, then headed across the street to the halfway house.

THE HALFWAY HOUSE looked like any of the fading mansions on the wrong side of Summit, a brown-brick three-story with a carriage house out back, a broad front porch with white pillars, now flaking paint, and an empty porch swing.

Dan Westchester somewhat resembled the house: he was on the wrong side of fifty, the fat side of two-twenty, and the short side of five-ten. He had a small gray ponytail, a gold earring in his left earlobe, and wore long cotton slacks, a golf shirt, and sandals. The name plaque on his desk showed a red-yellow-green Vietnam ribbon under his name.

"I already talked to St. Paul, and I talked to your guy at the BCA," he said unhappily. "What do you want from us?"

"Just trying to scc what's what," Lucas said. "We've got two murdered old ladies across the street from a halfway house full of convicted criminals. If we didn't talk to you, our asses would get fired."

"I know, but we've worked so hard . . ."

"I can believe that," Lucas said. "But . . ." He shrugged.

Westchester nodded. "The guys here . . . we've had exactly six complaints since we opened the facility, and they involved alcoholic relapses," he said. "None of the people were violent. The DOC made a decision early on that we wouldn't house violent offenders here."

Lucas: "Look. I'm not here to dragoon the house, I'm just looking for an opinion: If one of your guys did this, who would it be?"

"None of them," Westchester snapped.

"Bullshit," Lucas snapped back. "If this was a convent, there'd be two or three nuns who'd be more likely than the others to do a double murder. I'm asking for an assessment, not an accusation."

"None of them," Westchester repeated. "The guys in this house wouldn't beat two old ladies to death. Most of them are just unhappy guys . . ."

"Yeah." Unhappy guys who got drunk and drove cars onto sidewalks and across centerlines into traffic.

Westchester: "I'm not trying to mess with you. I'm not silly about convicted felons. But honest to God, most of the people here are sick. They don't intend to do bad, they're just *sick*. They're inflicted with an evil drug."

"So you don't have a single guy . . ."

"I can't give you a name," Westchester said. "But I'll tell you what: you or St. Paul can send over anyone you want, and I'll go over my guys, file by file, and I'll tell you everything I know. Then *you* make the assessment. I don't want a goddamn killer in here. But I don't think I've got one. I'm sure I don't."

Lucas thought about it for a moment: "All right. That's reasonable." He stood up, turned at the office door. "Not a single guy?"

"Not one."

"Where were *you* Friday night?"

Westchester sat back and grinned. "I'm in a foosball league. I was playing foosball. I got two dozen 'ballers to back me up."

LUCAS LEFT, a little pissed, feeling thwarted: he'd wanted a name, any name, a place to start. Halfway down the sidewalk, his cell phone rang, and when he looked at the number, saw that it came from the governor's office.

"Yeah. Governor," Lucas said.

"You catch them?"

"Not yet."

"Well, fuck 'em then, they're too smart for you," the governor said. "Now: I want you to talk to Neil tomorrow morning. He has some suggestions about the way you conduct the Kline investigation, okay?"

"Maybe not," Lucas said. "I hate the charge, 'suborning justice.'"

"We're not going to suborn anything, Lucas," said the governor, putting a little buttermilk in his voice. "You know me better than that. We're managing a difficult situation."

"Not difficult for me, at this point," Lucas said. "Could get difficult, if I talk to Neil."

"Talk to Neil. Talk. How can it hurt?" the governor asked.

"Ask the White House guys in federal minimum security . . . Listen, sir, there's a straightforward way to handle this."

"No, there isn't," the governor said. "We've gone over all the options. We need more. If you can think up some reasonable options, then we won't have to turn Neil loose. So talk to him."

———

AT DINNER, Lucas told the Bucher story to his wife, Weather; his fifteen-year-old ward, Letty; and his son, Sam, who was almost two feet tall now, and who'd developed an intense interest in spoons.

Weather was a short blonde with a bold nose, square shoulders, and shrewd Finnish eyes; she was a plastic and microsurgeon and spent her days fixing heads and faces, revising scars, and replacing skin and cutting out lesions. When he was done with the story, Weather said, "So it was a robbery."

"Odd robbery," Lucas said, with a shake of his head. "If they were after the jewelry, why did they trash the rest of the house? If they were after paintings, why were there terrific old paintings all over the place? Why would they take swoopy furniture? The kid said it looked like they took it off the *Star Trek* set. It's just weird: They stole a printer? They stole an Xbox but not the hottest game on the market?"

"That is definitely strange," Letty said. She was a lanky girl, dark haired, and was growing into a heart-stopper.

"All that other stuff was to throw you off, so you'd think dopers did it, but it's really a gang of serious antique and jewel thieves," Weather said. "They took a few special pieces and scattered the rest around to conceal it. It's as plain as the nose on your face."

"Weather . . ." Lucas said impatiently.

"Lucas," Weather snapped. "Look around, if you can get your head out of your butt long enough."

Letty giggled. ". . . head out of your butt." Sam pointed his spoon and yelled, "Butt!"

"We have three antiques," Weather said. "The most expensive one cost sixteen thousand."

"Sixteen thousand?" Lucas was appalled. "Which one was that?"

"The china cabinet," Weather said. "Most real antique people would tell you it is a piece of junk. When I redid the house, how much do you think I spent on furniture? Just give me a ballpark figure."

Lucas's eyes wandered down the dining room, toward the living room; thought about the new bedroom set, the couches in the den, the living room, the family room, and the TV room. The latter now needed new covers because he kept putting his feet on the arms. "I don't know. Forty, fifty thousand?"

It sounded high, but better high than low.

Weather stared at him, then looked at Letty, and back to Lucas. "Lucas, I mean, sweet-bleedin' . . ."

She looked at Letty again, who filled in, "Jesus."

Lucas said, "We're letting our mouths get a little out of control here . . ." That was an uphill fight he'd never win. He was laying down a smoke screen to cover his furniture-pricing faux pas, if that's what it was.

Weather said, "Lucas, I spent two hundred and ten thousand dollars, and that wasn't the really good stuff that I actually wanted."

His mouth didn't drop open, but he felt as if it had.

She continued: "Lucas, a fair-to-middling couch with custom coverings *starts* at five thousand dollars. This table"—she rapped with her knuckles on the dining table—"cost nine thousand dollars with eight chairs. And that's nothing. Nothing. Rich people would spit on this table."

"Not with me around," Lucas said.

Weather jabbed a fork at him. "Now. You say Bucher has as much money as your old pal Miller."

"Yeah. Same league," Lucas said. "Maybe some of the same ancestors."

"Those people were billionaires when a billion dollars was serious money," Weather said. "Everything in their houses would be top quality—and an eighty-year-old woman's house would be stuffed to the gills with antiques . . . Lucas, I don't know much about antiques, but I know you could get a million dollars' worth in a van. Paintings, who knows what they're worth? I thought maybe I'd buy a couple of nice old American paintings for the living room. But you know what old American impressionist-style paintings go for now? You could put twenty million dollars in the trunk of your Porsche. I'm not even talking about the biggest names. Painters you never heard of, you have to pay a half million dollars for their work."

Now he was impressed. He pushed back from the table: "I didn't . . . I gotta get a book."

Weather marched on: "This Lash kid, he said she had some old pots, and you said there were smashed pots lying around. They were covering up for what they took. Art Deco pots can go for fifty thousand dollars. Swoopy chairs with leather sets? There are Mies van der Rohe swoopy chairs that go for five thousand dollars each. I know, because Gloria Chatham bought two, and she never stops talking about it. Lucas, they could've taken millions out of this place. Not even counting those diamonds."

Lucas looked down at his roast, then back up to Weather: "You paid nine thousand dollars for this table? We could have gone over to IKEA."

"Fuck IKEA," Weather said.

Letty giggled. "I'd like to see that."

Sam hit a glass with a spoon; Weather looked at him and smiled and said, "Good boy."

WHEN THEY WERE done with dinner, Lucas hiked down to the Highland Park bookstore and bought a copy of Judith Miller's *Antiques Price Guide,* which was the biggest and slickest one. Back at home, sitting in the quiet of the den, he flipped through it. Weather hadn't been exaggerating. Lamps worth as much as $100,000; vases worth $25,000; Indian pots worth $30,000; a Dinky truck—*a Dinky truck like Lucas had played with new, as a kid, made in 1964!*—worth $10,000. Tables worth $20,000, $50,000, $70,000; a painting of a creek in winter, by a guy named Edward Willis Redfield, of whom Lucas had never heard, valued at $650,000.

"Who'd buy this shit?" he asked aloud. He spent another fifteen minutes with the book, made some notes, then got his briefcase, found his phone book, and called Smith at home.

"You catch 'em?" Smith asked.

"No. I've already been asked that," Lucas said. "By the governor."

"Well, shit."

"Listen, I've been doing some research . . ."

Lucas told Smith about the antiques book, and what he thought had to be done at the murder scene: "Interrogate the relatives. Try to nail down every piece of furniture and every painting. Get somebody who's good at puzzles, go over to that pot cupboard, whatever you call it, and glue those smashed pots back together. Get an antiques dealer in there to evaluate the place. My guys checked her insurance, but there's some bullshit about writs and privacy, so it'd probably be easier to check her safe-deposit box; or maybe there's a copy in one of those file cabinets. We need some paperwork."

Smith was uncertain: "Lucas, those pot pieces are smaller'n your dick. How in the hell are we going to get them back together?"

"The pots don't have to be perfect. We need to see what they are, and get somebody who knows what he's doing, and put a value on them. I've got this idea . . ."

"What?"

"If the people who hit the place are big-time antique thieves, if this is some kind of huge invisible heist, I'll bet they didn't bust up the good stuff," Lucas said. "I bet there's twenty thousand bucks worth of pots in the cupboard, there's a thousand bucks worth of busted pots on the floor, and the six missing pots are worth a hundred grand. That's what I think."

After a moment of silence, Smith sighed and said, "I'll freeze the scene, won't allow anybody to start cleaning anything out. Take pictures of everything, inch by inch. I'll get a warrant to open the safe-deposit box, get the insurance policies. I'll find somebody who can do the pots. I don't know any artists, but I can call around to the galleries. What was that the Lash kid said? A painting that said 'reckless'?"

"I put it in Google, and got nothing," Lucas said. "There's a guy here in town named Kidd, he's a pretty well-known artist. He's helped me out a couple of times, I'll give him a call, see if he has any ideas."

OFF THE PHONE with Smith, he considered for a moment. The media were usually a pain in the ass, but they could also be a useful club. If the robbery aspect of the murders were highlighted, it could have two positive effects: if the killers were local, and had already tried to dump the stuff, then some useful leads might pop up. If they were professionals, hitting Bucher for big money, it might freeze the resale of anything that was taken out. That'd be good, because it'd still be on their hands when the cops arrived.

There was no doubt in Lucas's mind that the cops would arrive, sooner or later. He looked in his address book again, and dialed a number. Ruffe Ignace, the reporter from the *Star Tribune,* said, without preface, "This better be good, because I could get laid tonight if I don't go back to the office. It's a skinny blonde with a deep need for kinky sex."

"You owe me," Lucas said. "Besides, I'm doing you another favor, and then you'll owe me two."

"Is this a favor that'll keep me from getting laid?" Ignace asked.

"You gotta work that out yourself," Lucas said. "What I'm going to tell you comes from an anonymous source close to the investigation."

"Are you talking about Brown? I got that."

"Not Brown," Lucas said. "But to me, it looks like a smart reporter might speculate that the murders and the trashing of the Bucher house were covers for one of the biggest arts and antiquities thefts in history, but one that's invisible."

Open cell phone: restaurant dishes clinking in the background. Then, hushed, "Holy shit. You think?"

"It could be speculated," Lucas said.

"How could I find out what they had in there?"

"Call Shelley Miller. Let me get you that number. Don't tell her that I gave it to you."

"Motherfucker," Ignace groaned. "The blonde just walked up to the bar. She's wearing a dress you can see her legs through. She's like wearing a thong? In Minneapolis? You know how rare that is? And she wants my body? You know how rare *that* is?"

"That number is . . . You gotta pen?"

"Davenport, man, you're killing me," Ignace said.

"Ruffe, listen: Tell her the story. The whole thing, the murders, everything. Tell her that Deep Throat called. Take her back to your office, drive as fast as you can, scream into your cell phone at the editors while you're driving. Fake it, if nobody's working. Then when you get there, sit her down, write the story, and ask her what she thinks. Then make some change she suggests; joke that she ought to get a share of the byline."

"Yeah, bullshit. The Ignace doesn't share bylines."

"Listen, Ruffe, she'll be all over you," Lucas said. "You'll nail her in the front seat of your car."

"I got a Prelude, man. With a stick shift. It'd hit her right in the small of the back."

"Whatever," Lucas said. "This will not mess up your night. I swear to God. You're good as gold—but try to get it in tomorrow morning, okay? I need this."

"You need that and I need this—" The phone clicked off.

But Lucas smiled.

He knew his reporters. No way Ignace wouldn't write the story.

AND LATE that night, in bed, Weather reading the latest Anne Perry, Lucas said, "I'm worried about the Kline thing. The governor's got me talking to Mitford tomorrow."

"I thought you liked him. Mitford."

"I do—but that doesn't mean that he's not a rattlesnake," Lucas said. "You gotta watch your ankles when he's around."

"You've never talked to the girl, have you?" Weather asked. "It's all been that fuckin' Flowers."

"No. I haven't talked to her. I should. But we've been trying to keep it at the cop level, apolitical. Now Kline's trying to cut a separate deal, but Rose Marie says that's not gonna fly. Nobody'll buy it. I expect I'm going to have to talk to Kline and then we're gonna bring in the Ramsey County attorney. That little chickenshit will do everything he can to turn it into a three-ring circus."

"Don't get in too deep, Lucas," Weather said. "This sounds like it'll require scapegoats."

"That worries me," he said.

"And sort of interests you, too."

He sat for a moment looking at the book in his lap. He was learning more about antiques. Then he grinned at her and admitted, "Maybe."

5

LUCAS READ the paper in the morning, over breakfast, and was happy to see Ignace's story on the possible theft; and he truly hoped that Ignace had gotten laid, which he, like most newspaper reporters, of both sexes, desperately needed.

In any case, the story should wake somebody up.

Sam was still working on his spoon technique, slopping oatmeal in a five-foot radius of his high chair; the housekeeper was cursing like a sailor, something to do with the faucet on the front of the house wouldn't turn off. Weather was long gone to work, where she spent almost every morning cutting on people. Letty was at school, the first summer session.

Lucas noticed a story on a zoning fight in the Dakota County suburbs south of the Twin Cities. One of the big shopping centers, the Burnsville Mall, was looking to expand, and some of its commercial neighbors thought that was a bad idea.

Lucas thought, "Hmmm," and closed his eyes. *Dakota County . . .*

LUCAS TOLD the housekeeper to call a plumber, kissed Sam on the head, dodged a spoonful of oatmeal, and went to look up Kidd's phone number. Kidd was the artist who might be able to help with the reckless painting. Lucas found his book, dialed, and got a dairy. Kidd had either changed numbers, or left town.

He glanced at his watch: Kidd's apartment was down by the river. He could drop by after he talked with Neil Mitford. Mitford was the governor's hatchet man; he tried to cut out at least one gizzard every morning before going out for a double latte grande.

Lucas finished his coffee and headed up the stairs to suit up; and once outside, it was another great day, puffy fair-weather clouds under a pale blue sky, just enough wind to ruffle the stars 'n' stripes outside an elementary school. He motored along Summit Avenue toward the Capitol, elbow out, counting women on cell phones making illegal turns.

MITFORD HAD a modest office down the hall from the governor's, in what he said had been a janitor's closet when the building was first put up. With just enough room for a desk, a TV, a computer, a thousand books, and a pile of paper the size of a cartoon doghouse, it might have been.

Mitford himself was short and burly, his dark hair thinning at the crown. He'd been trying to dress better lately, but in Lucas's opinion, had failed. This morning he was wearing pleated khaki slacks with permanent ironed-in wrinkles, a striped short-sleeved dress shirt, featureless black brogans with dusty toes, a chromed watch large enough to be a cell phone, and two actual cell phones, which were clipped to his belt like cicadas on a tree trunk.

Altogether, five or six separate and simultaneous fashion faux pas, in Lucas's view, depending on how you counted the cell phones.

"Lucas." Mitford didn't bother to smile. "How are we going to handle this?"

"That seems to be a problem," Lucas said, settling in a crappy chair across the desk from Mitford. "Everybody's doing a tap dance."

"You know, Burt backed us on the school-aid bill," Mitford said tentatively.

"Fuck a bunch of school-aid bill," Lucas said. "School aid is gonna be a bad joke if the word gets out that he'd been banging a ninth-grader."

Mitford winced. "Tenth-grader."

"Yeah, now," Lucas said. "But not when they started, if she's telling the truth."

"So . . ."

"I've got one possibility that nobody has suggested yet, and it's thin," Lucas said.

"Roll it out," Mitford said.

"The girl says Kline once took her to the Burnsville Mall and bought her clothes—a couple of blouses, skirts, some white cotton underpants, and a couple of push-up bras. She said he liked to have a little underwear-and-push-up-bra parade at night. Anyway, he got so turned on that they did a little necking and groping in the parking lot. She said she, quote, cooled him off, unquote."

"All right. So . . . the push-up bra?"

"She said he bought her gifts in return for the sex."

Mitford digressed: "He really said, 'Oh God, lick my balls, lick my balls'?"

"According to Virgil Flowers, Kline admits he might have said it, but he would've said it to Mom, not the daughter," Lucas said.

"Ah, Jesus," Mitford said. "This is dreadful."

"Kline said his old lady never . . ."

"Hey, hey—forget it." Mitford rubbed his face, and shuddered. "I know his old lady. Anyway, he took the kid to the Burnsville Mall and groped her and she cooled him off . . . Is that a big deal?"

"That'd be up to you," Lucas said. "We can make an argument that he was buying the clothes in return for sex, because of the kid's testimony. And then there was the touching in the car, what you call your basic manual stimulation. So one element of the crime happened at the mall."

"So what?"

"The mall is in Burnsville," Lucas said, "which happens to be in Dakota County. Dakota County, in its wisdom, elected itself a Republican as county attorney."

Mitford instantly brightened. "Holy shit! I knew there was a reason we hired you."

"That doesn't mean . . ." Lucas began.

Mitford was on his feet, circling his desk, shaking a finger at Lucas. "Yes, it does. One way or the other, it does. If we can get a Republican to indict this cocksucker . . ."

"Actually, *he* wasn't the . . ."

". . . then we're in the clear. Our hands are clean. There is no Democratic involvement in the process, no goddamn little intransigent Democratic cockroach publicity-seeking motherfucking horsefly Ramsey County attorney to drag us all down. It's a Republican problem. Yes, it is."

"Virgil is coming up here today to brief some people on the details," Lucas said.

"Yeah. I'll be going. I've been hearing some odd things about Flowers," Mitford said. "Somebody said he once whistled at a guy in an interrogation cell until the guy cracked and confessed."

"Well, yeah, you have to understand the circumstances, the guy belonged to a cult . . ."

Mitford didn't care about Flowers and whistling. "Goddamn! Lucas! A Republican county attorney! You my daddy!"

LUCAS WAS FEELING okay when he took the hill down into the St. Paul loop. He zigzagged southeast until he got to a chunky red-brick building that had once been a warehouse, then a loft association, and was now a recently trendy condominium.

One of the good things about the Bucher and Kline cases was that the major crime sites were so close to his house—maybe ten minutes on residential streets; and they were even closer to his office. He knew all the top cops in both cases, and even most of the uniformed guys. In the past couple of years he'd covered cases all over the southern half of Minnesota, on the Iron Range in the north, and in the Red River Valley, which was even farther north and west. Minnesota is a tall state, and driving it can wear a guy out.

Not these two cases. These were practically on his lawn.

He was whistling as he walked into the condo. An elderly lady was coming through the inner doors with a shopping bag full of old clothes. He held it for her, she twinkled at him, and he went on inside, skipping past the apartment buzzers.

KIDD CAME to the door looking tired and slightly dazed. He had a wrinkled red baby, about the size of a loaf of Healthy Choice bread, draped over one shoulder, on a towel. He was patting the baby's back.

"Hey . . ." He seemed slightly taken aback. Every time Lucas had seen him, he'd seemed slightly taken aback.

"Didn't know you had children," Lucas said.

"First one," Kidd said. "Trying to get a burp. You want to take him?"

"No, thanks," Lucas said hastily. "I've got a two-year-old, I just got done with that."

"Uh . . . come on in," Kidd said, stepping back from the door. Over his shoulder he called, "Lauren? Put on some pants. We've got company. It's the cops."

Kidd led the way into the living room. He was a couple inches shorter than Lucas, but broader through the shoulders, and going gray. He'd been a scholarship wrestler at the university when

Lucas played hockey. He still looked like he could pull your arms off.

He also had, Lucas thought, the best apartment in St. Paul, a huge sprawling place put together from two condos, bought when condos were cheap. Now the place was worth a million, if you could get it for that. The balcony looked out over the Mississippi, and windows were open and the faint smell of riverbank carp mixed with the closer odor of spoiled milk, the odor that hangs around babies; and maybe a touch of oil paint, or turpentine.

"Ah, God," Kidd called. "Lauren, we're gonna need a change here. He's really wet. Ah . . . shit."

"Just a minute . . ." Lauren was a slender, dark-haired, small-hipped woman with a wide mouth and shower-wet hair down to her shoulders. She was barefoot, wearing a black blouse and faded boot-cut jeans. She came out of the back, buttoning the jeans. "You could do it, you ain't crippled," she said to Kidd.

Kidd said, "Yeah, yeah. This is Detective Davenport . . . He's probably got an art problem?" This last was phrased as a question, and they both looked at Lucas as Lauren took the baby.

Lucas nodded. "You heard about the killings up on Summit?"

"Yeah. Fuckin' maniacs," Kidd said.

"We're wondering if it might not be a cover for a crime . . ." Lucas explained about the murders, about the china cabinet swept of pots, and his theory that real art experts wouldn't have broken the good stuff, and about getting restorers and antique experts. "But there's this kid, the nephew of one of the dead women, who said he thinks a couple of old paintings are missing from the attic. All he knows is that they're old, and one of them had the word 'reckless' written on the back. Actually, he said it was painted on the back. I wonder if that might mean something to you? You know of any paintings called *Reckless*? Or databases that might list it? Or anything?"

Kidd's eyes narrowed, then he said, "Capital *r* in 'reckless'?"

"I don't know," Lucas said. "Should there be?"

"There was an American painter, first half of the twentieth century named Reckless. I might have something on him . . ."

Lucas followed him through a studio, into a library, a narrow, darker space, four walls jammed with art books, Lauren and the baby trailing behind. Kidd took down a huge book, flipped through it . . . "Alphabetical," he muttered to himself, and he turned more pages, and finally, "Here we go. Stanley Reckless. Sort of funky impressionism. Not bad, but not quite the best."

He showed Lucas a color illustration, a riverside scene. Next to them, the baby made a bad smell and seemed pleased. Lucas asked, "How much would a painting like that be worth?"

Kidd shook his head: "We'll have to go to the computer for that . . . I subscribe to an auction survey service."

"I want to hear this," Lauren said. "Bring the laptop into the baby's room while I change the diaper." To the baby: "Did you just poop? Did you just poop, you little man? Did you just . . ."

Kidd had a black Lenovo laptop in the living room, and they followed Lauren to the baby's room, a bright little cube with its own view of the river. Kidd had painted cheerful, dancing children all around the lemon-colored walls.

"Really nice," Lucas said, looking around.

"Uh." Kidd brought up the laptop and Lauren began wiping the baby's butt with high-end baby-butt cleaner that Lucas recognized from his own changing table. Then Kidd started typing, and a moment later he said, "Says his paintings are rare. Auction record is four hundred fifteen thousand dollars, that was two years ago, and prices are up since then. He had a relatively small oeuvre. The range is down to thirty-two thousand dollars . . . but that was for a watercolor."

"Four hundred fifteen thousand dollars," Lucas repeated.

"Yup."

"That seems like a lot for one painting, but then, my wife tells me that I'm out of touch," Lucas said.

"Shoot, Kidd makes that much," Lauren said. "He's not even dead."

"Not for one painting," Kidd said.

"Not yet . . ."

"Jeez, I was gonna ask you how much you'd charge to paint my kid's bedroom," Lucas said, waving at the walls of the room. "Sorta be out of my range, huh?"

"Maybe," Kidd said. "From what I've read, your range is pretty big."

LUCAS WROTE *Stanley Reckless* and *$415,000* in his notebook as they drifted out toward the door. "You know," Lauren said, squinting at him. "I think I met you once, a long time ago, out at the track. You gave me a tip on a horse. This must have been . . . what? Seven or eight years ago?"

Lucas studied her face for a minute, then said, "You were wearing cowboy boots?"

"Yes! I went off to place the bet, and when I got back, you were gone," Lauren said. She touched his arm. "I never got to thank you."

"Well . . ."

"Enough of that," Kidd said, and they all laughed.

"You know, these killings . . . they might be art pros, but they aren't professional thieves," Lauren said. "A pro would have gone in there, taken what he wanted, maybe trashed the place to cover up. But he wouldn't have killed anybody. You guys would have sent some new detective over there to write everything down, and he would have come back with a notebook that said, 'Maybe pots stolen,' and nobody would care."

Lucas shrugged.

"Come on. Tell the truth. Would they care? Would anybody really care if some old bat got her pots stolen, and nobody got hurt? Especially if she didn't even know which pots they were?"

"Probably not," Lucas said.

"So they might be art pros, but they weren't professional burglars," Lauren said. "If you kill an old lady, everybody gets excited. Though, I suppose, it could be a couple of goofy little amateur crackheads. Or maybe acquaintances or relatives, who *had* to kill them."

Lucas's forehead wrinkled. "What do you do, Lauren? You weren't a cop?"

"No, no," she said. "I'm trying to be a writer."

"Novels?"

"No. I don't have a fictive imagination. Is that a word? *Fictive?*"

"I don't know," Lucas said.

She bounced the baby a couple of times; stronger than she looked, Lucas thought. "No," she said. "If I can get something published, it'll probably be more on the order of true crime."

WHEN LUCAS LEFT, Lauren and Kidd came to the door with the baby, and Lauren took the baby's hand and said, "Wave goodbye to the man, wave goodbye . . ."

Lucas thought, hmm. A rivulet of testosterone had run into his bloodstream. She was the kind of skinny, cowgirl-looking woman who could make you breathe a little harder; and she did. Something about the tilt of her eyes, as well as her name, reminded him of Lauren Hutton, the best-looking woman in the world. And finally, she made him think about the killers. Her argument was made from common sense, but then, like most writers, she probably knew jack-shit about burglars.

THERE WERE a half-dozen cops at Bucher's, mostly doing cler-ical work—checking out phone books and answering-machine logs, looking at checks and credit cards, trying to put together a picture of Bucher's financial and social life.

Lucas found Smith in the music room. He was talking to a woman dressed from head to toe in black, and a large man in a blue seer-sucker suit with a too-small bow tie under his round chin.

Smith introduced them, Leslie and Jane Little Widdler, antique ex-perts who ran a shop in Edina. They all shook hands; Leslie was six-seven and fleshy, with fat hands and transparent braces on his teeth. Jane was small, had a short, tight haircut, bony cold hands, and a strangely stolid expression.

"Figure anything out yet?" Lucas asked.

"Just getting started," Jane Widdler said. "There are some very nice things here. These damn vandals . . . they surely don't realize the damage they've done."

"To say nothing of the killings," Lucas said.

"Oh, well," Jane said, and waved a hand. She somehow mirrored Lucas's guilty attitude: old ladies came and went, but a Louis XVI gilt-bronze commode went on forever.

Lucas asked Smith, "Get the insurance papers?"

"Yeah." Smith dipped into his briefcase and handed Lucas a sheaf of papers. "Your copy."

Lucas told him about Kidd's take on Stanley Reckless. "Between the jewelry and this one painting, we're talking big money, John. We don't even know what else is missing. I'm thinking, man, this is way out of Nate Brown's league."

Smith said, "Ah, Brown didn't do it. I don't think he's bright enough to resist the way he has been. And I don't think he's mean enough to kill old ladies. He's sort of an old hangout guy."

"What's the Reckless painting?" Leslie Widdler asked, frowning. "It's not on the insurance list."

"Should it be?"

"Certainly. A genuine Stanley Reckless painting would be extremely valuable. Where was it hung? Did they take the frame, or . . ."

"Wasn't hung," Lucas said. "It would have been in storage."

"In storage? You're sure?"

"That's what we've been told," Lucas said. "Why?"

Widdler pursed his lips around his braces. "The thing is, some of these paintings here, I mean . . . frankly, there's a lot of crap. I'm sure Mrs. Bucher had them hung for sentimental reasons."

"Which are purely legitimate and understandable," Jane Widdler said, while managing to imply that they weren't.

". . . but a genuine Reckless shouldn't have been in storage. My goodness . . ." Widdler looked at the high ceiling, his lips moving, then down at Lucas: "A good Reckless painting, today, could be worth a half-million dollars."

Smith to Lucas: "It's piling up, isn't it? A pro job."

"I think so," Lucas said. "Professional, but maybe a little nuts. No fight, no struggle, no sounds, no signs of panic. Whack. They're dead. Then the killers take their time going through the house."

"Pretty goddamned cold."

"Pretty goddamned big money," Lucas said. "We both know people who've killed somebody for thirty bucks and for no reason at all. But this . . ."

Smith nodded. "That Ignace guy from the *Star Tribune* really nailed us. We've got calls coming in from all over."

"*New York Times?*"

"Not yet, but I'm waiting," Smith said.

"Best find the killer, John," Lucas said.

"I know." Smith wasn't happy: still didn't have anything to work with, and the case was getting old. "By the way, Carol Ann Barker's upstairs, checking out Bucher's stuff."

"Barker?" Lucas didn't remember the name.

"The niece, from L.A.," Smith said. "She's the executor of the will. She's, uh, an actress."

"Yeah?"

"Character actress, I think. She's got a funny nose." He glanced at the Widdlers. "I didn't actually mean that . . ."

"That's all right," Jane Widdler said, with a wooden smile. "Her nose *is* quite small."

LUCAS WANTED to talk to Barker. On the way up the stairs, he thumbed through the insurance papers, which, in addition to the standard boilerplate, included a ten-page inventory of household items. Ten pages weren't enough. He noticed that none of the furniture or paintings was valued at less than $10,000, which meant that a lot of stuff had been left off.

He counted paintings: ten, twelve, sixteen. There were at least thirty or forty in the house. Of course, if Widdler was right, many of them had only sentimental value. Lucas would have bet that none of the sentimental-value paintings were missing . . .

LUCAS FOUND Barker sitting on the floor of Bucher's bedroom, sorting through family photo albums. She was a little too heavy, her hair was a little too big, and she had glasses that were three fashions ahead of anything seen in the Twin Cities.

The glasses were perched on one of the smallest noses Lucas had ever seen on an adult; its carefully sculpted edges suggested a major nose job. Weather would have been interested. She had a whole rap on rhinoplasties, their value, and the problems that come up. Barker had been ill served by her surgeon, Lucas thought.

She looked up when Lucas loomed over her. The glasses slipped a quarter inch, and she peered at him over the black plastic frames. "There are way too many pictures, but this should give us a start."

"On what?" Lucas asked.

She pushed the glasses back up her tiny nose. "Oh, I'm sorry— you're not with the police?"

"I'm with the state police, not St. Paul," Lucas said. "Give us a start on what?"

She waved her hand at three stacks of leather-bound photo albums. "Aunt Connie used to have big Christmas and birthday parties. There were Easter-egg hunts both inside and outside, and a lot of pictures were taken," Barker said. "We can probably get most of the furniture in one picture or another."

"Great idea," Lucas said, squatting next to her, picking up one of the photos. Connie Bucher, much younger, with a half-dozen people and a drinks cabinet in the background. "What about her jewelry?" Lucas asked. "One of her friends said even the bedside jewelry was worth a lot."

"She's right. Unfortunately, most of it was old, so there aren't any microphotographs. All we have is descriptions in the insurance rider and those are essentially meaningless. If the thieves are sophisticated, the loose stones might already be in Amsterdam."

"But we could probably find out weights and so on?" Lucas asked.

"I'm sure."

"Have you ever heard of a painter called Stanley Reckless?"

She shook her head. "No."

"Huh. There supposedly was a painting up in the storage rooms that had 'reckless' written on the back," Lucas said. "There's an artist named Stanley Reckless, his paintings are worth a bundle."

Barker shook her head: "It's possible. But I don't know of it. I could ask around the other kids."

"If you would."

A cop came in with a handful of photographs. "We're missing one," he said. "The photograph was taken in the music room, but I can't find it anywhere."

Lucas and Barker stood up, Barker took the photo and Lucas looked at it over her shoulder. The photo showed a diminutive brown table, just about square on top. The top was divided in half, either by an inlaid line or an actual division. Below the tabletop, they could make out a small drawer with a brass handle.

After looking at it for a moment, Barker said, "You know, I remember that. This was years and years ago, when I was a child. If you folded the top back, there was a checkerboard inside. I think it was a checkerboard. The kids thought it was a secret hiding place, but there was never anything hidden in it. The checkers were kept in the drawer."

"Is it on the insurance list?" Lucas asked. "Any idea what it's worth?" He thumbed his papers.

The cop shook his head: "I checked John's list. Doesn't look like there's anything like it. Checkers isn't mentioned, that's for sure."

"There are some antique experts downstairs," Lucas said. "Maybe they'll know."

HE AND BARKER took the photos down to the Widdlers. Barker coughed when they were introduced, and pressed her knuckles against her teeth for a moment, and said, "Oh, my. I think I swallowed a bug."

"Protein," Jane Widdler said. She added, still speaking to Barker, "That's a lovely necklace . . . Tiffany?"

"I hope so," Barker said, smiling.

Lucas said to the dealers, "We've got a missing table. Think it might be a folding checkerboard." He handed the photograph of the table to Leslie Widdler, and asked, "Any idea what it's worth?"

The two dealers looked at it for a moment, then at each other, then at the photograph again. Leslie Widdler said to his wife, "Fifty-one thousand, five hundred dollars?"

She ticked an index finger at him: "Exactly."

"You can tell that closely?" Lucas asked.

Leslie Widdler handed the photograph back to Lucas. "Mrs. Bucher donated the table—it's a China-trade backgammon table, not a checkerboard, late eighteenth century—to the Minnesota Orchestra Guild for a fund-raising auction, let's see, must've been two Decembers ago. It was purchased by Mrs. Leon Cobler, of Cobler Candies, and she donated it to the Minneapolis Institute." He stopped to take a breath, then finished, "Where it is today."

"Shoot," Lucas said.

THE GOVERNOR CALLED and Lucas drifted down a hallway to take it. "Good job. Your man Flowers was here and gave an interesting presentation," the governor said. His name was Elmer Henderson. He was two years into his first term, popular, and trying to put together a Democratic majority in both houses in the upcoming elections. "We pushed the Dakota County proposal and Flowers agreed that it might be feasible. We—you—could take the evidence to Dakota County and get them to convene a grand jury. Nice and tidy."

"If it works."

"Has to," the governor said. "This girl . . . mmm . . . the evidentiary photos would suggest that she is not, uh, entirely undeveloped. I mean, as a woman."

"Governor . . . sir . . ."

"Oh, come on, loosen up, Lucas. I'm not going to call her up," Henderson said. "But that, 'Oh God, lick my balls'—that does tend to attract one's attention."

"I'll talk to Dakota County," Lucas said.

"Do so. By the way, why does everybody call your man 'that fuckin' Flowers'?"

6

Earlier that morning, Leslie Widdler had been sitting on his marigold-rimmed flagstone patio eating toast with low-calorie butter substitute and Egg Beaters, looking out over the brook, enjoying the sun, unfolding the *Star Tribune*; his wife, Jane, was inside, humming along with Mozart on Minnesota Public Radio.

A butterfly flapped by, something gaudy, a tiger swallowtail, maybe, and Leslie followed it for a second with his eyes. This was typical, he thought, of the kind of wildlife experience you had along the creek—no, wait, it was the *brook;* he had to remember that—and he rather approved.

A butterfly wasn't noisy, like, for instance, a crow or a blue jay; quite delicate and pretty and tasteful. A plane flew over, but well to the east, and he'd become accustomed to the sound. A little noise wasn't significant if you lived on the brook. Right *on* the brook—it was right there in his backyard when he shook open the paper, and at night he could hear it burbling, when the air conditioner wasn't running.

Jane was working on her own breakfast, consumed by the music, projected across the kitchen by her Bang & Olufsen speakers; it was like living inside an orchestra, and by adjusting the speakers according to the Bang & Olufsen instructions, she could vary her position from, say, the violas, back through the woodwinds, and all the way around the violins. It was lovely. She never referred to the speakers as speakers; she always referred to them as the Bang & Olufsens.

Jane Widdler, née Little. At Carleton College, where she and Leslie had met and become a couple, Leslie had been known to his roommates as Big Widdler, which the roommates had found hilarious for some obscure reason that Leslie had never discovered.

And when he courted and then, halfway through his senior year, married a woman named Little, of course, they'd become Big and Little Widdler. For some reason, the same ex-roommates thought that was even more hilarious, and could be heard laughing at the back of the wedding chapel.

Jane Little Widdler disapproved of the nicknames; but she rarely thought of it, since nobody used them but long-ago acquaintances from Carleton, most of whom had sunk out of sight in the muck of company relations, widget sales, and circus management.

Jane was putting together her breakfast smoothie. A cup of pineapple juice, a cup of strawberries, a half cup of bananas, a little of this, a little of that, and some yogurt and ice, blended for one annoying minute, the whining of the blender drowning out the Mozart. When it stopped, she heard Leslie's voice, through the sliding screen door: "Oh, my God!"

She could tell from his tone that it was serious. She couldn't frown, exactly, because of the Botox injections, but she made a frowning look and stepped to the door: "What? Is it the brook?"

The Widdlers were leading a petition drive to have the name officially changed from Minnehaha Creek to Minnehaha Brook, a combination they felt was more euphonic. They'd had some trashy kayakers on the brook lately—including one who was, of course, a left-wing lawyer, who had engaged in a shouting match with Leslie. Paddling for the People. Well, fuck that. The brook didn't belong to the people.

But it wasn't the creek, or the brook, that put the tone in Big Widdler's voice. Leslie was on his feet. He was wearing a white pullover Egyptian long-staple cotton shirt with loose sleeves, buttoned at the wrists with black mother-of-pearl buttons, madras plaid shorts, and Salvatore Ferragamo sandals, and looked quite good in the morning sunlight, she thought. "Check this out," he said.

He passed her the *Star Tribune*.

The big headline said: *Did Murders Conceal Invisible Heist?* Under that, in smaller type, *Millions in Antiques May Be Missing.*

"Oh, my gosh," Jane said. Her frowning look grew deeper as she read. "I wonder who Ruffe Ignace is?"

"Just a reporter. That's not the problem," said Big Widdler, flapping his hands like a butterfly. "If they do an inventory, there may be items . . ." The Bang & Olufsen slimline phone started to ring from its spot next to the built-in china cabinet, and he reached toward it. ". . . on the list that can be identified, and we won't know which ones they are. If there are photos . . ."

He picked up the phone and said, "Hello?" and a second later, "Uh, Detective? Well, sure . . ."

Jane was shaken, placed one hand on her breast, the other on the countertop. This could be it: everything they'd worked for, gone in the blink of an eye.

Leslie said, "Hello, yes, it is . . . uh huh, uh huh . . ." Then he smiled, but kept his voice languid, professional. "We'd be delighted to help, as long as it wouldn't prejudice our position in bidding, if there should be an estate auction. I can't see why it would, if all you want is an opinion . . . Mmm, this afternoon would be fine. I'll bring my wife. Our assistant can watch the shop. One o'clock, then. See you after lunch."

He put down the phone and chuckled: "We've been asked to advise the St. Paul police on the Bucher investigation."

Jane made a smiling look. "Leslie, that's *too rich*. And you know what? It's really going to piss off Carmody & Loan."

Carmody & Loan were their only possible competition, in terms of quality, in the Cities. If C&L had been asked to do the valuations, Jane would have been *royally* pissed. She couldn't *wait* to hear what Melody Loan had to say about *this*. She'd be furious. She said, "Maybe we could find a way to get the news of the appointment to this Ruffe Ignace person."

Leslie's eyebrows went up: "You mean to rub it in? Mmmm. You are such a *bitch* sometimes. I like it." He moved up to her, slipped his hand inside her morning slacks, which were actually the bottoms of a well-washed Shotokan karate gi, down through her pubic hair.

She widened her stance a bit, put her butt back against the counter, bit her lip, made a look, the best she could, considering the Botox, of semi-ecstasy. "Rub it in, big guy," she whispered, the smoothie almost forgotten.

BUT AS LESLIE was inclined to say, the Lord giveth, and the Lord is damn well likely to taketh it away in the next breath. They spent the morning at the shop, calling customers and other dealers, dealing with bills, arguing with the State Farm agent about their umbrella policy. At noon, they stopped at a sandwich shop for Asiago roast-beef sandwiches on sourdough bread, then headed for St. Paul.

They were driving east on I-494 in Jane's Audi A4, which she now referred to as "that piece of junk," when another unwelcome call came in. Jane fumbled her cell phone out and looked at the screen. The caller ID said *Marilyn Coombs*.

"Marilyn Coombs," she said to Leslie.

"It's that damned story," Leslie said.

Jane punched the answer button, said, "Hello?"

MARILYN COOMBS WAS an old lady, who, in Jane's opinion, should have been dead a long time ago. Her voice was weak and thready: she said, "Jane? Have you heard about Connie Bucher?"

"Just read it in the paper this morning," Jane said. "We were shocked."

"It's the same thing that happened to Claire Donaldson," Coombs whimpered. "Don't you think we should call the police?"

"Well, gosh, I'd hate to get involved with the police," Jane said. "We'd probably have to wind up hiring lawyers, and we wouldn't want . . . you know."

"Well, we wouldn't say anything about *that*," Coombs said. "But I got my clipping of when Claire was killed, and Jane, they're just *alike*."

"I thought Claire was shot," Jane said. "That's what I heard."

"Well, except for that, they're the same," Coombs said. Jane rolled her eyes.

"You know, I didn't know Claire that well," Jane said.

"I thought you were friends . . ."

"No, no, we knew who she was, through the quilt-study group, but we didn't really *know* her. Anyway, I'd like to see the clipping. I could probably tell you better about the police, if I could see the clipping."

"I've got it right here," Coombs said.

"Well. Why don't we stop by this evening," Jane suggested. "It'll probably be late, we're out on an appointment right now. Let me take a look at it."

"If you think that'd be right," Coombs said.

"Well, we don't want to make a mistake."

"Okay, then," Coombs said. "After dinner."

"It'll be later than that, I'm afraid. We're on our way to Eau Claire. What time do you go to bed?"

"Not until after the TV news."

"Okay. We'll be back before then. Probably . . . about dark."

THAT GAVE THEM something to talk about. "Is it all falling apart, Leslie? Is it all falling apart?" Jane asked. She'd been in drama club, and was a former vice president of the Edina Little Theater.

"Of course not," Leslie said. "We just need to do some cleanup."

Jane sighed. Then she said, "Do you think the Hermès is too much?" She was wearing an Hermès scarf with ducks on it, and the ducks had little red collars and were squawking at each other.

"No, no. I think it looks quite good on you."

"I hope it's not falling apart on us," Jane said.

"Most cops are dumber than a bowl of spaghetti," Leslie said. "Not to worry, sweet."

Still, Jane, with her delicate elbow on the leather bolster below the Audi's window, her fingers along her cheek, couldn't help think, if it *were* all coming to an end, if there might not be some way she could shift all the blame to Leslie.

Perhaps even . . . She glanced at him, speculatively, at his temple, and thought, *No. That's way premature.*

Then they met the cops. And talked about missing antiques, including a painting by Stanley Reckless.

ON THE WAY out of Oak Walk, Jane said, "That Davenport person is *not* dumber than a bowl of spaghetti."

"No, he's not," Leslie said. He held the car door for her, tucked her in, leaned forward and said, "We've got to talk about the Reckless."

"We've got to get rid of it. Burn it," Jane said.

"I'm not going to give up a half-million-dollar painting," Leslie said. "But we have to do something."

They talked it over on the way home. The solution, Jane argued, was to destroy it. There was no statute of limitations on murder, and, sometime, in the future, if the call of the money was too strong, they might be tempted to sell it—and get caught.

"A new, fresh Reckless—that's going to attract some attention," she said.

"Private sale," Leslie said.

"I don't know," Jane said.

"Half-million dollars," Leslie said, and when he said it, Jane knew that she wanted the money.

They went home, and after dinner, Leslie stood on a stool and got the Reckless out of the double-secret storage area in the rafters of the attic.

"Gorgeous piece?" he said. He flipped it over, looked at the name slashed across the back of the canvas. Though Leslie ran to fat, he was still strong. Gripping the frame tightly, he torqued it, wiggled the sides, then the top and bottom, and the frame began to spread. When it was loose enough, he lifted the canvas, still on stretchers, out of the frame, and put it under a good light on the dining room table.

"Got a strong signature," he said. Reckless had carefully signed the front of the painting at the lower right, with a nice red signature over a grassy green background. "Don't need the one on the back."

"Take it off?"

"If we took it off, then it couldn't be identified as the Bucher painting," Leslie said.

"There'd always be some . . . remnants."

"Not if you don't want to see it," Leslie said. He looked at the painting for a moment, then said. "Here's what we do. We stash it at the farm for now. Wrap it up nice and tight. Burn the frame. When I get time, I'll take the 'Reckless' off the back—it'll take me a couple of weeks, at least. We get some old period paint—we should be able to get some from Dick Calendar—and paint over the area where the 'Reckless' was. Then we take it to Omaha, or Kansas City, or even Vegas, rent a safe-deposit box, and stick it away for five years. In five years, it's good as gold."

Bad idea, Jane thought: but she *yearned* for the money.

THREE HOURS LATER, the Widdlers were rolling again.

"There is," Leslie said, his hands at ten o'clock and four on the wood-rimmed wheel of his Lexus, "a substantial element of insanity in this. No coveralls, no gloves, no hairnets. We are shedding DNA every step we take."

"But it's eighty percent that we won't have to do anything," Jane said. "Doing nothing would be best. We pooh-pooh the newspaper clipping, we scare her with the police, with the idea of a trial. Then, when we get past the lumpy parts, we might come back to her. We could do that in our own good time. Or maybe she'll just drop dead. She's old enough."

They were on Lexington Avenue in St. Paul, headed toward Como Park, a half hour past sunset. The summer afternoon lingered, stretching toward ten o'clock. Though it was one of the major north-south streets, Lexington was quiet at night, a few people along the sidewalks, light traffic. Marilyn Coombs's house was off the park, on Iowa, a narrower, darker street. They'd park a block away, and walk; it was a neighborhood for walking.

"Remember about the DNA," Leslie said. "Just in case. No sudden moves. They can find individual hairs. Think about *gliding* in there. Let's not walk all over the house. Try not to touch anything. Don't pick anything up."

"I have as much riding on this as you do," Jane said, cool air in her voice. "Focus on what we're doing. Watch the windows. Let me do most of the talking."

"The DNA . . ."

"Forget about the DNA. Think about anything else."

There was a bit of a snarl in her voice. Leslie glanced at her, in the little snaps of light coming in from the street, and thought about what a delicate neck she had . . .

THEY WERE coming up on the house. They'd been in it a half-dozen times with the quilt-study group. "What about the trigger?" Leslie asked.

"Same one. Touch your nose. If I agree, I'll touch my nose," Jane said.

"I'll have to be behind her. Whatever I do, I'll have to be be-hind her."

"If that finial is loose . . ." The finial was a six-inch oak ball on the bottom post of Coombs's stairway banister. The stairway came down in the hallway, to the right of the inner porch door. "If it's just plugged in there, the way most of them are . . ."

"Can't count on it," Leslie said. "I'm not sure that a competent medical examiner would buy it anyway."

"Old lady, dead at the bottom of the stairs, forehead fracture that fits the finial, hair on the finial . . . What's there to argue about?" Jane asked.

"I'll see when I go in," he said. "We might get away with it. They sure as shit won't believe she fell on a kitchen knife."

"Watch the language, darling. Remember, we're trying." Trying for elegance. That was their watchword for the year, written at the top of every page of their Kliban Cat Calendar: *Elegance!* Better business through *Elegance!* Jane added, "Two things I don't like about the knife idea. First, it's not instantaneous. She could still scream . . ."

"Not if her throat was cut," Leslie said. Leslie liked the knife idea; the idea made him hot.

"Second," Jane continued, "She could be spraying blood all over the place. If we track it, or get some on our clothes . . . it could be a mess. With the finial, it's *boom*. She goes down. We won't even have to move her, if we do it right."

"On the way out."

"On the way out. We're calm, cool, and collected while we're there," Jane said. She could see it. "We talk. If it doesn't work, we make nice, and we get her to take us to the door."

"I walk behind her, get the glove on."

"Yes. If the finial comes loose, you either have to hit her on the back of her skull, low, or right on her forehead. Maybe . . . I'm thinking of how people fall. Maybe we'll have to break a finger or something. A couple of fingers. Like she caught them on the railing on the way down."

Leslie nodded, touched the brakes for a cyclist in the street. "I could pick her up, and we could scratch her fingernails on the railing, maybe put some carpet fiber in the other hand. She's small, I could probably lift her close enough, all we need to do is get some varnish under a fingernail . . ."

"It's a plan," Jane said. "If the finial comes loose."

"STILL, the knife has a certain appeal," Leslie said, after a moment of silence. "Two older women, their skulls crushed, three days apart. *Somebody* is going to think it's a pretty heavy coincidence. The knife is a different MO and it looks stupid. Another little junkie thing. And if *nothing* is taken . . ."

"Probably be better to take something, if we do it with the knife," Jane said. "I mean, then there'll be no doubt that it's murder. Why kill her? To rob her. We don't want a mystery. We want a clear story. Kill her, take her purse. Get out. With the finial, if they figure out it was murder, there'll be a huge mystery."

"And they'll see it as *smart*. They'll know it wasn't some little junkie."

Jane balanced the two. "I think, the finial," Jane said. "If the finial works, we walk away clear. Nobody even suspects. With the knife, they'll be looking for something, chasing down connections."

Then, for about the fifteenth time since they left home, Leslie said, "If the finial comes out . . ."

"Probably won't do it anyway," Jane said. "We'll scare the bejesus out of the old bat."

MARILYN COOMBS LIVED in a nice postwar home, the kind with a big picture window and two-car garage in back, once un-attached, now attached with a breezeway that was probably built in the '60s. The siding was newer plastic, with heated plastic gutters at the eaves. The front yard was narrow, decorative, and steep. Five concrete steps got you up on the platform, and another five to the outer porch door. The backyard, meant for boomers when they were babies, was larger and fenced.

They climbed the steps in the yard, up to the porch door, through the porch door; in these houses, the doorbell was inside the porch. On the way up, Leslie pulled a cotton gardening glove over his right hand, and pushed the doorbell with a glove finger, then slipped the hand into his jacket pocket.

COOMBS WAS EIGHTY, Jane thought, or even eighty-five. Her hair had a pearly white quality, nearly liquid, fine as cashmere, as she walked under the living room lights. She was thin, and had to tug the door open with both hands, and smiled at them: "How are you? Jane, Leslie. Long time no see."

"Marilyn . . ."

"I have cookies in the kitchen. Oatmeal. I made them this after-noon." Coombs squinted past Leslie at the sidewalk. "You didn't see any gooks out there, did you?"

"No." Leslie looked at Jane and shrugged, and they both looked out at the empty sidewalk.

"Gooks are moving in. They get their money from heroin," Coombs said, pushing the door shut. "I'm thinking about getting an alarm. All the neighbors have them now."

She turned toward the kitchen. As they passed the bottom of the stairs, Leslie reached out with the gloved hand, slipped it around the bottom of the finial, and lifted. It came free. It was the size of a slo-pitch softball, but much heavier. Jane, who'd turned her head, nod-ded, and Leslie let it drop back into place.

A PLATTER of oatmeal cookies waited on a table in the break-fast nook. They sat down, Coombs passed the dish, and Jane and Leslie both took one, and Leslie bolted his and mumbled, "Good."

"So, Marilyn," Jane said. "This newspaper clipping."

"Yes, yes, it's right here." Coombs was wearing a housecoat. She fumbled in the pocket, extracted a wad of Kleenex, a bottle of Aleve, and finally, a clipping. She passed it to Jane, her hand shaking a bit. Leslie took another cookie.

> A noted Chippewa Falls art collector and heir to the Thune brewing fortune was found shot to death in her home Wednesday morning by relatives . . .

"They never caught anybody. They didn't have any leads," Coombs said. She ticked off the points on her fingers: "She came from a rich family, just like Connie. She was involved in quilting, just like Connie. She collected antiques, just like Connie. She lived with a maid, like Connie, but Claire's maid wasn't there that night, thank goodness for her."

"She was shot," Jane said. "Connie was killed with a pipe or a baseball bat or something."

"I know, I know, but maybe they had to be quieter," Coombs said. "Or maybe they wanted to change it, so nobody would suspect."

"We really worry about getting involved with the police," Jane said. "If they talk to you, and then to us, because of the quilt connection, and they say, 'Look, here's some people who know all of the murdered people . . . then they'll begin to suspect. Even though we're innocent. And then they might take a closer look at the Armstrong quilts. We really don't want that."

Coombs's eyes flicked away. "I'd feel so guilty if somebody else got hurt. Or if these people got away scot-free because of me," she said.

"So would I," Jane said. "But . . ."

And Coombs said, "But . . ."

They talked about it for a while, trying to work the old woman around, and while she was deferential, she was also stubborn. Finally, Jane looked at Leslie and touched her nose. Leslie nodded, rubbed the side of his nose, and said to Coombs, "I have to say, you've talked me around. We've got to be really, really careful, though. They've got some smart police officers working on this."

He stopped and stuffed another oatmeal cookie in his mouth, mumbling around the crumbs. "We need to keep the quilts out of it. Maybe I could send an anonymous note mentioning the antique connection, and leave the quilts out of it."

Coombs brightened. She liked that idea. Jane smiled and shook her head and said, "Leslie's always liked you too much. I think we should stay away from the police, but if you're both for it . . ."

———

COOMBS SHUFFLED OUT to the front door as they left, leading the way. In the rear, Leslie pulled on the cotton gloves, and at the door, Jane stepped past Coombs as Leslie pulled the finial out of the banister post. He said, "Hey, Marilyn?"

When she turned, he hit her on the forehead with the finial ball. Hit her hard. She bounced off Jane and landed at the foot of the stairs. They both looked at her for a moment. Her feet made a quivering run, almost as though dog-paddling, then stopped.

"She dead?" Jane asked.

Leslie said, "Gotta be. I swatted her like a fuckin' fly with a fuckin' bowling ball."

"Elegance!" Jane snapped.

"Fuck that . . ." Leslie was breathing hard. He squatted, watching the old lady, watching her, seeing never a breath. After a long two minutes, he looked up and said, "She's gone."

"Pretty good. Never made a sound," Jane said. She noticed that Leslie's bald spot was spreading.

"Yeah." Leslie could see hair, a bit of skin and possibly a speck of blood on the wood of the finial ball. He stood up, turned it just so, and slipped it back on the mounting down in the banister post, and tapped it down tight. The hair and skin were on the inside of the ball, where Coombs might have struck her head if she'd fallen. "Fingers?" he asked. "Break the fingers?"

"I don't think we should touch her," Jane said. "She fell perfectly . . . What we could do . . ." She pulled off one of Coombs's slippers and tossed it on the bottom stair. "Like she tripped on the toe."

"I'll buy that," Leslie said.

"So . . ."

"Give me a minute to look around," Jane said. "Just a minute."

"Lord, Jane . . ."

"She was an old lady," Jane said. "She might have had something good."

OUT IN THE CAR, they drove fifty yards, turned onto Lexington, went half a mile, then Leslie pulled into a side street, continued to a dark spot, killed the engine.

"What?" Jane asked, though she suspected. They weren't talking Elegance here.

Leslie unsnapped his seat belt, pushed himself up to loosen his pants, unzipped his fly. "Gimme a little hand, here. Gimme a little hand."

"God, Leslie."

"Come on, goddamnit, I'm really hurtin'," he said.

"I won't do it if you continue to use that kind of language," Jane said.

"Just do it," he said.

Jane unsnapped her own seat belt, reached across, then said, "What did you do with that package of Kleenex? It must be there in the side pocket . . ."

"Fuck the Kleenex," Leslie groaned.

7

THE NEXT TWO DAYS were brutal. Kline was hot, and Lucas
had no time for the Bucher case. He talked to Smith both days, getting updates, but there wasn't much movement. The papers were
getting bad tempered about it and Smith was getting defensive.

Reports came in from the insurance companies and from the
Department of Corrections; the halfway house was looking like a
bad bet. The St. Paul cops did multiple interviews with relatives,
who were arriving for the funeral and to discuss the division of the
Bucher goodies. There were rumors of interfamilial lawsuits.

Despite the onset of bad feelings, none of the relatives had accused any of the others of being near St. Paul at the time of the murder. They'd been more or less evenly divided between Santa Barbara
and Palm Beach, with one weirdo at his apartment in Paris.

All of them had money, Smith said. While Aunt Connie's inheri-
tance would be a nice maraschino cherry on the sundae, they already had the ice cream.

LUCAS HAD three long interviews over the two days, and twice
as many meetings.

The first interview went badly.

Kathy Barth had both tits and ass: and perhaps a bit too much of each, as she slipped toward forty. Her daughter, Jesse, had gotten her momma's genes, but at sixteen, everything was tight, and when she walked, she quivered like a bowl of cold Jell-O.

While she talked like a teenager, and walked like a teenager, and went around plugged into an iPod, Jesse had the face of a bar-worn thirty-year-old: too grainy, too used, with a narrow down-turned sullen mouth and eyes that looked like she was afraid that somebody might hit her.

At the first interview, she and Kathy Barth sat behind the shoulder of their lawyer, who was running through a bunch of mumbo-jumbo: ". . . conferring to see if we can decide exactly *what* happened and *when,* and if it really makes any sense to continue this investigation . . ."

Virgil Flowers, a lean, tanned blond man dressed in jeans, a blue cotton shirt with little yellow flowers embroidered on it, and scuffed black cowboy boots, said, "We've already got her on tape, Jimbo."

"That would be 'James' to *you,* Officer," the lawyer said, pretending to be offended.

Flowers looked at Lucas, "The old Jimster here is trying to put the screws to Kline." He looked back at the lawyer. "What'd you find? He's got some kind of asset we didn't know about?" His eyes came back to Lucas: "I say we take a research guy, pull every tax record we can find, run down every asset Kline has got, and attach it. Do a real estate search, put Kline on the wall . . ."

"Why do you want to steal the rightful compensation from this young woman?" the lawyer demanded. "It's not going to do her any good if Burt Kline goes to jail and that's it. She may need years of treatment—years!—if it's true that Mr. Kline had sexual contact with her. Which, of course, we're still trying to determine."

"Motherfucker," Flowers said.

The lawyer, shocked—*shocked*—turned to Jesse and said, "Put your hands over your ears."

Jesse just looked at Flowers, twisted a lock of her hair between her fingers, and stuck a long pink tongue out at him. Flowers grinned back.

"SHE'S HOT," Flowers said when they left the house. They had to step carefully, because a yellow-white dog with bent-over ears, big teeth, and a bad attitude was chained to a stake in the center of the yard.

"She's sixteen years old," Lucas said, watching the dog.

"Us Jews bat mitzvah our women when they're fourteen, and after that, they're up for grabs," Flowers said. "Sixteen's no big thing, in the right cultural context."

"You're a fuckin' Presbyterian, Virgil, and you live in Minnesota."

"Oh, yeah. Ya got me there, boss," Flowers said. "What do we do next?"

THE SECOND INTERVIEW was worse, if you didn't like to see old men cry.

Burt Kline sat in his heavy leather chair, all the political photos on the walls behind him, all the plaques, the keys, the letters from presidents, and put his face in his hands, rocked back and forth, and wept. Nothing faked about it. His son, a porky twenty-three-year-old and heir apparent, kept smacking one meaty fist into the palm of the other hand. He'd been a football player at St. Johns, and wore a St. Johns T-shirt, ball cap, and oversized belt buckle.

Burt Kline, blubbering: "She's just a girl, how could you think . . ."

Flowers yawned and looked out the window. Lucas said, "Senator Kline . . ."

"I-I-I d-d-didn't do it," Kline sobbing. "I swear to God, I never touched the girl. This is all a lie . . ."

"It's a fuckin' lie, he didn't do it, those bitches are trying to blackmail us," Burt Jr. shouted.

"There's that whole thing about the semen and the DNA," Flowers said.

The blubbering intensified and Kline swiveled his chair toward his desk and dropped his head on it, with a thump like a pumpkin hitting a storm door. "That's got to be some kind of mistake," he wailed.

"*You're* trying to frame us," Burt Jr. said. "You and that whole fuckin' bunch of tree-hugging motherfuckers. That so-called lab guy is probably some left-wing nut . . ."

"Here's the thing, Senator Kline," Lucas said, ignoring the kid. "You know we've got no choice. We've got to send it to a grand jury. Now we can send it to a grand jury here in Ramsey County, and you know what *that* little skunk will do with it."

"Oh, *God* . . ."

"Just not right," Burt Jr. said, smacking his fist into his palm. His face was so red that Lucas wondered about his blood pressure. Lucas kept talking to the old man: "Or, Jesse Barth said you once took her on a shopping trip to the Burnsville Mall and bought her some underwear and push-up bras . . ."

"Oh, *God* . . ."

"If you did that for sex, or if we feel we can claim that you did, then that aspect of the crime would have taken place in Dakota County. Jim Cole is the county attorney there, and runs the grand jury."

The sobbing diminished, and Kline, damp faced, looked up, a line of calculation back in his eyes. "That's Dave Cole's boy."

"I wouldn't know," Lucas said. "But if you actually took Jesse over to Burnsville . . ."

"I never had sex with her," Kline said. "But I might've taken her to Burnsville once. She needed back-to-school clothes."

"They wear push-up bras to high school?" Lucas asked.

"Shit, yes. And thongs," Flowers said. "Don't even need Viagra with that kind of teenybopper quiff running around, huh, Burt?"

"You motherfucker, I ought to throw you out the fuckin' window," Burt Jr. snarled at Flowers.

"You said something like that last time," Flowers said. He didn't move, but his eyes had gone flat and gray like stones. "So why don't you do it? Come on, fat boy, let's see what you got."

The kid balled his fists and opened and shut his mouth a couple of times, and then Kline said to him, "Shut up and sit down," then asked Lucas, "What do I gotta do?"

"Agree that you took her to Burnsville. Agent Flowers will put that in his report and we will make a recommendation to the county attorney."

"Dave Cole's boy . . ."

"I guess," Lucas said. "Neil Mitford would like to talk to you. Just on the phone."

"I bet he would," Kline said.

ON THE STREET, Flowers said, "I don't like the smell of this, Lucas."

Lucas sighed. "Neither do I, Virgil. But there's a big load of crap coming down the line, no matter what we do, and there's no point in *our* people getting hurt, if we can confine the damage to Kline."

"And the Republicans."

"Well, Kline's a Republican," Lucas said.

"Fuck me," Flowers said.

Lucas said, "Look, I've got loyalties. People have helped me out, have given me a job chasing crooks. I like it. But every once in a while, we catch one of these. If you can tell me who we ought to put in jail here—Burt Kline or Kathy Barth—then I'll look into it. But honest to God, they're a couple of dirtbags and nobody else ought to get hurt for it."

"Yeah, yeah." Flowers was pissed.

Lucas continued rambling. "There's a guy I talk to over at the *Star Tribune*. Ruffe Ignace. He's a guy who can sit on a secret, sit on a source. I'd never talk to Ruffe about something like this—I've got those loyalties—but we go out for a sandwich, now and then, and we always argue about it: Who has the right to know what? And when? And what about the people who get hurt? Is it going to help Jesse to get her ass dragged through the courts?"

"Yeah, yeah," Flowers said again.

"So I gotta go talk to this Cole guy, down in Dakota County," Lucas said.

"Sounds like another in a long line of assholes," Flowers said.

"Probably," Lucas said.

They walked along for a while and then Flowers grinned, clapped Lucas on the shoulder, and said, "Thanks, boss. I needed the talk."

THE THIRD INTERVIEW was better, but not much, and Lucas left it feeling a little more grime on his soul.

Jim Cole was a stiff; a guy who'd get out of the shower to pee. He said, "That all sounds a little thin, Agent Davenport, on the elements, but I'll assign my best person to it." Behind him, on the wall, among the political pictures, plaques, and a couple of gilt tennis trophies, was a photo-painting that said, "Dave Cole—A Man for the Ages."

Lucas thought the elder Cole looked like a woodpecker, but, that was neither here nor there. Dave's boy, Jim, bought the case.

"I would assume there's been a lot of concern about this," Cole said. "It seems like a touchy affair."

"Yes, it is."

"Why don't you ask Neil Mitford to give me a call—I'd like to discuss it. Purely off the record, of course."

"Sure," Lucas said.

ALL OF THAT took two days. On the third day, Lucas made a quick call to Smith about the Bucher case. She was still dead.

"I'm gonna get eaten alive if something doesn't break," Smith said. "Why don't you do some of that special-agent shit?"

"I'll think about it," Lucas said.

He did, and couldn't think of anything.

HE HAD his feet on his top desk drawer, and was reading *Strike! Catch Your River Muskie!*, a how-to book, when his secretary came into the office and shut the door behind her.

"There's a hippie chick here to see you," she said. The secretary was a young woman named Carol, with auburn hair and blue eyes. She had been overweight, but recently had gone on a no-fat diet, which made her touchy. Despite her youth, she was famous in the BCA for her Machiavellian ruthlessness. "About the Bucher case, and about her grandmother, who fell down the stairs and died."

Lucas was confused, his mind still stuck in how to fish the upstream side of a wing dam without losing your lower unit; something, in his opinion, that all men should know. "A hippie? Her grandmother died?"

She shrugged. "What can I tell you? But I know you're attracted to fucky blondes, especially the kind with small but firm breasts . . ."

"Be quiet," Lucas said. He peered through the door window past the secretary's desk into the waiting area. He couldn't see anybody. "Is she nuts?"

"Probably," Carol said. "But she made enough sense that I thought you should talk to her."

"Why doesn't she talk to Smith?" Lucas asked.

"I don't know. I didn't ask her."

"Ah, for Christ's sakes . . ."

"I'll send her in," Carol said.

GABRIELLA COOMBS HAD an oval face and blue-sky eyes and blond hair that fell to her small but firm breasts. Lucas couldn't tell for sure—she was wearing a shapeless shift of either gingham or calico, he could never remember which one was the print, with tiny yellow coneflowers, black-eyed Susans—but from the way her body rattled around in the shift, he suspected she could, as his subordinate Jenkins had once observed of another slender blond hippie chick, "crack walnuts between the cheeks of her ass."

She had a string of penny-colored South American nuts around her neck, and silver rings pierced both the lobes and rims of her ears, and probably other parts of her body, unseen, but not unsuspected.

Given her dress and carriage, her face would normally be as un-clouded as a drink of water, Lucas thought, her *wa* smooth and round and uninflected by daily trials. Today she carried two hori-zontal worry lines on her forehead, and another vertically between her guileless eyes. She sat down, perched on the edge of Lucas's vis-itor's chair, and said, "Captain Davenport?"

"Uh, no," Lucas said. "I'm more like a special agent; but you can call me Lucas."

She looked at him for a moment, then said, "Could I call you mis-ter? You're quite a bit older than I am."

"Whatever you want," Lucas said, trying not to grit his teeth.

She picked up on that. "I want us both to be comfortable and I think appropriate concepts of life status contribute to comfort," she said.

"What can I do for you? You are . . . ?"

"Gabriella Coombs. Ruffe Ignace at the *Star Tribune* said I should talk to you; he's the one who told me that you're a captain. He said that you were into the higher levels of strategy on the Bucher case, and that you provide intellectual guidance for the city police."

"I try," Lucas said modestly, picked up a pen and scrawled, *Get Ruffe,* on a notepad. "So . . ."

"MY MOTHER, Lucy Coombs, two fifty-seven . . ." She stopped, looked around the room, as if to spot the TV cameras. Then, "Do you want to record this?"

"Maybe later," Lucas said. "Just give me the gist of it now."

"My mom didn't hear from Grandma the night before last. Grandma had a little stroke a few months ago and they talk every night," Coombs said. "So anyway, she stopped by Grandma's place the morning before last, to see what was up, and found her at the bottom of the stairs. Dead as a doornail. The cops say it looks like she fell down the stairs and hit her head on one of those big balls on the banister post. You know the kind I mean?"

"Yup."

"Well, I don't believe it. She was murdered."

LUCAS HAD a theory about intelligence: there was critical intelligence, and there was silly intelligence. Most people tended toward one or the other, although everybody carried at least a little of both. Einstein was a critical intelligence in physics; with women, it was silly.

Cops ran into silly intelligences all the time—true believers without facts, who looked at a cocaine bust and saw fascism, or, when somebody got killed in a back-alley gunfight, reflexively referred to the cops as murderers. It wasn't that they were stupid—they were often wise in the ways of public relations. They were simply silly.

Gabriella Coombs . . .

"I THINK the medical examiner could probably tell us one way or the other, Miss Coombs," Lucas said.

"No, probably not," Coombs said, genially contradicting him. "Everybody, including the medical examiner, is influenced by environmental and social factors. The medical examiner's version of science, and figuring out what happened, is mostly a social construct, which is why all the crime-scene television shows are such a load of crap."

"Anyway." He was being patient, and let it show.

"Anyway, the police tell the medical examiner that it looks like a fall," she said. "The medical examiner doesn't find anything that says it wasn't a fall, so he rules it a fall. That's the end of the case. Nobody's curious about it."

Lucas doodled a fly line with a hook, with little pencil scratches for the fly's body, around the *Get Ruffe*. "You know, a person like yourself," he said. ". . . have you studied psychology at all?"

She nodded. "I majored in it for three quarters."

He was not surprised. "You know what Freud said about cigars?"

"That sometimes they're just cigars? Frankly, Mr. Davenport, your point is so simple that it's moronic."

He thought, *Hmm, she's got teeth.*

She asked, "Are you going to listen to what I have to say, or are you going to perform amateur psychoanalysis?"

"Say it," Lucas said.

She did: "My grandmother was killed by a blow to the head that fractured her skull. Last Friday or Saturday, Constance Bucher and Sugar-Rayette Peebles died the same way. Grandma and Connie were friends. They were in the same quilt group; or, at least, they had been. A story in the *Star Tribune* said that Mrs. Bucher's murder might have been a cover-up for a robbery. When Grandma died, I was supposed to inherit a valuable music box that her grandmother—my great-great-grandmother—brought over from the Old Country. From Switzerland."

"It's missing?" Lucas asked, sitting up, listening now.

"We couldn't find it," Coombs said. "It used to be in a built-in bookshelf with glass doors. The police wouldn't let us look everywhere, and she could have moved it, but it's been in that bookcase since she bought the house. Everything else seems to be there, but the music box is gone."

"Do you have a description?" Lucas asked. "Was it insured?"

"Wait a minute, I'm not done," Coombs said, holding up an index finger. Lucas noticed that all her fingers, including her thumbs, had rings, and some had two or three. "There was another woman, also rich, and old, in Chippewa Falls. That's in Wisconsin."

"I know," Lucas said. "I've been there."

Her eyes narrowed. "To drink beer, I bet."

"No. It was for a police function," Lucas lied. He'd gone on a brewery tour.

She was suspicious, but continued: "Sometimes Grandma and Connie Bucher would go over to this other lady's house for quilt group. They weren't in the same quilt groups, but the two groups intersected. Anyway, this other woman—her name was Donaldson—was shot to death in her kitchen. She was an antique collector. Grandma said the killers were never caught. This was four years ago."

Lucas stared at her for a moment, then asked, "Is your grandma's house open? Have the St. Paul police finished with it?"

"No. We're not allowed in yet. They took us through to see if there was anything unusual, or disturbed, other than the blood spot on the carpet. But see, the deal always was, when Grandma died, her son and daughter would divide up everything equally, but since I was the only granddaughter, I got the music box. It was like, a woman-thing. I looked for it when the police took us through, and it was missing."

LUCAS DID a drum tap with his pencil. "How'd you get down here?"

She blinked a couple of times, and then said, "I may look edgy to you, Mr. Davenport, but I *do* own a car."

"All right." Lucas picked up the phone, said to Carol, "Get me the number of the guy who's investigating the death of a woman named Coombs, which is spelled . . ."

He looked at Coombs and she nodded and said, "C-O-O-M-B-S."

". . . In St. Paul. I'll be on my cell." He dropped the phone on the hook, took his new Italian leather shoulder rig out of a desk drawer, put it on, took his jacket off the file cabinet, slipped into it. "You can meet me at your grandma's house or you can ride with me. If you ride with me, you can give me some more detail."

"I'll ride with you," she said. "That'll also save gasoline."

As they headed out of the office, Carol called after them, "Hey, wait. I've got Jerry Wilson on his cell phone."

Lucas went back and took the phone. "I'd like to take a look at the Coombs place, if you're done with it. I've got her granddaughter over here, she thinks maybe something else is going on . . . uh-huh. Just a minute." He looked at Coombs. "Have you got a key?"

She nodded.

Back to the phone: "She's got a key. Yeah, yeah, I'll call you."

He hung up and said, "We're in."

COOMBS HAD PARKED on the street. She got a bag and a bottle of Summer Sunrise Herbal Tea from her salt-rotted Chevy Cavalier and carried it over to the Porsche. The Porsche, she said, as she buckled in, was a "nice little car," and asked if he'd ever driven a Corolla, "which is sorta like this. My girlfriend has one."

"That's great," Lucas said, as they eased into traffic.

She nodded. "It's nice when people drive small cars. It's ecologically sensitive." Lucas accelerated hard enough to snap her neck, but she didn't seem to notice. Instead, she looked around, fiddling with her bottle of tea. "Where're the cup holders?"

"They left them off," Lucas said, not moving his jaw.

Halfway to Grandma's house, she said, "I drove a stick shift in Nepal."

"Nepal?"

"Yeah. A Kia. Have you ever driven a Kia?"

Being a detective, Lucas began to suspect that Gabriella Coombs, guileless as her cornflower eyes might have been, was fucking with him.

THE STREETS WERE quiet, the lawns were green and neat, the houses were older but well kept. Lucas might have been in a thousand houses like Marilyn Coombs's, as a uniformed cop, trying to keep the peace, or to find a window peeper, or to take a break-in report, or figure out who stole the lawn mower. They left the car on the street at the bottom of the front lawn, and climbed up to the porch.

"Not a bad place," Lucas said. "I could see living my life around here."

"She got very lucky," Coombs said. The comment struck Lucas as odd, but as Coombs was pushing through the front door, he let it go.

———

THEY STARTED WITH a fast tour, something Lucas did mostly to make sure there was nobody else around. Marilyn Coombs's house was tidy without being psychotic about it, smelled of cooked potatoes and cauliflower and eggplant and pine-scent spray, and old wood and insulation. There were creaking wooden floors with imitation oriental carpets, and vinyl in the kitchen; brown walls; doilies; three now-dried-out oatmeal cookies sitting on a plate on the kitchen table.

An old electric organ was covered with gilt-framed photographs of people staring at the camera, wearing clothes from the '40s, '50s, '60s, '70s, '80s, and '90s. The earliest were small, and black-and-white. Then a decade or so later, color arrived, and now was fading. The organ looked as though it probably hadn't been played since 1956, and sat under a framed painting of St. Christopher carrying the Christ Child across the river.

There was a blood spot, about the size of a saucer, on the floor next to the bottom of the stairway.

"They took the ball," Coombs said, pointing to the bottom post on the stairway. The post had a hole in it, where a mounting pin would fit. "They supposedly found hair and blood on it."

"Huh."

He looked up the stairs, and could see it. Had seen it, once or twice, an older woman either killing or hurting herself in a fall down the stairs. The stairs were wooden, with a runner. The runner had become worn at the edges of the treads, and Coombs might have been hurrying down to the phone and had caught her foot on a worn spot . . .

"Could have been a fall," Lucas said.

"Except for the missing music box," Coombs said. "And her relationships with the other mysteriously murdered women."

"Let's look for the box."

————

THEY LOOKED and didn't find it. The box, Coombs said, was a distinctive black-lacquered rectangle about the size of a ream of paper, and about three reams thick. On top of the box, a mother-of-pearl inlaid decoration showed a peasant girl, a peasant boy, and some sheep. "Like the boy was making a choice between them," Coombs said, still with the guileless voice.

When you opened the box, she said, four painted wooden figures, a boy, a girl, and two sheep, popped up, and then shuttled around in a circle, one after the other, as music played from beneath them.

"Is the boy following the girl, or the sheep?" Lucas asked.

"The girl," Coombs said, showing the faintest of smiles.

"I think we're okay, then," Lucas said.

Although they didn't find the box, they did find what Coombs said, and Lucas conceded might possibly be, a faint rectangle in the light dust on the surface of the bookshelf where the box should have been.

"Right there," Coombs said. "We need a light . . ." She dragged a floor lamp over, pulled off the shade, replugged it, turned it on. "See?"

The light raked the shelf, which had perhaps a week's accumulation of dust. There may have been a rectangle. "Maybe," Lucas said.

"For sure," she said.

"Maybe."

"Only two possibilities," Coombs said. "Grandma was killed for the music box, or the cops stole it. Pick one."

THE HOUSE DIDN'T have anything else that looked to Lucas like expensive antiques or pottery, although it did have a jumble of cracked and reglued Hummel figurines; and it had quilts. Coombs had decorated all the rooms except the living room with a variety of quilts—crib quilts and single-bed crazy quilts, carefully attached to racks made of one-by-two pine, the racks hung from nails in the real-plaster walls.

"No quilts are missing?" Lucas asked.

"Not that I know of. My mom might. She's started quilting a bit. Grandma was a fanatic."

"It doesn't seem like there'd be much more space for them," Lucas said.

"Yeah . . . I wish one of the Armstrongs were left. I'd like to go to India for a while."

"The Armstrongs?"

"Grandma . . . this was ten years ago . . . Grandma bought a bunch of quilts at an estate sale and they became famous," Coombs said. "Biggest find of her life. She sold them for enough to buy this house. I mean, I don't know exactly how much, but with what she got for her old house, and the quilts, she bought this one."

They were at the top of the stairs, about to come down, and Coombs said, "Look over here."

She stepped down the hall to a built-in cabinet with dark oak doors and trim, and pulled a door open. The shelves were packed with transparent plastic cases the size of shoe boxes, and the cases were stuffed with pieces of fabric, with quilting gear, with spools of thread, with needles and pins and scissors and tapes and stuff that Lucas didn't recognize, but that he thought might be some kind of pattern-drawing gear.

The thread was sorted by hue, except for the stuff in two sewing containers. Containers, because only one of them was the traditional woven-wicker sewing basket; the other was a semitransparent blue tackle box. All the plastic boxes had been labeled with a black Sharpie, in a neat school script: "Threads, red." "Threads, blue."

"A lot of stuff," Lucas said. He put a finger in the wicker sewing basket, pulled it out an inch. More spools, and the spools looked old to him. Collector spools? Which tripped off a thought. "Do you think these Armstrongs, would they have been classified as antiques?"

"No, not really," Coombs said. "They were made in what, the 1930s? I don't think that's old enough to be an antique, but I really don't know. I don't know that much about the whole deal, except that Grandma got a lot of money from them, because of the curse thing."

"The curse thing."

"Yes. The quilts had curses sewn into them. They became . . . what?" She had to think about it for a second, then said, "I suppose they became feminist icons."

LIKE THIS, SHE SAID:

Grandma Coombs had once lived in a tiny house on Snelling Avenue. Her husband had died in the '70s, and she was living on half of a postal pension, the income from a modest IRA, and Social Security. She haunted estate sales, flea markets, and garage sales all over the Upper Midwest, buying cheap, reselling to antique stores in the Cities.

"She probably didn't make ten thousand dollars a year, after expenses, but she enjoyed it, and it helped," Coombs said. Then she found the Armstrong quilts at an estate sale in northern Wisconsin. The quilts were brilliantly colored and well made. Two were crazy quilts, two were stars, one was a log-cabin, and the other was unique, now called "Canada Geese."

None of that made them famous. They were famous, Coombs said, because the woman who made them, Sharon Armstrong, had been married to a drunken sex freak named Frank Armstrong who beat her, raped her, and abused the two children, one boy and one girl, all in the small and oblivious town of Carton, Wisconsin.

Frank Armstrong was eventually shot by his son, Bill, who then shot himself. Frank didn't die from the gunshot, although Bill did. The shootings brought out all the abuse stories, which were horrific, and after a trial, Frank was locked up in a state psychiatric hospital and died there twenty years later.

Sharon Armstrong and her daughter moved to Superior, where first the mother and then the daughter got jobs as cooks on the big interlake ore ships. Sharon died shortly after World War II. The daughter, Annabelle, lived, unmarried and childless, until 1995. When she died, her possessions were sold off to pay her credit-card debts.

"There were six quilts. I was in Germany when Grandma found them, and I only saw them a couple of times, because I was moving around a lot, but they were beautiful. The thing is, when Grandma bought them, she also bought a scrapbook that had clippings about Frank Armstrong, and Sharon Armstrong, and what happened to them.

"When Grandma got home, she put the quilts away for a while. She was going to build racks, to stretch them, and then sell them at an art fair. She used to do that with old quilts and Red Wing pottery.

"When she got them out, she was stretching one, and she noticed that the stitching looked funny. When she looked really close, she saw that the stitches were letters, and when you figured them out, they were curses."

"Curses," Lucas said.

"Curses against Frank. They were harsh: they said stuff like 'Goddamn the man who sleeps beneath this quilt, may the devils pull out his bowels and burn them in front of his eyes; may they pour boiling lead in his ears for all eternity' . . . They went on, and on, and on, for like . . . hours. But they were also, kind of, *poetic*, in an ugly way."

"Hmmm." Lucas said. "Grandma sold them for what?"

"I don't know, exactly. Mom might. But enough that she could sell her old house and buy this one."

"All this quilt stuff ties to Connie Bucher."

"Yeah. There are thousands of quilt groups all over the country. They're like rings, and a lot of the women belong to two rings. Or even three. So there are all these connections. You can be a quilter on a dairy farm in Wisconsin and you need to go to Los Angeles for something, so you call a friend, and the friend calls a friend, and the next thing you know, somebody's calling you from Los Angeles, ready to help out. The connections are really amazing."

"They wouldn't be mostly Democrats, would they?" Lucas asked.

"Well . . . I suppose. Why?"

"Nothing. But: your grandma was connected to Bucher. And there was another woman killed. Do you have a name?"

"Better than that. I have a newspaper story."

LUCAS DIDN'T WANT to sit anywhere in the room where the elderly Coombs had died, in case it became necessary to tear it apart. He took Gabriella Coombs and the clipping into the kitchen, turned on the light.

"Ah, God," Coombs stepped back, clutched at his arm.

"What?" Then he saw the cockroaches scuttling for cover. A half dozen of them had been perched on a cookie sheet on the stove. He could still see faint grease rings from a dozen or so cookies, and the grease had brought out the bugs.

"I've gotta get my mom and clean this place up," Gabriella said. "Once you get the bugs established, they're impossible to get rid of. We should call an exterminator. How long does it take the crime-scene people to finish?"

"Depends on the house and what they're looking for," Lucas said.

"I think they're pretty much done here, but they'll probably wait until there's a ruling on the death."

"You think I could wash the dishes?" she asked.

"You could call and ask. Tell them about the bugs."

THEY SAT AT the kitchen table, and Lucas took the newspaper clip. It was printed on standard typing paper, taken from a website. The clip was the top half of the front page in the *Chippewa Falls Post*, the text running under a large headline, *Chippewa Heiress Murdered*.

> A noted Chippewa Falls art collector and heir to the Thune brewing fortune was found shot to death in her home Wednesday morning by relatives, a Chippewa Falls police spokesman said Wednesday afternoon.
>
> The body of Claire Donaldson, 72, was discovered in the kitchen of her West Hill mansion by her sister, Margaret Donaldson Booth, and Mrs. Booth's husband, Landford Booth, of Eau Claire.
>
> Mrs. Donaldson's secretary, Amity Anderson, who lives in an apartment in Mrs. Donaldson's home, was in Chicago on business for Mrs. Donaldson, police said. When she was unable to reach Mrs. Donaldson by telephone on Tuesday evening or Wednesday morning, Anderson called the Booths, who went to Donaldson's home and found her body.
>
> Police said they have several leads in the case.
>
> "Claire Donaldson was brilliant and kind, and that this should happen to her is a tragedy for all of Chippewa Falls," said the Rev. Carl Hoffer, pastor of Prince of Peace Lutheran Church in Chippewa Falls, and a longtime friend of Mrs. Donaldson . . .

Lucas read through the clip, which was long on history and short on crime detail; no matter, he could get the details from the

Chippewa cops. But, he thought, if you changed the name and the murder weapon, the news story of Claire Donaldson's death could just as easily have been the story of Constance Bucher's murder.

"WHEN WE get back to the office, I'll want a complete statement," he told Coombs. "I'll get a guy to take it from you. We'll need a detailed description of that music box. This could get complicated."

"God. I wasn't sure you were going to believe me," Coombs said. "About Grandma being murdered."

"She probably wasn't—but there's a chance that she was," Lucas said. "The idea that somebody hit her with that ball . . . That would take some thought, some knowledge of the house."

"And a serious psychosis," Coombs said.

"And that. But it's possible."

"On the TV shows, the cops never believe the edgy counterculture person the first time she tells them something," Coombs said. "Two or three people usually have to get killed first."

"That's TV," Lucas said.

"But you have to admit that cops are prejudiced against us," she said.

"Hey," Lucas said. "I know a guy who walks around in hundred-degree heat in a black hoodie because he's always freezing because he smokes crack all day, supports himself with burglary, and at night he spray-paints glow-in-the-dark archangels on boxcars so he can send Christ's good news to the world. He's an edgy counterculture person. You're a hippie."

She clouded up, her lip trembling. "That's a cruel thing to say," she said. "Why'd you have to say that?"

"Ah, man," Lucas said. "Look, I'm sorry . . ."

She smiled, pleased with herself and the trembling lip: "Relax. I'm just toyin' with you."

———

ON THE WAY out of the house, they walked around the blood spot, and Coombs asked, "What's a doornail?"

"I don't know."

"Oh." Disappointed. "I would have thought you'd have heard it a lot, and looked it up. You know, dead as a doornail, and you being a cop."

He got her out of the house, into the Porsche, fired it up, rolled six feet, then stopped, frowned at Coombs, and shut it down again.

"Two things: If your grandma's name was Coombs, and your mother is her daughter, how come your name . . . ?"

"I'm a bastard," Coombs said.

"Huh?"

"My mom was a hippie. I'm second-generation hippie. Anyway, she slept around a little, and when the bundle of joy finally showed up, none of the prospective fathers did." She flopped her hands in the air. "So. I'm a bastard. What was the second thing?"

"Mmm." He shook his head, and fished his cell phone out of his pocket. "I'm going to call somebody and ask an unpleasant question about your grandmother. If you want, you could get out and walk around the yard for a minute."

She shook her head. "That's okay. I'd be interested in hearing the question."

Lucas dialed, identified himself, and asked for the medical examiner who'd done the postmortem on Coombs. Got her and asked, "What you take out of her stomach. Uh-huh? Uh-huh? Very much? Okay . . . okay."

He hung up and Coombs again asked, "What?"

"Her stomach was empty. If she fell when she was by herself, I wonder who ate nine oatmeal cookies?" Lucas asked.

―――――

BACK AT BCA headquarters, he briefed Shrake, put Coombs in a room with him, and told them both that he needed every detail. Five minutes later he was on the line with an investigator with the Chippewa County Sheriff's Office, named Carl Frazier, who'd worked the Donaldson murder.

"I saw the story in the paper and was going to call somebody, but I needed to talk to the sheriff about it. He's out of town, back this afternoon," Frazier said. "Donaldson's a very touchy subject around here. But since you called *me* . . . "

"It feels the same," Lucas said. "Donaldson and Bucher."

"Yeah, it does," Frazier said. "What seems most alike is that there was never a single lead. Nothing. We tore up the town, and Eau Claire, we beat on every asshole we knew about, and there never was a thing. I've gotten the impression that the St. Paul cops are beating their heads against the same wall."

"You nail down anything as stolen?"

"Nope. That was another mystery," Frazier said. "As far as we could tell, nothing was touched. I guess the prevailing theory among the big thinkers here was that it was somebody she knew, they got in an argument . . . "

"And the guy pulled out a gun and shot her? Why'd he have a gun?"

"That's a weak point," Frazier admitted. "Would have worked better if she'd been killed like Bucher—you know, somebody picked up a frying pan and swatted her. That would have looked a little more spontaneous."

"This looked planned?"

"Like D-Day. She was shot three times in the back of the head. But what for? A few hundred dollars? Nobody who inherited the money needed it. There hadn't been any family fights or neighbor-hood feuds or anything else. The second big-thinker theory was that it was some psycho. Came in the back door, maybe for food or booze, killed her."

"Man . . ."

"I know," Frazier said. "But that's what we couldn't figure out: *What for?* If you can't figure out *what for,* it's harder than hell to fig-ure out *who.*"

"She's got these relatives, a sister and brother-in-law, the Booths," Lucas said. "They still around?"

"Oh, yeah. The sheriff hears from them regularly."

"Okay. Then, I'll tell you what, I'm gonna go talk to them," Lucas said. "Maybe I could stop by and look at your files?"

"Absolutely," Frazier said. "If you don't mind, I'd like to ride along when you do the interview. Or, I'll tell you what. Why don't we meet at the Donaldson house? The Booths still own it, and it's empty. You could take a look at it."

"How soon can you do it?"

"Tomorrow? I'll call the Booths to make sure they'll be around," Frazier said.

WEATHER AND LUCAS spent some time that night fooling around, and when the first round was done, Lucas rolled over on his back, his chest slick with sweat, and Weather said, "That wasn't so terrible."

"Yeah. I was fantasizing about Jesse Barth," he joked. She swatted him on the stomach, not too hard, but he bounced and complained, "Ouch! You almost exploded one of my balls."

"You have an extra," she said. "All we need is one." She was try-ing for a second kid, worried that she might be too old, at forty-one.

"Yeah, well, I'd like to keep both of them," Lucas said, rubbing his stomach. "I think you left a mark."

She made a rude noise. "Crybaby." Then, "Did you hear what Sam said today . . . ?"

AND LATER, she asked, "What happened with Jesse Barth, anyway?"

"It's going to the grand jury. Virgil's handling most of it."

"Mmm. Virgil," Weather said, with a *tone* in her voice.

"What about him?"

"If I was going to fantasize during sex, which I'm not saying I'd do, Virgil would be a candidate," she said.

"Virgil? Flowers?"

"He has a way about him," Weather said. "And that little tiny butt."

Lucas was shocked. "He never . . . I mean, made a *move* or anything . . ."

"On me?" she asked. "No, of course not. But . . . mmm."

"What?"

"I wonder why? He never made a move? He doesn't even flirt with me," she said.

"Probably because I carry a gun," Lucas said.

"Probably because I'm too old," Weather said.

"You're not too old, believe me," Lucas said. "I get the strange feeling that Virgil would fuck a snake, if he could get somebody to hold its head."

"Sort of reminds me of you, when you were his age," she said.

"You didn't know me when I was his age."

"You can always pick out the guys who'd fuck a snake, whatever age they are," Weather said.

"That's unfair."

"Mmm."

A MINUTE LATER, Lucas said, "Virgil thinks that going to Dakota County was a little . . . iffy."

"Politically corrupt, you mean," Weather said.

"Maybe," Lucas admitted.

"It is," Weather said.

"I mentioned to Virgil that I occasionally talked to Ruffe over at the *Star Tribune.*"

She propped herself up on one arm. "You suggested that he call Ruffe?"

"Not at all. That'd be improper," Lucas said.

"So what are the chances he'll call?"

"Knowing that fuckin' Flowers, about ninety-six percent."

She dropped onto her back. "So you manipulated him into making the call, so the guy in Dakota County can't bury the case."

"Can you manipulate somebody into something, if he knows that you're manipulating him, and wants to be?" Lucas asked, rolling up on his side.

"That's a very feminine thought, Lucas. I'm proud of you," Weather said.

"Hey," Lucas said, catching her hand and guiding it. "Feminine *this.*"

8

ANOTHER GREAT DAY, blue sky, almost no wind, dew sparkling on the lawn, the neighbor's sprinkler system cutting in. Sam loved the sprinkler system and could mimic its *chi-chi-chi-chiiiii* sound almost perfectly.

Lucas got the paper off the porch, pulled it out of the plastic sack, and unrolled it. Nothing in the *Star Tribune* about Kline. Nothing at all by Ruffe. Had he misfired?

LUCAS NEVER LIKED to get up early—though he had no problem staying up until dawn, or longer—but was out of the house at 6:30, nudging out of the driveway just behind Weather. Weather was doing a series of scar revisions on a burn case. The patient was in the hospital overnight to get some sodium numbers fixed, and was being waked as she left the driveway. The patient would be on the table by 7:30, the first of three operations she'd do before noon.

Lucas, on the other hand, was going fishing. He took the truck north on Cretin to I-94, and turned into the rising sun; and watched it rise higher for a bit more than an hour as he drove past incoming rush-hour traffic, across the St. Croix, past cows and buffalo and small towns getting up. He left the interstate at Wisconsin Exit 52, continuing toward Chippewa, veering around the town and up the Chippewa River into Jim Falls.

A retired Minneapolis homicide cop had a summer home just below the dam. He was traveling in Wyoming with his wife, but told Lucas where he'd hidden the keys for the boat. Lucas was on the river a little after eight, in the cop's eighteen-foot Lund, working the trolling motor with his foot, casting the shoreline with a Billy Bait on a Thorne Brothers custom rod.

LUCAS HAD always been interested in newspapers—thought he might have been a reporter if he hadn't become a cop—and had gotten to the point where he could sense something wrong with a newspaper story. If a story seemed reticent, somehow; deliberately oblique; if the writer did a little tap dance; then, Lucas could say, "Ah, there's something going on." The writer knew something he couldn't report, at least, not yet.

Lucas, and a lot of other cops, developed the same sense about crimes. A solution was obvious, but wasn't right. The story was hinky. Of course, cops sometimes had that feeling and it turned out that they were wrong. The obvious *was* the truth. But usually, when it seemed like something was wrong, something was.

There'd been a car at the murder scene—if there hadn't been, then somebody had been running down the street with a sixty-pound printer on his back. So there'd been a car. But if there'd been a car, why wasn't a lot of the other small stuff taken? Like the TV in the bedroom, a nice thirty-two-inch flat screen. Could have carried it out under one arm.

Or those video games.

On the other hand, if the killers were professionals after cash and easy-to-hock jewelry, why hadn't they found the safe, and at least tried to open it? It wasn't that well hidden . . . Why had they spent so much time in the house? Why did they steal that fuckin' printer?

The printer bothered him. He put the fishing rod down, pulled his cell phone, was amazed to see he actually had a signal, and called back to the office, to Carol.

"Listen, what's that intern's name? Sandy? Can you get her? Great. Get the call list going: I want to know if anybody in the Metro area found a Hewlett-Packard printer. Have her call the garbage haulers, too. We're looking for a Hewlett-Packard printer that was tossed in a dumpster. You can get the exact model number from John Smith. And if somebody saw one, ask if there's anything else that might have come from Bucher's place, like a DVD player. Yeah. Yeah, tell everybody it's the Bucher case. Yeah, I know. Get her started, give her some language to explain what we're doing."

HE'D NO MORE THAN hung up when he had another thought, fished out the phone, and called Carol again. "Has anyone shown Sandy how to run the computer? Okay. After she does the call list, get her to pull every unsolved murder in the Upper Midwest for the last five years. Minnesota, Iowa, Wisconsin. Might as well throw in the Dakotas. Don't do Illinois, there'd be too much static from Chicago. Have her sift them for characteristics similar to the Bucher case. But don't tell her where I am—don't tell her about Donaldson. I want to see if she catches it. No, I'm not trying to fuck her over, I just want to know how good a job she did of sifting them. Yeah. Goodbye."

FEELING AS THOUGH he'd accomplished something, he floated the best part of a mile down the river, and then, with some regret, motored back up the opposite shore to the cop's house and the dock.

The river was cool, green, friendly. He could spend a lot of time there, he thought, just floating. Hadn't seen a single muskie; usually didn't—which meant that he didn't smell like fish slime, and wouldn't have to stop at a McDonald's to wash up.

Despite the interruption of the cell-phone call, he *had* seen a mink, several ducks, a brooding Canada goose, and a nearly empty Fanta orange bottle, floating down the river. He'd hooked it out, emptied it, and carried it up to the truck. Returned the keys to their hiding spot, put away the rod, wrote a thank-you note to the cop, and left it in the mailbox.

Not a bad way to start the day, he thought, rumbling up the hill to the main road. Took a right and headed into Chippewa.

THE DONALDSON MANSION was on the hill on the west side of town. There were other big houses scattered around, but the Donaldson was the biggest. Frazier was already there, leaning against an unmarked car that everyone but a blind man would recognize as a cop car, talking on a cell phone. Lucas parked, got out of the truck, locked it, and walked over.

Frazier was a short man in his fifties, stout, with iron gray hair cut into a flattop. He was wearing khaki slacks, a red golf shirt, and a blue sport coat. His nose was red, and spidery red veins webbed his cheekbones. He looked like he should be carrying a bowling bag. He took the phone away from his mouth and asked, "Davenport?"

Lucas nodded and Frazier said into the phone, "Could be a while, but I don't know how long." He hung up, grinned at Lucas as they shook hands, and said, "My old lady. My first priority is to get the dry cleaning and the cat food. My second priority is to solve the Donaldson killing."

"You gotta have your priorities," Lucas said. He looked up at the mansion. "That's a hell of a house," Lucas said. "Just like the Bucher house. When are the Booths . . . ?"

"Probably about seven minutes from now," Frazier said, looking at his watch. "They always keep me waiting about seven or eight minutes, to make a point, I think. We're the public servants, and they are . . . I don't know. The Dukes of Earl, or something."

"Like that," Lucas said.

"Yup." He handed Lucas a brown-paper portfolio, as thick as a metropolitan phone book. "This is every piece of paper we have on the Donaldson case. Took me two hours to Xerox it. Most of it's bullshit, but I thought you might as well have it all."

"Let me put it in the truck," Lucas said.

He ran the paper back to the truck, then caught Frazier halfway up the sidewalk to the house. "Isn't a hell of a lot to see, but you might as well see it," Frazier said.

FRAZIER HAD KEYS. Inside, the house smelled empty, the odor of dry wallpaper and floor wax. The furniture was sparse and to Lucas's eye, undistinguished, except that it was old. The few paintings on the walls were mostly oil portraits gone dark with age. As they walked around, their footfalls echoed down the hallways; the only other sound was the mechanical whir of an air-conditioner fan.

"What's going on here is that the house isn't worth all that much," Frazier said. "It'd need a lot of updating before you'd want to take out a mortgage on it. New wiring, new plumbing, new heating system, new roof, new windows, new siding. Basically, it'd cost you a million bucks to get the place into tip-top shape."

"But the woman who lived here was rich?"

"Very rich. She was also very old," Frazier said. "Her friends say she didn't want to be annoyed by a lot of renovation when she only had a few years left. So. She didn't do some things, and the house was perfectly fine for the way she used it. Went to Palm Beach in the winter, and so on."

After Donaldson was murdered, Frazier said, the Booths tried to sell it, but it didn't sell. Then somebody came up with the idea that the Booths could donate the place to the city as a rich-lumber-family museum. That idea limped along and then somebody else suggested it could be a venue for arts programs.

"Basically, what was going on is, the Booths couldn't sell it, so they were encouraging all this other bullshit. They'd donate the house and a few paintings and old tables to the city at some ridiculous valuation, like two million bucks, which they would then deduct from their income tax," Frazier said. "That'd save them, what, about eight hundred thousand dollars? If they can't get that done, if the house just sits here and rots . . . well, what they've got is about two city lots at fifty thousand dollars each, and it'd probably cost them half of that to get the place torn down and carted away. In the meantime, they pay property tax."

"Life is tough and then you die," Lucas said.

"Wasn't tough for the Booths," Frazier grunted. "They've been rich forever . . . You want to see where the murder was?"

Donaldson had been killed in the kitchen. There was nothing to see but slightly dusty hardwood floors and appliances that had stepped out of 1985. The refrigerator and stove were a shade of tobacco-juice yellow that Lucas remembered from his first house.

"Very cold," Frazier said. "I'd talked myself into the idea that it was a traveling killer, passing through, saw a light and wanted money and a sandwich, and went up and killed her with a crappy .22. Stood there and ate the sandwich and looked at the body and never gave a shit. In my brain-movie, he *so* doesn't give a shit, he doesn't even give a shit if he was caught."

"Any proof on the sandwich?" Lucas asked, joking.

Frazier wasn't joking: "Yeah. There was a bread crumb in the middle of Donaldson's back. Loose. Not stuck on her blouse, or any-thing. It was like it fell on her, after she hit the floor. Sea-Bird brand sourdough bread. There was a loaf of it on the counter."

"Huh." Lucas scratched his forehead. "Let me tell you about these oatmeal cookies . . ."

THE BOOTHS ARRIVED ten minutes later, in a black Mercedes-Benz S550. Landford Booth looked like a terrier, as short as Frazier, but thin, with small sharp eyes, a bristly white mustache, and a long nose with oversized pores. He wore a navy blue double-breasted jacket with silver buttons, and gray slacks. Margaret Booth had silvery hair, a face tightened by cosmetic surgery, and pale blue eyes. She wore a cranberry-colored dress and matching shoes, and blinked a lot, as though she were wearing contact lenses. Landford was a well-tended seventy-five, Lucas thought. His wife about the same, or possibly a bit older.

Lucas and Frazier had just come back from the kitchen and found the Booths standing in the open front door, Margaret's hand on Landford's arm, and Landford cleared his throat and said, "Well? Have you discovered anything new?"

THE BOOTHS KNEW almost nothing—but not quite nothing.

Lucas asked about missing antiques.

Margaret said, "Claire was a collector—and a seller. Pieces would come and go, all the time. One day there'd be a sideboard in the front hall, and the next week, there'd be a music cabinet. One week it'd be Regency, the next week Gothic Revival. She claimed she al-ways made a profit on her sales, but I personally doubt that she did. I suspect that what she really wanted was the company—people buying and selling. People to argue with and to talk about antiques with. She considered herself a connoisseur."

"Was anything missing, as far as you know?" Lucas asked.

"Not as far as we know—but we don't know that much. We have an insurance list, and of course we had to make an inventory of her possessions for the IRS," Landford said. "There were items on the insurance list that weren't in the house, but there were things in the house that weren't on the insurance list. The fact is, it's difficult to tell."

"How about sales records?"

"We have a big pile of them, but they're a mess," Landford said. "I suppose we could go back and check purchases, and what she had when she died, against sales. Might be able to pinpoint something that way," Landford said.

"Could you do that?" Lucas asked.

"We could get our accountant to take a look, she'd be better at it," Landford said. "Might take a couple of weeks. The papers are a mess."

THE BOOTHS MADE one claim, and made it to Lucas, ignoring Frazier as though he were an inconvenient stump: "Somebody should look carefully at Amity Anderson. I'm sure she was involved," Margaret Booth said.

Landford quivered: "There is no doubt about it. Although our sheriff's department seems to doubt it."

Behind their backs, Frazier rolled his eyes. Lucas said to Margaret: "Tell me why she must have been involved."

"It's obvious," she said. "If you go through all the possibilities, you realize, in the end, that the killer-person, whoever he was, *was inside the house with Claire*." She put the last phrase in vocal italics. "Claire would *never* let anybody inside, not when she was alone, unless she knew them well."

Landford: "The police checked all her friends, and friends-of-friends, and everybody was cleared. There was no sign of forced entry, and Claire always kept the doors locked. Ergo, Amity Anderson gave somebody a key. She had quite the sexual history, Claire used to tell me. I believe Amity gave the house key to one of her boyfriends, told him where Claire kept her cash—she always liked to have some cash on hand—and then went to Chicago as an alibi. It's perfectly clear to me that's what happened."

"Exactly," Margaret said.

"How much cash?" Lucas asked.

"A couple of thousand, maybe three or four, depending," Landford said. "If she'd just gotten back from somewhere, or was about to go, she'd have more on hand. That doesn't sound like much to you and me . . ." He hesitated, looking at the cops, as though he sensed that he might have insulted them. Then he pushed on, ". . . but to a person like Amity Anderson, it probably seemed like a fortune."

"Where is Anderson now?" Lucas asked.

Frazier cleared his throat. "Her address is in the file I gave you. But you know where the Ford plant is, the one by the river in St. Paul?"

"Yes."

"She lives maybe . . . six, seven blocks . . . straight back away from the river, up that hill. Bunch of older houses. You know where I mean?"

"It's about a ten-minute walk from my house," Lucas said, "If you're walking slow."

"How far from Bucher's?" Landford asked.

"Five minutes, by car," Lucas said.

"Holy shit," Frazier said.

THEY TALKED for another ten minutes, and spent some more time looking around the house with the Booths, but the crime had been back far enough that Lucas could learn nothing by walking through the house. He said goodbye to the Booths, gave them a card, and when they'd left, waited until Frazier had locked up the house.

"Why isn't Amity Anderson involved?" Lucas asked.

"I'm not saying it's impossible," Frazier said. "But Amity Anderson is a mousy little girl who majored in art and couldn't get a job. She wound up being Donaldson's secretary, though really, she was more like a servant. She did a little of everything, and got paid not much. One reason we don't think her boyfriend did it is that there's no evidence that she had a boyfriend."

"Ever?"

"Not when she lived here. Mrs. Donaldson had a live-in maid, and she told us that Amity never went anywhere," Frazier said. "Couldn't afford it, apparently had no reason to. In any case, she had no social life—didn't even get personal phone calls. Go talk to her. You'll see. You'll walk away with frost on your dick."

ON THE WAY back to the Cities, Lucas got a call from Ruffe Ignace.

"I got a tip that you've been investigating Burt Kline for statutory rape," Ignace said. "Can you tell me when you're gonna bust him?"

"Man, I don't know what you're talking about," Lucas said, grinning into the phone.

"Ah, c'mon. I've talked to six people and they all say you're in it up to your hips," Ignace said. "Are you going to testify for the Dakota County grand jury?"

"They've got themselves a grand jury?" Lucas eased the car window down, and held the phone next to the whistling slipstream. "Ruffe, you're breaking up. I can barely hear you."

"I'll take that as a 'no comment,'" Ignace said. "Davenport said, 'No comment, you worthless little newspaper prick,' but confirmed that he has sold all of his stock in Kline's boat-waxing business."

"You get laid the other night?" Lucas asked.

"Yes. Now: will you deny that you're investigating Kline?" Lucas kept his mouth shut, and after ten seconds of silence, Ignace said, "All right, you're not denying it."

"Not denying or confirming," Lucas said. "You can quote me on that."

"Good. Because that confirms. Is this chick . . ." Pause, paper riffling, ". . . Jesse Barth . . . Is she really hot?"

"Ah, fuck."

"Thank you," Ruffe said. "That'd be Jesse with two esses."

"Listen, Ruffe, I don't know where you're getting this, but honest to God, you'll never get another word out of me if you stick me with the leak," Lucas said. "Put it on Dakota County."

"I'm not going to put it on anybody," Ignace said. "It's gonna be like mystery meat—it's gonna come out of nowhere and wind up on the reader's breakfast plate."

"That's not good enough, because people are going to draw conclusions," Lucas argued. "If they conclude that I leaked it, I'll be in trouble, and you won't get another word out of me or anybody else in the BCA. Let people think it's Dakota County. Whisper it in their ear. You don't have to say the words."

"I'm going after the mother this afternoon," Ignace said. "Let's see, it's . . . Kathy? Is she hot?"

"Ruffe, you're breaking up really bad. I'm hanging up now, Ruffe."

DESPITE HIS WEASELING, Lucas was pleased. Flowers had done the job, and Ignace would nail Kline to a wall. Further, Ignace wouldn't give up the source, and if the game was played just right, everybody would assume the source was Dakota County.

He called Rose Marie Roux. He didn't like to lie to her, but sometimes did, if only to protect her; necessity is a mother. "I just talked to Ruffe Ignace. He knows about Kline. He's got Jesse Barth's name, he's going to talk to Kathy Barth. I neither confirmed nor denied and I am not his source. But his source is a good one and it comes one day after we briefed Dakota County. We need to start leaking around that Dakota County was talking to Ignace."

"We can do that," she said, also pleased. "This is working out."

"Tell the governor. Maybe he could do an off-the-record joke with some of the reporters at the Capitol, about Dakota County leaks," Lucas said. "Maybe get Mitford to put something together. A quip. The governor likes quips. And metaphors."

"A quip," she said. "A quip would be good."

LUCAS CALLED John Smith. Smith was at the Bucher mansion, and would be there for a while. "I'll stop by," Lucas said.

THE WIDDLERS were there, finishing the inventory. "There's a lot of good stuff here," Leslie told Lucas. He was wearing a pink bow tie that looked like an exotic lepidopteran. "There's two million, conservatively. I really want to be here when they have the auction."

"Nothing missing?"

He shrugged and his wife picked up the question. "There didn't seem to be any obvious holes in the decor, when you started putting things back together—they trashed the place, but they didn't move things very far."

"Did you know a woman named Claire Donaldson, over in Eau Claire?"

The Widdlers looked at each other, and then Jane said, "Oh my God. Do you think?"

Lucas said, "There's a possibility, but I'm having trouble figuring out a motive. There doesn't seem to be anything missing from the Donaldson place, either."

"We were at some of the Donaldson sales," Leslie Widdler said. "She had some magnificent things, although I will say, her taste wasn't as extraordinary as everybody made out." To his wife: "Do you remember that awful Italian neoclassical commode?"

Jane poked a finger at Lucas's chest. "It looked like somebody had been working on it with a wood rasp. And it obviously had been refinished. They sold it as the original finish, but there was no way . . ."

THE WIDDLERS went back to work, and Lucas and John Smith stepped aside and watched them scribbling, and Lucas said, "John, I've got some serious shit coming down the road. I'll try to stick with you as much as I can, but this other thing is political, and it could be a distraction."

"Big secret?"

"Not anymore. The goddamn *Star Tribune* got a sniff of it. I'll try to stay with you . . ."

Smith flapped his hands in frustration: "I got jack-shit, Lucas. You think this Donaldson woman might be tied in?"

"It feels that way. It feels like this one," Lucas said. "We might want to talk to the FBI, see if they'd take a look."

"I hate to do that, as long as we have a chance," Smith said.

"So do I."

Smith looked glumly at Leslie Widdler, who was peering at the bottom of a silver plant-watering pot. "It'd spread the blame, if we fall on our asses," he said. "But I want to catch these mother-fuckers. Me."

ON THE WAY out the door, Lucas asked Leslie Widdler, "If we found that there were things missing, how easy would it be to locate them? I mean, in the antiques market?"

"If you had a good professional photograph and good documentation of any idiosyncrasies—you know, dents, or flaws, or repairs—then it's *possible*," Widdler said. "Not likely, but possible. If you don't have that, then you're out of luck."

Jane picked it up: "There are literally hundreds of thousands of antiques sold every year, mostly for cash, and a lot of those sales are to dealers who turn them over and over and over. A chair sold here might wind up in a shop in Santa Monica or Palm Beach after going through five different dealers. They may disappear into somebody's house and not come out for another twenty or thirty years."

And Leslie: "Another thing, of course, is that if somebody spends fifty thousand dollars for an armoire, and then finds out it's stolen, are they going to turn it over to the police and lose their money? That's really not how they got rich in the first place . . . So I wouldn't be too optimistic."

"There's always hope," Jane said. She looked as though she were trying to make a perplexed wrinkle in her forehead. "But to tell you the truth, I'm beginning to think there's nothing missing. We haven't been able to identify a single thing."

"The Reckless painting," Lucas said.

"If there was one," she said. "There are a number of Reckless sales every year. If we find no documentation that suggests that Connie owned one, if all we have is the testimony of this one young African-American person . . . well, Lucas . . . it's gone."

9

RUFFE IGNACE'S STORY wasn't huge, but even with a one-column head, and thirty inches of carefully worded text, it was big enough to do all the political damage that Kline had feared.

Best of all, it featured an ambush photograph of Dakota County attorney Jim Cole, whose startled eyes made him look like a raccoon caught at night on the highway. Kline was now a Dakota County story.

Ignace had gotten to Kathy Barth. Although she was identified only as a "source close to the investigation," she spoke from the point of view of a victim, and Ignace was skilled enough to let that bleed through. "*. . . the victim was described as devastated by the experience, and experts have told the family that she may need years of treatment if the allegations are true.*"

NEIL MITFORD LED Lucas and Rose Marie Roux into the governor's office and closed the door. The governor said, "We're all clear, right? Nobody can get us on leaking the story?" He knew that Lucas had ties with the local media; that Lucas did, in fact, share a daughter with the leading Channel Three editorialist.

"Ruffe called me yesterday and asked for a comment and I told him I couldn't give him one," Lucas said, doing his tap dance. "It's pretty obvious that he got a lot of his information from the victim's mother."

"Is Kathy Barth still trying to cut a deal with Burt?" Mitford asked Lucas.

"They want money. That was the whole point of the exercise," Lucas said. "But now, she's stuck. She can't cut a deal with the grand jury."

"And Burt's guilty," the governor said. "I mean, he did it, right? We're not simply fucking him over?"

"Yeah, he did it," Lucas said. "I think he might've been doing the mother, too, but he definitely was doing the kid."

Rose Marie: "Screw their negotiations. They can file a civil suit later."

"Might be more money for the attorney," Mitford said. "If he's taking it on contingency."

"Lawyers got to eat, too," the governor said with satisfaction. To Rose Marie and Lucas: "You two will be managing the BCA's testimony before the grand jury? Is that all set?"

"I talked to Jim Cole, he'll be calling with a schedule," Rose Marie said. "There's a limited amount of testimony available—the Barths, Agent Flowers, Lucas, the technical people from the lab. Cole wants to move fast. If there's enough evidence to indict, he wants to give Kline a chance to drop out of the election so another Republican can run."

"Burt might get stubborn . . ." the governor suggested.

"I don't think so," Rose Marie said, shaking her head. "Cole won't indict unless he can convict. He wants to nail down the mother, the girl, the physical evidence, and then make a decision. With this newspaper story, he's got even more reason to push. If he tells Burt's lawyer that Burt's going down, and shows him the evidence, I think Burt'll quit."

The governor nodded: "So. Lucas. Talk to your people. We don't want any bleed-back, we don't want anybody pointing fingers at us, saying there's a political thing going on. We want this straightforward, absolutely professional. We regret this kind of thing as much as anybody. It's a tragedy for everybody involved, including Burt Kline."

"And especially the child. We have to protect the children from predators," Mitford said. "Any contacts with the press, we always hit that point."

"Of course, absolutely," the governor said. "The children always come first. Especially when the predators are Republicans."

Nobody asked about the Bucher case, which was slipping off the front pages.

WHEN THEY were finished, Lucas walked down the hall with Rose Marie, heading for the parking garage. "Wonder why with Republicans, it's usually fucking somebody that gets them in trouble. And with the Democrats, it's usually stealing?"

"Republicans have money. Most of them don't need more," she suggested. "But they come from uptight, sexually repressed backgrounds, and sometimes, they just go off. Democrats are looser about sex, but half the time, they used to be teachers or government workers, and they're desperate for cash. They see all that money up close, around the government, the lobbyists and the corporate guys, they can smell it, they can taste it, they see the rich guys flying to Paris for the weekend, and eating in all the good restaurants, and buying three-thousand-dollar suits. They just want to reach out and take some."

"I see money in this, for my old company," Lucas said. He'd once started a software company that developed real-time emergency simulations for 911 centers. "We could make simulation software that would teach Republicans how to fuck and Democrats how to steal."

"Jeez, I don't know," Rose Marie said. "Can we trust Republicans with that kind of information?"

BACK AT HIS OFFICE, Carol told him that the intern, Sandy, had been up half the night preparing a report on Hewlett-Packard printers and on murders in the Upper Midwest. He also had a call from one of Jim Cole's assistant county attorneys.

Lucas called the attorney, and they agreed that Lucas and Flowers would testify before the grand jury the following day. The assistant wanted to talk to Flowers before the grand-jury presentation, but said it would not be necessary to review testimony with Lucas himself.

"You'll do the basic bureaucratic outline, confirm the arrival of the initial information, the assignment of Agent Flowers to the case, and Flowers's delivery of the technical evidence to the crime lab. We'll need the usual piece of paper that says the evidence was properly logged in. That's about it."

"Excellent," Lucas said. "I'll call Agent Flowers now and have him get back to you."

Lucas called Flowers: "You're gonna have to carry the load, Virgil, so you best memorize every stick of information you put in the files. I wouldn't be surprised if somebody from Kline's circle has been talking to somebody from Cole's circle, if you catch my drift."

"After that newspaper story, I don't see how Cole could bail out," Flowers said.

"I don't see it, either. But depending on what may have been said behind the chicken house, we gotta be ready," Lucas said. "Tell them what you got, don't get mousetrapped into trying out any theories."

"Gotcha," Flowers said. "Gonna get my mind *tightly* wrapped around this one, boss. Tightly."

Lucas, exasperated, said, "That means you're going fishing, right?"

"I'll talk to the lab people and make sure the paperwork is right, that we got the semen sample and the pubic hair results, the photos of Kline's nuts. Copies for everyone. And so on, et cetera. I'll polish my boots tonight."

"You're not going fishing, Virgil," Luca said. "This is too fuckin' touchy."

"How's the little woman?" Flowers asked.

"Goddamnit, Virgil . . ."

LUCAS GOT his share of the paperwork done, reviewed it, then gave it to Carol, who had a nose for correct form. "Look it over, see if there are any holes. Same deal as the Carson case. I'll be back in five."

"Sandy's been sitting down in her cubicle all day, waiting for you . . ."

"Yeah, just a few more minutes."

While Carol was looking over the paperwork, he walked down to the lab and checked the evidence package, making sure everything was there. Whatever else happened, Lucas didn't want Kline to walk because of a bureaucratic snafu. Back at his office, he sat at his desk, kicked back, tried to think of anything else he might need. But the prosecutor had said it: Lucas was essentially the bureaucrat-in-charge, and would be testifying on chain-of-evidence, rather than the evidence itself.

Carol came in and said, "I don't see any holes. How many copies do you want? And you want me to call Sandy?"

"Just give me a minute. I gotta call John Smith."

SMITH WAS LEAVING a conference on the stabbing of a man at Regions Hospital a few weeks earlier. The stabbed man had died, just the day before, of an infection, that might or might not have been the result of the stabbing. The screwdriver-wielding drunk might be guilty of a minor assault, or murder, depending.

"Depending," Smith said, "on what eight different doctors say, and they're all trying to tap-dance around a malpractice suit."

"Good luck," Lucas said. "Anything new on Bucher?"

"Thanks for asking," Smith said.

"Look, I'm going to interview this Amity Anderson. I told you about her, she was the secretary to the Wisconsin woman."

"Yeah, yeah . . . Hope something comes out of it."

AMITY ANDERSON WORKED at the Old Northwest Foundation in Minneapolis. Lucas tracked her through a friend at Minnesota Revenue, who took a look at her tax returns. Her voice on the phone was a nasal soprano, with a touch of Manhattan. "I have clients all afternoon. I could talk to you after four o'clock, if it's really urgent," she said.

"I live about a half mile from you," Lucas said. "Maybe I could drop by when you get home? If you're not going out?"

"I'm going out, but if it won't take too long, you could come at five-fifteen," she said. "I'd have to leave by six."

"See you at five-fifteen."

HE HUNG UP and saw a blond girl standing by Carol's desk, peeking at him past the edge of his open door. He recognized her from a meet-and-greet with the summer people. Sandy.

"Sandy," he called. "Come in."

She was tall. Worse, she thought she was *too* tall, and so rolled her shoulders to make herself look shorter. She had a thin nose, delicate cheekbones, foggy blue eyes, and glasses that were too big for her face. She wore a white blouse and a blue skirt, and black shoes that were wrong for the skirt. She was, Lucas thought, somebody who hadn't yet pulled herself together. She was maybe twenty years old.

She hurried in and stood, until he said, "Sit down, how y'doing?"

"I'm fine." She was nervous and plucked at the hem of her skirt. She was wearing nylons, he realized, which had to be hot. "I looked up that information you wanted. They let me stay late yesterday."

"You didn't have to . . ."

"No, it was really interesting," she said, a spot of pink appearing in her cheeks.

"What, uh . . ."

"Okay." She put one set of papers on the floor by her feet, and fumbled through a second set. "On the Hewlett-Packard printers. The answer is, probably. Probably everybody saw a Hewlett-Packard printer, but nobody knows for sure. The thing is, there are all kinds of printers that get thrown away. Nobody wants an old printer, and there are supposed to be restrictions on how you get rid of them, so people put them in garbage sacks and hide them in their garbage cans, or throw them in somebody else's dumpster. There are dozens of them every week."

"Shit . . . " He thought about the word, noticed that she flushed. "Excuse me."

"That's okay. The thing is, because so many printers are in garbage sacks, they don't get seen until they're already in the trash flow, and they wind up getting buried at the landfill," she said.

"So we're out of luck."

"Yes. I believe so. There's no way to tell what printer came from where. Even if we found the right printer, nobody would know what truck it came from, or where it was picked up."

"Okay. Forget it," Lucas said. "I should have known that."

———

SHE PICKED UP the second pack of papers. "On the unsolved murders, I looked at the five states you asked about, and I also looked at Nebraska, because there are no big cities there. I found one unsolved that looks good. A woman name Claire Donaldson was murdered in Chippewa Falls, Wisconsin. I told Carol as soon as I found it, but she said I wouldn't have to work anymore on that, because you already knew about it."

Lucas nodded. "Okay. Good job. And that was the only one?"

"That was the only unsolved," Sandy said. "But I found one solved murder that also matches everything, except the sex of the victim."

Lucas frowned. "Solved?"

She nodded. "In Des Moines. An elderly man, wealthy, living alone, house full of antiques. His name was Jacob Toms. He was well known, he was on a lot of boards. An art museum, the Des Moines Symphony, an insurance company, a publishing company."

"Jeez, that sounds pretty good. But if it's solved . . ."

"I pulled the newspaper accounts off LexisNexis. There was a trial, but there wasn't much of a defense. The killer said he couldn't remember doing it, but wouldn't be surprised if he had. He was high on amphetamines, he'd been doing them for four days, he said he was out of his mind and couldn't remember the whole time he was on it. There wasn't much evidence against him—he was from the neighborhood, his parents were well-off, but he got lost on the drugs. Anyway, people had seen him around the neighborhood, and around the Toms house . . ."

"Inside?"

"No, outside, but he knew Toms because he'd cut Toms's lawn when he was a teenager. Toms had a big garden and he didn't like the way the lawn services cut it, because they weren't careful enough, so he hired this guy when he was a teenager. So the guy knew the house."

"There had to be more than that."

"Well, the guy admitted that he might have done it. He had cuts on his face that might have been from Toms defending himself . . ." She leaned forward, her eyes narrowing: "But the interesting thing is, the stuff that was stolen was all stuff that could be sold on the street, including some jewelry and some electronics, but none of it was ever found."

"Huh."

"An investigator for the public defender's office told the *Register* that the case was fabricated by the police because they were under pressure to get somebody, and here was this guy," Sandy said.

"Maybe he did it," Lucas said.

"And maybe he didn't," Sandy said.

Lucas sat back in his chair and stared at her for a moment, until she flinched, and he realized that he was making her even more nervous. "Okay. This is good stuff, Sandy. Now. Do you have a driver's license?"

"Of course. My car is sorta iffy."

"I'll get you a state car. Could you run down to Des Moines today and Xerox the trial file? I don't think the cops would be too happy about our looking at the raw stuff, but we can get the trial file. If you have to, you could bag out in a Des Moines hotel. I'll get Carol to get you a state credit card."

"I could do that," she said. She scooched forward on the chair, her eyes brightening. "God, do you think this man might have gone to prison for something he didn't do?"

"It happens—and this sounds pretty good," Lucas said. "This sounds like Bucher and Donaldson and Coombs . . ."

"Who?"

"Ah, a lady named Coombs, here in the Cities. Anyway. Let's go talk to Carol. Man, looking at *solved* cases. That was *terrific*. That was a terrific idea."

———

LATER, as Lucas left the office, Carol said, "You really got Sandy wound up. She'd jump out of an airplane for you."

"It'll wear off," Lucas said.

"Sometimes it does, and sometimes it doesn't," Carol said.

AMITY ANDERSON probably would not have jumped out of an airplane for him, Lucas decided after meeting her, but she might be willing to push him.

He saw her unlocking the front door of her house, carrying a purse and what looked like a shopping bag, as he walked up the hill toward her. She looked down the hill at him, a glance, and disappeared inside.

SHE LIVED in a cheerful postwar Cape Cod–style house, with yellow-painted clapboard siding, white trim, and a brick chimney in the middle of the roof. The yard was small, but intensely cultivated, with perennials pushing out of flower beds along the fences at the side of the house, and bright annuals in two beds on either side of the narrow concrete walk that led to the front door. A lopsided one-car garage sat off to the side, and back.

Lucas knocked, and a moment later, she answered. She was a mid-sized woman, probably five-six, Lucas thought, and in her early to middle thirties. Her dark hair was tied in a severe, schoolmarmish bun, without style; she wore a dark brown jacket over a beige blouse, with a tweedy skirt and practical brown shoes. Olive-complected, she had dark brown eyes, overgrown eyebrows, and three small frown wrinkles that ran vertically toward her forehead from the bridge of her short nose. She looked at him through the screen door; her face had a sullen aspect, but a full lower lip hinted at a concealed sensuality. "Do you have any identification?"

He showed her his ID. She let him in, and said, "I have to go back to the bathroom. I'll be just a minute."

The inside of the house was as cheery as the outside, with rugs and quilts and fabric hangings on the brightly painted plaster walls and the spotless hardwood floors. A bag sat on the floor, next to her purse. Not a shopping bag, but a gym bag, with three sets of handball gloves tied to the outside, stiff with dried sweat. A serious, sweating handball player . . .

A toilet flushed, distantly, down a back hallway, and a moment later Anderson came out, tugging down the back of her skirt. "What can I do for you, Mr. Davenport?"

"You worked for Claire Donaldson when she was killed," Lucas said. "The most specific thing I need to know is, was anything taken from the house? Aside from the obvious? Any high-value antiques, jewelry, paintings, that sort of thing?"

She pointed him at a sofa, then perched on an overstuffed chair, her knees primly tight. "That was a long time ago. Has something new come up?"

Lucas had no reason not to tell her: "I'm looking at connections between the Donaldson murder and the murder of Constance Bucher and her maid. You may have read about it or seen it on television . . ."

Anderson's hand went to her cheek. "Of course. They're very similar, aren't they? In some ways? Do you think they're connected?"

"I don't know," Lucas said. "We can't seem to find a common motive, other than the obvious one of robbery."

"Oh. Robbery. Well, I'm sure the police told you she usually had some money around," Anderson said. "But not enough to kill somebody for. I mean, unless you were a crazy junkie or something, and this was in Chippewa Falls."

"I was thinking of antiques, paintings . . ."

She shook her head. "Nothing like that was taken. I was in charge of keeping inventory. I gave a list of everything to the police and to Claire's sister and brother-in-law."

"I've seen that," Lucas said. "So you don't know of anything specific that seemed to be missing, and was valuable."

"No, I don't. I assume the Booths told you that I was probably involved, that I gave a key to one of my many boyfriends, that I went to Chicago as an alibi, and the boyfriend then came over and killed Claire?"

"They . . ." He shrugged.

"I know," she said, waving a hand dismissively.

"So you would categorize that as 'Not true,'" Lucas suggested with a grin.

She laughed, more of an unhappy bark: "Of course it's not true. Those people . . . But I will tell you, the Booths didn't have as much money as people think. I know that, from talking to Claire. I mean, they had enough to go to the country club and pay their bills, and go to Palm Springs in the winter, but I happen to know that they rented in Palm Springs. A condo. They were very tight with money and they were *very* happy to get Claire's—and they got all of it. She had no other living relatives."

"You sound unhappy about that," Lucas said. "Were you expecting something?"

"No. Claire and I had a businesslike arrangement. I was a secretary and I helped with the antiques, which was my main interest. We were friendly, but we had no real emotional connection. She was the boss, I was the employee. She didn't pay much, and I was always looking for another job."

They looked at each other for a moment, then Lucas said, "I suppose you've been pretty well worked over by the sheriff's investigators. They found no boyfriends, no missing keys . . ."

"Officer Davenport. Not to put too fine a point on it, I'm gay."

"Ah." He hadn't gotten that vibe. Getting old.

"At that moment, I had no personal friend. Chippewa is not a garden spot for lesbians. And I wasn't even sure I was gay."

"Okay." He slapped his knees, ready to get up. "Does the name Jacob Toms mean anything to you? Ever heard of him? From Des Moines?"

"No, I don't think so. I've never been to Des Moines. Is he another . . . ?"

"We don't know," Lucas said. "How about a woman named Marilyn Coombs. From here in St. Paul?"

Her eyes narrowed. "God. I've heard of the name. Recently."

"She was killed a couple of days ago," Lucas said.

Anderson's mouth actually dropped: "Oh . . . You mean there are three? Or four? I must've heard Coombs's name on television. Four people?"

"Five, maybe, including Mrs. Bucher's maid," Lucas said.

"That's . . . crazy," Anderson said. "Insane. For what?"

"We're trying to figure that out," Lucas said. "About the Booths. Do you think *they* were capable of killing Mrs. Donaldson? Or of planning it?"

"Margaret was genuinely horrified. I don't doubt that," Anderson said, her eyes lifting toward the ceiling, as she thought about it. "Glad to get the money, but horrified by what happened. Landford wasn't horrified. He was just glad to get the money."

Then she smiled for the first time and looked back at Lucas. "Thinking that Landford . . . no. He wouldn't do it himself, because he might get blood on his sleeve. Thinking that he might know somebody who'd do it for him, you know, a killer—that's even more ridiculous. You have to know them. Deep in their hearts, way down in their souls, the Booths are twits."

He smiled back at her and stood up. She was right about the twits.

"One last question, just popped into my head. Did you know Connie Bucher? At all? Through antiques, or whatever?"

"No." She shook her head. "One of my jobs at the foundation is roping in potential donors, especially those who are old and infirm and have buckets of cash, but she was well tended by other people. She was surrounded, really. I bet she got twenty calls a week from 'friends,' who were really calling about money. Anyway, I never met her. I would never have had a chance to clip her money, under any circumstances, but I would have liked to have seen her antiques."

" 'Clip her money,' " Lucas repeated.

"Trade talk," she said.

LUCAS'S CELL PHONE RANG.

He dug it out of his pocket, looked at the screen, and said to Anderson, "Excuse me. I have to take this . . ."

He stepped away from her, toward the front door, turning a shoulder in the unconscious pretend-privacy that cell-phone users adopt. In his ear, Flowers said, "I'm at the Barths with Susan Conoway—have you talked to her, she's from Dakota County?"

"No. I talked to somebody. Lyle Pender?"

"Okay, that's somebody else. Anyway, Susan was assigned to prep the Barths, but Kathy's heard that she can take the Fifth, if she thinks she might have committed a crime. Or might be accused of one. So now she says she doesn't want to talk to Susan, and Susan's got a date that she doesn't want to miss. The whole fuckin' thing is about to go up in smoke. I could use some weight over here."

"Damnit. What does Barth's lawyer say?"

"He's not here. Kathy's nervous—I don't think this is coming from her lawyer," Flowers said. "It might be coming from somewhere else."

"I'm sure Kline wouldn't have . . . Ah, Jesus. You think Burt Jr. might have talked to her?"

"Maybe. The thought occurred to me, that fat fuck," Flowers said. "If he has, I'll put his ass in jail. I told Kathy that the grand jury could give her immunity and that she'd have to testify, or go to jail. Nobody told her that. But if she decides to take the Fifth, it's gonna mess up the schedule and it could create some complications. If Cole started getting cold feet, or Kline's buddies in the legislature got involved . . . We need to get this done."

"Why doesn't Conoway talk to her?" Lucas asked.

"Says she can't. Says the Barths have an attorney, and without the other attorney here, she's not comfortable examining a reluctant witness. That's not exactly what she said, but that's what she means."

"Listen: It'll take me at least ten or fifteen minutes to get there. I have to walk home, I'm six or seven minutes away from my car," Lucas said. "What is Jesse saying? Is she letting Kathy do the talking, or can you split them, or what?"

"They were both sitting on the couch. It's all about the money, man."

Lucas groaned. "I don't know why the Klines are holding on like this. You'd think they'd try to deal. Suborning a witness . . . they'd have to be crazy. How could they think they'd get away with it?"

Flowers said, "Burt's a fuckin' state legislator, Lucas."

"I know, but I'm always the optimist."

"Right," Flowers said. "Ten minutes?"

Lucas glanced at Anderson, who at that moment tipped her wrist to look at her watch. "I need a minute or two to finish here, then walk home, so . . . give me fifteen."

HE RANG OFF and stepped back into the living room, took a card from his pocket, and handed it to Anderson. "I've got to run. Thanks for your time. If you think of *anything* . . . About Donaldson, about Bucher, about possible ties between them, I'd like to hear it."

She took the card, said, "I'll call. I've got what we call a grip-and-grin, trying to soak up some money. So I've got to hurry myself."

"Seems like everything is about money," Lucas said.

"More and more," Anderson said. "To tell you the truth, I find it more and more distasteful."

LUCAS HURRIED HOME, waved at a neighbor, stuck his head into the kitchen, blurted, "Got something going, I'll tell you when I get back," to Weather, and took off; Weather called after him, "When?" He shouted back, "Half an hour. If it's longer, I'll call."

There was some traffic, but the Barths lived only three miles away, and he knew every street and alley. By chopping off a little traffic, and taking some garbage-can routes, he made it in the fifteen minutes he'd promised Flowers.

FLOWERS WAS LEANING in a doorway, chatting with a solid dishwater-blond woman with a big leather bag hanging from her shoulder: Conoway. Lucas had never met her, but when he saw her, he remembered her, from a lecture she gave at a child-abuse convention sponsored by the BCA.

A small-town cop, working with volunteer help and some sheriff's deputies who lived in the area, and a freelance social therapist, had busted a day-care center's owner, her son, and two care providers and charged them with crimes ranging from rape to blasphemy.

Conoway, assigned as a prosecutor, had shredded the case. She'd demonstrated that the day-care center operators were innocent, and had shown that if the children had been victimized by anyone, it had been the cops and the therapist, who were involved in what amounted to an anti-pederasty cult. She hadn't endeared herself to the locals, but she had her admirers, including Lucas.

Lucas came up the walk, noticed that the yellow-white dog was gone, the stake sitting at an angle in the yard. He wondered if the dog had broken loose.

Conoway looked tired; like she needed to wash her hair. She saw Lucas coming, through the screen door, cocked an eyebrow, said something to Flowers, and Flowers stepped over and pushed open the door.

"You know Susan Conoway . . ."

Conoway smiled and shook hands, and Lucas said, "We haven't met, but I admired your work in the Rake Town case."

"Thank you," she said. "The admiration isn't universal."

Lucas looked at Flowers: "What do you need?"

Flowers said, "We just need you—somebody—to talk to the Barths in a polite, nonlegal way, that would convince them to cooperate fully with Ms. Conoway, who has a hot date tonight with somebody who couldn't possibly deserve her attentions."

Lucas said, "Huh."

Conoway said, "Actually, he *does* deserve my attentions. If they're not going to talk, I'm outa here."

"Give me a minute," Lucas said. "I've got to work myself into a temper tantrum."

KATHY AND JESSE BARTH were perched side by side on a green corduroy sofa, Kathy with a Miller Lite and a cigarette and Jesse with Diet Pepsi. Lucas stepped into the room, closed the door, and said, "Kathy, if Ms. Conoway leaves, and this thing doesn't go down tomorrow, you'll have messed up your life. Big-time. You'll wind up in the women's prison and your daughter will wind up in a juvie home. It pisses me off, because I hate to see that happen to a kid. Especially when her mom does it to her."

Kathy Barth was cool: "We've got a lawyer."

Lucas jabbed a finger at her, put on his hardest face: "Every ass-hole in Stillwater had a lawyer. Every single fuckin' one of them." She opened her mouth to say something, but Lucas waved her down, bullying her. "Have you talked to your lawyer about this?"

"Doesn't answer his cell. But we figured, what difference do a few hours make?"

"I'll tell you what difference it makes—it means somebody either got to you, or tried to get to you," Lucas said. "You can't sell your testimony, Kathy. That's a felony. That's mandatory jail time."

Jesse shifted on her seat, and Kathy glanced at her, then looked back at Lucas. "Burt owes us." She didn't whine, she just said it.

"So sue him," Lucas said. "Kline broke a state law and he has to pay for it. Pay the state. If you interfere with the state getting justice, then you're committing a crime. Judges don't fool around with peo-ple who mess with witnesses, or witnesses who sell their testimony. They get the max, and they don't get time off for good behavior. You don't fuck with the courts, Kathy, and that's what you're doing."

Jesse said, "Mom, I don't want to go to jail."

"He's bullshitting us, hon," Kathy said, looking at Lucas with skep-ticism; but unsure of herself.

Lucas turned to Jesse and shook his head. "If your mom goes down this road, you've got to take care of yourself. I can't even ex-plain how stupid and dangerous this is. You won't get any money *and* you'll be in jail. If your lawyer were here, he'd tell you that. But if Conoway leaves—she's got a date tonight—she's going to pull the plug on your testimony tomorrow, then she's going to turn off her cell phone, and then you are truly fucked. You've got about one minute to decide. Then she's gonna walk."

"She can't do that . . ." Kathy said.

"Horseshit," Lucas said. "She's already after-hours, working on her own time. She's got a right to a life. This isn't the biggest deal of her career, it's not even the biggest deal of her week. She doesn't have to put up with some crap where somebody is trying sell her daughter's ass to a pederast. She's gonna walk."

"I'm not trying to sell anybody . . ." Kathy said.

"I'll talk to her," Jesse blurted. To her mother: "I'm gonna talk to her, Mom. I don't care if we don't get any money from Burt. I'm not going to jail."

"Smart girl," Lucas said.

BACK IN THE HALLWAY, Lucas said to Conoway, "Give them a minute."

"What're they doing," Flowers asked, "sopping up the blood?"

"Jesse's telling Kathy what's what," Lucas said. "I think we're okay."

A moment later Jesse stuck her head into the hall, looked at Conoway. Kathy was a step behind her. "We'll talk to you," Jesse said.

Conoway sighed, said, "I thought I was outa here. Okay, let's go, girls . . ." And to Lucas: "Thanks. You must throw a good tantrum."

10

AMITY ANDERSON WAS ANNOYED: with life, with art, with rich people, with Lucas Davenport. So annoyed that she had to suppress a little hop of anger and frustration as she drifted past the Viking warrior. The warrior was seven feet tall, made of plaster, carried an ax with a head the size of a manhole cover, and wore a blond wig. He was dressed in a furry yellow skin, possibly from a puma, if puma hides are made of Rayon, and his carefully draped loins showed a bulge of Scandinavian humor.

Anderson wasn't amused. The reception was continuing. If she ate even one more oat cracker with goat cheese, she'd die of heart congestion. If she had one more glass of the Arctic Circle Red Wine, her taste buds would commit suicide.

She moved slowly through the exhibit, clutching the half-empty wineglass, smiling and nodding at the patrons, while avoiding eye contact, and trying, as much as she could, to avoid looking at the art itself. Scandinavian minimalism. It had, like all minimalism, she thought, come to the museum straight from a junkyard, with a minimal amount of interference from an artist.

An offense to a person of good taste. If somebody had pointed a gun at her head and told her that she had to take a piece, she'd have asked for the Viking warrior, which was *not* part of the show.

Anderson had changed into her professional evening dress: a soft black velvet blouse, falling over black velvet pants, which hid the practical black shoes. The Oslo room was built from beige stone with polished stone floors. The stone look good, but killed your legs, if you had to stand on it too long. Thank God foundation staffers weren't expected to wear high heels. Heels would have been the end of her.

THE VIKING WARRIOR guarded the entrance. The art exhibit itself, mostly sculpture with a few paintings, spread down the long walls. The end wall was occupied by a fifteen-foot model of a Viking ship, which appeared to have been built of scrap wood by stupid unskilled teenagers. The best thing about the ship was that the stern concealed a door. The door led onto the patio, and once every fifteen minutes or so, Anderson could slip outside and light up.

So the art sucked. The people who were looking at the art also sucked. They were rich, but not rich enough. Millionaires, for sure, but a million wasn't that much anymore. A million dollars well invested, taking inflation and taxes into account, would generate an income about like a top-end Social Security check.

That was nothing. That was chicken feed. You couldn't lease a BMW for that; you'd be lucky to get a Chrysler minivan. You needed ten million; or twenty million. And if you were one of these guys, you sure as shit weren't going to give a million of it to some unknown gay chick at an exhibit of bent-up car fenders, or whatever this was.

Anderson knew all that, but her bosses wanted somebody at the show. Somebody to smile and nod and eat goat-cheese oat crackers. No skin off their butt. She wasn't getting paid for the time. This was a required voluntary after-hours function; most small foundations had work rules that would have appalled the owners of a Saigon sweatshop.

She looked at her watch. She'd given it fifty-four minutes. Not nearly enough. She idled toward the Viking ship, turned and checked the crowd, and when she judged that no one was looking at her, stepped backward and went out the door.

The evening air was like a kiss, after the refrigerated air of the gallery. Night was coming on. The patio looked over a maple-studded lawn toward the evening lights of downtown Minneapolis, a pretty sight, lights like diamonds on a tic-tac-toe grid. She fumbled the Winstons out of her purse, lit one, blew smoke, trying to keep it away from her hair, and thought about Davenport and Claire Donaldson and Constance Bucher and Marilyn Coombs.

Goddamn money. It all came down to money. The wrong people had it—heirs, car dealers, insurance men, corporate suits who went through life without a single aesthetic impulse, who thought a duck on a pond at sunset was *art*.

Or these people, who bought a coffee-table book on minimalism, because they thought it put them out on the *cutting edge*. Made them mini-Applers. But they were still the same bunch of parvenu buck-lickers, the men with their washing-machine-sized Rolexes and the women with the "forever" solitaire hanging between their tits, not yet figuring out that "forever" meant until something fifteen years younger, with bigger tits, came along.

Damn, she was tired of this.

THE DOOR popped open and she flinched. A red-haired woman, about Anderson's age, stepped outside, and said, "I thought I saw you disappear." She took a pack of Salems out of her purse. "I was just about to start screaming."

"I saw you talking to the Redmonds," Anderson said. "Do any good?"

"Not much. I'm working on the wife," the redhead said. A match flared, the woman inhaled, and exhaling, said, "I'll get five thousand a year if I'm lucky."

"I'd take that," Anderson said. "We could get a new TV for the employee lounge."

"Well, I'll *take* it. It's just that . . ." She waved her hand, a gesture of futility.

"I know," Anderson said. "I was pitching Carrie Sue Thorson. She had her DNA analyzed. She's ninety percent pure Nazi. The other ten percent is some Russian who must've snuck in the back door. I was over there going, 'It's so *fascinating* to know that our ancestors reach back to the *European Ice Age*.' Like, 'Thank Christ they didn't come from Africa in the last hundred generations or so.' "

"Get anything?" the redhead asked.

"Not unless you count a pat on the ass from her husband," Anderson said.

"You might work *that* into something."

"Yeah. A whole-life policy," Anderson said.

The redhead laughed, blew smoke and screeched, "Run away, run away."

ANDERSON WOUND UP staying for almost two hours and failed to raise a single penny—but she scored in one way. An hour and forty-five minutes into the reception, she took a cell-phone call from her supervisor, who "just wanted to check how things were going."

"I've eaten too much cheese," Anderson said, sweetly. She understood her dedication was being tested and she'd aced the test. "But the art's okay. Carrie Sue is right over here, isn't she a friend of yours?"

"No, no, not really," her supervisor said hastily. "I'd hate to bother her. Good going, Amity. I'll talk to you tomorrow."

Five minutes later, she was out of there. She drove a Mazda, cut southwest across town, down toward Edina. Time for a gutsy move. She knew the truth, and now was the time to use it.

AND SHE didn't want much.

A couple of years in France, or maybe a year in France and another Italy. She could rent her own house, bank the money, come back in a couple of years with the right languages, she could talk about Florence and Venice and Aix and Arles. With a little polish, with the background, she could move up in the foundation world. She could get an executive spot, she could take a shortcut up the ladder, she wouldn't have to go to any more Arctic Circle Red receptions.

Worth the risk. Of course, she needed to be prepared. As she turned the corner at the top of the last block, she reached under the car seat, found the switchblade, and slipped it into the pocket of her velvet pants.

THE WIDDLER HOUSE was an older two-story, with cedar shingles and casement windows, built on a grassy lot, with the creek behind. She glanced at her watch: ten-fifteen. There was a light in an upstairs bedroom and another in the back of the house. An early night for the Widdlers, she thought.

She parked in the drive, went to the front door, and rang the bell. Nothing. She rang it again, and then felt the inaudible vibrations of a heavy man coming down a flight of steps. Leslie Widdler turned on a light in the hallway, then the porch light, squinted at her through the triple-paned, armed-response-alarmed front door. Widdler was wearing a paisley-patterned silk robe. As fucked up and crazy as the

Widdlers might be, there was nothing inhibited about their sex life, Anderson thought.

Widdler opened the inner door, unlocked and pushed open the screen door, and said, "Well, well. Look what washed up on our doorstep. Nice to see you."

Anderson walked past him and Widdler looked outside, as though he might see somebody else sneaking along behind. Nobody. He shut the door and locked it, turned to Anderson, pushed her against the wall, slipped one big hand up under her blouse, pulled her brassiere down, and squeezed her breast until the pain flared through her chest. "How have you been?" he asked, his face so close that she could smell the cinnamon toothpaste.

Her own hand was inside his robe, clutching at him. "Ah, Leslie. Where's Jane?"

"Upstairs," Leslie said.

"Let's go up and fuck her."

"What a good idea," Widdler said.

AND THAT'S WHAT they did, the three of them, on the Widdlers' king-sized bed, with scented candles burning all around.

Then, when the sweat had dried, Anderson rolled off the bed, found her purse, dug out a cigarette.

"Please don't smoke," Jane said.

"I'll go out on the back porch, but I need one," she said. She groped for her pants, said, "Where's that lighter?" She got both the lighter and the switchblade. "We need to talk."

They didn't bother with robes; they weren't done with the sex yet. Anderson led the way down the stairs in the semidarkness, Leslie poured more wine for himself and Jane, and got a fresh glass from the cupboard and gave a glass to Anderson. They moved out to the porch, and Jane and Anderson settled on the glider, the soft summer air flowing around them, while Leslie pulled a chair over.

"Well," Jane said. She took a hit of the wine, then dipped a finger in it, and dragged a wet finger-pad over one of Anderson's nipples. "You were such a pleasant surprise."

"I want a cut," Anderson said. "Of the Connie Bucher money. Not much. Enough to take me to Europe for a couple of years. Let's say . . . a hundred and fifty thousand. You can put it down to consulting fees, seventy-five thousand a year."

"Amity . . ." Leslie said, and there was a cold thread in the soft sound of her name.

"Don't start, Leslie. I know how mean and cruel you are, and you know I like it, but I just don't want to deal with it tonight. I spotted the Bucher thing as soon as it happened. It had your names written all over it. But I wouldn't have said a thing, I wouldn't have asked for a nickel, except that you managed to drag *me* into it."

After a moment of silence, Jane said, *"What?"*

"I got a visit from a cop named Lucas Davenport. This afternoon. He's an agent with the state police . . ."

"We know who he is. We're police consultants on the Bucher murder," Leslie said.

Anderson was astonished; and then she laughed. "Oh, God, you might know it."

But Jane cut through the astonishment: "How did he get to you?"

"He hooked the Bucher murder to the Donaldson case. He's looking at the Coombs murder. He *knows*."

"Oh, shit." Anderson couldn't see it, but she could feel Jane turn to her husband. "He's a danger. I told you, we've got to do something."

Leslie was on his feet and he moved over in front of Anderson and put a hand on her head and said, "Why shouldn't we just break Amity's little neck? That would close off that particular threat."

Anderson hit the button on the switchblade and the blade *clack*ed open. She pressed the side of the blade against him. "Take your hand off my head, Leslie, or I swear to God, I will cut your cock off."

Jane snorted, amused, and said, "A switchblade. You know, you *should* take off about four inches, just to make him easier to deal with."

"I'll take off nine inches if he doesn't take his hand off my head," Anderson snarled. She could feel the heat coming off Leslie's thighs.

"Fuck you," Leslie said, but he moved away and sat down again.

Anderson left the blade extended. "One good reason for you not to break my neck: Davenport will then know that the thieves are close. And when they investigate either my death or disappearance, the police will unlock the center drawer of my desk, where they will find a letter."

"The old letter ploy," Jane said, still amused, but not as amused as she'd been with the switchblade.

"It's what I had to work with," Anderson said. "About Davenport. He's working on the Bucher case and now on Donaldson and Coombs, but he's also working on a sex scandal. There was a story in the paper this morning. Some state legislator guy has been screwing some teenager."

"I saw it," Leslie said. "So what?"

"So Davenport is running that case, too, and that's apparently more important. He was interviewing me and he had to run off to do something on the other one. Anyway, I heard him talking on his cell phone, and I know the name of the people involved. The girl's name."

"Really," Jane said. "Is that a big deal?"

"It could be," Anderson said, "If you want to distract Davenport."

11

SANDY THE INTERN was sitting next to Carol's desk when Lucas came in. He was running a little late, having taken Sam out for a morning walk. He was wearing his grand-jury suit: navy blue with a white shirt, an Hermès tie with a wine-colored background and vibrating commas of a hard blue that the saleslady said matched his eyes; and cap-toed black tie-shoes with a high shine. His socks had clocks and his shorts had paisleys.

Sandy, on the other hand, looked like she'd been dragged through hell by the ankles—eyes heavy, hair flyaway, glasses smudged. She was wearing a pink blouse with plaid pants, and the same scuffed shoes she'd worn the day before. Somebody, Lucas thought, should give her a book.

She stood up when she saw him, sparks in her eyes: "He's innocent."

Lucas thought, "Ah, shit." He didn't need a crusader, if that's what she was morphing into. But he said, "Come on in, tell me," and to Carol, "I've gotta be at the Dakota County courthouse at one o'clock and it's a trip. I'm gonna get out of here soon as I can and get lunch down there, with Virgil."

"Okay," Carol said. "Rose Marie called, she's got her finger in the media dike, but she says the leakers are going crazy and she doesn't have enough fingers. The governor's gone fishing and can't be reached. Kline has issued a statement that said the charges are without foundation and that he can't be distracted because he's got to work up a budget resolution for a special session in July."

"I bet the papers jumped on *that* like a hungry trout," Lucas said. "You're in a news meeting and you have the choice of two stories. A—President of the Senate works on budget resolution. B—President of the Senate bangs hot sixteen-year-old and maybe her mother, too, and faces grand-jury indictment. Whatta you going to do?"

"You think he did them both at the same time? I mean, simultaneously?" Carol asked.

"I don't want to think about why you want to know," Lucas said. "Sandy, let's talk."

SHE SAT ACROSS the desk from him with a four-inch-thick file. "Lots of people have sex when they're sixteen," she ventured. "Probably, now, most."

"Not with the president of the Minnesota Senate," Lucas said. He dropped into his chair and leaned back. "When did you get in?"

"I came back last night, about midnight. Then I stayed up reading until five . . . I had some luck down there."

"Start from the beginning," Lucas said.

She nodded. "I went down and found the Polk County Courthouse. Des Moines is in Polk County. Anyway, I went to the clerk's office, and there was this boy there—another intern. I told him what I was looking for, and he really helped a lot. We got the original trial file, and Xeroxed that, and then we discovered that Duane Child—that was the man who was convicted of killing Toms—we found out that Child *appealed*. His attorney appealed.

They claimed that the investigation was terrible, and that the trial judge let a lot of bad information get in front of the jury."

"What happened with the appeal?" Lucas asked.

"They lost it. Child is in prison. But the appeals court vote was six to three for a new trial, and the three judges who voted for it wrote that there was no substantial evidence, either real or circumstantial, that supported conviction."

"So . . ."

She held up a finger: "The main thing, from our point of view, that Bill showed me . . . Bill is the other intern . . . is that when they appealed, they got the entire police investigative file entered as evidence. So I got that, too."

"Excellent!" Lucas said.

"Reading through it, I cannot figure out two things: I cannot figure out why he was indicted, and I cannot figure out how he was convicted," Sandy said. "It was like all the cops testified that he did it and that was good enough. But there was almost no evidence."

"None?"

"Some. Circumstantial," she said.

"Circumstantial is okay . . ." Lucas said.

"Sure. Sometimes. But if that's all you've really got . . ."

"What about connections between the Toms murder and the others?" Lucas asked.

"That's another thing, Mr. Davenport . . ." she began.

"Call me Lucas, please."

"That's another thing, Lucas. They are almost identical," she said. "It's a perfect pattern, except for two things. Mr. Toms was male. All the others are female. And he was strangled with a piece of nylon rope, instead of being shot, or bludgeoned. When I was reading it last night, I thought, 'Aha.' "

"Aha."

"Yes. The killers are smart enough to vary the method of murder, so if you're just looking at the murders casually, on paper, you've got one woman clubbed to death, one woman shot, one woman dies in a fall, and one man is strangled," Sandy said. "There's no consistent method. But if you look at the killings structurally, you see that they are otherwise identical. It looks to me like the killers deliberately varied the method of murder, to obscure the connections, but they couldn't obscure what they were up to. Which was theft."

"Very heavy," Lucas said.

"Yes. By the way, one of the things that hung Duane Child is that he was driving an old Volkswagen van, yellow, or tan," Sandy said. "The night that Toms was murdered, a man was out walking his dog, an Irish setter. Anyway, he saw a white van in the neighborhood, circling the block a couple of times. This man owns an appliance company, and he said the van was a full-sized Chevrolet, an Express, and he said he knew that because he owns five of them. The cops said that he just *thought* the van was white, because of the weird sodium lights around there, that the lights made the yellow van look whiter. But the man stuck with it, he said the van was a Chevy. A Chevy van doesn't look anything like the Volkswagen that Child drove. I know because I looked them up on Google. I believe the van *was* the killers' vehicle, and they needed the van to carry away the stuff they were stealing."

"Was there a list of stolen stuff?"

"Yes, and it's just like the list Carol showed me, of the stuff taken from Bucher's house. All small junk and jewelry. Obvious stuff. And in Toms's case, a coin collection which never showed up again. But I think—and Carol said you think this happened at Bucher's—I think they took other stuff, too. Antiques and artworks, and they needed the van to move it."

"Have you read the entire file?" Lucas asked.

She shook her head. "Most of it."

"Finish it, and then go back through it. Get some of those sticky flag things from Carol, and every time you find another point in the argument, flag it for me," Lucas said. "I've got to do some politics, but I'll be back late in the afternoon. Can you have it done by then?"

"Maybe. There's an ocean of stuff," she said. "We Xeroxed off almost a thousand pages yesterday, Bill and I."

"Do as much as you can. I'll see you around four o'clock."

BEFORE HE LEFT, he checked out with Rose Marie, and with Mitford, the governor's aide. Mitford said, "I had an off-the-record with Cole. He doesn't plan to do any investigation. He's says it'll rise or fall on the BCA presentation. They could possibly put it off for a couple of weeks, if you need to develop some elements, but his people are telling him they should go ahead and indict. That they've got enough, as long as the Barths testify."

"Everybody wants to get rid of it; finish it, except maybe the Klines," Lucas said.

VIRGIL FLOWERS was waiting in the parking lot of the Dakota County courthouse. Lucas circled around, picked him up, and they drove into the town of Hastings for lunch. Like Lucas, Flowers was in his grand-jury suit: "You look more like a lawyer than I do," Lucas said.

"That's impossible."

"No, it's not. My suit's in extremely good taste. Your suit looks like a lawyer suit."

"Thanks," Flowers said. "I just wasted thirty bucks on it, and you're putting it down."

They went to a riverside café, sitting alone on a back patio with checkered-cloth-covered tables, looking toward the Mississippi; ordered hamburgers and Cokes. "Everything is arranged," Lucas said, when the waitress had gone.

"Yes. The whole package is locked up in the courthouse. The jury starts meeting at one o'clock, Cole and Conoway will make the first presentation, then they'll bring in Russell from Child Protection to talk about the original tip. Then you go on, testify about assigning the investigation to me, and you'll also testify about chain-of-custody on the evidence that came in later, that everything is okay, bureaucratically. Then I go on and testify about the investigation, then we have the tech people coming up, then they get the Barths. After that, they go to dinner. They reconvene at six-thirty, Conoway summarizes, and then they decide whether they need more, or to vote an indictment."

"Does Conoway think they'll vote?"

"She says they'll do what she tells them to do, and unless something weird happens, they're gonna vote," Flowers said.

"Okay. You've done a good job on this, Virgil."

"Nice to work in the Cities again," Flowers said, "but I gotta get back south. You know Larry White from Jackson County?"

"Yeah. You're talking about that body?"

"Down the riverbank. Yeah. It was the girl. DNA confirms it, they got it back yesterday," Flowers said. "The thing is, she went to school with Larry's son and they were friendly. Not dating, but the son knew her pretty well since elementary school, and Larry doesn't want to investigate it himself. He wants us carrying the load, because . . . you know, small town."

"Any chance his kid actually did it?" Lucas asked.

"Nah," Flowers said. "Everybody in town says he's a good kid, and he's actually got most of an alibi, and like I said, he wasn't actually seeing the girl. Didn't run with her crowd. Larry's just trying to avoid talk. He's got the election coming up, and they haven't got the killer yet . . . if there is one."

"Any ideas? She didn't get on the riverbank by herself."

The waitress came back with the Cokes, and said, with a smile, "I haven't seen you fellas around before. You lawyers?"

"God help us," Flowers said. When she'd gone, Flowers said, "There's a guy name Floyd. He's a couple years older than the girl, he's been out of school for a while. Does seasonal work at the elevator and out at the golf course, sells a little dope. I need to push him. I think he was dealing to the girl, and I think she might have been fooling around with him."

"Any dope on the postmortem?"

"No. She'd been down way too long. When they pulled her off the riverbank, they got most of her clothes and all of the bones except from one foot and a small leg bone, which probably got scattered off by dogs or coyotes or whatever. There's no sign of violence on the bones. No holes, no breaks, hyoid was intact. I think she might have OD'd."

"Can you crack the kid?"

"That's my plan . . ."

THEY SAT SHOOTING the breeze, talking about cases, talking about fishing. Flowers had a side career going as an outdoor writer, and was notorious for dragging a fishing boat around the state while he was working. Lucas asked, "You go fishing last night?"

"Hour," Flowers admitted. "Got a line wet, while I was thinking about the grand jury."

"You're gonna have to decide what you want to do," Lucas said. "I don't think you can keep writing and keep working as a cop. Not full-time, anyway."

"I'd write, if I could," Flowers said. "Trouble is, I made fifteen thousand dollars last year, writing. If I went full-time, I could probably make thirty. In other words, I'd starve."

"Still . . ."

"I know. I think about it," Flowers said. "All I can do is, keep juggling. You see my piece last month in *Outdoor Life?*"

"I did, you know?" Lucas said. "Not bad, Virgil. In fact, it was pretty damn good. Guys were passing it around the office."

THE FIRST SESSION of the grand jury was as routine as Flowers had suggested it would be. Lucas sat in a waiting room until 1:45, got called in. The grand jury was arrayed around a long mahogany-grained table, with two assistant county attorneys managing files. The lead attorney, Susan Conoway, had Lucas sworn in by a clerk, who then left. She led him through his handling of the original tip, to the assignment of Flowers, and through the BCA's handling procedures for evidence. After checking to make sure the signatures on the affidavits were really his, she sent him on his way.

In the hallway, Flowers said, "I'll call you about that Jackson case," and Lucas said, "See ya," and he was gone.

BACK AT THE OFFICE, Sandy had gone.

"I sent her home," Carol said, as she trailed Lucas into his office. The file was sitting squarely in front of Lucas's chair, with a dozen blue plastic flags sticking out of it. "She was about to fall off the chair. She said you could call her there, and she'd come in . . . but I think you could let it go until tomorrow. She's really beat."

"Did she finish the file?" Lucas took off his jacket, hung it on his coatrack, and began rolling up his shirtsleeves.

"Yes. She flagged the critical points. She said she flagged them both pro and con, for and against it being the same killers."

"She's pretty good," Lucas said. "I hope she doesn't go overboard, start campaigning to free this Child guy. If his appeal got turned down, we'd be better off working it from the other end. Find the real killers."

HE STARTED on the file, looking first at the flagged items, and going back to the original arrest, the interviews, and immediately saw how Child got himself in trouble: He hadn't denied anything. He had, in fact, meekly agreed that he might have done it. He simply didn't know—and he stuck to that part of the story.

There were other bits of evidence against him. He'd been in the neighborhood the night of the murder; he'd stopped to see if he could get some money from his father. His father had given him thirty dollars, and Child had spent some of it at a Subway, on a sandwich, and had been recognized there by a former schoolmate.

He knew the Toms house. He was driving a van, and a van had been seen circling the block. He had cuts on his face and one arm, which he said he got from a fall, but which might have been defensive cuts received as he strangled Toms. On the other hand, Toms had no skin under his fingernails—there'd been no foreign DNA at all.

Child had what the police called a history of violence, but he'd never been arrested for it—as far as Lucas could tell, he'd had a number of fights with another street person near the room where he lived, and Child had said that the other bum had started the fights: *"He's a crazy, I never started anything."*

But it had been the lack of any denial that had hung him up.

At the sentencing, he made a little speech apologizing to the victim's family, but still maintained that he couldn't remember the crime.

The judge, who must have been running for reelection, if they reelected judges in Iowa, said in a sentencing statement that he rejected Child's memory loss, believed that he did remember, and condemned him as a coward for not admitting it. Child got life.

CAROL STUCK her head in, said, "I forgot to tell you, Weather got done early and she was heading home. She wants to take the kids out to the Italian place."

"I'll call her . . ."

THE ITALIAN place at six, Weather said; she'd load the kids up, and meet him there. Lucas looked at his watch. Four-twenty. He could get to the Italian place in ten minutes, so he had an hour and a half to read. It'd be quiet. People were headed out of the building, Carol was getting her purse together, checking her face.

He heard the phone ring, and then Carol called, "You got Flowers on one. Flowers the person."

Lucas picked up: "Yeah."

"We got another problem."

"Ah, shit. What is it?" Lucas asked.

"Jesse didn't come home from school," Flowers said.

"*What?*"

"Didn't come home. She left school on time, Kathy checked with her last class and some friends of hers, they saw her on the street, but she never showed up at home. Kathy might be bullshitting us, but she seems pretty stressed. Conoway doesn't know whether to be pissed or worried. The grand jury's been put on hold for a while, but if we don't find her in the next hour or so, they're gonna send them home. I'm headed up that way, but it's gonna take a while. If you've got a minute, you could run over to their house . . ."

"Goddamnit," Lucas said. "If they're fucking with us, I'm gonna break that woman's neck."

"Hope that's what it is, but Kathy . . . I don't know, Lucas. Didn't sound like bullshit," Flowers said. "Of course, it could be something that Jesse thought up on her own. But she was set to go, she seemed ready . . ."

"I'm on my way," Lucas said. "Call me when you get close."

12

KATHY BARTH WAS STANDING in front of her house talking to a uniformed St. Paul cop and a woman in a green turban. Lucas parked at the curb and cut across the small front lawn. They all turned to look at him. Barth called, "Did you find her?" and Lucas knew from the tone of her voice that she wasn't involved in whatever had happened to her daughter; wherever she'd gone.

"I just heard," Lucas said. "Virgil Flowers was down at the grand jury, he's on his way up." To the cop: "You guys looking?"

The cop shrugged, "Yeah, we're looking, but she's only a couple hours late. We don't usually even look this soon, for a sixteen-year-old."

"Get everybody looking," Lucas said. "She was supposed to be talking to a grand jury about now. If there's a problem, I'll talk to the chief. We need everybody you can spare." To Barth: "We need to know what she was wearing . . . the names of all her friends. I need to talk to her best friend right now."

The woman in the turban hadn't said anything, but now spoke to Barth: "Kelly McGuire."

"I called, but she's not home yet," Barth said. Her face was taut with anxiety. She'd seen it all before, on TV, the missing girl, the frantic mother. "She's at a dance place and the phone's off the hook. She won't be home until five-thirty."

"You know what dance place?" Lucas asked.

"Over on Snelling, by the college," Barth said. "Just south of Grand."

"I know it," Lucas said to the cop, "I'm going over there. Let me give you my cell number . . ." The cop wrote the number on a pad. "If you need any more authority, call me. I'll call the governor if I have to. Talk to whoever you need to, and tell them that this could be serious. You want everybody out there looking, because the press is gonna get on top of this and by tomorrow, if we don't have this kid, the shit is gonna hit the fan."

"All right, all right," the cop said. And to Barth: "You said she had a yellow vest . . ."

Lucas hustled back to his car, cranked it, and took off. The dance studio was called Aphrodite, the name in red neon with green streaks around it. The windows were covered by venetian blinds, but through the slots between the blinds and the window posts, you could see the hardwood floor and an occasional dancer in tights.

Lucas parked at a hydrant and pushed through the studio's outer door. An office was straight ahead, the floor to the right, with a door in the back leading to the locker rooms; it smelled like a gym. An instructor had a half-dozen girls working from a barre, the girls all identically dressed in black. Another woman, older, sat behind a desk in the office, and peered at Lucas over a pair of reading glasses. Lucas stepped over and she said, "Can I help you?"

Lucas held out his ID. "I'm with the state Bureau of Criminal Apprehension. We have a missing girl, and I need to talk to one of your students. A Kelly McGuire?"

"Who's missing?" the woman asked.

"One of her classmates. Is Kelly still here?"

"Yes . . . Just a minute." She got up, stepped onto the floor, and called, "Kelly? Could you come over here for a moment?"

McGuire was a short, slender, dark-haired girl who actually looked like professional dancers Lucas had met. She frowned as she stepped away from the barre and walked across the floor: "Did something happen?"

Everybody paused to listen. Lucas said, "Ah, I'm a police officer, I need to talk to you for a second about a friend of yours. Could you step outside, maybe?"

"I'll have to get my shoes . . . Or, it's nice, I could go barefoot . . ." She took off her dance shoes and followed Lucas outside. "What happened?"

"Have you seen Jesse Barth today?" Lucas asked.

"Yes. When school got out." Her eyes were wide; she'd see it all on TV, too. "I talked to her, we usually walk home, but I had a band practice and then my dance lesson . . . Is she hurt?"

"We can't locate her at the moment," Lucas said. "She was . . ."

"She was going to testify to a jury today, tonight," McGuire said. "She was pretty nervous about it."

"If she decided to chicken out, where would she go?" Lucas asked. "Does she have any special friends, a boyfriend?"

McGuire was troubled: "Jeez, I don't know . . ."

"Look, Kelly: if she doesn't want to testify, she doesn't have to. But. We can't find her. That's what we're worried about," Lucas said. "Somebody saw her on the street, walking home, but she never showed up. We've got to know where she might've gone. If she's okay, we can work it out. But if she's not . . ."

"Ah . . ." She stared at Lucas for a moment, then turned and looked at a bus, and then said, "Okay. If she hid out, it'd be either Mike Sochich's house, or she might have gone to Katy Carlson's—or she might have taken a bus to Har Mar, to go to a movie. Sometimes she goes up to Har Mar and sits there for hours."

"Where can I find these people . . . ?"

MᴄGᴜɪʀᴇ ᴡᴀs an assertive sort: She said, "Give me two min-utes to change. I'll show you. That'd be fastest."

She took five minutes, and hustled out with a bag of clothes. In the car, she said, "Turn around, we want to go over to the other side of Ninety-four, into Frogtown. Mike would be the best possi-bility . . . Best to go down Ninety-four to Lexington, then up Lex-ington. I'll show you where to turn . . ."

He did a U-turn on Snelling, caught a string of greens, accelerated down the ramp onto I-94, then up at Lexington, left, and north to Thomas, right, down the street a few blocks until McGuire pointed at a gray-shingled house behind a waist-high chain-link fence. Lucas pulled over and McGuire slumped down in her seat and said, "I'll wait here."

Lucas said, with a grin, "If she's here, she's gonna know you rat-ted her out. Might as well face the music." He popped the door to get out, and heard her door pop a second later. She followed him across the parking strip to the gate. There was a bare spot in the yard with a chain and a stake, and on the end of the chain, the same yellow-white dog he'd seen at the Barth's.

"Jesse's dog," Lucas said.

"Naw, that's Mike's dog," McGuire said. "Sometimes Jesse walks home with it. Dog likes her better than Mike."

Again, they stepped carefully. The dog barked twice and snarled, but knew where the end of the chain was. And a good thing, Lucas thought. All he needed this afternoon was a pitbull-wannabe hang-ing on his ass.

Mike's house had a low shaky porch, with soft floorboards going to rot. The aluminum storm door was canted a bit, and didn't close completely. Lucas rang the doorbell, then knocked on the door. He heard a thump from inside, and a minute later, saw the curtain move in a window on the left side of the porch.

He felt the tension unwind a notch. He banged on the door, pissed off now. "Jesse. Goddamnit, Jesse, answer the door. Jesse . . ."

There was a moment's silence, then Lucas said to McGuire, "If she comes to the door, yell for me."

He stepped off the porch, circled the dog, and hurried around to the back of the house: five seconds later, Jesse Barth came sneaking out the back door, carrying a backpack.

"Goddamnit, Jesse," he said.

Startled, she jerked around, saw him at the corner of the house. Gave up: "Oh, shit. I'm sorry."

"Come on—I've got to call your mom," Lucas said. "She's freaked out, half the cops in St. Paul are out looking for you. People thought you were kidnapped."

"I was just scared," Jesse said as he led her through the ankle-deep grass back around the house. "What if I make a mistake?" Her lip trembled. "I don't want to make a mistake and go to jail."

"Did Conoway say she was going to put you in jail?" Lucas asked. "Who said they were gonna put you in jail?"

"Well, you did, for one."

"That's if you tried to sell your testimony," Lucas said. "If you just go down and tell the truth, you're fine. You're the *victim* here."

"But if I make a mistake . . ."

"There's a difference between lying and making a mistake," Lucas told her. "They're not gonna put you in jail for making a mistake. You have to deliberately lie, and know you're lying, and it's gotta be an important lie. You talked to Conoway about what you're going to say. Just say that, and you're fine."

They cleared the front of the house and found McGuire on the porch, talking to a tall, bespectacled kid wearing a Seal T-shirt and jeans: Mike. McGuire said: "Jesse, they were afraid you were kidnapped. I'm sorry, I was so worried, you know, you see on the news all the time . . ."

"That's okay," Jesse said. "I'm just fucked up."

LUCAS CALLED KATHY BARTH: "I got her. She was hiding out with a friend. You've still got time to get down to Dakota County."

"I've got to talk to Jesse," Barth said.

"She's willing to go. You're holding up a lot of people here," Lucas said.

"Oh, God." Long silence, as though she were catching her breath. "Well, I've got to change . . ."

Lucas called Flowers, who was just crossing the Mississippi bridge into South St. Paul. He was ten minutes away: "Man, I thought she was gone," Flowers said. "I was thinking all this shit about the Klines and finding her body under a bridge . . ."

"Can you pick her up? That'd be best: I'm here with the Porsche and I got a rider."

"Fast as I can get there. If we turn right around, we'll just about be on time."

He told Flowers how to find the house, then called the St. Paul cops and canceled the alert: "Yeah, yeah, so I'll go kill myself," he told a cop who was inclined to pull his weenie.

THE THREE younger people sat on the porch, waiting for Flowers, and Lucas gave Jesse a psychological massage, telling her of various screw-ups with grand juries, and explained the difference between grand juries and trial juries. Jesse unsnapped the dog, whose name, it turned out, was Screw. She put it on a walking leash and the dog rolled over in the dirt and panted and licked its jaws and whimpered when Jesse scratched its stomach. "You're gonna make him come," Mike said.

"No . . ." Jesse was embarrassed.

Lucas moved and the dog twitched. "I don't think he likes me."

"Bit a paperboy once," Mike said. "They were gonna sue us, but Mom said, 'For what?' so they didn't."

"That's great," Lucas said.

Flowers arrived, towing a boat. He got out of his car, ambled over, shaking his head, and said to Jesse, "I ought to turn you over my knee."

"Oo. Do me, do me," McGuire said.

IN THE CAR, McGuire said she might as well go home, since her class would be ending. "Hope the neighbors see me coming home in a Porsche. They'll think I'm having a fling."

"Maybe I oughta put a bag over my head," Lucas said.

"That'd be no fun," she said. "I want people to see it's a big tough old guy."

LUCAS WAS still cranked from Flowers's original call, and, in the back of his head, couldn't believe that they'd found Jesse so quickly. He dropped McGuire off at her home in Highland. She waved goodbye going up the walk, and he thought she was a pretty good kid. He looked at his watch. If he took a little time, rolled down Ford Parkway with his arm out the window, enjoying the day and the leafy street, and maybe blowing the doors off the Corvette that had just turned onto the parkway in front of him, he'd just about make dinner with the wife and kids.

He was done with Kline and the Barths.

Now he had a motherfucker who was killing old people, and he was going to run him down like a skunk on a highway.

DINNER WITH the kids was fine; in the evening, he read a Chuck Logan thriller novel. Late at night, Flowers called: "We got an indictment. They're going to process the paper tomorrow, talk to Kline's attorney, set up a surrender late tomorrow afternoon, and then make the announcement day after tomorrow. Cole's set it up so they can arrest and book him before the press finds out, he'll make bail, then go hide out. Then the announcement."

"Sounds good to me," Lucas said. "You headed back south?"

"I'm here tonight, I'm heading back tomorrow at the crack of dawn."

IN THE MORNING, after a few phone calls, Lucas took a meeting at Bucher's house. He'd asked Gabriella Coombs to come over, to sit in.

The Widdlers had almost finished the appraisals of the contents of the house, with negative results. "In other words," Smith said, "there's nothing missing."

"There are a few things missing, John," Lucas said. "The Reckless painting, for one. A couple of chairs."

"According to a kid, who admitted that he hadn't been up there for a while, and that maybe Bucher got rid of them herself," Smith said.

"The whole thing smells. And we've now got a couple of other deals . . ."

"Lucas, I'm not saying you're wrong," Smith said. "What I'm saying is, you've got a killing years ago in Eau Claire where a woman was shot and nothing was taken but some money. An old man was strangled in Des Moines and the case was cleared. Another woman probably fell, according to the medical examiner, with all respect to Miss Coombs here. We've got nothing to work with. It's been a while since you worked at the city level, but I'll tell you what, it has gotten worse. I'm up to my ass in open investigations, and until we get more to go on . . ."

"That's not right," Coombs said. "My grandmother was murdered and her house was robbed."

"That's not what . . ." Smith shook his head.

Leslie Widdler came in, carrying a white paper bag. He said, "We've got a bunch of sticky buns from Frenchy's. Who wants one?"

Lucas held up his hand and Leslie handed him the sack. Lucas took out a sticky bun and passed the bag to Smith, who took one and passed it to Coombs, who took one, and then they all sat chewing and swallowing and Lucas said, "Thanks, Les . . . John tells me you haven't found a single goddamn stick of furniture missing. Is that right?"

"We've gone through the photographs one at a time, and we've found two pieces that are not actually here," Widdler said. "We've accounted for both of them. Both were given away."

"What about the swoopy chairs that the Lash kid was talking about?"

Widdler shrugged. "Can't put our finger on them. 'Swoopy' isn't a good enough description. He can't even tell us the color of the upholstery, or whether the seats were leather or fabric. All he ever looked at were the legs."

"Well . . . if he's right, how much would they be worth?"

"I can't tell you that, either," Widdler said. "Everything depends on what they were, and condition. A pristine swoopy chair, of a certain kind, might be worth a thousand dollars. The same chair, in bad shape, might be worth fifty. Or, it might be a knockoff, which is very common, and be worth zero. So—I don't know. What I do know is, there's a lot of furniture here that's worth good money, and they didn't take it. There are some old, old oriental carpets, especially one up in Mrs. Bucher's bedroom, that would pull fifty thousand dollars on the open market. There are some other carpets rolled up on the third floor. If these people were really sophisticated, they could have brought one of those carpets down and unrolled it in Mrs. Bucher's bedroom, taken the good one, and who would have known? Really?"

They chewed some more, and Smith said, "One more bun. Who wants it? I'm all done . . ."

Widdler said, "Me." Smith passed him the sack and Widdler retrieved the bun, took a bite, and said, "The other thing is, we know for sure that Mrs. Bucher gave things away from time to time. There may have been some swoopy chairs and a Reckless painting. Has anybody talked to her accountants about deductions the last couple of years?"

"Yeah, we did," Smith said. "No swoopy chairs or Reckless anything."

"Well . . ." Widdler said. And he pressed the rest of the bun into his face as though he were starving.

"Not right," Coombs said again, turning away from Widdler and the sticky bun.

Lucas sighed, and said, "I'll tell you what. I want you to go over every piece of paper you can find in your grandma's house. *Anything* that could tie her to Bucher or Donaldson or Toms. I'll do the same thing here, and I'll get Donaldson's sister working on it from her end."

"The St. Paul cops won't let me into the house yet," Coombs said. "They let me clean up the open food, but that's it."

"I'll call them," Lucas said. "You could get in tomorrow."

"Okay," Coombs said.

"Hope you come up with something, because from my point of view, this thing is drifting away to never-never land," Smith said. "We need a major break."

"Yeah," Lucas said. "I hear you."

"How much time can you put into it?" Smith asked.

"Not much," Lucas said. "I've got some time in the next two weeks, but with this election coming up, any sheriff with a problem case is gonna try to shift it onto us—make it look like something is getting done. The closer we get to the election, the busier we'll be. "

"Not right," said Coombs. "I want Grandma's killer found."

"We're giving it what we can," Lucas said. "I'll keep it active, but John and I know . . . we've been cops a long time . . . it's gonna be tough."

"Bucher's gonna be tough," Smith said. "With your grandma and the others . . . hell, we don't even know that they're tied together. At all. And Donaldson and Toms are colder than ice." He finished the sticky bun and licked the tips of his fingers. "Man, that was good, Les."

"The French aren't all bad," Widdler said, using his tongue to pry a little sticky bun out of his radically fashionable clear-plastic braces.

LUCAS WALKED COOMBS out to her car. "You can't give up," she said.

Lucas shook his head. "It's not like we're giving up—it's that right now, we don't have any way forward. We'll keep pushing all the small stuff, and maybe something will crack."

She turned at the car and stepped closer and patted him twice on the chest with an open hand. "Maybe I'm obsessive-compulsive; I don't think I can get on with life until this is settled. I can't stop thinking about it. I need to get something done. I spent all those years screwing around, lost. Now I've finally got my feet on the ground,

I've got some ideas about what I might want to do, I'm getting some friends . . . it's like I'm just getting started with real life. Then . . . *this*. I'm spinning my wheels again."

"You got a lot of time, you're young," Lucas said. "When I was your age, everything seemed to move too slow. But this will get done. I'll keep working on Grandma, St. Paul will keep working. We'll get somebody, sooner or later."

"You promise?" She had a really nice smile, Lucas thought, soft, and sadly sexy. Made you want to protect her, to take her someplace safe . . . like a bed.

"I promise," he said.

THE ST. PAUL COPS had gone through the papers in the Bucher house on-site, and not too closely, because so much of it was clearly irrelevant to the murders.

With Coombs agreeing to comb through her grandmother's papers, Lucas established himself in the Bucher house-office and began going through the paper files. Later, he'd move on to the computer files, but a St. Paul cop had told him that Bucher rarely used the computer—she'd learned to call up and use Microsoft Word for letter-writing, but nothing more—and Peebles never used it.

Lucas had no idea what he was looking for: something, anything, that would reach outside the house, and link with Donaldson, Toms, or Coombs. He'd been working on it for an hour when it occurred to him that he hadn't seen any paper involving quilts.

There was an "art" file, an inventory for insurance, but nothing mentioned the quilts that hung on the walls on the second floor. And quilts ran through all three murders that he knew of. He picked up the phone, dialed his office, got Carol: "Is Sandy still free?"

"If you want her to be."

"Tell her to call me," Lucas said.

He walked out in the hall where the Widdlers seemed to be packing up. "All done?"

"Until the auction," Jane Widdler said. She rubbed her hands. "We'll do well off this, thanks to you police officers."

"We now know every piece in the house," Leslie Widdler explained. "We'll work as stand-ins for out-of-state dealers who can't make it."

"And take a commission," Jane Widdler said. "The family wants to have the auction pretty quickly, after they each take a couple of pieces out . . . This will be fun."

"Hmm," Lucas said. "My wife is interested in antiques."

"She works for the state as well?" Leslie Widdler asked.

Lucas realized that Widdler was asking about income. "No. She's a plastic and microsurgeon over at Hennepin General."

"Well, for pete's sake, Lucas, we're always trying to track down people like that. Give her our card," Jane Widdler said, and dug a card out of her purse and passed it over. "We'll talk to her anytime. Antiques can be great investments."

"Thanks." Lucas slipped the card in his shirt pocket. "Listen, did you see any paper at all on the quilts upstairs? Receipts, descriptions, anything? All these places . . . I don't know about Toms . . ."

His cell phone rang and he said, "Excuse me . . ." and stepped away. Sandy. "Listen, Sandy, I want you to track down the Toms relatives, whoever inherited, and ask them if Toms had any quilts in the place. Especially, collector quilts. Okay? Okay."

He hung up and went back to the Widdlers. "These murders I'm looking at, there seems to be a quilt thread . . . Is that a joke? . . . Anyway, there seems to be a quilt thing running through them."

Leslie Widdler was shaking his head. "We didn't see anything like that. Receipts. And those quilts upstairs, they're not exactly collector quilts . . . I mean, they're collected, but they're not antiques. They're worth six hundred to a thousand dollars each. If you see a place that says 'Amish Shop,' you can get a quilt just like them. Traditional designs, but modern, and machine-pieced and quilted."

"Huh. So those aren't too valuable."

Leslie Widdler shook his head. "There's a jug in the china cabinet in the music room that's worth ten times all the quilts put together."

Lucas nodded. "All right. Listen. Thanks for your help, guys. And thanks for those sticky buns, Les. Sorta made my morning."

OUT OF THE HOUSE, Leslie Widdler said, "We've got to take him out of it."

"God, we may have overstepped," Jane said. "If we could only go back."

"Can't go back," Leslie said.

"If they look into the Armstrong quilts, they'll find receipts, they'll find people who remember stuff . . . I don't know if they can do it, but they might find out that Coombs didn't get all the money she should have. Once they get on that trail—it'd be hard, but they might trace it on to us."

"It's been a long time," Leslie said.

"Paperwork sticks around. And not only paperwork—there's that sewing basket. If Jackson White still has a receipt, or a memory, he could put us in prison." Jackson White sold them the sewing basket. "I should have looked for the sewing basket instead of that damn music box. That music box has screwed us."

"What if we went back to Coombs's place, put the music box someplace that wasn't obvious, and took the basket? That'd solve that thing," Leslie said.

"What about Davenport?"

"There's Jesse Barth," Leslie said. "Amity might have been right."

"So dangerous," Jane said. "So dangerous."

"Have to get the van, have to steal another plate."

"That's no problem. That's fifteen seconds, stealing the plate," Jane said. She was thinking about it.

"Davenport said he has a week or two to work on it—if we can push him through another week, we could be good," Leslie said. "He's the dangerous one. Smith already wants to move on. It's Davenport who's lingering . . ."

"He could come back to it," Jane said. "He smells the connection."

"Yes, but the older things get, and the fuzzier . . . Maybe Jackson White could have a fire," Leslie said. "If they find the music box, that might erase the Coombs connections. If he has to go chasing after Jesse Barth, that'll use a lot of time. All we need is a little time."

"So dangerous to go after Jesse Barth," Jane said. "We almost have to do it tonight."

"And we can. She's not the early-to-bed kind. And she walks. She walked over to her boyfriend's yesterday, maybe she'll be walking again."

"We should have taken her yesterday," Jane said.

"Never had a clear shot at her . . . and it didn't seem quite so necessary."

"Oh, God . . ." Jane scrubbed at her deadened forehead. "Can't even think."

"Be simpler to wait for Davenport outside his house, and shoot him. Who'd figure it out?" Leslie said. "There must be dozens or hundreds of people who hate him. Criminals. If he got shot . . ."

"Two problems. First, he's not an old lady and he's not a kid and he carries a gun and he's naturally suspicious. If we missed, he'd kill us. Look at all those stories about him," Jane said. "Second, we only know two cases he's working on. One of them is almost over. If the cops think the Bucher killers went out and killed a cop, especially a cop like Davenport who has been working as long as he has . . . they'd tear up everything. They'd never let go. They'd work on it for years, if they had to."

THEY RODE in silence for a while. Then Jane said, "Jesse Barth."

"Only if everything is perfect," Leslie said. "We only do it if every-thing is exactly right. We don't have to pull the trigger until the last second, when we actually stop her. Then if we do it, we've got an hour of jeopardy until we can get her underground. They don't have to know she's dead. They can think she ran away. But Davenport'll be working it forever, trying to find her."

"Only if everything is perfect," Jane said. "Only if the stars are right."

13

LUCAS WAS STILL PORING over paper at Bucher's when Sandy called back. "I talked to Clayton Toms. He's the grandson of Jacob Toms—the murdered man," she said. "He said there were several quilts in the house, but they were used as bedspreads and weren't worth too much. He still has one. None of them were these Armstrong quilts. None of them were hung on walls. He's going to check to see if there's anything that would indicate that he knew Mrs. Bucher or Mrs. Donaldson or Mrs. Coombs."

"Thanks," Lucas said. Maybe quilts weren't the magic bullet.

GABRIELLA COOMBS DECIDED to put off her research into Grandma's quilts. She had a date, the fifth in a series. She liked the guy all right, and he definitely wanted to get her clothes off, and she was definitely willing to take them off.

Unfortunately, he wanted them off for the wrong reason. He was a painter. The owner of the High Plains Drifter Bar & Grill in Minneapolis wanted a naked-lady painting to hang over his bar, and the painter, whose name was Ron, figured that Gabriella would be perfect as a model, although he suggested she might want to "fill out your tits" a little.

She didn't even mind *that* idea, as long as she got laid occasionally. The problem was, he worked from photographs, and Gabriella's very firm sixteenth Rule of Life was Never Take Off Your Clothes Around a Camera.

Ron had been pleading: "Listen, even if I did put your picture on the Internet, who'd recognize it? Who looks at faces? The facts are, one in every ten women in the United States, and maybe the world, is naked on the Internet. Nobody would look at your face. Besides, I won't put it on the Internet."

On that last part, his eyes drifted, and she had the bad feeling that she'd be on the Internet about an hour after he took the picture. And three hours after that, the wife of some friend would call up to tell her that everyone was ordering prints from Pussy-R-Us.

So the question was, was he going to make a move? Or did he only want her body in a computer file?

Coombs was a lighthearted sort, like her mother, and while she carefully chose her clothing for the way it looked on her, she didn't use much in the way of makeup. That was trickery, she thought. She *did* use perfume: scents were primal, she believed, and something musky might get a rise out of the painter. If not, well, then, Ron might be missing out on a great opportunity, she thought.

She dabbed the perfume on her mastoids, between her breasts, and finally at the top of her thighs. As she did it, her thoughts drifted to Lucas Davenport. The guy was growing on her, even though he was a cop and therefore on the Other Side, but he had a way of talking with women that made her think photography wouldn't be an issue. And she could feel little attraction molecules flowing out of him; he liked her looks. Of course, he was married, and older. Not that marriage always made a difference. And he wasn't *that* much older.

"Hmm," she said to herself.

———

JESSE BARTH USED a Bic lighter to fire up two cigarettes at once, handed one of them to Mike. The evening was soft, the cool humid air lying comfortably on her bare forearms and shoulders. They sat on the front porch, under the yellow bug light, and Screw, the pooch, came over and snuffed at her leg and then plopped down in the dirt and whimpered for a stomach scratch.

Two blocks away, Jane Widdler, behind the wheel, watched for a moment with the image-stabilizing binoculars, then said, "That's her."

"About time," Leslie said. "Wonder if the kid's gonna walk her home?"

"If he does, it's off," Jane said.

"Yeah," Leslie said. But he was hot. He had a new pipe, with new tape on the handle, and he wanted to use it.

LUCAS WAS DRINKING a caffeine-free Diet Coke out of the bottle, his butt propped against a kitchen counter. He said to Weather, "There's a good possibility that whoever killed Coombs didn't have anything to do with the others. The others fit a certain profile: they were rich, you could steal from them and nobody would know. They were carefully spaced both in time and geography— there was no overlap in police jurisdictions, so there'd be nobody to compare them, to see the similarities. Still: Coombs knew at least two of them. And the way she was killed . . ."

Weather was sitting at the kitchen table, eating a raw carrot. She pointed it at him and said, "You *might* be wasting your time with Coombs. But in the lab, when we're looking at a puzzle, and we get an interesting outlier in an experiment—Coombs would be an outlier—it often cracks the puzzle. There's something going on with it, that gives you a new angle."

"You think I might be better focusing on Coombs?"

"Maybe. What's the granddaughter's name?" Weather asked.

"Gabriella."

"Yes. You say she's looking at all the paper. That's fine, but she doesn't have your eye," Weather said. "What you should do, is get her to *compile* it all. Everything she can find. Then *you* read it. The more links you can find between Coombs and the other victims, the more likely you are to stumble over the solution. You need to pile up the data."

A STRETCH of Hague Avenue west of Lexington was perfect. The Widdlers had gone around the block, well ahead of Jesse, and scouted down Hague, spotted the dark stretch.

"If she stays on this street . . ." Jane said.

They circled back, getting behind her again, never getting closer than two blocks. The circling also gave them a chance to spot cop cars. They'd seen one, five minutes earlier, five blocks away, quickly departing, as though it were on its way somewhere.

That was good.

They could see Jesse moving between streetlights, walking slowly. Leslie was in the back of the van, looking over the passenger seat with the glasses. He saw the dark stretch coming and said, "Move up, move up. In ten seconds, she'll be right."

"Nylons," Jane said.

They unrolled dark nylon stockings over their heads. They could see fine, but their faces would be obscured should there be an unexpected witness. Better yet, the dark stockings, seen from any distance, made them look as though they were black.

"Why is she walking so slow?" Jane asked.

"I don't know . . . she keeps stopping," Leslie said. "But she's get-ting there . . ."

"So dangerous," Jane said.

"Do it, goddamnit," Leslie snarled. "She's there. Put me on her."

JESSE HEARD the sudden acceleration of the van coming up be-hind her. In this neighborhood, that could be a bad thing. She turned toward it, her face a pale oval in the dark patch. The van was com-ing fast, and just as quickly lurched to a stop. Now she was worried, and already turning away, to run, when the van's sliding door slammed open, and a big man was coming at her, running, one big arm lifting overhead, and Jesse screamed . . .

LESLIE HOPED to be on her before she could scream, realized somewhere in the calculating part of his brain that they'd done it wrong, that they should have idled up to her, but that was all done now, in the past. He hit the grass verge, running, before the van had even fully stopped, his chin hot from his breath under the nylon stocking, his arm going up, and he heard the girl scream "Shoe," or "Shoot," or "Schmoo."

Or "Screw"?

He was almost there, the girl trying to run, he almost had her when he became aware of something like a soccer ball flying at his hip, he had the pipe back ready to swing, and cocked his head toward whatever it was . . .

Then Screw hit him.

Leslie Widdler hit the ground like a side of beef, a solid *thump*, thrashing at the dog, the dog's snarls reaching toward a ravening lupine howl, Leslie thrashing at it with the pipe, the dog biting him on the butt, the leg, an upper arm, on the back, Leslie thrashing, finally kicking at the dog, and dog fastening on his ankle. Leslie managed to stagger upright, could hear Jane screaming something, hit the dog hard with the pipe, but the dog held on, ripping, and Leslie hit it again, still snarling, and, its back broken, the dog launched itself with its front paws, getting Leslie's other leg, and Leslie, now picking up Jane's "Get in get in get in . . ." threw himself into the back of the van.

The dog came with him, and the van accelerated into a U-turn, the side door still open, almost rolling both Leslie and the dog into the street, and Leslie hit the dog on the skull again, and then again, and the dog finally let go and Leslie, overcome with anger, lurched forward, grabbed it around the body, and threw it out in the street.

Jane screamed, "Close the door, close the door."

Leslie slammed the door and they were around another corner and a few seconds later, accelerating down the ramp onto I-94.

"I'm hurt," he groaned. "I'm really hurt."

LUCAS AND LETTY were watching *Slap Shot* when Flowers called. "I'm down in Jackson. Kathy Barth just called me and said that somebody tried to snatch Jesse off the street. About twenty minutes ago."

"You gotta be shittin' me." Lucas was on his feet.

"Jesse said somebody in a white van, a really big guy, she said, pulled up and tried to grab her. She was walking this dog home from her boyfriend's . . ."

"Screw," Lucas said.

"What?"

"That's the dog's name," Lucas said. "Screw."

"Yeah. That yellow dog. Anyway, she said Screw went after the guy, and the guy wound up back in the van with Screw and that's the last she saw of them," Flowers said. "She said the van did a U-turn and headed back to Lexington and then turned toward the interstate and she never saw them again. She ran home and told Kathy. Kathy called nine-one-one and then called me. She's fuckin' hysterical."

"Call Kathy, tell her I'm coming over," Lucas said. "Are the cops looking for a van?"

"I guess, but the call probably didn't go out for ten minutes after Jesse got jumped," Flowers said. "She said the guy was big and beefy and mean, like a football player. Who do we know like that?"

"Junior Kline . . . Can you get back on this?" Lucas asked.

"I could, but I'm a long way away," Flowers said.

"All right, forget it," Lucas said. "I'll get Jenkins or Shrake to find Junior and shake his ass up."

"Jesus, tell them not to beat on the guy unless they know he's guilty," Flowers said. "Those guys can get out of hand."

"Tell Barth I'm on the way," Lucas said.

THE ARTIST was wearing a black T-shirt, black slacks, and a black watch cap on his shaven head, a dramatic but unnecessary touch, since it was probably seventy degrees outside, Coombs thought, as she peered at him over the café table.

There was tension in the air, and it involved who was going to be the first to look at the check. The photographer was saying, "Camera had eight-bit color channels, and I'm asking myself, eight-bit? What the hell is that all about? How're you gonna get any color depth with eight-bit channels? Furthermore, they compress the shit out of the files, which means that the highlights get absolutely blown out, and the blacks fill up with noise . . ."

Coombs knew it was a lost cause. Almost without any personal volition, her fingertips crawled across the table toward the check.

JANE PULLED THE VAN into the garage and said, "Let's go look. Can you walk?"

"Yeah, I can walk," Leslie said. "Ah, God, bit me up. The fuckin' dog. That's why the kid was walking so slow. She had the dog on a goddamn leash, why didn't you see that? You had the binoculars . . ."

"The dog was just too close to the ground, or the leash was too long, or something, but I swear to God, I never had a hint," Jane said.

They went inside, Jane leading the way, up to the master bath. Leslie was wearing the anti-DNA coveralls, which were showing patches of blood on the back of his upper right arm, his right hip, and down both legs. He stripped the coveralls off and Jane gaped: "Oh, my God."

Probably fifteen tooth-holes, and four quarter-sized chunks of loose flesh. Leslie looked at himself in the mirror: he'd stopped leaking, but the wounds were wet with blood. "No arteries," he said. "Can't get stitches, the cops will call the hospitals looking for dog bites."

"So what do you think?" Jane asked. She didn't want to touch him.

"I think we use lots of gauze pads and tape and Mycitracin, and you tape everything together and then . . . When you had that bladder infection, you had some pills left over, the ones that made you sick."

"I've still got them," Jane said. The original antibiotics had given her hives, and she'd switched prescriptions.

"I'll use those." He looked at himself in the mirror, and a tear popped out of one eye and ran down his cheek. "It's not just holes, I'm going to have bruises the size of saucers."

"Time to go to Paris," Jane said. "Or Budapest, or anywhere. Antique-scouting. If anybody should take your shirt off in the next month . . ."

"But we're not done yet," Leslie said. "We've got to get that music box back in place, we've got to get the sewing basket."

"Leslie . . ."

"I've been hurt worse than this, playing ball," Leslie said. Another tear popped out. "Just get me taped up."

A ST. PAUL COP CAR was sitting at the curb at Barth's house. Every light in the house was on, and people who might have been neighbors were standing off the stoop, smoking. Lucas pulled in behind the cop car, got out, and walked up to the stoop.

"They're pretty busy in there," one of the smokers said.

"I'm a cop," Lucas said. He knocked once and let himself into the house. Two uniformed cops were standing in the living room, talking with the Barths, who were sitting on the couch. Lucas didn't recognize either of the cops, and when they turned to him, he said, "Lucas Davenport, I'm with the BCA. I worked with the Barths on the grand jury."

One of the cops nodded and Lucas said to Jesse, "You all right?"

"They got Screw," she said.

"But *you're* all right."

"She's scared *shitless*, if that's all right," Kathy snapped.

"We just got a call from another squad," one of the cops said. "There's a dead dog on the side of the road, just off Lexington. It's white, sounds like . . . Screw."

"All right," Lucas said. Back to Jesse. "You think you could come down with me, look at the dog?"

She snuffled.

The cop said, "We called Animal Control, they're gonna pick it up."

Lucas to Jesse: "What do you think?"

"I could look," she said. "He saved my life."

"Tell me exactly what happened . . ."

SHE TOLD the story in an impressionistic fashion—touches of color, touches of panic, not a lot of detail. When the dog hit the big man, she said, she was already running, and she was fast. "I didn't look back for a block and then I saw him jump in the van and Screw was stuck on his leg. Then the van went around in a circle, and that's the last I saw. They turned on Lexington toward the interstate. Then I ran some more until I got home."

"So there had to be at least two people," Lucas said.

"Yeah. Because one was driving and the other one tried to hit me," she said.

"What'd he try to hit you with?" Lucas asked.

"Like a cane."

"A cane?"

"Yeah, like a cane," she said.

"Could it have been a pipe?"

She thought for a minute, and then said, "Yeah. It could have been a pipe. About this long." She held her hands three feet apart.

Lucas turned away for a second, closed his eyes, felt people looking at him. "Jesus."

"What?" Kathy Barth was peering at him. "You havin' a stroke?"

"No, it's just . . . Never mind." He thought: the van guys were in the wrong case. To Jesse: "Honey, let's go look at the dog, okay?"

THEY FOUND the dog lying in the headlights of a St. Paul squad car. The cop was out talking to passersby, and broke away when Lucas pulled up. This cop he knew: "Hey, Jason."

"This your dog?" Jason was smiling, shaking his head.

"It's sorta mine," Jesse said. She looked so sad that the cop's smile vanished. She got up close and peered down at Screw's body. "That's him. He looks so . . . dead."

The body was important for two major reasons: it confirmed Jesse's story; and one other thing . . .

Lucas squatted next to it: the dog was twisted and scuffed, but also, it seemed, broken. Better though: its muzzle was stained with blood.

Lucas stood up and said to the cop, "Somebody said Animal Control was coming?"

"Yeah."

"I don't know how to do this, exactly, but I want an autopsy done," Lucas said. "I'd like to have it done by the Ramsey medical examiner, if they'll do it."

"An autopsy?" Jason looked doubtfully at the dead dog.

"Yeah. I want to know how he was killed. Specifically, if it might have been a pipe," Lucas said. "I want the nose, there, the mouth, checked for human blood. If there is human blood, I want DNA."

"Who'd he bite?" the cop asked.

"We don't know. But this is seriously important. When I find this guy, I'm gonna hang him up by his . . . I'm gonna hang him up," Lucas said.

"By his balls," said Jesse.

GABRIELLA DIDN'T NOTICE the broken window in the back door until she actually pushed the door open and was reaching for the kitchen light switch. The back door had nine small windows in it, and the broken one was bottom left, above the knob. The glass was still there, held together by transparent Scotch tape, but she could see the cracks when the light snapped on. She frowned and took a step into the kitchen and the other woman was right there.

JANE WIDDLER had just come down the stairs, carrying the sewing basket. She turned and walked down the hall into the kitchen, quiet in running shoes, Leslie twenty feet behind, when she heard the key in the back door lock and the door popped open and the light went on and a woman stepped into the kitchen and there they were.

The woman froze and blurted, "What?" and then a light of recognition flared in her eyes.

Jane recognized her from the meeting at Bucher's. The woman shrank back and looked as though she were about to scream or run, or scream *and* run, and Jane knew that a running fight in a crowded neighborhood just wouldn't work, not with the dog bites in Leslie's legs, and Leslie was still too far away, so she dropped the basket and launched herself at Coombs, windmilling at her, fingernails flying, mouth open, smothering a war shriek.

Coombs put up a hand and tried to backpedal and Jane hit her in the face and the two women bounced off the doorjamb and went down and rolled across the floor, Coombs pounding at Jane's midriff and legs, then Leslie was there, trying to get behind Coombs, and they rolled over into the kitchen table, and then back, and then Leslie plumped down on both of them and got an arm around Coombs and pulled her off of Jane like a mouse being pulled off flypaper.

Coombs tried to scream, her mouth open, her eyes bulging as Leslie choked her, and she was looking right in Jane's eyes when her spine cracked, and her eyes rolled up and her body went limp.

Jane pushed the body away and Leslie said, "Motherfucker," and backed up to the door, then turned around and closed it.

Jane was on her hands and knees, used the table to push herself up. "Is she dead?"

"Yeah." Leslie's voice was hoarse. He'd been angry with the world ever since the dog. His arms, ass, and legs burned like fire, and his heart was pounding from the surprise and murder of Coombs.

Coombs lay like a crumpled rag in the nearly nonexistent light on the kitchen floor; a shadow, a shape in a black-and-white photograph. "We can't leave her," Leslie said. "She's got to disappear. She's one too many dead people."

"They'll know," Jane said, near panic. "We've got to get out of here."

"We've got to take her with us. We'll go back to the house, get the van, we've got to move the van anyway. We'll take her down to the farm, like we were gonna do with the kid," Leslie said.

"Then what? Then what?"

"Then tomorrow, we go to see John Smith at Bucher's, give him some papers of some kind, tell him we forgot something," Leslie said "We let him see us: see that I'm not all bitten up. I can fake that. We tell him we're thinking of a scouting trip . . . and then we take off."

"Oh, God, Leslie, I'm frightened. I think . . ." Jane looked at the shadow on the floor. What she thought was, *This won't work.* But better not to tell Les. Not in the mood he was in. "Maybe. Maybe that's the best plan. I don't know if we should go away, though. Going away won't help us if they decide to start looking for us . . ."

"We can talk about that later. Get your flashlight, see if there're some garbage bags here. We gotta bag this bitch up and get rid of her. And we've gotta pick up this sewing shit . . . What'd you do, you dumbshit, *throw* it at her?"

"Don't be vulgar. Not now. Please."

THEY SCRABBLED AROUND in the dark, afraid to let the light of the flash play against the walls or windows. They got the sewing basket back together, hurriedly, and found garbage bags in a cleaning closet next to the refrigerator. They stuffed the lower half of Coombs's limp body into a garbage bag, then pulled another over the top of her body.

Leslie squatted on the floor and sprayed around some Scrubbing Bubbles cleaner, then wiped it up with paper towels and put the towels in the bags with the body. He did most of the kitchen floor that way, waddling backward away from the wet parts until he'd done most of the kitchen floor.

"Should be good," he muttered. Then: "Get the car. Pull it through the alley. I'll meet you by the fence."

She didn't say a word, but went out the back door, carrying the wicker sewing basket. And she thought, *Won't work. Won't work.* She moved slowly around the house, in the dark, then down the front lawn and up the street to the car. She got in, thinking, *Won't work.* Some kind of dark, disturbing mantra. She had to break out of it, had to think. Leslie didn't see it yet, but he would.

Had to think.

THE ALLEY WAS a line of battered garages, with one or two new ones, and a broken up, rolling street surface. She moved through it slowly and carefully, around an old battered car, maybe Coombs's, paused by the back gate to Coombs's house, popped the trunk: felt the weight when the body went in the trunk. Then Leslie was in the car and said, "Move it."

She had to think. "We need supplies. We need to get the coveralls. If we're going to dig . . . we need some boots we can leave behind. In the ground. We need gloves. We need a shovel."

Leslie looked out the window, at the houses passing on Lexington Avenue, staring, sullen: he got like that after he'd killed someone. "We've got to go away," he said, finally. "Someplace . . . far away. For a couple of months. Even then . . . these goddamn holes in me, they're pinning us down. We don't dare get in a situation where somebody wants to look at my legs. They don't even have to suspect us—if they start looking at antique dealers, looking in general, asking about dog bites, want to look at my legs . . . We're fucked."

Maybe you, Jane thought. "We can't just go rushing off. There's no sign that they'll be looking at you right away, so we'll tell Mary Belle and Kathy that we're going on a driving loop, that we'll be gone at least three weeks. Then, we can stretch it, once we're out there. Talk to the girls tomorrow, get it going . . . and then leave. End of the week."

"Just fuckin' itch like crazy," Leslie said. "Just want to pull the bandages off and scratch myself."

"Leslie, could you please . . . watch the language? Please? I know this is upsetting, but you know how upset *I* get . . ."

LESLIE LOOKED OUT the window and thought, *We're fucked.* It was getting away from them, and he knew it. And with the bites on his legs, he was a sitting duck. He could run. They had a good bit of cash stashed, and if he loaded the van with all the highest-value stuff, drove out to L.A., and was very, very careful, he could walk off with a million and a half in cash.

It'd take some time; but he could buy an ID, grow a beard, lose some weight. Move to Mexico, or Costa Rica.

Jane was a problem, he thought. She required certain living standards. She'd run with him, all right, but then she'd get them caught. She'd talk about art, she'd talk about antiques, she'd show off . . . and she'd fuck them. Leslie, on the other hand, had grown up on a dairy farm and had shoveled his share of shit. He wouldn't want to do that again, but he'd be perfectly content with a little beach cantina, selling cocktails with umbrellas, maybe killing the occasional tourist . . .

He sighed and glanced at Jane. She had such a thin, delicate neck . . .

AT THE HOUSE, Jane went around and rounded up the equipment and they both changed into coveralls. She was being calm. "Should we move the girl into the van?"

Leslie shook his head: "No point. The police might be looking for a van, after the thing with the kid. Better just to go like we are. You follow in the car, I take the van, if I get stopped . . . keep going."

BUT THERE was no problem. There were a million white vans. The cops weren't even trying. They rolled down south through the countryside and never saw a patrol car of any kind. Saw a lot of white vans, though.

THE FARM WAS a patch of forty scraggly acres beside the Cannon River, with a falling-down house and a steel building in back. When they inherited it, they'd had some idea of cleaning it up, someday, tearing down the house, putting in a cabin, idling away summer days waving at canoeists going down the river. They'd have a vegetable garden, eat natural food . . . And waterfront was always good, right?

Nothing ever came of it. The house continued to rot, everything inside was damp and smelled like mice; it was little better than a place to use the bathroom and take a shower, and even the shower smelled funny, like sulfur. Something wrong with the well.

But the farm was well off the main highways, down a dirt road, tucked away in a hollow. Invisible. The steel building had a good concrete floor, a powerful lock on the only door, and was absolutely dry.

The contractor who put in the building said, "Quite the hideout."

"Got that right," Leslie had said.

———

THEY PUT the van in the building, then got a flashlight, and Jane carried the shovel and Leslie put the girl in a garden cart and they dragged her up the hill away from the river; got fifty yards with Leslie cursing the cart and unseen branches and holes in the dark, and finally he said, "Fuck this," and picked up the body, still wrapped in garbage bags, and said, "I'll carry her."

DIGGING THE HOLE was no treat: there were dozens of roots and rocks the size of skulls, and Leslie got angrier and angrier and angrier, flailing away in the dark. An hour after they started, taking turns on the shovel, they had a hole four feet deep.

When Leslie was in the hole, digging, Jane touched her pocket. There was a pistol in her pocket, their house gun, a snub-nosed .38. A clean gun, bought informally at a gun show in North Dakota. She could take it out, shoot Leslie in the head. Pack him into the hole under the girl. Go to the police: "Where's my husband . . . ? What happened to Leslie?"

But there were complications to all that. She hadn't thought about it long enough. This was the perfect opportunity, but she just couldn't see far enough ahead . . .

She relaxed. Not yet.

THEY PACKED the body in, and Leslie started shoveling the dirt back.

"Stay here overnight," Leslie said. "Tomorrow, we can come up and spread some leaves around. Drag that stump over it . . . Don't want some hunter falling in the hole. Or seeing the dirt."

"Leslie . . ." She wanted to say it, wanted to say, "This won't work," but she held back.

"What?"

"I don't know. I hate to stay here. It smells funny," she said.

"Gotta do it," he grunted. He was trampling down the dirt. "Nothing has been working, you know? Nothing."

THE BED they slept in was broken down; tended to sag in the middle. Neither could sleep much; and Leslie woke in the middle of the night, his eyes springing open.

Two people in the world knew about him and the killings. One was Amity Anderson, who wanted money. They'd promised her a cut, as soon as they could move the furniture, which was out in the steel building.

The other one was Jane.

A tear dribbled down his face; good old Jane. He unconsciously scratched at a dog bite. He could pull Anderson in with the promise of money—come on out to the house, we've got it. Kill her, bring her out here.

And Jane . . . Another tear.

14

JENKINS WAS ASLEEP in the visitor's chair when Lucas arrived at his office the next morning. Carol said, "He was asleep when I got here," and nodded toward the office. Lucas eased the door open and said, quietly, "Time to work, bright eyes."

Jenkins was wearing a gray suit, a yellow shirt, and black shoes with thick soles, and, knowing Jenkins's penchant for kicking suspects, the shoes probably had steel toes. He'd taken off his necktie and gun and placed them under his chair.

He didn't move when Lucas spoke, but Lucas could tell he was alive because his head was tipped back and he was snoring. He was tempted to slam the door, give him a little gunshot action, but Jenkins might return fire before Lucas could slow him down. So he said, louder this time: "Hey! Jenkins! Wake up."

Jenkins's eyes popped open and he stirred and said, "Ah, my back . . . This is really a fucked-up chair, you know that?" He stood up and slowly bent over and touched his toes, then stood up again, rolled his head and his hips, smacked his lips. "My mouth tastes like mud."

"How long you been here?" Lucas asked.

"Ahhh . . . Since six? I found the Kline kid last night, then I went out with Shrake and had a few."

"Until six?"

"No, no. Five-thirty, maybe," Jenkins said. "Farmer's market was open, I ate a tomato. And one of those long green things, they look like a dildo . . ."

"A cucumber?" Lucas ventured.

"Yeah. One of those," Jenkins said.

"What about the kid?"

"Ah, whoever was in the truck, it wasn't Kline," Jenkins said. He yawned, scratched his head with both hands. "He was out with some of his business-school buddies. They're not the kind to lie to the cops. Stuffy little cocksuckers. They agree that he was with them from eight o'clock, or so, to midnight."

"That would have been too easy, anyway." Jenkins yawned again, and that made Lucas yawn.

"Girl have any kind of description?" Jenkins asked.

"The guy had a nylon on his head," Lucas said. "She was too scared to look for a tag number. All we got is the dead dog and a white van, and we don't know where the van is."

"Well, the dog's something. I bet they're doing high-fives over at the ME's office," Jenkins said. He yawned and shuffled toward the door. "Maybe I'll go out for a run. Wake myself up."

"Call nine-one-one before you start," Lucas said. Jenkins was not a runner. The healthiest thing he did was sometimes smoke less than two packs a day.

"Yeah." He coughed and went out. "See ya."

"Eat another tomato," Lucas called after him.

LUCAS COULDN'T THINK of what to do next, so he phoned John Smith at the St. Paul cops: "You going up to Bucher's?"

"Yeah, eventually, but I don't know what I'm going to do," Smith said.

"Anybody up there?"

"Barker, the niece with the small nose, an accountant, and a real estate appraiser. They're doing an inventory of contents for the IRS—everything, not just what the Widdlers did. Widdlers are finished. School got out, and the Lash kid called to see if he could go over and pick up his games. He'll be up there sometime . . . probably some people in and out all day, if you want to go over. If there's nobody there when you get there, there's a lockbox on the door. Number is two-four-six-eight."

"All right. I'm gonna go up and look at paper," Lucas said.

"I understand there'll be some excitement in Dakota County this morning, and you were involved," Smith said.

"Oh, yeah. Almost forgot," Lucas said. "Where'd you hear that?"

"*Pioneer Press* reporter," Smith said. "He was on his way out to Dakota County. Politicians don't do good in Stillwater."

"Shouldn't fuck children," Lucas said.

HE CHECKED OUT of the office and headed over to Bucher's, took a cell-phone call from Flowers on the way. Flowers wanted the details on Jesse Barth: "Yeah, it happened, and no, it wasn't the Kline kid," Lucas said. He explained, and then asked about the girl's body on the riverbank. Flowers was pushing it. "Keep in touch," Lucas said.

IN HIS MIND'S EYE, Lucas could see the attack of the night before. A big man with a pipe—or maybe a cane—in a white van, going after Jesse. A man with a pipe, or a cane, killed Bucher. But as far as he knew, there hadn't been a van.

A van had figured into the Toms case, but Toms had been strangled.

Coombs's head had hit a wooden ball, which St. Paul actually had locked up in the lab—and it had a dent, and hair, and blood, and even smudged handprints, but the handprints were probably from people coming down the stairs. But then, Coombs probably had nothing to do with it anyway . . . except for all those damn quilts. And the missing music box. He hadn't heard from Gabriella Coombs, and made a mental note to call her.

There was a good possibility that the van was a coincidence. He remembered that years before, during a long series of sniper attacks in Washington, D.C., everybody had been looking for a white van, and after every attack, somebody remembered seeing one. But the shooters hadn't been in a white van. They'd been shooting through a hole in the trunk of a sedan, if he remembered correctly. The fact is, there were millions of white vans out there, half the plumbers and electricians and carpenters and roofers and lawn services were working out of white vans.

BARKER AND THE ACCOUNTANT and the real estate appraiser had set up in the main dining room. Lucas said hello, and Barker showed him some restored pots, roughly glued together by the wife of a St. Paul cop who'd taken pottery lessons: "Just pots," she said. "Nothing great."

"Huh."

"Does that mean something?" she asked.

"I don't know," he said.

In the office, he started flipping through paper, his heart not in it. He really didn't feel like reading more, because he hadn't yet found anything, and he'd looked through most of the high-probability stuff. Weather had said that he needed to pile up more data; but he was running out of data to pile up.

The pots. No high-value pots had been smashed, but the cabinet had been full of them. Maybe not super-high value, but anything from fifty to a couple of hundred bucks each.

The pots on the floor were worth nothing, as if only the cheaper pots had been broken. If a knowledgeable pot enthusiast had robbed the place, is that what he'd do? Take the most valuable, put the somewhat valuable back—perhaps out of some aesthetic impulse—and then break only the cheap ones as a cover-up? Or was he, as Kathy Barth suggested the night before, simply having a stroke?

THE WIDDLERS CAME IN, Leslie cheerful in his blue seersucker suit and, this time, with a blue bow tie with white stars; Jane was dressed in shades of gold.

"Bringing the lists to Mrs. Barker," Jane called, and they went on through. Five minutes later, they went by the office on the way out. Lucas watched them down the front walk, toward their Lexus. Ronnie Lash rode up on a bike as they got to the street, and they looked each other over, and then Lash turned up the driveway toward the portico.

Lash walked in, stuck his head in the office door, and said, "Hi, Officer Davenport."

"Hey, Ronnie."

Lash stepped in the door. "Figured anything out yet?"

"Not yet. How about you?" Lucas asked.

"You know when we discovered that whoever did it, had to have a car?"

"Yeah?"

"Detective Smith said they'd check the security camera at the Hill House to see what cars were on it. Did he do it?" Lash asked.

"Yup. But the cameras operate on a motion detector that cover the grounds," Lucas said. "They didn't have anything in the time frame we needed."

"Huh. How about that halfway house?"

Lucas said, "They're mostly drunks. We've been looking at their histories . . ."

"I mean the camera," Lash said. "They've got a camera on their porch roof pointing out at the street."

Lucas scratched his chin: "Really?"

"Yeah. I just came by there," Lash said.

"I'll call John Smith. Ask him to look into it. Thanks, Ronnie."

"You're welcome."

LUCAS CALLED SMITH. Smith said he would check it right away. "If it's there, what I'm interested in would be a van," Lucas said.

"Probably won't be anything," Smith said. "Nothing goes longer than about forty-eight hours, you know, those tapes. But I'll give them a call."

RONNIE CAME BACK THROUGH, carrying a shopping bag full of video games. "I talked to Mrs. Barker, and she showed me those vases. Those pots, the ones that got glued back together."

"You recognize them?" Lucas asked.

"Yeah. Last time I saw them, they were upstairs. On a table upstairs. They were never in that glass cabinet."

"You sure?"

"I'm sure," Lash said. "They were in a corner, in a jog of the hallway, on a little table. I dusted them off myself, when I was helping Aunt Sugar."

LUCAS PACED AROUND the office, impatient with himself for not getting anywhere. He watched Lash go down the walk, get on his bike, and wobble off, the games bag dangling from one hand. There *had* been a robbery. He didn't give a shit what the Widdlers said.

His cell phone rang, and he glanced at the screen: Smith.

"Yeah?"

"We got a break—they archive the tapes for a month, in case they've got to see who was with who. I'm gonna run over there and take a look."

"Van," Lucas said.

His shut the phone, but before he could put it in his pocket, it rang again: Carol, from the office. He flipped it open. "Yeah?"

"You need to make a phone call. A Mrs. Coombs . . ."

"Gabriella. I've been meaning to call her."

"This is Lucy Coombs. The mother. She's calling about Gabriella. Lucy says Gabriella's disappeared, and she's afraid something happened to her."

LUCY COOMBS WAS at her mother's house. She was tall, thin, and blond, like her daughter, with the same clear oval face, but threaded with fine wrinkles; a good-looking woman, probably now in her late fifties, Lucas thought. She met him on the front lawn, twisting a key ring in her hands.

"I called you because Gabriella said she was working with you," she said. "I can't find her. I've been looking all over, I called the man she was dating, and he said he dropped her off at her apartment last night and that she planned to come over here to look at papers and so I came over here and I . . ."

She paused to take a breath and Lucas said, "Slow down, slow down. Have you been inside?"

"Yes, there's no sign of anything. But there's a broken window on the back door, right by the latch. And I found these by the back porch." She held up the key ring. "They're her keys."

Lucas thought, *Oh, shit.* Out loud, he said, "Let's go look around. Does she have a cell phone?"

"No, we don't believe in cell phones," Coombs said. "Because of EMI."

"Okay . . . Has she done this before? Wandered off?"

"Not lately. I mean she did when she was younger, but she's been settling down," Coombs said. "She's been in touch every day since my mom died. I mean, I found her *keys*." She was no fool; the keys were a problem, and there was fear in her eyes.

They went around the house and through the back door, Coombs showing Lucas where she'd found the keys, off the back steps, as if they'd been dropped or thrown. "Maybe she dropped them in the dark and couldn't find them," Lucas suggested. "Did you look for her car?"

"No, I didn't think to. I wonder . . . sometimes she parked in the alley, behind the fence." They walked out through the backyard, to a six-foot-high woven-board privacy fence that separated Marilyn Coombs's house from the alley. The gate was hanging open, and as soon as Lucas pushed through, he saw Gabriella's rusty Cavalier.

"Oh, God," Lucy Coombs said. She hurried past Lucas and then almost tiptoed up to the car, as if she were afraid to look in the windows. But the car was empty, except for some empty herbal tea bottles on the floor of the backseat. The car wasn't locked; but then, Lucas thought, why would it be? There was nothing in it, and who would steal it?

"Back to the house," he said.

"What do you think happened?"

"I don't know," Lucas said. "She's probably just off somewhere. Maybe I oughta go talk to her boyfriend."

"I think you should," Lucy Coombs said. "I know it wasn't going very well. I think Gabriella was about to break it off."

"Let's check the house and then I'll go talk to the guy," Lucas said. "Do you have any relatives or know any girlfriends or other boyfriends . . . ?"

THEY WALKED through the house: nobody there. Lucas looked at the broken window. He'd never actually seen it done, but he'd read about it in detective novels—burglars making a small break in a window, usually by pushing the point of a screwdriver against the glass, to get a single pressure crack. Then they'd work the glass out, open the door with a wire, then put the pane back in place and Scotch-tape it. With any luck, the owners didn't notice the break for a while—sometimes a long while—and that would obscure the date and time of the break-in . . .

It did suggest a certain experience with burglary. Or perhaps, with detective novels.

"I'm going to make a call, get the St. Paul cops to go over the place," Lucas said. "If you could give me the boyfriend's name . . ."

They were talking in the kitchen, next to the phone, and the color caught his eye: a flash of red. He thought it might be blood, but then instantly knew that it wasn't. Blood was purple or black. This was scarlet, in the slot between the stove and refrigerator. He hadn't seen it when he and Gabriella Coombs were in the kitchen, and he'd looked—he'd been doing his typical crime-scene check, casually peering into cracks and under tables and chairs.

"Excuse me," he said. He went over to the stove and looked down.

"What?"

"Looks like . . . Just a minute." He opened a kitchen cabinet, took out a broom, and used the handle to poke out the red thing.

A spool of thread.

The spool popped out of the stove space, rolled crookedly in a half circle, and bumped into his shoe. He used a paper towel to pick it up, by the spool edge on one end, and put it on the stove. They both looked at it for a moment.

"How'd it get there?" Lucy asked.

"I don't know," Lucas said. "Wasn't there before. There was a closetful of quilting stuff upstairs. Maybe Gabriella came and took it?"

Lucy frowned. "She doesn't quilt. I've been trying to get her interested, but she's more interested in a social life. Besides, if she took it, where'd she put it? It's not in her car."

"Neither is she. Maybe she came over with a girlfriend, who quilts . . ." Lucas was bullshitting, and he knew it. Making up fairy stories.

"That's from the old basket," Lucy said. "It's old thread, see? I don't think they even make it anymore. This says Arkansas on it. Now, most of it comes from China or Vietnam."

"Let's go look at the basket," Lucas said.

They climbed the stairs together, to the big linen closet, and Lucas used the paper towel to open the door.

"Ah, fuck me," he said.

No wicker sewing basket.

But there, under a neat stack of fabric clippings, where the basket had been, was a black lacquer box with mother-of-pearl inlay.

The music box.

15

LUCAS CALLED JERRY WILSON, the St. Paul cop who'd caught the investigation of Marilyn Coombs's death, and told him about the disappearance of Gabriella Coombs, about the keys and the car, about the broken window with the Scotch tape, about the spool of thread and the music box.

Wilson said, "That sounds like an Agatha Christie book."

"I know what it sounds like," Lucas said. "But you need to cover this, Jerry—we need to find Gabriella. I'll talk to her boyfriend, but I could use some cops spread out behind me, talking to her other friends."

"Okay. You got names? And I'll tell you what—that window wasn't broken day before yesterday."

"I'll get you names and phone numbers," Lucas said. "If you find her, God bless you, but I've got a bad feeling about this." Lucas was on his cell phone, looked back to the house, where Lucy Coombs was locking the front door. "I've got a feeling she's gone."

LUCY COOMBS wanted to come along when Lucas confronted Ron Stack, the artist boyfriend. Lucas told her to go home and get on the phone, and he lied to her: "There's an eighty percent chance that she's at a friend's house or out for coffee. We've just got to run her down, and anything you can do to help . . ."

On the way to Stack's place, Lucas called Carol: "Have you seen Shrake?"

"Yes, but I'm not sure he saw me. He's getting coffee, and he needs it. His eyes are the color of a watermelon daiquiri."

"Fuck him. Tell him to meet me at the Parkside Lofts in Lowertown. Ten minutes."

WHEN LUCAS got back downtown, Shrake was sitting on a park bench across the street from Stack's apartment building. He got shakily to his feet when Lucas pulled into the curb. He was a tall man in a British-cut gray suit and white shirt, open at the collar. His eyes, as Carol said, were Belgian-hare pink, and he was hungover.

"I hope we're gonna kill something," he said, when Lucas got out of the car. "I really need to kill something."

"I know. I talked to Jenkins this morning," Lucas said. "We're looking for an artist. His girlfriend disappeared last night." Lucas told him about it as they crossed the street.

The Parkside was a six-story building, a onetime warehouse, un-profitably converted to loft apartments, with city subsidies, and was now in its fourth refinancing. They rode up to the top floor in what had been a freight elevator, retained either for its boho cool or for lack of money. For whatever reason, it smelled, Lucas thought, like the inside of an old gym shoe.

As they got off the elevator, Lucas's cell phone rang. Lucas looked at the Caller ID: the medical examiner's office. He said, "I've got to take this."

The ME: "You know, I like doing dogs," he said. "It's a challenge."

"Find anything good?" Lucas asked.

"A lot of people think all we can do is routine, run-of-the-mill dis-sections and lab tests, like it's all cut-and-dried," the ME said. "That's not what it's about, is it? It's a heck of a lot more than that . . ."

"Listen, we'll have lunch someday and you can tell me about it," Lucas said. "What happened with the dog?"

"You're lying to me about the lunch. You're just leading me on . . ."

"What about the fuckin' dog?" Lucas snarled.

"Pipe," the ME said. "I did Bucher—and man, if it ain't the *same* pipe, it's a brother or a cousin. The dog's skull was crushed, just like Bucher's and Peebles's, and the radius of the crushing blow is identical. I don't mean somewhat the same, I mean, *identical*. We got mucho blood samples, but I don't know yet whether they're human or dog."

"Give me a guess," Lucas suggested.

"My guess is, it's human," the ME said. "It looks to me like the mutt was chewing on somebody. We've got enough for DNA, if it's human."

"That's great," Lucas said. "And the pipe . . ."

"You're hot," the ME said. "You're onto something."

"Get a break?" Shrake asked, when Lucas rang off.

"Maybe, but not on Gabriella."

RON STACK was in 610. Lucas knocked on the door, and a moment later a balding, bad-tempered, dark-complected man peered out at them over a chain. He was wearing a nasal spreader on his nose, the kind football players use to help them breathe freely. He was holding a cup of coffee and had a soul patch under his thin lower lip. "What?"

Lucas held up his ID. "Bureau of Criminal Apprehension. We're investigating the disappearance of Gabriella Coombs," Lucas said.

Stack's chin receded into his throat. "Disappearance? She disappeared?"

"You're the last person we know for sure who saw her. Can we come in?"

Stack turned and looked back into his loft, then at Lucas again. "I don't know. Maybe I should call my lawyer."

"Well, whatever you want to do, Mr. Stack, but we aren't going anywhere until you talk to us. I can have a search warrant down here in twenty minutes if you want to push us. But it'd be a lot easier to sit on the couch and talk, than having you on the floor in handcuffs, while we tear the place apart."

"What the fuck? Is that a threat?" His voice climbed an octave.

From behind Stack, a woman's voice said, "Who's that, Ron?"

Stack said, "The police."

"What do they want?" the woman asked.

"Shut up. I'm trying to think." Stack scratched his chin, then asked, "Am I a suspect?"

"Absolutely," Lucas said.

Shrake, the nice guy: "Look, all we're doing is trying to find Gabriella. We don't know where she's gone. She's involved in another case, and now . . ."

"Okay," Stack said. "I'm gonna push the door shut a little so I can take the chain off."

He did, and let them in.

THE LOFT WAS an open cube with floor-to-ceiling windows along one wall. The other three walls were concrete block, covered with six-foot-wide oil paintings of body parts. The place smelled of turpentine, broccoli, and tobacco.

A kitchen area, indicated by a stove, refrigerator, and sink gathered over a plastic-tile floor, was to their left; and farther to the left, a sitting area was designated by an oriental carpet. A tall blond woman, who looked like Gabriella Coombs, but was not, sat smoking on a scarlet couch.

At the other end of the cube, a door stood open, and through the open door, Lucas could see a towel rack: the bathroom. Overhead, a platform was hung with steel bars from the fifteen-foot ceiling, with a spiral staircase going up. Bedroom.

At the center of the cube was an easel, on a fifteen-foot square of loose blue carpet; against the right wall, three battered desks with new Macintosh computer equipment.

Shrake wandered in, following Lucas, sniffed a couple of times, then tilted his head back and took in the paintings. "Whoa. What *is* this?"

"My project," Stack said, looking around at all the paintings. There were thirty of them, hung all the way to the ceiling, all along one wall and most of the end wall. One showed the palm of a hand, another the back of the hand. One showed a thigh, another a hip, one the lower part of a woman's face. "I unwrapped a woman." He paused, then ventured, "Deconstructed her."

"It's like a jigsaw puzzle," Shrake asked.

Stack nodded. "But conceptually, it's much more than that. These are views that you could never see on an actual woman. I took high-resolution photographs of her entire body, so you could see every pore and every hair, and reproduced them here in a much bigger format, so you *can* see every hair and pore. You couldn't do that, just looking at somebody. I call it *Outside of a Woman*. It was written up last month in *American Icarus*."

"Wow, it's like being there," Shrake enthused. He pointed: "Like this one: you're right there inside her asshole."

WRONG FOOT, Lucas thought. To Stack: "We can't find Gabriella. Her mother tells us that you were out together last night, and Gabriella broke it off with you . . ."

"Who's Gabriella?" the woman asked.

"How ya doing?" Shrake asked. He winked at her, and pointed up at the paintings. "Is this you?"

"No," the woman said, with frost.

"Gabriella's a potential model," Stack said to her. Then to Lucas: "Look, she didn't break anything off, because there was nothing to break off. We went down to Baker's Square and had a sandwich, and we couldn't make a deal on my new project, and I said, 'Okay,' and she said, 'Okay,' and that was it. She took off." He shrugged and pushed his hands into his jeans pocket.

"You go there together?" Shrake asked.

"No. We met there."

"Where were you last night?" Lucas asked.

"Here," Stack said. He turned to the woman: "With her."

"He was," the woman said. To Stack: "This Gabriella's just a model?"

"Just a model," Stack agreed.

"What kind of a car do you drive?" Lucas asked.

"An E-Class Mercedes-Benz station wagon."

"What color?" Lucas asked.

"Black," Stack said.

"You must do pretty well for yourself," Shrake said. "A Benz."

"It's a 'ninety-four," Stack said. "I bought it used, with eighty-nine thousand miles on it."

"Where's the van—the one you use for moving paintings?" Lucas asked.

Stack was mystified: "What van? I have a friend with a blue pickup, when I'm moving big sheets of plywood, but I never used a van."

"Did you know Marilyn Coombs?" Lucas asked.

"No. Gabriella told me about her dying and about you guys investigating," Stack said. "In fact, I think she sorta had the hots for you."

"For Lucas?" Shrake asked skeptically.

"If you're the guy who took her around her grandmother's house," Stack said to Lucas. "Yeah."

"What'd you mean by 'had'?" Shrake asked. "You said she 'had' the hots for Lucas. Do you think she's dead? Or just stopped having the hots?"

"Hell, *you're* the guys who think she's dead," Stack said. "That's the way you're talking."

"Did she say where she was going last night?" Lucas asked.

"Well, yeah," Stack said. "She said she had to go because you—or somebody—asked her to go through her grandma's papers. Looking for clues, or something. Is that, uh . . . Where'd she disappear from, anyway?"

Lucas looked at Shrake, felt an emotional squeeze of fear and the cold finger of depression. "Bad," he said. "Bad. Goddamnit to hell, this is bad."

THEY PUSHED the painter for another ten minutes, then Lucas left Shrake with Stack and the woman, to get details of where they were overnight, to get an ID on the woman, to probe for holes in their stories.

On the way out to the car, Smith called: "We got a van. A two thousand one Chevy Express, looks to be a pale tan, but one of the geniuses here tells me that could be the light. It might be white. It went past the halfway house three times on Friday night, the night the storm came in. Can't see the occupants, but we think the tag is Wisconsin and we think we know two letters, but we can't make out the other letter or the numbers. We're going to send it off to the feds, see if they can do some photo magic with it. In the meantime, we're sorting vans out by the letters we know."

"That's something," Lucas said. "Listen, feed every name you've got associated with Bucher into the computer. I'll get you all the names I can pull out of the Donaldson and Toms files, and the Coombs stuff. Find that van . . . Once we know who we're looking for . . ."

"Get me the names," Smith said.

"And listen: do me a favor," Lucas said. "Go see this girl in the Kline case, her name is Jesse Barth. She lives up on Grand, her mother is Kathy, they're in the phone book. Have her look at the van. See if she thinks it might be the same one."

"If it is . . . what does that mean?" Smith asked.

"I don't know. I'm freakin' out here, man. Just have her look at it, okay?"

"Okay," Smith said. "I'll tell you something else: I'm gonna get that fuckin' Ronnie Lash and turn his ass into a cop."

LUCAS WAS in a hurry now, with Gabriella missing.

He kept thinking, *The quilts, the van, the pipe; the quilts, the van, the pipe. The quilts, the van, the pipe . . .*

He couldn't get at the van. Too many of them and he didn't have a starting place, unless Smith or the feds came up with something. The pipe didn't make any difference, unless he found the actual pipe that did the killing; a killer could buy as much pipe as he wanted at Home Depot.

That left the quilts. Gabriella had said that her mother was messing with quilts. He got in the car, and pointed it toward the Coombs house, got Lucy Coombs on the phone: "Her friends say anything?"

"Nobody's seen her. Oh, God, *where's my baby?*"

"I'm coming over," Lucas said.

LUCY COOMBS LIVED in the Witch Hat neighborhood off University Avenue, in an olive-green clapboard house with a stone wall separating the front yard from the sidewalk. The yard had no grass, but was an overgrown jumble of yellow and pink roses, and leggy perennials yet to flower. The house had a damp, mossy, friendly look, with a flagstone pathway running from the front stoop around the side of the house and out of sight.

The front door was open and Lucas banged on the loosely hung screen door. He could hear people talking, and felt a twitch of hope: Had Gabriella shown up? Then a heavyset woman in a purple shift and long dangly earrings came to the door, said, "Yes?"

Lucas identified himself and the woman pushed the door open and whispered, "Anything?"

"No."

"Lucy is terrified," she said.

Lucas nodded. "I have to talk to her about her mother . . ."

THERE WERE THREE more unknown women in the kitchen with Coombs. Lucy Coombs saw him and shuffled forward, shoulders rounded, hands up in front of her as though she might punch him: "Where is she?"

"I don't know," Lucas said. "We're looking, I've got the St. Paul cops out looking around, we're pushing every button we know."

She wanted to shout at him, and to cry; she was crippled with fear: "You've got to find her. I can't stand this, you've *got* to find her."

Lucas said, "Please, please, talk to me about your mother."

"She was murdered, too, wasn't she?" Coombs asked. "They killed her and came back and took my baby . . ."

"Do you have any idea . . . who're *they*?"

"I don't know—the people who killed her."

Lucas said, intent on Coombs: "This thing is driving me crazy. We have three dead women, and one missing. Two of them were involved in antiques, but your mother wasn't—but she had one antique that was taken, and then maybe returned, by somebody who may also have taken a quilting basket."

"And Gabriella," Coombs blurted.

Lucas nodded. "Maybe."

"It's the Armstrong quilts," one of the women said. "The curses."

Lucas looked at her: She was older, thin, with dry skin and a pencil-thin nose. "The curses . . . the ones sewn into the quilts? Gabriella told me . . ."

The woman looked at the others and said, "It's the curses working. Not only three women dead, but the son who committed suicide, the father dies in the insane asylum."

Another of the women shivered: "You're scaring me."

"Did Bucher and Donaldson have something to do with the Armstrong quilts?" Lucas asked, impatient. He didn't believe in witchcraft.

Coombs said, "Yes. They both bought one from my mom, after Mom found them."

Lucas said, "There were what, five quilts? Six, I can't remember . . ."

"Six," the thin-nosed woman said. "One went to Mrs. Bucher, one went to Mrs. Donaldson, the other four were sold at auction. Big money. I think two of them went to museums and two went to private collectors. I don't know who . . ."

"Who did the auction?"

Coombs said, "One of the big auction houses in New York. Um, I don't know how to pronounce it, Sotheby's?"

"Are there any here in Minneapolis?" Lucas asked.

The dangly-earring woman said, "At the Walker Gallery. Mrs. Bucher donated it."

"Good. I'll go look at it, if I have time," Lucas said. "Have you ever heard the name Jacob Toms?"

The women all looked at each other, shaking their heads. "Who's he?"

H E   W A S   on his way out the door, intent on tracing the Armstrong quilts, when he was struck by a thought and turned around, asked Coombs: "The music box. You don't think Gabriella had it, do you? That she just used it to get an investigation going?"

Coombs shook her head: "No. I found Mom, and called the police, and then called Gabriella. The police were already there when she came over. She was sad and mentioned the music box, and we went to look at it, and it wasn't there."

"Okay. So somebody brought back the music box and took the sewing basket," Lucas said. "Why did they do that? Why did they take the sewing basket? Was that part of the Armstrong quilt thing?"

"No, she just bought that kind of thing when she was hunting for antiques—I don't know where she got it."

"I remember her talking about it at quilt group," said the big woman in the purple shift. "She said she might see if she could sell it to a museum, or somewhere that did restorations, because the thread was old and authentic. Nothing special, but you know—worth a few dollars and kinda interesting."

Coombs said, "There might be a . . . clue . . . wrapped up in the quilts. But that won't save Gabriella, will it? If they took her? A clue like that would take forever to work out . . ." Tears started running down her face.

Lucas lied again: "I still think it's better than fifty-fifty that she went off someplace. She may have lost her keys in the dark, called somebody over to pick her up. She's probably asleep somewhere . . ."

He looked at his watch: she'd been gone for sixteen or eighteen hours. Too long.

"I'm running," he said. "We'll find her."

FROM HIS OFFICE, he looked up Sotheby's in New York, called, got routed around by people who spoke in hushed tones and non–New York accents, and finally wound up with a vice president named Archie Carton. "Sure. The auctions are public, so there's no secret about who bought what—most of the time, anyway. Let me punch that up for you . . ."

"What about the rest of the time?" Lucas asked.

"Well, sometimes we don't know," Carton said. "A dealer may be bidding, and he's the buyer of record, but he's buying it for somebody else. And sometimes people bid by phone, to keep their identify confidential, and we maintain that confidentiality—but in a police matter, of course, we respond to subpoenas."

"So if one of these things was a secret deal . . ."

"That's not a problem. I've got them on-screen, and all four sales were public," Carton said. "One went to the Museum of Modern Art here in New York, one went to the National Museum of Women's Art in Washington, D.C., one went to the Amon Carter in Fort Worth, Texas, and one went to the Modern in San Francisco."

"Does it say how much?"

"Yup. Let me run that up for you . . ." Lucas could hear keys clicking, and then Carton said, "The total was four hundred seventy thousand dollars. If you want, I could send you the file. I could have it out in five minutes."

"Terrific," Lucas said. "If my wife ever buys another antique, I'll make sure she buys it from you."

"We'll be looking forward to it," Carton said.

THAT'D BEEN EASY. Lucas leaned back and looked at the number scrawled on his notepad: $470,000. He thought about it for a moment, then picked up the phone and called Carton back.

"I'm sorry to bother you again, but I was looking in an antiques book, and I didn't see any quilts that sold for this much," Lucas said. "Was there something really special about these things?"

"I could get you to somebody who could answer that . . ."

Two minutes later, a woman with a Texas accent said, "Yes, the price was high, but they were unique. The whole history of them pushed the price, and the curses themselves have almost a poetic quality to them. Besides, the quilts are brilliant. Have you seen one?"

"No. Not yet," Lucas said.

"You should," she said.

"So you'd pay, what, a hundred and twenty-five thousand for one?"

The woman laughed. "No. Not exactly. What happened, was, the owner of the quilts, a Mrs. Coombs, put them up for sale, and we publicized the sale. Now, as it happened, two of the original six quilts had already been acquired by museums . . ."

"Two?"

"Yes. One was donated to the Art Institute of Chicago, and the other to the Walker Gallery in Minneapolis," she said.

"I knew about the Walker."

"The Walker and Chicago. Their original sales price established a price *level*. Then, when the other four came up, the museums that were interested would have reached out to their donor base, informed them of the Armstrong quilt history, and they would have asked for support on this specific acquisition. All of these museums have thousands of supporters. All they had to do was find a hundred and thirty women interested in donating a thousand dollars each.

Remember: these quilts commemorate a woman fighting for her freedom and safety, for her very life, the only way she knew how. And how many affluent veterans of the feminist wars do we have donating to museums? Many, many."

"Ah." That made sense, he thought.

"Yes. So raising the money wouldn't have been a problem," the woman said. "There were a dozen bids on each of them, mostly other regional museums, and, we had the four winners."

"Thank you."

WHO'D SAID IT? The woman with the dangly earrings? The thin-nosed woman? One of them had said, *"Big money."* Lucas turned and looked up at the wall over his bookcase, at a map of St. Paul. Gabriella Coombs had told him that her grandmother "got lucky" with the quilts, and with the money, and the money she had in her former house, and been able to buy in the Como neighborhood.

But houses on Coombs's block didn't cost $470,000, certainly not when she bought, and not even now, after the big price run-up. They might cost $250,000 now, probably not more than two-thirds of that when Coombs bought. Maybe $160,000, or $175,000. And Gabriella said she'd put in money from her old house . . .

There was money missing. Where was it?

FOR THE FIRST TIME, Lucas had the sense of moving forward. Most murders didn't involve big money. Most involved too many six-packs and a handy revolver. But if you had a murder, and there was big money missing . . . the two were gonna be related.

Bucher and Donaldson and Coombs, tied by quilts and methods.

As for the kidnap attempt on Jesse Barth, by somebody in a van, that was most likely a coincidence, he thought now. An odd coincidence, but they happened—and as he'd thought earlier, there were many, many vans around, especially white vans.

The two cases were separate: Coombs/Bucher on one side, Barth/Kline on the other.

ALL OF MARILYN COOMBS'S papers were in her house. He had Gabriella's keys in a bag in his car, he could use them to get in. All that time at Bucher's house, looking at paper, had been wasted. He'd been looking at the wrong paper. He needed Coombs's.

He was on his way north in the Porsche, when John Smith called.

"We showed the tape to Jesse Barth. She swears it's the same van."

"What?"

"That's what she says. The van in the film shows what looks like a dent in the front passenger-side door, and she swears to God, she remembers the dent."

Lucas had no reply, and after a moment, Smith asked, "So. What does that mean? Lucas?"

16

MARILYN COOMBS'S HOUSE was not as organized as Bucher's. There were papers all over the place, some in an old wooden file cabinet, others stuffed in drawers in the kitchen, the living room, and the bedroom. Lucas found a plastic storage bin full of checkbooks trailing back to the '70s, but tax returns going back only four years.

He finally called his contact at the state tax office, and asked her to check Coombs's state returns, to see when she'd gotten the big money.

He had the answer in five minutes—computers made some things easier: "She had a big bump in income for one year, a hundred eighty-six thousand dollars and then, let's see, a total of thirty-three thousand dollars the year before, and thirty-five thousand nine hundred dollars the year after. We queried the discrepancy, and there's an accountant's letter reporting it as a onetime gain from the sale of antique quilts bought two years earlier. I don't have the letter, just the notation. Does that help?"

"I'll call you later and tell you," Lucas said.

He spent an hour scratching through the pile of check registers, stopping now and again to peer sightlessly at the living room wall, thinking about the van. What the fuck was it? Where was the van coming from?

The checks were in no particular order—it seemed that she'd simply tossed the latest one in a drawer, and then, when the drawer got full, dumped the old ones in a plastic tub and started a new pile in the drawer.

He finally found one that entered a check for $155,000. The numbers were heavily inked, as though they'd been written in with some emotion. He went through check registers for six months on either side of the big one, and found only two exceptionally large numbers: a check for $167,500 to Central States Title Company. She'd bought the house.

A few months later, she registered a check for $27,500; and then, a week later, a check payable to U.S. Bank for $17,320. The $27,500 was the sale of her old house, Lucas thought. She'd taken out a swing loan to cover the cost of her new house, and the check to U.S. Bank was repayment.

HE'D BEEN SITTING on a rug as he sorted through the checks, and now he rocked back on his heels. Not enough coming in. There'd been $470,000 up for grabs, and she only showed $155,000 coming in as a lump sum. He closed one eye and divided $470,000 by $155,000 . . . and figured the answer was very close to three.

He got a scrap of paper and did the actual arithmetic: $470,000 divided by three was $156,666. If Marilyn Coombs had gotten a check for that amount, and to use the $1,666 as a little happy-time mad money . . . then she might have deposited $155,000.

Where was the rest? And what the fuck was that van all about?

HE CALLED Archie Carton at Sotheby's, and was told that Carton had left for the day, that the administrative offices were closed, and no, they didn't give out Carton's cell-phone number. Lucas pressed, and was told that they didn't *know* Carton's cell-phone number, which sounded like an untruth, but Lucas was out in flyover country, on the end of a long phone line, and the woman he was talking to was paid to frustrate callers.

"Thanks for your help," he snarled, and rang off. Carton would have to wait overnight: he was obviously the guy to go to. In the meantime . . .

ALICE SCHIRMER WAS the folk art curator at the Walker. She was tall and too thin with close-cropped dark hair and fashionable black-rimmed executive glasses. She wore a dark brown summer suit with a gold silk scarf as a kind of necktie. She said, "I had two of our workpersons bring it out; we've had it in storage."

"Thank you."

"You said there was a woman missing . . . ?" Schirmer asked. She did a finger twiddle at a guy with a two-day stubble and a $400 haircut.

"Yeah. One of the heirs to the Armstrong fortune, in a way," Lucas said. "Granddaughter of the woman who found them. That woman may also have been murdered."

"Mrs. Coombs?"

"Yup."

"Good God," Schirmer said, touching her lips with three bony fingers. "They really do hold a curse. Like the tomb of Tutankhamen."

"Maybe you could palm it off on another museum," Lucas suggested. "Get a picture or a statue back."

"I don't think . . . we'd get enough," Schirmer said, reluctantly. She pointed: "Through here."

They walked past a painting that looked like a summer salad. "Why wouldn't you get enough?"

"I'm afraid the value of the Armstrongs peaked a while ago. Like, the year we got it."

"Really."

"First the stock market had problems, and art in general cooled off, and then, you know, we began to get further and further from the idealism of the early feminists," she said. "The cycle turns, women's folk art begins to slip in value. Here we go."

THEY STEPPED PAST a sign that said GALLERY CLOSED, IN-STALLATION IN PROGRESS, into an empty, white-walled room. The quilt was stretched between naturally finished timber supports; it was a marvel of color: black, brown, red, blue, and yellow rectangles that seemed to shape and reshape themselves into three-dimensional tri-angles that swept diagonally across the fabric field.

"Canada Geese," Schirmer said. "You can almost see them flap-ping, can't you?"

"You can," Lucas agreed. He looked at it for a moment. He didn't know anything about art, but he knew what he liked, and he liked the quilt.

"This was donated by Ms. Bucher?" Lucas asked.

"Yes."

"Where are the curses?" he asked.

"Here." Schirmer's suit had an inside pocket, just like a man's, and she slipped out a mechanical pencil and a penlight. They stood close to the quilt and she pointed out the stitches with the tip of the pencil. "This is an *M*. See it? You read this way around the edge of the piece, 'Let the man who lies beneath this quilt . . .' "

Lucas followed the curse around the quilted pieces, the letters like hummingbird tracks across fallen autumn leaves. "Jesus," he said after a moment. "She was really pissed, wasn't she?"

"She was," Schirmer said. "We have documents from her life that indicate exactly *why* she was pissed. She had the right to be. Her husband was a maniac."

"Huh." A thread of scarlet caught Lucas's eye. He got closer, his nose six inches from the quilt. "Huh."

Had to be bullshit. Then he thought, *no it doesn't*—as far as he could tell, the thread was exactly the same shade as the thread on the spool he'd found behind the stove at Marilyn Coombs's. But that thread had come from Arkansas . . .

He said, "Huh," a third time, and Schirmer asked, "What?"

Lucas stepped back: "How do you authenticate something like this?"

"Possession is a big part of it. We know where Mrs. Coombs bought them, and we confirmed that with the auctioneer," she said. "A couple of Mrs. Armstrong's friends verified that she'd once been a pretty busy quilter, and that she'd made these particular quilts. She signed them with a particular mark." She pointed at the lower-left-hand corner of the quilt. "See this thing, it looks like a grapevine? It's actually a script SA, for Sharon Armstrong. We know of several more of her quilts without the curses, but the same SA. She used to make them when she was working on the ore boats . . . You know about the ore boats?"

"Yeah, Gabriella . . . the missing woman . . . mentioned that Armstrong worked on the boats."

"Yes. She apparently had a lot of free time, and not much to do, so she made more quilts. But that was after Frank was in the asylum, so there was no need for curses."

"Huh." Lucas poked a finger at the quilt. "Can you tell by the fabric, you know, that they're right? For the time? Or the style, or the cloth, or something?"

"We could, if there was any doubt," she said.

Lucas looked at her. "What would I have to do," he asked, "to get a little teeny snip of this red thread, right here?"

AN ACT OF CONGRESS, it turned out, or at least of a judge from the Hennepin County district court.

Schirmer escorted him to the elevator that went down to the parking garage. "If it had been up to me, I'd let you have the snip. But Joe thinks there's a principle involved."

"Yeah, I know. The principle is, 'Don't help the cops,'" Lucas said.

He said it pleasantly and she smiled: "I'm sure it won't be any trouble to get a piece of paper."

"If I weren't looking for Gabriella Coombs . . ."

"You think the snip of thread would make a difference?" she asked.

"Maybe . . . hell, probably not," Lucas admitted. "But I'd like a snip. I'll talk to a judge, send the paper."

"Bring it yourself," she said. "I'd be happy to show you around. I haven't seen you here before . . ."

"When I was in uniform, with the Minneapolis cops, I'd go over to the spoon-and-cherry . . ." He was talking about the Claes Oldenburg spoon bridge in the sculpture garden across the street. He smiled reflexively, and then said, "Never mind."

"You did not *either!*" she said, catching his sleeve. What she meant was, *You did not either fuck in the spoon.*

He shrugged, meaning to tell her that he'd chased people off the spoon a couple of times. Before he could, she leaned close and said, "So'd I." She giggled in an uncuratorlike way. "If I'd been caught and fired, it still would have been worth it."

"Jeez, you crazy art people," Lucas said.

He said goodbye and went down to the car, rolled out of the ramp. A white van was just passing the exit; he cut after it, caught the Minnesota plates—wrong state—and then a sign on the side that said "DeWalt Tools."

Getting psycho, he thought.

WITH NOBODY behind him, he paused at the intersection, fished through his notebook, and found a number for Landford and Margaret Booth, the Donaldson brother-in-law and sister. He dialed and got Margaret: "I need to know the details of how your sister acquired one of the Armstrong quilts, which she donated to the Milwaukee Art Museum."

"Do you think it's something?" she asked.

"It could be."

"I bet Amity Anderson is involved," she said.

"No, no," Lucas said. "This thing is branching off in an odd direction. If you could look through your sister's tax records, though, and let me know how she acquired it, and when she donated it, I'd appreciate it."

"I will do that this evening; but we are going out, so could I call you back in the morning?"

"That'd be fine," Lucas said.

HE LOOKED at his watch. Five o'clock. He called Lucy Coombs, and from the way the phone was snatched up after a partial ring, knew that Gabriella had not been found: "Any word at all?" he asked.

"Nothing. We don't have anybody else to call," Lucy Coombs sobbed. "Where is she? Oh, my God, where is she?"

SMITH COULDN'T tell him. He did say the St. Paul cops were going door-to-door around Marilyn Coombs's neighborhood, looking for anything or anybody who could give them a hint. "And what about the van? Still no thoughts?"

"Not a thing, John. Honest to God, it's driving me nuts."

HE THOUGHT about going over to Bucher's, and looking at her tax records. But he knew the valuation and the date of the donation, and couldn't think of what else he might find there. With a sense of guilt, he went home. Home to dinner, wondering where Gabriella Coombs might be; or her body.

AFTER DINNER, Weather said, "You're really messed up."

"I know," Lucas said. He was in the den, staring at a TV, but the TV was turned off. "Gabriella Coombs is out there. I'm sitting here doing nothing."

"That thread," Weather said. Lucas had told her about the spool of thread at Marilyn Coombs's house, and the thread in the quilt. "If that's the same thread, you're suggesting that something is wrong with the quilts?"

"Yeah, but they all wound up in museums, and the woman who benefited is dead," Lucas said. "It seems like some of the money is missing. She didn't get enough money. Maybe. It's all so long ago. Maybe the Sotheby's guy could tell me about it tomorrow, but Gabriella's out there now . . . And what about the van?"

"You're going crazy sitting here," Weather said. "Why don't you go over to Bucher's place, and see if she has anything on the quilt she donated to the Walker? You'll need to look sooner or later. Why not now? You'd be doing something . . ."

"Because it feels like the wrong thing to do. I feel like I ought to be out driving down alleys, looking for Gabriella."

"You're not going to find her driving up and down alleys, Lucas."

He stood up. "I'm going to eat some cheese and crackers."

"Why don't you take them with you?"

HE DID, a bowl of sliced cheese and water crackers on the passenger seat of the Porsche, munching through them as he wheeled down to Bucher's house. The mansion was brightly lit. Inside, he found the Bucher heirs, six people, four women and two men, dividing up the goodies.

Carol Ann Barker, the woman with the tiny nose, came to greet him. "The St. Paul people said we could begin some preliminary marking of the property," she explained. "People are getting ready to go back home, and we wanted to take this moment with the larger pieces."

Lucas said, "Okay—I'll be in the office, looking at paper. Have you seen check registers anywhere? Stuff going back a few years? Or tax returns . . . ? Anything to do with the buying and donation of the Armstrong quilt?"

"The Armstrong quilt?"

She didn't know what it was, and when Lucas explained, pursed her lips, and said, "She had an annual giving program. There are some records in her office, we looked to see if we could find anything about the Reckless painting. We didn't find anything, but there are documents on donations. Check registers are filed on the third floor, there's a room with several old wooden file cabinets . . . I don't know what years."

Barker showed him the file: it was an inch thick, and while Barker went back to marking furniture, he thumbed through it, looking for the quilt donation. Not there. Looked through it again. Still found nothing.

He had the date of the quilt donation, and found donations of smaller items on dates on either side of it. Scratched his head. Rummaged through the files, looking for more on art, or donations. Finally, gave up and climbed the stairs to the third floor.

The file room was small and narrow and smelled of crumbling plaster; dust and small bits of plaster littered the tops of the eight file cabinets. The room was lit by a row of bare bulbs on the ceiling. Lucas began opening drawers, and in the end cabinets, the last ones he looked at, found a neat arrangement of check registers, filed by date. There was nothing of interest that he could see around the time of the quilt donation; but as he worked backward from the donation, he eventually found a check for $5,000 made out to Marilyn Coombs.

For the quilt? Or for something else Coombs had found? He looked in his notebooks for the date of the quilt auction in New York. The check to Coombs had been issued seven months earlier. Maybe not related; but why hadn't there been any other check to Coombs? In fact, the only large check he'd seen had been to a car dealer.

He was still stuck. Stuck in a small room, dust filtering down on his neck. He ought to be out looking for Gabriella . . .

THE HEIRS were finishing up when Lucas came back down the stairs. Barker asked, "Find anything?"

"No. Listen, have you ever heard of a woman named Marilyn Coombs?"

Barker shook her head: "No . . . should I have?"

"She was an acquaintance of your aunt's, the person who originally found the Armstrong quilts," Lucas said. "She was killed a few days ago . . . If you find anything with the name 'Coombs' on it, could you call me?"

"Sure. Right away. You don't think there's a danger to us?" The other heirs had stopped looking at furniture, and turned toward him.

"I don't think so," he said. "We've got a complicated and confusing problem, we may have had a couple of murders and maybe a kidnapping. I just don't know."

There was a babble of questions then, and he outlined the known deaths. One man asked anxiously, "Do you think it's just random? Or is there a purpose behind the killings? Other than money?"

"I don't know that, either," Lucas said. "Part of this may be coincidence, but I'm starting to think not. If these killings are connected somehow, I would think it would have to do with some special knowledge that would give away the killers. In addition to the money angle, the robbery aspect."

The man exhaled: "Then I'm good. I don't know nothin' about nothin'."

DISCOURAGED, Lucas went back to the car, making a mental list of things to do in the morning, calls to make. He didn't want to call Lucy Coombs, because he didn't want to talk to her again. Instead, he called John Smith, who was home watching television. "Not a thing," Smith said. "I'll get a call as soon as anybody finds anything. Finds a shoelace. So far, we haven't found a thing."

Heading toward home, a fire truck, siren blasting away, went by on a cross street. He could hear more sirens to the south, not far away, and halfway home, with the windows in the car run down, he could smell the distinctive odor of a burning house. He'd never figured out what it was, exactly—insulation, or plaster, or old wood, or

some combination—but he'd encountered it a dozen times in his career, and it never smelled good.

Back at home, he found Weather in the kitchen, sitting at the
counter with a notepad. She asked, "You have time to run to
the store?"

"Yeah, I guess," he said. Ought to be doing something.

"I'm making a list . . ."

He was waiting for the list when his cell phone rang. He looked
at the caller ID: Flowers.

"Yeah?"

"I just got a call from Kathy Barth," Flowers said. "Somebody just
firebombed her house."

17

THE FIRE WAS OUT by the time Lucas got back. He'd driven right past it on the way home, but a block north, hadn't seen the smoke against the night sky, and the flames had been confined to the back side of the house.

Kathy and Jesse Barth were standing in the front yard talking to firemen when Lucas walked across the fire line. Jesse Barth saw him coming and pointed him out to her mother, who snapped something at her daughter, and then started toward Lucas.

"My house is burned down because of you assholes," she shouted.

Lucas thought she was going to hit him, and put his hands up, palms out. "Wait, wait, wait . . . I just heard. Tell me what happened."

"Somebody threw a firebomb through my back window, right in the kitchen, right through the window, everything's burned and screwed up and there's water . . ."

She suddenly went to her knees on the dirty wet grass, weeping. Jesse walked up to stand next to her, put her hand on her mother's shoulder. "Virgil said nothing would happen," the kid said. "Virgil said you'd look out for us."

Lucas shook his head: "We don't know what's going on here," he said. "We can't find anybody who might have tried to pull you off the street, who killed Screw . . ."

"It's those fuckin' Klines, you fuckin' moron," Kathy Barth shouted, trying to get back on her feet. The fireman caught her under one arm, and helped her get up.

Lucas said, "Ah, Jesus, I'm sorry about this . . ."

"It's all my pictures, all of Jesse's things from when she was a kid, all of her school papers, my wedding dress . . ." She took a step toward the house, and the fireman said, "Whoa. Not yet."

Lucas asked him, "How bad is it?"

"The kitchen's a mess. Miz Barth used a fire extinguisher on it, which was pretty brave, and that held it down some, and we got here pretty quick," the fireman said. "The actual fire damage is confined to the kitchen, but there's smoke damage, and foam. Some of the structure under the back of the house could be in trouble."

Lucas asked Kathy Barth, "Do you have insurance?"

"Yes. Part of the mortgage."

"Then you'll get it fixed. Better than it was," Lucas said. "A new kitchen. If it's only smoke, you can save a lot of your stuff, but as soon as the fire guys let you, you've got to get in, and get your photo stuff out."

She came back at him: "Why can't you stop those guys? They're crazy." And to Jesse: "We should never have gotten involved with them. We should never have gone to the cops. Now our house . . . Oh, jeez, our house . . ."

"Tell me what happened," Lucas said.

"We were watching television, and there was a crash in the kitchen—" Jesse began.

Kathy interrupted: "One minute before that I was in the kitchen getting Cheez-Its. I would have been exploded and burned up."

Jesse, continuing: "—and we heard this window crash, this glass, and boom, there was fire all over the kitchen and I was screaming—"

"I ran and got the fire extinguisher from the closet—" Kathy said.

Jesse: "I called nine-one-one and got the fire department to come—"

"I squirted the fire extinguisher but there was fire all over, I could smell the gasoline and it wouldn't go out, the whole kitchen was full of fire and we had to run," Kathy said. She was looking anxiously at the house.

Jesse: "The fire department took forever to get here . . ."

"Six minutes from when the call came in," the fireman said. "Fire was out in seven."

LUCAS FOUND the fireman in charge in the backyard. He was talking with another fireman, pointing up at the roof, broke off when Lucas came up. Lucas flashed his ID: "These folks were part of an investigation we did at the BCA."

"The Klines—they told us," the fireman said.

"Yeah. They say it was a bomb, came in through the window. What do you think?" Lucas asked.

"Our arson guy'll look it over when he gets here, but it could have been. There was a big flash all over the kitchen, all at once. You can still smell the propellant if you get close. Gas and oil."

"A Molotov cocktail?"

"Something on that order," the fireman said. "Maybe like a gallon cider jug."

"Be pretty heavy to throw," Lucas said.

The fireman nodded. "You ever in the Army?"

"No."

"Well, in the Army they've got this thing in Basic Training where you try to throw a dummy grenade through a window from twenty or thirty feet. Most guys can't do it, even with three chances. You got grenades bouncing all over the place," the fireman said. "Most guys couldn't throw a bottle any better. I'd say somebody ran up to the window, and dunked it, like a basketball." He hesitated, then added, "If it was an outsider who did it."

"The alternative would be . . . ?"

The fireman shrugged. "The owner wants a vacant lot. This is a nice piece of property, and it might even be worth more if the house wasn't here. The house isn't so hot. You take the insurance, you sell the lot . . . you move to Minnetonka."

Lucas looked back at the house. He could see Kathy Barth on the front lawn, arms wrapped tight around herself.

"Uh-uh." He shook his head. "She was worried about their pictures being burned, Jesse's school stuff, her wedding dress."

"Well, that's something," the fireman agreed. "You don't see people burning up that kind of thing, not unless it's a revenge trip. They don't burn up their own stuff that much."

The second fireman chipped in: "There was a lot of damage right over the kitchen sink. There are dishes in the sink, and we haven't gone through it yet, but I betcha that bottle landed in the sink, and a lot of the gas wound up in the sink, instead of shooting all over the place. That helped confine it; the arson guys'll know better."

"So who's your arson guy?"

Lucas took down the name of the head arson investigator, and thanked them for their time. Back in the front yard, he asked Kathy, "You got a credit card?"

"Why?"

"Gonna have to stay in a motel tonight," Lucas said. "Probably for a few nights."

She nodded. "Yeah. Okay."

"Got some cash, got an ATM card?"

She nodded again. "We're okay. We're just . . . we just . . ."

"We're just really scared," Jesse finished.

———

LUCAS CALLED the Radisson in downtown St. Paul, got them a room. Told them not to tell anyone else where they were staying. A fireman said he would take them inside to get what they could out of the house. A neighbor volunteered space in her garage, where they temporarily could store whatever they could get out of the house.

The fireman suggested a couple of cleaning companies that could clean up the part of the house that wasn't damaged. "If you guys hadn't been home, if it'd taken another five minutes before somebody reported it, if you hadn't used that fire extinguisher to slow it down, you'd be looking at a hole in the ground. You get it cleaned up, you could be living in it again in a week," he said. "I see it all the time."

LUCAS CALLED Jenkins and Shrake. They were at the White Bear Yacht Club, having a few drinks after a round of golf, part of what they said was an investigation into gambling on golf courses. "Get your asses out of the country club, and get onto the Klines. Jack those fuckers up. My gut feeling is that they're not involved, but I want you to prove it," Lucas told Jenkins.

"Can't prove a negative," Jenkins said.

"Not before this," Lucas said. "You guys are gonna do it, though, or we're gonna do a gay prostitution sting, and your ass will be on the corner."

"We get to wear nylons?" Jenkins asked. He didn't threaten well.

Lucas's voice went dark: "I'm not fuckin' around here, man. We had an attempted kidnapping, we got a dead dog, now we got a firebomb."

"We'll jack them up, no shit," Jenkins promised. "We're on the case."

"Flowers is coming up. He'll get in touch."

OFF THE PHONE, Lucas started walking around the neighborhood, checking the houses on each side of the Barths' house, then across the alley in back, and so on, up and down both streets and the houses on the alley. Four houses up from the Barths, and across the alley, he found an elderly man named Stevens.

"I was cooking some Weight Watchers in the microwave, and I saw a car go through the alley," Stevens said. He was tall, and too thin, balding, with a dark scab at the crest of his head, as if he'd walked into something. They were in the kitchen, and he pointed a trembling hand at the window over the sink, the same arrangement as in the Barths'. "Then, maybe, ten minutes later I was just finished eating, and I took the dish to the trash, and saw more lights in the alley. I didn't see the car, but I think it was the same one. They both had blue headlights."

"Blue?"

"Not blue-blue, but bluish. Like on German cars. You know, when you look in your rearview mirror on the interstate, and you see a whole bunch of yellow lights, and then, mixed in, some that look blue?"

"Yeah. I've got blue lights myself," Lucas said.

"Like that," Stevens said. "Anyway, I'd just sat back down again, and I heard the sirens."

"That was right after you saw the blue headlights."

"I got up to take the dish to the trash during a commercial," Stevens said. "Saw the lights, came in, sat back down. The sirens came before there was another commercial."

"You didn't see what kind of a car it was? The time you actually saw it?"

"Nope. Just getting dark," Stevens said. "But it was a dark-colored car, black, dark blue, dark green, and I think a sedan. Not a coupe."

"Not a van."

"No, no. Not a van. A regular, generic car. Maybe bigger than most. Not a lot bigger, a little bigger. Not an SUV. A car."

"You see many cars back in the alley?" Lucas asked.

"Between five and six o'clock, there are always some, with the garages off the alley. But not with blue lights. None with blue lights. That's probably why I noticed it."

That was all he'd seen: he hadn't heard the bomb, the screaming, hadn't heard anything until the sirens came up. He'd been watching *Animal Planet*.

"Live here alone?" Lucas asked, as he went out.

"Yeah. It sucks."

LUCAS CONTINUED WALKING, found a woman who thought she'd seen a car with bluish lights, but wasn't exactly certain what time. She'd seen it coming out of the alley at least sometime before the sirens, and added nothing to what Stevens said, except to confirm it.

HE CHECKED OUT with the firemen at the Barths'. The arson investigator had shown up, and said he'd have some preliminary ideas in the morning. "But I can tell you, there was gasoline." He sniffed. "Probably from BP. I'd say, ninety-two octane." Lucas frowned and the arson guy grinned: "Pulling your weenie. Talk to you in the morning."

————

LUCAS GOT HOME at midnight and found Weather in bed, reading a book on cottage gardens. "I think we live in a cottage," she said.

"Good to know," he grunted.

"So, I think we should hire a couple of gardeners next year, and get a cottage garden going," she said. "Maybe a white picket fence."

"Picket fence would be nice," he said, grumpily.

She put the book down. "Tell me about it."

HE TOLD her about it, walking back and forth from the bathroom, waving his arms around, getting into his pajamas. He'd brought up a bottle of caffeine-free Diet Coke, with a shot of rum. He sat on the edge of the bed drinking it as he finished, and finally said, "The ultimate problem is, there is no connection between the two cases. But we've got a serious psycho killing people over quilts, and another serious psycho trying to get at the Barths, and they seem to be driving the same van, and goddamnit . . . I can't find a single fuckin' thing in common between the two cases. There is nothing. The Barths—straight political bullshit. Bucher is a robbery-murder, by people who killed at least one and maybe two other people, and somehow involves quilts. They've got jack-shit to do with each other."

He calmed down after a while, and Weather turned out the lights. Lucas usually lay awake in the dark for a while, brooding, even when there wasn't anything to brood about, while Weather dropped off after three deep breaths. This night, she took a half-dozen deep breaths, then lifted her head, said sleepily, "I can think of one thing the cases have in common."

"What's that?"

"You." She rolled back over, and went to sleep.

THAT GAVE HIM something to brood about, so he did, for half an hour, coming up with nothing before he drifted away to sleep. At three-fourteen in the morning, his eyes popped open—he knew it was three-fourteen, exactly, because as soon as he woke up, he reached out and touched the alarm clock, and the illuminated green numbers popped up.

The waking state had not been created by an idea, by a concept, by a solution—rather, it had come directly from bladder pressure, courtesy of a late-night twenty-ounce Diet Coke. He navigated through the dark to the bathroom, shut the door, turned on the light, peed, flushed, turned off the light, opened the door, and was halfway across the dark bedroom when another light went on, this one inside his head:

"That fuckin' Amity Anderson," he said aloud.

HE LAY AWAKE AGAIN, thinking about Amity Anderson. She'd worked for Donaldson, lived only a couple of miles from Bucher, and even closer to the Barths. She was an expert on antiques, and must have been working for Donaldson about the time the Armstrong quilt went through.

But the key thing was, she'd heard him talking about the Kline investigation, and he was almost certain that he'd mentioned the Barths' names. At that same time, Ruffe Ignace had published the first Kline story, mentioning Lucas by name. Amity Anderson could have put it all together.

He had, at that point, already hooked the Donaldson killing to Bucher, and he'd told her that. If he had frightened her, if her purpose had been to distract him from Bucher and Donaldson, to push him back at Kline . . . then she'd almost done it.

He kicked it around for forty-five minutes or so, before slipping off to sleep again. When he woke, at eight, he was not as sure about Anderson as when he'd gone to sleep. There were other possibilities, other people who knew he was working both cases.

But Anderson . . . did she have, or had she ever had, a van?

18

WEATHER WAS in the backyard, playing with Sam, who had a toy bulldozer that he was using as a hammer, pounding a stick down into the turf. "He's got great hand-eye coordination," Weather said, admiring her son's technique. She was wearing gardening gloves, and had what looked like a dead plant in her hand.

"Great," Lucas said. "By the way, you're a genius. That tip last night could turn out to be something."

Sam said, "Whack! Whack!"

Lucas told him, "Go get the football."

Sam looked around, spotted the Nerf football, dropped the bulldozer, and headed for the ball.

"What tip?" Weather asked.

"That I was the common denominator in these cases," Lucas said.

She looked puzzled. "I said that?"

"Yeah. Just before you went to sleep."

"I have no memory of it," she said.

Sam ran up with the ball, stopped three feet from Lucas, and threw it at Lucas's head. Lucas snatched it out of the air and said, "Okay, wide receiver, down, juke, and out."

Sam ran ten feet, juked, and turned in. He realized his mistake, continued in a full circle, went out, and Lucas threw the ball, which hit the kid in the face and knocked him down. Sam frowned for a moment, uncertain whether to laugh or cry, then decided to laugh, and got up and went after the ball.

"Medical school," Lucas said. "On a football scholarship."

"Oh, no. He can play soccer if he's interested in sports," Weather said.

"Soccer? That's not a sport, that's a pastime," Lucas said. "Like whittling or checkers."

"We'll talk about it some other year."

DOWN AT HIS OFFICE, Lucas began a list:

• *Call Archie Carton at Sotheby's.*

• *Call the Booths about the quilt donation to the Milwaukee Art Museum.*

• *Get a court order for a snip of red thread from the Walker Gallery quilt.*

• *Call Jenkins and Shrake, and find out where Flowers is.*

• *Find out exactly when Amity Anderson worked for Donaldson, and how she would have known Bucher, Coombs—through the quilts, probably—and Toms, the dead man in Des Moines.*

• *Start a biography on Amity Anderson.*

"Carol!"

Carol popped her head in the door. "Yup?"

"Is that Sandy kid still around?"

"Yeah."

"Get her ass in here."

BOTH SHRAKE'S and Flowers's cell phones were off. Jenkins answered his and said, "Lucas, Jesus, Kline is gonna get a court order to keep us away from him."

"What happened? Where are you?"

"I'm up in Brainerd. Kline Jr. was four-wheeling yesterday up by the family cabin," Jenkins said. "He and his pals went around drinking in the local bars in the evening."

"What about his old man?" Lucas asked.

"Shrake looked him up last night. He says he was home the whole time, talked to a neighbor late, about the Twins game when they were taking out the garbage, the game was just over. Shrake checked, and that was about the time of the fire."

"So they're alibied up."

"Yeah. And they're not smug about it. They're not like, 'Fuck you, figure this out.' They're pissed that we're still coming around. Junior, by the way, is gonna run for his old man's Senate seat, and says they're gonna beat the sex charge by putting Jesse on the stand and making the jurors figure out about how innocent she was."

"That could work," Lucas admitted. "You know where Flowers is?"

"I talked to him last night," Jenkins said. "He was on his way to see the Barths. He'd be getting in really late, he might still be asleep somewhere."

"Okay. That's what I needed. Go home," Lucas said.

"One more thing."

"Yeah?"

Jenkins said, "I don't know if this means anything to you. Probably not."

"What?"

"I was talking to Junior Kline. He and his buddies were all wrapped up in Carhartt jackets and boots and concho belts and CAT hats, and they all had Leathermans on their belts and dirt and all that, and somehow . . . I got the feeling that they might be singin' on the other side of the choir. A bunch of butt-bandits."

"Really?"

"Yeah. And you know what? I don't think I'm wrong," Jenkins said. "I don't know how that might reflect on the attacks on the Barths . . . I mean, I just don't know."

"Neither do I," Lucas said.

HE GOT CAROL started on getting a court order for a snip of thread from the quilt.

SANDY HURRIED IN. "You called?"

Lucas said, "There's a woman named Amity Anderson. I've got her address, phone number, and I can get her Social Security number and age and all that. I need the most complete biography you can get me. I need it pretty quick. She can't know about it."

Sandy shrugged: "No problem. I can rip most of it off the Net. Be nice if I could see her federal tax returns."

"I can't get you the federals, but I can get you the state . . ."

THE BOOTHS CAME through with a date on the donation to the Milwaukee museum. "The woman who handled the donation for the museum was Tricia Bundt. B-U-N-D-T. She still works there and she'll be in this morning. Her name is on all the letters to Claire," Landford Booth said.

"She related to the Bundt-cake Bundts?" Lucas asked.

Booth chuckled, the first time Lucas had seen anything that resembled humor in him. "I asked her that. She isn't."

ARCHIE CARTON CAME through on the quilts. "The quilts had two owners. One was a Mrs. Marilyn Coombs, who got a check for one hundred sixty thousand dollars and fifty-nine cents, and one to Cannon Associates, for three hundred and twenty thousand dollars."

"Who's Cannon Associates?"

"That I don't know," Carton said. "All we did was give them a check. The dealings on the quilts were mostly between our folk art specialist at the time, James Wilson, and Mrs. Coombs. The company, Cannon, I don't know . . . Let me see what I can get on the check."

"Can I talk to Wilson?" Lucas asked.

"Only if you're a really good Anglican," Carton said.

"What?"

"I'm afraid James has gone to his final reward," Carton said. "He was an intensely Anglican man, however, so I suspect you'd find him in the Anglican part of heaven. Or hell, depending on what I didn't know about James."

"That's not good," Lucas said.

"I suspect James would agree . . . I'm looking at this check, I actually have an image of it, it was deposited to a Cannon Associates account at Wells Fargo. Do you want the account number?"

"Absolutely . . ."

"CAROL!"

She popped in: "What?"

"I need to borrow Ted Marsalis for a while," Lucas said. "Could you call over to Revenue and run him down? I need to get an old check traced."

"Are we hot?"

"Maybe. I mean, we're always hot, but right now, we're maybe *hot*."

H E   G O T Tricia Bundt on the phone, explained that he was investigating a murder that might somehow involve the Armstrong quilts. "We're trying to track down what happened at the time they were disposed of . . . at the time they were donated. I know you got the donation from Claire Donaldson, but could you tell me, was there anybody else on the Donaldson side involved in the transaction? Or did Mrs. Donaldson handle all of it?"

"No, she didn't," Bundt said. Bundt sounded like she had a chipped front tooth, because all of her sibilant *S*s whistled a bit. "Actually, I only talked to her twice. Once, when we were working through the valuation on the quilts, and then at the little reception we had with our acquisitions committee, when it came in."

"So who handled it from the Donaldson side?"

"Her assistant," Bundt said. "Let me see, her name was something like . . . Anita Anderson? That's not quite right . . ."

"Amity Anderson." He got a little thrill from saying the name.

"That's it," Bundt said. "She handled all the paperwork details."

Lucas asked, "Could you tell me, how did you nail down the evaluation on the quilt?"

"That's always difficult," Bundt said. "We rely on experienced appraisers, people who operate quilt galleries, previous sales of similar quilts, and so on," she whistled.

"Then let me ask you this," Lucas said. "Do museums really care about what the appraisal is? I mean, you're getting it for free, right?"

"Oh, we *do* care," Bundt said. "If we simply inflated everything, so rich people could get tax write-offs, then pretty soon Congress would change the rules and we wouldn't get anything."

"Hmph."

"Really," she said. But she said "really" the way a New Yorker says "really," which means "maybe not really."

"Does the quilt still have its original value?" Lucas asked.

"Hard to say," she said. "There are no more of them, and their creator is dead. That always helps hold value. They're exceptional quilts, even aside from the curses."

Lucas thanked her for her help, and just before he rang off, she said, "You didn't ask me if I was related to the Bundt-cake Bundts."

"Didn't occur to me," he said.

"Really."

AS SOON AS he hung up, his phone rang again, and Carol said, "I'm ringing Ted Marsalis for you."

Marsalis came on a minute later, and Lucas said, "I need you to check with your sources at Wells Fargo. I'm looking to see what happened to an account there, and who's behind it . . ."

LUCAS SAT BACK at his desk and closed his eyes. He was beginning to see something back there: a major fraud. Two rich old ladies, both experienced antique buyers, buy quilts cheaply from a well-known quilt stitcher, and then turn around and donate them to museums.

For this, they get a big tax write-off, probably saving $50,000 or $60,000 actual dollars from their tax bills. Would that mean anything to people as rich as they were? Of course it would. That's how rich people stayed rich. Watch your pennies and the dollars take care of themselves.

The donations established the value of the quilts and created a stir in the art community. The remaining quilts are then moved off to Sotheby's, where they sell for equally large prices to four more museums. Why the museums would necessarily be bidding, he didn't know. Could be fashion, could be something he didn't see.

In any case, Marilyn Coombs gets enough money to buy a house, and put a few bucks in her pocket. Two-thirds of the money disappears into Cannon Associates, which, he would bet, was none other than Amity Anderson.

How that led to the killings, he didn't know yet. Anderson had to have an accomplice. Maybe the accomplice was even the main motivator in the whole scheme . . .

He got on the phone to Jenkins again: "How would you feel about around-the-clock surveillance?"

"Oh, motherfucker . . . don't do this to me."

MORE DOODLING on a notepad, staring out a window. Finally, he called up the Amon Carter Museum in Fort Worth, and got the head of the folk arts department, and was told that the curator who had supervised the acquisition of the quilt had moved on; she was now at the High Museum in Atlanta.

Lucas got the number, and called her. Billie Walker had one of the smooth Southern Comfort voices found in the western parts of the Old South, where the word *bug* had three vowels between the *b* and *g* and they all rhymed with *glue.*

"I remember that clearly," she said. "No, we wouldn't have bought it normally, but an outside foundation provided much of the money. A three-to-one match. In other words, if we came up with thirty thousand dollars, they would provide ninety thousand."

"Is this pretty common?"

"Oh my, yes. That's how we get half of our things," Walker said.

"Find some people willing to chip in, then find a foundation willing to come up with a matching grant. There are many, many foundations with an interest in the arts."

"Do you remember the name of this one?" Lucas asked.

"Of course. In my job, you don't forget a funding source. It was the Thune Foundation of Chicago." Lucas asked her how she spelled it. "T-h-u-n-e."

"Did you have to dig them out of the underbrush to get the donation? Or did they come to you?"

"That's the odd thing. They volunteered. Never heard from them before," she said. "Took no sucking-up at all."

Lucas scribbled *Thune* on his desk pad. "Have you ever heard of a woman named Amity Anderson?"

"No . . . not that I recall. Who is she?"

HE'D HEARD the name Thune, he thought. He didn't know where, but he'd heard it, and recently. At Bucher's, one of the relatives? He couldn't put his finger on it, and finally dialed Chicago directory assistance, got a number for the Thune Foundation, and five minutes later, was talking to the assistant director.

He explained, briefly, what he was up to, and then asked, "Do the names Donaldson, Bucher, or Toms mean anything to you?"

"Well, Donaldson, of course. Mr. Thune owned a large brewery in Wisconsin. He had no sons, but one of his daughters married George Donaldson—this would have been way back—and they became the stalwarts of this foundation."

"Really."

"Yes."

"Claire Donaldson?" Lucas asked. "I believe she was the last Donaldson?"

"Yes, she was. Tragic, what happened. She was on our board for several years, chairwoman, in fact, for many years, although she'd stepped aside from that responsibility before she died."

"Did she have anything to do with grants? Like, to museums?"

"She was on our grants committee, of course . . ."

LUCAS GOT OFF the phone and would have said, "Ah-ha!" if he hadn't thought he'd sound like a fool.

A new piece: even the prices paid for the quilts in the auction were a fraud. He'd bet the other purchases were similarly funded. He'd have Sandy nail it down, but it gave him the direction.

A very complicated scheme, he thought, probably set up by Anderson and her accomplice.

Create the quilts. Create an ostensible value for them by donating them to museums, with appraisals that were, he would bet, as rigged as the later sales.

Sell the quilts at Sotheby's to museums who feel that they're getting a great deal, because most of the money is coming from charitable foundations. Why would the foundations give up money like that? Because of pressure from their founders . . .

The founders would be banned from actually getting money from the foundations themselves. That was a definite no-no. But this way, they got it, and they got tax write-offs on top of it.

HE PUT DOWN boxes with arrows pointing to the boxes: Anderson sets it up for a cut; the funders, Bucher and Donaldson, get tax write-offs. At the Sotheby's sale, the money is distributed to Coombs and Cannon Associates—Amity Anderson. Anderson kicks back part of it—a third?—to Donaldson and Bucher . . .

What a great deal. Completely invisible.

Then maybe, Donaldson cracks, or somebody pushes too hard, and Donaldson has to go. Then Bucher? That would be . . . odd.

And what about Toms? Where did he fit in?

TED MARSALIS called back. "The Wells Fargo account was opened by a woman named Barbra Cannon," he said. "Barbra without the middle *a*, like in Barbra Streisand. There was a notation on the account that said the owners expected to draw it down to much lower levels fairly quickly, because they were establishing an antiques store in Palm Springs, and were planning to use the money for original store stock. Did I tell you this was all in Las Vegas?"

"Las Vegas?"

"In Nevada," Marsalis said.

"I know where it is. So what happened?"

"So they drew the money down, right down to taking the last seven hundred dollars out of the account from an ATM, and that's the last Wells Fargo heard from them," Marsalis said. "After the seven hundred dollars, there were six dollars left in the account. That was burned up by account charges over the years, so now, there's nothing. Account statements sent to the home address were returned. There's nobody there."

"Shit."

"What can I tell you?" Marsalis said.

"What'd the IRS have to say about that?" Lucas asked.

"I don't think they said anything. You want me to call them?"

"Yeah. Do that. That much money can't just go up in smoke." Lucas said.

"Sure it can," Marsalis said. "You're a cop. You ever heard of drug dealers? This is how they make money go away."

———

DRUG DEALERS? He didn't even want to think about that. He had to focus on Amity Anderson. Jenkins and Shrake would stake her out, see who she hung with. He needed as much as he could get, because this was all so obscure . . . He was pretty sure he had it right, but what if the red thread came back as something made only in Wisconsin? Then the whole structure would come down on his head.

HE CALLED SANDY: "Anything on Anderson?"

"A lot of raw records, but I haven't coordinated them into a report, yet," she said.

"I don't want a fu . . . friggin' PowerPoint—where'd she work? You look at her tax stuff?"

"She worked at her college as a teaching assistant, at Carleton College in Northfield, and then she worked at a Dayton's store in St. Paul," Sandy said. "Then she worked for Claire Donaldson, which we know about, and then she went straight to the Old Northwest Foundation, where she still is," Sandy said. "Also, I found out, she has a little tiny criminal record."

"What was it?" Something involving violence, he hoped.

"She got caught shoplifting at Dayton's. That's why she left there, I think. The arrest is right at the time she left."

"Huh."

"Then I've got all kinds of tax stuff, but I have to say, I don't think there's anything that would interest you," Sandy said. "She does claim a mortgage exemption. She bought her house six years ago for a hundred and seventy thousand dollars, and she has a mortgage for a hundred and fifty thousand, so she put down about the minimum—like seventeen thousand dollars."

"Any bank records?"

"Not that I've gotten, but she only got like forty dollars in interest on her savings account last year. And she doesn't report interest or capital gains on other investments accounts."

"Car?" Lucas asked.

"I ran her through DMV," Sandy said. "She has a six-year-old Mazda. One speeding ticket, three years ago."

"Ever own a van?"

"There's no record of one."

THERE WAS MORE of the same—but overall, Amity Anderson's biography seemed to paint a picture of a woman who was keeping her head above water, but not easily.

"This does not," Lucas said to Sandy, "seem like the biography of a woman who came into an untaxed quarter-million bucks a few years ago."

"It isn't," Sandy said. "I'll keep looking, but if she's got the money, she's hidden it pretty well. Did you ever think about the possibility that she just bought antiques? That her house is her bank?"

"I've been in her house. It's not full of antiques."

"Well, maybe there's a big lump of cash moldering in the basement. But if I were her, I would have spent at least some of it on a new car."

"Yeah. Damnit. This isn't turning out the way I thought it would," Lucas said.

HE SENT SANDY back to the salt mines—actually, an aging Dell computer and a stool—to continue the research, and called Jenkins: "You talk to Shrake?"

"Yeah. We figure to start tracking her tonight. We don't

know what she looks like, so trying to pick her up outside that foundation . . . that'd be tough."

"Tonight's fine. I wasn't serious about twenty-four hours . . . put her to bed, keep her there for half an hour, pick her up in the morning," Lucas said. "Mostly, I want to know who she hangs with. Need a big guy: somebody who could snatch Jesse Barth off the street."

FLOWERS LOUNGED in the door, looking too fresh. "Sat up most of the night with the Barths. They're scared spitless," he said.

"Well, they got a firebomb through the kitchen window. They say."

"Oh, they did," Flowers said. He moved over to the visitor's chair, sat down, and propped one foot on the edge of Lucas's desk. "I talked to the arson guy—there was no glass in the sink, but there was some burned stuff that he thinks is what's left of a half-gallon paper milk jug. Probably had a burning rag stuck in the spout. Said it'd be like throwing a ball of gas through the window; better than a bottle."

"Yeah?"

"Yes." He propped another foot over the first. "He says wine bottles work fine if you're throwing them onto tanks, but if you throw them onto an ordinary kitchen floor, half the time they'll just bounce along, and not break."

"Really," Lucas said.

"Yup. So what're we doing?"

"I got this concept . . ."

"We needed a concept," Flowers said. "Like, bad."

Lucas explained about Amity Anderson. Flowers listened and said, "So call this chick at the Walker and find out if she dealt with Amity Anderson on the Bucher deal."

Lucas nodded: "I was about to do that."

ALICE SCHIRMER was mildly pissed: "Well, we got the court order, and your lab person was here, and we butchered the quilt. Hope you're happy."

Lucas had the feeling that she was posing. He had no time for that, and snapped: "There are several people dead, and one missing and probably dead. For an inch of thread or whatever . . ."

"I'm sorry, let's start over," she said quickly. "Hello, this is Alice."

Lucas took a breath. "When you dealt with Bucher on the quilt, did you ever meet a woman named Amity Anderson?"

"Amity? I know Amity Anderson, but she wasn't involved in the Bucher bequest," Schirmer said.

"Where do you know her from? Amity?" Lucas asked.

"She works for a foundation here that provides funding for the arts."

"That's it? You don't know her socially, or know who she hangs with, or know about any ties that might take her back to Bucher?"

"No, I've never mixed with her socially," Schirmer said. "I know she was associated for a while with a man named Don Harvey, but Don moved to Chicago to run the New Gallery there. That was a couple of years ago."

"A boyfriend?"

"Yes. They were together for a while, but I don't know what she's been up to lately," Schirmer said.

"Uh, just a moment." Lucas took the phone away from his face and frowned.

Flowers asked, "What?"

Lucas went back to the phone. "I had understood . . . from a source . . . that Amity Anderson is gay."

"Amity? No-o-o, or maybe, you know, she likes a little of both," Schirmer said. "She definitely had a relationship with Don, and knowing Don, there was nothing platonic about it. With good ol' Don, it was the more, the merrier."

"Huh. What does Don look like? Football-player type?"

She laughed. "No. He's a little shrimp with a big mouth and sup- posedly, a gargantuan . . . You know. I doubt that he ever lifted any- thing heavier than a glass of scotch."

"You say he runs a gallery," Lucas said. "An antique gallery? Or would he know about antiques?"

"He's a paintings-and-prints guy. Amity's an antique savant, though," Schirmer said. "I expect she'll wind up as a dealer someday. If she can get the capital."

"Okay. Listen, keep this conversation to yourself," Lucas said.

"Sure," she said.

"And that thread . . ."

"From the butchered quilt?" Now she was kidding.

"That one. Is it on the way back here?" Lucas asked.

"It is. Your man left here more than an hour ago."

LUCAS SAID to Flowers, "Amity Anderson lied to me, in a way most people wouldn't do. I asked her about boyfriends and she said she's gay. I bought it at the time—but it turns out she's not."

"That make's a difference?" Flowers asked.

"It does if you need somebody large to carry a fifty-thousand-dollar table," Lucas said. "Somebody you can trust with murder."

THE LAB MAN SAID, "We've got tests to do, but I took a look at it with a 'scope: it's identical. I mean, identical. I'd be ninety-seven percent surprised if it didn't come off the same spool. We're gonna do some tests on the dye, and so on, just to nail it down."

"The curator said you really butchered the quilt."

"Yeah. We took a half-inch of loose thread off an overturned corner. You couldn't find the same spot without a searchlight and a bloodhound."

LUCAS HUNG UP. Flowers again asked, "What?"

"There was a major fraud, probably turned over a half-million dollars or so, involving all these people. Think that's enough to kill for?"

"You can go across the river in the wintertime and get killed for a ham sandwich," Flowers said. "But you told me it was a theft, not a fraud."

"Here's what I think now," Lucas said. "I think they all got to know each other through this fraud. That may have seemed like a little game. Or maybe, the rich people didn't even know the quilts were fake. But that opened the door to these guys, who looked around, and cooked up another idea—get to know these people a little, figure out what they had, and how much it was worth, and then, kill them to get it."

"Kind of crude, for arty people."

"Not crude," Lucas said. "Very selective. You had to know exactly what you were doing. You take a few high-value things, but it has to be the obscure stuff. Maybe the stuff kept in an attic, and forgotten about. An old painting that was worth five hundred dollars, when you bought it fifty years ago, but now it's worth half a million. They looked for people who were isolated by time: old, widows and widowers, with heirlooms going back a hundred or a hundred and fifty years. So a few pieces are missing, a pot here, a table there, a painting from the attic, who's going to know? Some distant nephew? Who's going to know?"

Flowers stood up, stuffed his hands in his pockets, wandered over and looked at a five-foot-tall wall map of Minnesota. "It's the kind of thing that could piss you off," he said. "If you're civilized at all."

"Yeah. You can't get crazier than that, except that, for money . . . you can kind of understand it, in its own insane way. But now they're starting to swat people who just get in the way." He peered past Flowers at the wall map. "Where the fuck is Gabriella Coombs? Where are you, honey?"

19

LUCAS WAS SITTING in the den with a drawing pad and pen, trying to figure how to get at Amity Anderson, when his cell phone rang. He slipped it out of his pocket and looked at the caller ID: Shrake. He glanced at his watch: ten minutes after midnight. Shrake had taken over the surveillance of Amity Anderson, and was due to go home. He flipped open the phone: "Yeah?"

"What, you put me and Jenkins on the gay patrol, right? We pissed you off, so you sent Jenkins to watch Boy Kline, and now . . ."

"What are you talking about?"

"Amity Anderson went on a date, lot of kissy-face, had dinner, spent three hours at her date's town house, and now we're headed back to Anderson's house. Soon as I get her in bed, I'm going back to her date's place and see if *I* can get a date," Shrake said.

"She *is* gay?"

"Either that or she's dating the swellest looking guy I've ever seen," Shrake said. "World-class ass, and red hair right down to it."

"Goddamnit. Anderson's supposed to have a boyfriend," Lucas said.

"I can't help you there, Lucas. Her date tonight definitely wasn't a boy," Shrake said. "What do you want me to do?"

"Go home."

"You don't want an overnight?"

"Nah. We're looking for her friends," Lucas said. "Give it half an hour after lights-out . . . Hell, give it an hour . . . then go on home. Jenkins'll pick her up in the morning."

IN THE MORNING, after Weather and Letty had gone, and the housekeeper had settled in with Sam, Lucas went out to the garage, and walked around the nose of the Porsche to a door in the side wall. The door opened to the flight of steps that went up to what the builders called a "bonus room"—a semi-finished warm-storage loft above the garage.

Lucas had supervised the construction of the house from top to bottom, had driven the builders crazy with questions and unwanted advice, had issued six dozen change orders, and, in the end, had gotten it right; and when the builders had walked away, satisfied, he'd added a couple things on his own.

He looked back over his shoulder to the entry from the house, then knelt on the bottom landing, groped under the edge of the tread of the first step, felt the metal edge. He worked it for a moment with his fingernail, and it folded out, like the blade of a pocketknife.

He pulled on the blade, hard, and the face of the step popped loose. A drawer. He would have bet that not even a crime-scene crew could have found it. Inside, he kept his special cop stuff: two cold pistols with magazines; a homemade silencer that fit none of his guns, and that he kept meaning to throw away, but never had; an old-fashioned lead-and-leather sap; a hydraulic door-spreader that he'd picked up from a burglary site; five thousand dollars in twenty-dollar bills in a paper bank envelope; an amber-plastic bottle of amphetamines; a box of surgical gloves lifted from Weather's office; and a battery-powered lock rake.

The rake was about the size and shape of an electric toothbrush. He took it out of the drawer, along with a couple of latex gloves, slipped the drawer back in place, pushed the blade-grip back in place, and took the rake and gloves to his truck.

Back inside the house, he got Weather's digital camera, a pocket-sized Canon G7, got his jacket, and told the housekeeper he was leaving. Kissed Sam.

On the phone to Jenkins: "You still got her?"

"YEAH. She just got in the elevator. So what do I do now, sit on my ass?"

"Ah . . . yeah," Lucas said. "Go on over and sit in the Starbucks."

"Listen, if she wants to get out, there's a back stairs that comes out on the other side of the building," Jenkins said. "Or she can walk down into the Skyways off the elevators on the second floor, or she could come all the way down and walk out the front door. There's too much I can't see, and if I guess wrong, I'll be standing here with my dick in my hand."

"She shouldn't have any idea that we're watching her, so she's not gonna be sneaking around," Lucas said.

"I'm just saying," Jenkins warned. "We either get three or four guys over here, or she could walk on us."

"I know what you're saying. Just . . . sit. Call me if you see her moving."

HER HOUSE WAS two minutes away in the truck. He parked under a young maple tree, a half block out, watched the street for a moment, then slipped the rake in one pocket, the camera and gloves in the other, and walked down to her door. The door was right out in the open, but with tall ornamental cedars on each side. A dental office building was across the street, with not much looking at him.

He rang the doorbell, holding it for a long time, listening to the muffled buzz. No reaction; no movement, no footfalls. He rang it again, then pulled open the storm door, as if talking to somebody inside, and pushed the lock-snake into the crappy 1950s Yale. The rake chattered for a moment, then the lock turned in his hand. He was in.

"Hello?" he called. "Hello? Amity? Amity?"

Nothing. A little sunlight through the front window, dappling the carpet and the back of the couch; little sparkles of dust in the light of the doorway to the kitchen. "Amity?"

He stepped inside, shut the door, pulled on the latex gloves, did a quick search for a security system. Got a jolt when he found a keypad inside the closet next to the front door. And then noticed that the '80s-style liquid-crystal read-out was dead.

He pushed a couple of number-buttons: nothing.

He could risk it, he thought. If the cops came, maybe talk his way out of it. But still: move quick. He hurried through the house, looking for anything that might be construed as an antique. Found a music box—was she a music-box collector? That would be interesting. He took a picture of it. Up to the bedroom, taking shots of an oil painting, a rocking chair, a drawing, a chest of drawers that seemed too elegant for the bedroom.

Into the bathroom: big tub, marijuana and scented candle wax, bottles of alprazolam and Ambien in the medicine cabinet. Stress? Under the sink, a kit in a velvet bag. He'd seen kits like that, from years ago, but what . . . He opened it: ah, sure. A diaphragm. So she swung both ways. Or had, at one time.

His cell phone rang, and vibrated at the same time, in his pocket, nearly giving him a heart attack.

Carol: "Mrs. Coombs called. She wants to talk to you. She's really messed up."

"I'll get back to her later," Lucas said.

"She's pretty messed up," Carol said.

Not a goddamn thing he could do about it, either. He snapped: "Later. Okay?"

QUICK THROUGH the bedroom closet, through the chest of drawers, under the bed; looked down the basement, called "Hello?" and got nothing but a muffled echo. Back up the stairs, into a ground-floor bedroom used as an office. He'd been inside a long time now—five, six minutes—and the pressure was growing.

The office had an ornate table used as a desk; everything expensive looked like mahogany to Lucas, and this looked like mahogany, with elaborately carved feet. He took a picture of it. The desk had one center drawer, full of junk: paper clips, envelopes, ticket stubs, a collection of old ballpoints, pencils, rubber bands. He had noticed with the upstairs closets that while the visible parts of the house were neatly kept, the out-of-sight areas were a mess.

The office had two file cabinets, both wooden. Neither looked expensive. He opened a drawer: papers, paid bills. Not enough time to check them. Another drawer: taxes, but only going back four years. He pulled them out, quickly, looked at the bottom numbers on the federal returns: all in the fifties. Two more drawers full of warranties, car-maintenance records—looked at the maintenance records, which covered three different cars, all small, no vans—employment stuff and medical records.

No time, no time, he thought.

He checked a series of personal photographs on the wall behind the desk. One showed a much younger Amity in a graduation gown with several other people, also in gowns, including a guy large enough to carry a $50,000 table. The guy looked familiar, somehow, but Lucas couldn't place him. He turned off the camera's flash, so that it wouldn't reflect off the protective glass, and took a picture of the photograph.

Inside too long.

Damn. If he could have half an hour with the desk drawers . . . But then, he had the sense that she was careful.

He took a last look around, and left, locking the door behind himself.

BACK IN THE TRUCK, he called Jenkins. "I drank about a gallon of coffee. If my heart quits, it's your fault," Jenkins said. "I ain't seen her, but I called her office ten minutes ago, and she was in a conference. I told them I'd call back."

"Don't want to make her curious," Lucas said.

"I'll take care."

TEN MINUTES to a Target store. He pulled the memory card out of the camera and at the Kodak kiosk, printed five-by-sevens of Amity Anderson's furniture. In the photos, it sure didn't look like much; but what'd he know?

But he did know somebody who'd know what it was. He looked up John Smith's cell-phone number and called him: "I need to talk to the Widdlers about some furniture. Want to see if it's worth something."

"On the case? Or personal?"

"Maybe semirelated to the case, but I don't know. I think they're done at Bucher's, right?"

"Yup. They're out in Edina. You need to see them right away?"

"I'm over on the airport strip, I can be there in ten minutes."

"Let me get you the address . . ."

THE WIDDLERS HAD a neat two-story building in old Edina, brown brick with one big display window in front. A transparent shade protected the window box from sunlight, and behind the window, a small oil painting in an elaborate wood frame sat on a desk something like Amity Anderson's, but this desk was smaller and better-looking. The desk, made from what Lucas guessed was mahogany, sat on a six-by-four-foot oriental carpet. The whole arrangement looked like a still-life painting.

Lucas pushed through the front door; a bell tinkled overhead. Inside, the place was jammed with artifacts. He couldn't think of another word for the stuff: bottles and pottery and bronze statues of naked girls with geese, lamps and chairs and tables and desks and busts. The walls were hung with paintings and rugs and quilts and framed maps.

He thought, *quilts*. Hum.

A stairway went up to the second floor, and looking up the stairwell, he could see even more stuff behind the second-floor railing. A severe-looking portrait of a woman, effective, though it was really nothing more than an arrangement in gray and black, hung on the first landing of the stairway. She was hatchet-faced, but broad through the shoulders, and as with the photograph he'd seen that morning, he had the feeling that he'd seen her before.

He was peering at it when a woman's voice said, "Can I help you?"

He jumped and turned. A motherly woman, white haired and sixtyish, had snuck up behind him from the back room, and was looking pleased with herself for having done it; or at least, amused that she'd startled him. He said, "Uh, jeez, is Leslie around? Or Jane?"

"No. They're in Minnetonka on an appraisal. They won't be back until after lunch, and they'll be in tomorrow . . . If there's anything I can help you with?"

"Oh, I had some questions about some furniture . . ." He looked back again at the painting. "That woman looks familiar, but I can't place her."

"That's Leslie's mom," the shop lady said. "Painted by quite a talented local artist, James Malone. Although I think he has since moved to New York City."

A LITTLE CLICK in the back of Lucas's mind.

Of course it was Leslie's mom. He could see Leslie's face in the woman's face, although the woman was much thinner than the Leslie that Lucas had met, who was running to fat.

But he hadn't always been fat, Lucas knew. Lucas knew that because Leslie wasn't fat in the picture in Amity Anderson's office. Amity Anderson and the Widdlers: and Leslie was easily big enough to carry a $50,000 table out of a house.

In fact, Leslie was a horse. You didn't see it, because of the bow ties and the fussy clothes and the fake antiquer-artsy accent he put on, but Leslie was a goddamn Minnesota farm boy, probably grew up humping heifers around the barn, or whatever you did with heifers.

The woman said, "So, uh . . ."

"I'll just come back tomorrow," Lucas said. "If I have time. No big deal, I was passing by."

"They should be in right at nine, because I'm off tomorrow," the woman said.

"I'll talk to them then," Lucas said. On the way out the door, he stopped, as with an afterthought: "Do you know, did they take the van?"

The woman was puzzled: "They don't have a van."

"Oh." Now Lucas put a look of puzzlement on *his* face. "Maybe I'm just remembering wrong, but I saw them at an auction and they were driving a van. A white van. I thought."

"Just a rental. They rent when they need one, it's a lot cheaper than actually owning," the woman said. "That's what I do, when I'm auctioning."

Lucas nodded: "Hey. Thanks for the help."

OUTSIDE IN the parking lot, he sat in the truck for a moment, then got on the phone to John Smith:

"If you happen to see them, don't tell the Widdlers I was going out to their place," Lucas said.

After a moment of silence, Smith said, "You gotta be shittin' me."

"Probably nothing, but I need to look them up," Lucas said. "How did they get involved in assessing the Bucher place?"

"I called them," Smith said. "I asked around, they were recommended. I called them and they took it on."

"But you didn't call them because somebody suggested them specifically?" Lucas asked. "Somebody at Bucher's?"

"Nope. I called a guy at the Minneapolis museum who knows about antiques, and he gave me two names. I looked them up in the Yellow Pages and picked the Widdlers because they were closer."

"All right," Lucas said. "So: if you talk to them, don't mention me."

NEXT, he got Carol at the office:

"Get somebody—not Sandy—and have him go out to all the local car-rental agencies and see if there's a record of a Leslie or Jane Widdler—W-I-D-D-L-E-R—renting a white van. Or any van.

"Then, Sandy is doing research on a woman named Amity Anderson. I want her to keep doing that, but put it on the back burner for today. Right now, I need to know everything about Leslie and Jane Widdler. They're married, they own an antique store in

Edina. I think they went to college at Carleton. I want a bunch of stuff figured out by the time I get back there."

"When are you getting back?"

"Half hour," Lucas said.

"Not much time," Carol said.

"Sandy's gotta hurry," Lucas said. "I'm in a really big fuckin' hurry. And get that rental check going. Going right now."

Carol got in the last word: "Lucy Coombs called again."

20

"HE WAS A BIG GUY, dark complexion, blue eyes. Asking about a white van."

"A van? We haven't had a van in years," Jane Widdler said. "I'm not getting a clear picture of him. You say, a big guy?"

The sales assistant nodded. "He looked . . . sort of French. Big shoulders, black hair with a little salt and pepper. Good-looking, but tough," she said. "He had a scar that started up in his hair and came down across his eye. Not an ugly scar, a white line."

"He wasn't as big as Leslie," Jane Widdler suggested.

"No . . . not as tall, and also . . ." Widdler's sales assistant groped for a word.

"Not so fat," Jane Widdler said.

"He looked like he was in really good shape," the sales assistant said, staying away from the topic of Leslie's heft. "He didn't look like an antiques person."

"I might know who he is," Jane Widdler said. She smiled, just a little, because of the Botox. "It might be better if you didn't mention him to Leslie. I think this man is . . . an old friend of mine. There's nothing going on, but I don't want Leslie to get upset."

The sales assistant nodded. "Okay. I'll let you deal with it." She *definitely* didn't like the idea of upsetting Leslie.

"That would be best," Jane Widdler said.

———

JANE THOUGHT about it for a long time, until a headache began creeping down her neck from the crown of her head. Finally, she got her BlackBerry from her purse, looked up a number, and punched it in.

"Hello, Jane," Amity Anderson said.

"We've got to get together. Right now. Without Leslie," Jane said.

"Why?"

"Because," Jane Widdler said.

"I just want out," Amity said.

"That's all I want," Jane Widdler said. "But things may be getting . . . difficult."

THEY HOOKED UP in a coffee shop in the Skyway. Widdler arrived on the street level, before going up to the Skyway, walking right past Jenkins who sat behind a window in Starbucks, but he'd never seen her before. Anderson came down to the second floor to the Skyway, never going to the street, leaving Jenkins sitting in the Starbucks, with, at least metaphorically, his dick in his hand.

The Skyway shop, a Caribou, had a selection of chairs and tables and Widdler and Anderson both got medium light-roasts and chocolate raspberry thumbprint cookies, and hunched over a table in the corner. Widdler said, "This state agent who talked to you, Davenport. He came to the shop and he asked about a white van. He knows."

"Knows what?" Amity Anderson took a bite of her thumbprint.

"You know," Widdler said irritably. They'd never talked about it, but Anderson *knew*.

"The only thing I know is that we went to college together and you recommended that Mrs. Donaldson buy a rare Armstrong quilt, which was later donated to the Milwaukee, and that's all I know," Anderson said. She popped the last of the thumbprint in her mouth and made a dusting motion with her hands.

"I really didn't want to be unpleasant about this," Widdler said, "but I've got no choice. So I will tell you that if they take me off to prison, you will go with me. I will make a deal to implicate the rest of the gang, in exchange for time off. Meaning you and Marilyn Coombs."

Anderson's faced tightened like a fist: "You bitch. I did *not* . . ."

"You knew. You certainly knew about the quilts, and if you knew about the quilts, then any jury is going to believe you knew about the rest of it," Widdler said. "You *worked* for Donaldson, for Christ's sake. You live five minutes from Bucher. Now, if Davenport knows, and he does, he will eventually be able to put together a fairly incriminating case. We dealt with all those people—Donaldson, Bucher, Toms. There are records, somewhere. Old checks."

"Where's my money? You were going to get me the money." Anderson hissed. "I'm going to Italy."

"I'll get you the money and you can go to Italy," Jane said. "But we've got to get out of this."

"If you're talking about doing something to Davenport . . ."

Widdler shook her head. "No, no. Too late for that. Maybe, right back at the beginning . . ." She turned away from Anderson, her eyes narrowing, reviewing the missed opportunity. Then back to Anderson: "The thing is, cops are bureaucrats. My stepfather was a cop, and I know how they work. Davenport's already told somebody what he thinks. If we did something to him, there'd be eight more cops looking at us. They'd never give up."

"So who . . ." Anderson had the paper cup at her lips, looking into Widdler's eyes, when the answer came to her. "Leslie?"

Widdler said, "I never signed anything. He endorsed all the checks, wrote the estimates. He did the scouting while I watched the shop. They could make a better case against him than they could against me."

"So what are you thinking?"

Widdler glanced around. A dozen other patrons were sitting in chairs or standing at the counter, but none were close enough to hear them over the chatter and dish-and-silverware clank of the shop. Still, she leaned closer to Anderson. "I'm thinking Leslie could become despondent. He could talk to me about it, hint that he'd done some things he shouldn't have. I could get the feeling that he's worried about something."

"Suicide?"

"I have some small guns . . . a house gun, and car guns, for self-protection. Leslie showed me how they work," Widdler said.

"So . . ."

"I need a ride. I don't just want him to *shoot* himself, I want him to . . . do it on a stage, so to speak. I want people looking in a different direction."

"And you need a ride?" Anderson was astonished. They were talking about a murder, and the killer needed *a ride.*

"I can't think of any other way to do it—to get him where I need him, to get back home. I need to move quickly to establish an alibi . . . I need to be home if somebody calls. I can't take a taxi, it's just . . . it's just all too hard to work out, if you don't help."

"All I have to do is give you a ride?"

"That's all," Widdler said. "It's very convenient. Only a few minutes from your house."

THEY ARGUED for another five minutes, in hushed tones, and finally Anderson said, "I couldn't stand it in prison. I couldn't stand it."

"Neither could I," Widdler said. Anderson was watching her, and her lips trembled as much as they could. She reached out and put her hand on Anderson's. "Can you do this? Just this one thing?"

"Just the ride," Anderson said.

"That's all—and then . . . about the money. Leslie keeps all the controversial stuff in a building at our country place."

"I didn't know you had a country place," Anderson said.

"Just a shack, and a storage building. I'll give you the key. You can take whatever you want. If you can get it out to the West Coast . . . just the small things could be worth a half-million dollars. You could get enough to stay in Europe for ten years, if you were careful. You can take whatever you want."

"Whatever I want?" Eyebrows up.

"Whatever you want," Widdler said. "The police will find it sooner or later. I'm not going to get a penny of it, no matter what happens. If you can get there first, take what you want."

Anderson thought it over: Jane's offer seemed uncharacteristically generous. But then, she was in a serious bind. "So I don't have to do anything else: I just give you a ride."

"That's all," Jane said.

"When?"

"Right away. I've started talking to Leslie about it, letting him brood. His tendency, anyway . . ." She shrugged.

"Is to go crazy," Anderson finished. "Your husband is a fuckin' lunatic."

Widdler nodded.

Anderson pressed it: "So when?"

"Tonight. I want to do it tonight."

WIDDLER GAVE HER a key to what she said was the storage building. "I'll put a map in the mail this afternoon—Leslie's got one in his car." When they broke up, Widdler went back down the escalator and walked past the Starbucks, but Jenkins didn't see her.

Jenkins had gone. Lucas had pulled him.

———

LUCAS FOUND SANDY hunched in front of her ancient computer, chewing on a fingernail, and she looked up, her hair flyaway, and said, "We had some luck. The Widdlers were written up in a *Midwest Home* article on antiques, and they have a website with vitae. They both graduated from Carleton the year before Amity Anderson. They had to know each other—Jane Widdler majored in art history, and Amity Anderson in art, and Leslie Widdler had a scholarship in studio art. He did ceramics."

Lucas dragged a chair over and asked, "On their website, is there anything about clients?"

"No, it's just an ad, really—it's one of the preformatted deals where you just plug stuff in. The last change was dated a month ago."

"Motor vehicles?"

"Never owned a van," Sandy said. "Not even when they were in college. But: I looked at their tax records and they both had student loans. And the *Home* article says they both had scholarships. Leslie—this is funny—Leslie Widdler had an art scholarship, but I get the impression from the website and the *Home* article that all he did was play football."

"What's funny about that?" Lucas asked. He'd gone to the University of Minnesota on a hockey scholarship.

"Well, Carleton doesn't have athletic scholarships, see, so they get this giant guy to play football and they give him a scholarship in art . . ."

"Maybe he was a good artist," Lucas said, a bit stiff. "Athletes have a wide range of interests."

She looked at him: "You were a jock, weren't you?"

"So what were you saying?" Lucas asked.

"Did you get a free Camaro?"

"What were you saying?" Lucas repeated.

Unflustered—her self-confidence, Lucas thought, seemed to be growing in leaps and bounds—she turned back to the computer, tapped a few keys, and pulled up a page of notes. "So, about the scholarships. They apparently didn't have a lot of family money. They get married in their senior year, move to the Twin Cities, start an antique store. Here they are ten years later, starting from nothing, they've got to be millionaires. They own their store, they have a house on Minnehaha Creek, they drive eighty thousand dollars' worth of cars . . ."

"That's interesting. But: it could be that they're really smart," Lucas said.

"And maybe Leslie learned leadership by participating in football," she suggested.

Lucas leaned back: "Why do women give me shit?"

"Basically, because you're there," she said.

SANDY HAD DONE one more thing. "I made a graph of their income." She touched a few more keys, and the graph popped up. The income line started flat, then turned up at a forty-five-degree angle, then flattened a bit over the years, but continued up. "Here are the quilts." She tapped a flat area, just before an upturn. "The upturn in income would come a year later—it would take them a while to flow the money into their sales." She pointed out two other upturns: "Toms and Donaldson."

"Bless my soul," Lucas said. Then, "Can you go back to Des Moines? Right now?"

JENKINS WAS SITTING in Carol's visitor's chair when Lucas got back to his office, moving fast. "Come on in," Lucas said.

"What's going on?" He followed Lucas into the inner office. Lucas was studying a printout of Sandy's graph.

"I think we finally got our fingernails under something," Lucas said. "I want you to go to Eau Claire—I'd fly you if it were faster, but I think it would be faster to drive. You're going to talk to some people named Booth and look at some check duplicates and some purchase records for antiques."

Jenkins said, "Man, you're all cranked up—but you gotta know, if this Gabriella Coombs didn't take off with a boyfriend or something, then she's gone by now."

Lucas nodded. "I know. Now I just want to get the motherfuckers. You're looking for some people named Widdler . . ."

LUCAS BRIEFED HIM; Sandy stopped in, halfway through, and said, "I'm on my way. I'll call you tonight."

"Good. Try to get back here tonight, or early tomorrow. We're gonna have a conference about all of this, get everybody together. Tomorrow morning, I hope."

She nodded, and was gone.

He finished briefing Jenkins, who asked, "So you're gonna take Bucher?"

"Yeah, and I've got some politics to do with the St. Paul cops and I gotta go see Lucy Coombs. I'll be on my phone all night—until one in the morning, anyway. Call me."

"I'm outa here."

21

THE ST. PAUL POLICE DEPARTMENT is a brown-brick building that looks like a remodeled brewery, and it's built in a place where a brewery should have been built: across a lot of free-ways on the back side of the city.

Lucas parked in the cops' lot, put a sign on the dash, and found John Smith in a cubicle. Another detective sat three cubicles down, playing with a Rubik's Cube so worn that it might have been an orig-inal. A third was talking so earnestly on a telephone that it had to be to his wife, and he had to be in trouble. Either that, or she'd just found out that she was pregnant.

Lucas said, "Let's go somewhere quiet."

Smith sat up. "Widdlers?"

The second detective said, without looking up from the Rubik's Cube, "That's right, talk around me. Like I'm an unperson."

"You *are* an unperson," Smith said. To Lucas: "Come on this way." Lucas followed him down the hall to the lieutenant's office. Smith stuck his head inside, said, "I thought I heard him leave. Come on in."

LUCAS SAID, "We're going full steam ahead on the Widdlers. It's not a sure thing by a long way. At the very least, I'll talk to Leslie

Widdler and ask him to roll up his pant legs. See if he has any Screw bites."

"When?"

"Midday tomorrow. I've got people going to Eau Claire and Des Moines right now. I've hooked both Marilyn Coombs and Donaldson to Amity Anderson, and Anderson is a longtime friend of the Widdlers. I think they were involved in a tax fraud together, selling these fake quilts, and I think it went from there. We know the killers involve one very big man, and that they know a lot about antiques, and that they have a way to dispose of them. In other words, the Widdlers."

"You don't have them directly connected to anybody? I mean, the Widdlers to Donaldson, Bucher, or Toms?"

"Not yet," Lucas said.

"How about the van?" Smith asked.

"No van."

"Goddamnit. There's got to be a van," Smith said.

"I talked to a woman at the Widdlers' who said they rented vans," Lucas said. "That's being checked."

"The van in the tape on Summit was too old to be a rental— unless they went to one of the Rent-a-Wreck places."

"I don't know," Lucas said. "The van is like a loose bolt in the whole thing."

"Without a van, without a direct connection . . . I don't think you have enough to get a warrant to search Leslie."

Lucas grinned at him: "I was thinking *you* might want to get the warrant. You probably have more suck with one of the local judges."

Smith said, "I've got some suck, but I've got to have *something*."

"Maybe we will tomorrow morning," Lucas said. "And if we don't, I can always ask Leslie to roll up his pant leg. If he tells me to go fuck myself, then we'll know."

LUCAS GOT the key to Bucher's place, went out, sat in his car, stared at his cell phone, then sighed and dialed. Lucy Coombs snatched up the phone and said, "What?"

"This is Lucas Davenport . . ."

WHEN HE GOT to Coombs's house, she was sitting in the kitchen with a neighbor, eyes all hollow and black, and as soon as she saw Lucas, she started to cry again: "You think she's gone."

Lucas nodded: "Unless she's with a friend. But she was so intent on getting to the bottom of this, her relationship seemed to be breaking up, this is what she wanted to do. I don't think she would have simply dropped it. I think we have to be ready for . . . the worst."

"What do you mean 'we,'" Coombs sobbed. "This is your fuck-ing *job*. She's not your daughter."

"Miz Coombs . . . Ah, jeez, Gabriella got me going on this," Lucas said. "She probably was the key person who'll bring all these killers down—and they've killed more people than you know."

"My mother and my daughter," Coombs said, her voice drying out and going shrill.

"More than that—maybe three elderly people, they may have at-tacked a teenager, there may be people who we don't have any idea about," Lucas said.

"You know who they are?"

"We're beginning to get some ideas."

"What if they've just kidnapped her? What if they're just keeping her for . . . for . . ." She couldn't think of why they might be keeping her. Neither could Lucas.

He said, "That's always a possibility. That's what we hope for. We hope to make some kind of a move tomorrow—and I hope you'll keep that under your hat. Maybe we'll find out something fairly soon. One way or another."

"Oh, shit," Coombs said. She looked around the kitchen, then snatched a ceramic plate from where it was hanging on the wall, a plate with two crossed-fish, artsy-craftsy, and hurled it at the side wall, where it shattered.

"Miz Coombs . . ."

"Where is she . . . Where's my baby?"

OUT ON the street, he exhaled, looked back at Coombs's house, and shook his head. In her place, he thought, he wouldn't be screaming, or crying—and maybe that was bad. Maybe he should behave that way, but he knew he wouldn't. He could see Weather grieving as Coombs did; he could see most normal people behaving that way.

What Lucas would feel, instead, would be a murderous anger, an iceberg of hate. He would kill anyone who hurt Weather, Sam, or Letty. He'd be cold about it, he'd plan it, but the anger would never go away, and sooner or later, he would find them and kill them.

BUCHER'S HOUSE was dark as a tomb. Lucas let himself in, flipped on lights by the door, and headed for the office. This time, he spent two hours, looking at virtually every piece of paper in the place. Nothing. He moved to the third-floor storage room, with the file cabinets. A small, narrow room, cool; only one light, hanging bare from the ceiling, and no place to sit. Dusty . . .

He went down the hall, found a chair, and carried it back across the creaking plank floor. As he put the chair down, he thought he heard footsteps, down below, someplace distant, trailing off to silence. The hair rose on the back of his neck. He stepped to the doorway, called, "Hello? Hello?"

Nothing but the air moving through the air conditioners. A light seemed to flicker in the stairway, and he waited, but nothing else moved. The hair was still prickling on the back of his neck, when he went back to the paper.

An amazing amount of junk that people kept: old school papers, newspaper clippings, recipes, warranties and instruction books, notebooks, sketchpads, Christmas, Easter, and birthday cards, postcards from everywhere, old letters, theater programs, maps, remodeling contracts, property-tax notices. An ocean of it.

A current of cold air touched the back of his neck and he shivered; as though somebody had passed in the hallway. He stepped to the door again, looked down the silent hall.

Ghosts. The thought trickled through his mind and he didn't laugh. He didn't believe in them, but he didn't laugh, either, and had never been attracted to the idea of screwing around in a cemetery at night. Two people killed here, their killers not found, blood still drying in the old woodwork . . . the silence seemed to grow from the hallway walls; except for the soft flowing sound of the air conditioner.

He went back to the paper, feeling his skin crawl. There was nobody else in the house: he knew it, and still . . .

THE PHONE BUZZED, and almost gave him his second heart attack of the day.

He took it out of his pocket, looked at it: out-of-area. He said, "Hello?"

There was a pause and then a vaguely metallic man's voice said,

"Hi! This is Tom Drake! We'll be doing some work in your neighborhood next week, sealing driveways. As a homeowner . . ."

"Fuck you," Lucas said, slamming the phone shut. Almost killed by a computer voice.

He found a file, two inches thick, of receipts for furniture purchases. Began to go through it, but all the furniture had been bought through decorators, none of them the Widdlers. Still, he was in the right neighborhood, the furniture neighborhood.

The phone took a third shot at his heart: it buzzed again, he jumped again, swore, looked at the screen: out-of-area. He clicked it open: "Hello?"

"Lucas? Ah, Agent Davenport? This is . . ."

"Sandy. What's up?" Lucas thought he heard something in the hallway, and peeked out. Nobody but the spirits. He turned back into the room.

Sandy said, "I got your Widdlers. The Toms cousin had a file of purchases, and Mr. Toms, the dead man, bought three paintings from them, over about five years. He spent a total of sixteen thousand dollars. There's also a check for five thousand dollars that just says 'appraisals,' but doesn't say what was appraised."

The thrill shook through him. Gotcha. "Okay! Sandy! This is great! That's exactly what we need—we don't have to figure out what the appraisals were, all we have to do is show contact. Now, the originals on those papers, can you get them copied?"

"Yes. They have a Xerox machine right here," she said.

"Copy them," Lucas said. "Leave the originals with your guy there, tell him that the local cops will come get them tomorrow, or maybe somebody from the DCI."

"The who?"

"The Iowa Division of Criminal Investigation," Lucas said. "I got a friend down there, he can tell us how to deal with the documents. But bring the copies back with you. When can you get here?"

"Tonight. I can leave in twenty minutes," she said. "I'd like to get a sandwich or something."

"Do what you've got to," Lucas said. "Call me when you get back."

He slapped the phone shut. This was just exactly . . .

A MAN SPOKE from six inches behind his ear. "So what's up?"

Lucas lurched across the narrow room, nearly falling over the chair, catching himself on the file cabinet with one hand, the other flailing for his gun, his heart trying to bore through his rib cage.

John Smith, smile fading, stood in the doorway, looked at Lucas's face, and asked, "What?"

"Jesus Christ, I almost shot you," Lucas rasped.

"Sorry . . . I heard you talking and came on up," Smith said. "I thought you might appreciate some help."

"Yeah." Lucas ran his hands through his hair, shook himself out. His heart was still rattling off his ribs. "It's just so damn quiet in here."

Smith nodded, and looked both ways down the hall: "I spent a couple of evenings by myself. You can hear the ghosts creeping around."

"Glad I'm not the only one," Lucas said. He turned back to the file cabinets. "I've done two of them, I'm halfway down the third."

"I'll take the bottom drawer and work up," Smith said. He went down the hall, got another chair, pulled open the bottom drawer. "You been here the whole time?"

Lucas glanced at his watch. "Three hours. Did the office, started up here. Went over and talked to Miz Coombs, before I came over. She's all messed up. Oh, and by the way—we put the Widdlers with Toms."

Smith, just settling in his chair, looked up, a light on his face, and said, "You're kidding."

"Nope."

Smith scratched under an arm. "This might not look good—you know, calling in the killers to appraise the estate. If they're the killers."

"I'm not gonna worry about it," Lucas said. "For one thing, there was no way to know. For another . . ." He paused.

Smith said, "For another?"

"Well, for another, I didn't do it." Lucas smiled. "*You* did."

"Fuck you," Smith said. He dipped into the bottom file drawer and pulled out a file, looked at the flap. "Here's a file that says 'Antiques.'"

"Bullshit," Lucas said.

"Man, I'm not kidding you . . ."

Lucas took the file and looked at the flap: "Antiques."

Inside, a stack of receipts. There weren't many of them, not nearly as many as there were in the furniture file. But one of them, a pink carbon copy, said at the top, "Widdler Antiques and Objets d'Art."

He handed it over to Smith who looked at it, then looked at Lucas, looked at the pink sheet again, and said, "Kiss my rosy red rectum."

"WE GOT THEM with Toms and Bucher, and we know that their good friend actually worked with Donaldson, and they pulled off a fraud. That's enough for a warrant," Smith said.

"At the minimum, we get Leslie to lift up his pant legs," Lucas said. "If he's got bite holes, we take a DNA and compare it to the blood on Screw. At that point, we've got him for attempted kidnapping . . ."

"And cruelty to animals."

"I'm not sure Screw actually qualified as an animal. He was more of a beast."

"Can't throw a dog out a car window. Might be able to get away with an old lady, but not a dog," Smith said. "Not in the city of St. Paul."

Lucas was a half block from his house when Jenkins called from Wisconsin. He fumbled the phone, caught it, said, "Yeah?"

"Got 'em," Jenkins said.

22

THE WHOLE STORY was so complicated that Jane Widdler almost couldn't contain it. She wrote down the major points, sitting at her desk while Leslie was upstairs in the shower, singing an ancient Jimmy Buffett song, vaguely audible through the walls.

Jane wrote:

- *No way out*
- *Arrested*
- *Disgraced*
- *Attorneys*
- *Prison forever*

Then she drew a line, and below it wrote:

- *Arrested*
- *Disgraced*
- *Attorneys*
- *Time in prison?*

Then she drew a second line and wrote:

- *Save the money*

The last item held her attention most of the afternoon, but she was working through the other items in the back of her head.

Davenport, she thought, was probably unstoppable. It was possible that he wouldn't get to them, but unlikely. She'd seen him operating.

She nibbled on her bottom lip, looked at the list, then sighed and fed it into the shredder.

If he did get to them, could Davenport convict? Not if Leslie hadn't been bitten by the dog. But with the dog bites, Leslie was cooked. If she hadn't taken some kind of preemptive action before then, she'd be cooked with him.

From watching her stepfather work as a cop, and listening to him talk about court cases, she felt the most likely way to save herself was to give the cops another suspect. Build reasonable doubt into the case. As much reasonable doubt as possible.

As for the money . . .

They had a safe-deposit box in St. Paul where they had more than $160,000 in hundreds, fifties, and twenties. The cash came from stolen antiques, from four dead old women and one dead old man, each in a different state. The Widdlers had worked the cash slowly back through the store, upgrading their stock, an invisible laundry that the mafia would have appreciated.

With Leslie looking at a china collection in Minnetonka, Jane, after talking to Anderson, had gone alone to the bank, retrieved the money, and wrapped it in Ziploc bags. Where to put it? She'd eventually taken it home and buried it in a flower garden, carefully scraping the bark mulch back over it.

AMITY ANDERSON, Jane knew, was on the edge of cracking. One big fear: that Anderson would crack first, and go to the cops hoping to make a deal. Anderson knew herself well enough to know that she couldn't tolerate prison. She was too fragile for that. Too much of a free spirit. All she wanted was to go to Italy; look at Cellini and Caravaggio. Amity believed that if she could only get to Italy, somehow, the problems would be left behind.

Magical thinking. Jane Widdler had no such illusions. The victims had been too rich, the money too big, the publicity too great. The cops would be all over them once they had a taste; and Davenport had gotten a taste.

Still, Jane could pull it off, if she had time.

LESLIE CALLED, said he was on the way home. Jane hurried over to the shop, opened the safe in the back, and took out the coin collection and a simple .38-caliber pistol.

The coin collection came from the Toms foray, fifty-eight rare gold coins from the nineteenth century, all carefully sealed in plastic grading containers, all MS66 through MS69—so choice, in fact, that they'd been a little worried about moving the coins. They still had all but two, but if necessary, she could take them to Mexico and move them there.

The coins went deep in a line of lilacs, behind and to one side of the house, halfway to the creek. She dug them six inches down, covered them with sod, dusted her hands. If she didn't make it back . . . what a waste.

The pistol went into her purse. She'd never learned not to jerk the trigger, but that wouldn't matter if you were shooting at a range of half an inch.

SHE WONDERED where the jail was. Would it be Hennepin County, or Ramsey? Somehow, she thought it might be Ramsey, since that's where the murders occurred. And Ramsey, she thought, might be preferable, with a better class of felon. Surely they had separate cells, you were presumed innocent until proven guilty. And if Leslie had passed away, the house would be hers to use as a bond for bail . . .

She went inside. Leslie was perched on the couch in the den, wearing yellow walking shorts and a loose striped shirt from a San Francisco clothier, pale blue stripes on a champagne background that went well with the shorts and the Zelli crocodile slippers, $695. He said, "Hi. I heard you come in . . . Where'd you go?"

"I thought I saw the fox out back. I walked around to see. But he was gone."

"Yeah? I'd like a fox tail for the car."

"We've got to talk," Jane said. "Something awful happened today."

WHEN SHE TOLD him about Davenport visiting the shop, about his question about a white van, Leslie touched one fat finger to his fat nose and said, "He's got to go."

"There's no time," Jane said, pouring the anxiety into her voice. "If he was asking about the van this afternoon, he'll be looking at all the files tomorrow. Once that gets into the system . . ."

Leslie was digging in a pocket. He came up with a pack of breath mints and popped two. "Listen," he said, clicking the mints off his lower teeth, "we do it tonight. Just have to figure out how."

"I looked him up," Jane volunteered. "He lives on Mississippi River Boulevard in St. Paul. I drove by; a very nice house for a cop. He must be on the take."

"Maybe *that's* a possibility," Leslie suggested. "If he's crooked . . ."

"No. Too late, too late . . . The thing is, have you seen him with that gun? And he's going to be wary, I'd be afraid to approach him."

"So what do you think?" Leslie let her do most of the thinking.

"If you think we should do it, I suggest that rifle. God knows it's powerful enough. You shoot from the backseat, I drive. We'll ambush him right outside his house. If the opportunity doesn't present itself, we go back tomorrow morning."

"If we see him in a window—a .300 Mag won't even notice a piece of window glass," Leslie said.

"Whatever."

"If we're going to do it, we've got things to do," Leslie said cheerfully. The thought of killing always warmed him up. "I'm gonna take a shower, clean up the gun. Take my car, I'll sit in the back. We'll need earplugs, but I've got some. What's the layout?"

"We can't park on River Boulevard, it's all no-parking. But there's a spot on the side street, under a big elm tree. It looks sideways at his garage and front door. If he goes anywhere . . ."

"Too bad it's summer," Leslie said. "We'll be shooting in daylight."

"We can't go too early," Jane said. "It has to be dark enough that people can't read out faces."

"Not before nine-fifteen, then," Leslie said. "I've played golf at nine, but sometime around nine-fifteen or nine-thirty, you can't see the golf ball anymore."

"Get there at nine-thirty and hope for the best," Jane said. "Maybe there'd be some way to lure him out?"

"Like what?"

"Let me think about it."

HE WENT UP to take a shower, and she thought about it: how to get Davenport outside, with enough certainty that Leslie would buy the idea. Then she sat down and made her list, looked at the list, dropped it in the shredder, and thought about it some more.

Leslie was working on "Cheeseburger in Paradise" when she stepped into his office and brought up the computer. She typed two notes, one a fragment, the other one longer, taken from models on the Internet. When she was done, she put them in the Documents file, signed off, pushed the chair back in place, walked up the stairs, and called through the bathroom door, "I've got to run out: I'll be back in twenty minutes."

The water stopped. "Where're you going?"

"Down to Wal-Mart," she said through the door. "We need a couple of baseballs."

WHEN SHE GOT back home, Leslie was in the living room, sliding the rifle, already loaded, into an olive-drab gun case. He was dressed in a black golf shirt and black slacks.

"God, I hate to throw this thing away," he said. "We'll have to, but it's really a nice piece of machinery."

"But we have to," Jane said. She had a plastic bag in her hand, and took out two boxes with baseballs inside.

"Baseballs?"

"You think, being the big jock, that you could hit a house a hundred feet away with a baseball?"

"Hit a house?" Leslie was puzzled.

"Suppose you're a big-shot cop sitting in your house, and you hear a really loud thump on your front roof, or front side of the house at nine-thirty at night," Jane said. "Do you send your wife out to take a look?"

Leslie smiled at her. "I can hit a house. And you get smarter all the time."

"We're both smart," Jane said. "Let's just see if we can stay ahead of Davenport."

"Wish we'd done this first, instead of that harebrained dog thing," Leslie said. "You oughta see the holes in my legs."

"Maybe later." Jane looked at her watch. "I have to change, and we have to leave soon. Oh God, Leslie, is this the end of it?" That, she thought, was what Jane Austen would have asked.

———————

SHE TURNED to look back at the house when they left. She'd get back tonight, she thought, but then, if the police arrested her, she might not see it for a while. A tear trickled down one cheek, then the other. She wiped them away and Leslie growled, "Don't pussy out on me."

"You know how I hate that word," she said. She wiped her face again. "I'm so scared. We should never have done Bucher. Never have killed at home."

"We'll be okay," Leslie said. He reached over and patted her thigh. "We've just got to kill our way out of it."

"I know," she said. "It scares me so bad . . ."

THEY GOT to Davenport's at nine-fifteen and cruised the neighborhood. Still too light. They went out to a bagel place off Ford Parkway and got a couple of bagels with cream cheese for Leslie. Nine-thirty. There were more people around than they'd expected, riding out the last light of day on the River Boulevard bike trail, and walking dogs on the sidewalk. But the yards were big, and they could park well down the darker side street and still see Davenport's house, one down beyond the corner house.

There were lights all over Davenport's house; the family was *in.*

"I could probably kill him with the baseball from here," Leslie said, when they rolled into the spot Jane had picked. He had gotten in the backseat at the bagel shop. Now he slipped the rifle out of the case, and sitting with his back to the driver's side of the car, pointed the rifle through the raised back window at Davenport's front porch.

"No problem," he said, looking through the scope. Jane put the yellow plastic ear protectors in her ears. Leslie fiddled with the rifle for a moment, then snapped it back to his shoulder. "No problem.

A hundred and fifty feet, if these are hundred-foot lots, less if they're ninety feet . . ." His voice was muffled, but still audible.

"God. I'm so scared, Les," she said, slipping the revolver out of her purse. Checked the streets: nobody in sight. "I'm not sure I can do it."

"Hey," Leslie said. "Don't pussy out."

She lifted the gun to his temple and pulled the trigger. There was a one-inch spit of flame, not as bright as a flash camera, and a tremendous *crack*.

She recoiled from it, dropped the gun, hands to her ears, eyes wide. She looked out through the back window. The gunshot had sounded like the end of the world, but the world, a hundred feet away, seemed to go on. A car passed, and ten seconds later, a man on a bicycle with a leashed Labrador running beside him.

Leslie was lying back on the seat, and in the dim light, looked terrifically dead. "Damn gun," Jane muttered into the stench of gunpowder and blood. She had to kneel on the seat and reach over the back to get the revolver off the floor. She wiped it with a paper towel, then pressed it into one of Leslie's limp hands, rolling it, making sure of at least one print.

Leslie kept his cell phone plugged into the car's cigarette lighter. She picked it up, called Amity Anderson. When Anderson picked up, she said, "Can you come now?"

"Right now?" The anxiety was heavy in Anderson's voice.

"That would be good."

"Did you . . ."

"This is a radio," Widdler said. "Don't talk, just come."

SHE CHECKED for watchers, then let herself out of the car. Shut the door, locked it with the second remote. That was a nice piece of work, she thought. Locked from the inside, with the keys still in Leslie's pocket. These keys, the second set, would go back in the front key drawer, to be found by the investigators.

She walked away into the dark. She was sure she hadn't thought of everything, but she was confident that she'd thought of enough. All she wanted was a simple "Not guilty." Was that too much to ask?

AMITY FOUND her on the corner.

Jane wasn't all that cranked: Leslie had been on his way out. His actual passing was more a matter of *when* than *if*. And though she was calm enough, she had to seem cranked. She had to be frantic, flustered, and freaked. As she came up to the corner she brushed her hair forward, messing it up; her hair was never messed up. She slapped herself on the face a couple of times. She muttered to herself, bit her lip until tears came to her eyes. Slapped herself again.

Amity found her freshly slapped and teary eyed, on the corner, properly disheveled for a recent murderess.

JANE GOT in the car: "Thank God," she moaned.

"You did it."

"We have to go to your house," Jane said. "For one minute. I'm so scared. I'm going to wet my pants. I just . . . God, I can't hold it in."

"Hold it, hold it, we'll be there in two minutes," Amity said. Down Cretin, left on Ford, up the street past the shopping centers, up the hill, into the driveway.

IN THE BATHROOM, Jane pulled down her pants, listened, then stood up and opened the medicine cabinet. Two prescription bottles. She took the one in the back. Sat down, peed, waddled to the sink with her pants down around her ankles, looked in, then turned around and carefully and silently pried open the shower door. Hair near the drain. She got a piece of toilet paper, and cleaned up some hair, put it in her pocket.

Almost panting now. The cops might be on their way at any moment: a passerby happens to glance into the car, sees a shoe . . . and she had a lot to get done. She sat back on the toilet, flushed, stood up, pulled up her pants. Lot to get done.

AMITY WAS SHAKY. "When do you think, ah, what . . . ?"

"Let's go," Jane said. "Now, we're in a hurry."

IN THE CAR, headed west across the bridge, Jane said, "I mailed you the map. You should get it tomorrow. Don't wait too long before you go. Leslie owned the land through a trust, and they'll find it pretty quick. Make sure you're not being followed. Davenport's talked to you, if he knows anything else, if he's investigating the quilts . . . then you might be followed."

Amity looked in the rearview mirror. "How do you know we're not being followed now?"

Jane made a smile. "We can't be," she said.

"Why not?"

"Because if we are, we're finished."

AMITY LOOKED at her, white-faced. "That's it? We can't be because we can't be?"

"Actually, they'd be much more likely to be following Leslie and me," Jane said. "If they were, they probably would have picked me up back at Davenport's house, don't you think?"

Amity nodded. That made sense. "Maybe I should drop you off around the block from your place. Just in case."

"You could do that," Jane said. "Just to be perfectly clear about this, you're now an accomplice in whatever it is that happened to Leslie. I happen to think it was a suicide, and you should think that, too. Because if you ever even hint that I know something about it, well, then, you're in it, too."

"All I want to do is go to Italy," Amity said.

AMITY DROPPED HER off around the block, and Jane strolled home in the soft night light, listening to the insects, to the frogs, to the rustlings in the hedges: cats on their nightly missions, a possum here, a fox there, all unseen.

Nobody waiting. And she thought, *No Les, no more.* She made a smile-look, reflecting at her own courage, her own ability to operate under pressure. It was like being a spy, almost . . .

WITH ONE MORE mission that night. She backed the car out of the garage, took the narrow streets out to I-494, watching the mirror, took 494 to I-35, and headed south. The country place wasn't that far out, down past the Northfield turnoff to County 1, and east with a few jogs to the south, into the Cannon River Valley.

The country place comprised forty acres of senile maple and box elder along the west or north bank of the Cannon, depending on how you looked at it, with a dirt track leading back to it. Her lights bored a hole through the cornfields on either side of the track, the wheels dropping into washouts and pots, until she punched through to the shack.

When they first bought it, they talked of putting up a little cabin that didn't smell like mold—the shack smelled like it had been built from mold—with a porch that looked out over the river, and Leslie could fish for catfish and Jane could quilt.

In the end, they put up a metal building with good locks, and let the shack slide into ruin. The cabin was never built because, in fact, Leslie was never much interested in catfish, and Jane never got the quilt-making thing going. There was too much to do in the Cities, too much to see, too much to buy. Couldn't even get the Internet at the shack. It was like a hillbilly patch, or something.

But a good place to stash stolen antiques.

She let herself into the shed, fumbling in her headlights with the key. Inside, she turned on the interior lights and then went back and turned off the car lights. She took the amber prescription bottle from her pocket, and rolled it under the front seat of the van.

From her purse, she got a lint roller, peeled it to get fresh tape, and rolled it over the driver's seat. They were always fastidious about the van, wearing hairnets and gloves and jumpsuits, in case they had to ditch it. There shouldn't be a problem, but she was playing with her life.

She rolled it, and then rolled it again, and a third time.

Then she took the wad of hair from her pocket.

Looked at it, and thought, *soap*. Nibbled at her lip, sighed, thought, *do it right*, and walked over to the shack and went inside. They kept the pump turned off, so she had to wait for it to cycle and prime, and then to pump out some crappy, shitty water, waiting until it cleared. When it was, she rinsed the wad of hair—nasty—and then patted it dry on a paper towel.

When it was dry, she pulled out a few strands, pinched them in the paper towel, and carried them back to the van. Two here, curled over the back of the seat, not too obvious, and another one here, on the back edge of the seat. She took the rest of the hair and wiped it roughly across the back of the seat, hoping to get some breaks and split ends . . .

Good as she could do, she thought. That was all she had.

JANE WIDDLER was home in bed at two A.M. There were no calls on her phone, and the neighborhood was dark when she pulled into the garage. Upstairs, she lit some scented candles and sank into the bathtub, letting the heat carry away her worries.

Didn't work.

She lay awake in the night like a frightened bat, waiting for the day to come, for the police, for disgrace, for humiliation, for lawyers.

LUCAS, on the other hand, slept like a log until five-thirty, when his cop sense woke him up. The cop sense had been pricked by a flashing red light on the curtains at the side of the house, the pulsing red light sneaking in under the bottom of the blackout shades.

He cracked his eyes, thought, *the cops.* What the hell was it? Then he heard a siren, and another one.

He slipped out of bed—Weather had no cop sense, and would sleep soundly until six, unless Sam cried out—and walked to the window, pulled back one side of the shade. Two cop cars, just up the street, then a third arriving, all gathered around a dark sedan.

What the hell? It looked and smelled like a crime scene.

He got into his jeans and golf shirt, and slipped sockless feet into loafers, and let himself out the front door. As he came across the lawn, his ankles wet with dew, one of the St. Paul cops recognized him. "Where're you coming from?" the cop asked.

"I live right there," Lucas said. "What've you got?"

"Guy ate his gun," the cop said. "But he was up to something . . . You live right there?"

But Lucas was looking in the back window of what he now knew was a Lexus, a Lexus with a bullet hole in the roof above the back window, and at the dead fat face of Leslie Widdler.

"Ah, no," he said. "Ah, Jesus . . ."

"What? You know him?" the cop asked.

23

ROSE MARIE ROUX came steaming through the front door, high heels, nylons, political-red skirt and jacket, white blouse, big hair. She spotted Lucas and demanded, "Are you all right?"

Lucas was chewing on an apple. He swallowed and said, "I'm fine. My case blew up, but I'm fuckin' wonderful."

"What's this about a guy with a rifle?" Rose Marie said. "They said a guy with a rifle was waiting for you."

"Must have changed his mind," Lucas said. "Come on. Everything's still there. You saw the cops when you came in?"

"Of course. A convention. So tell me about it."

A GUY WAS out running shortly after first light, Lucas told her. He was a marathoner, running out of his home, weaving down the Minneapolis side of the Mississippi, across the Ford Bridge into St. Paul, weaving some more—he tried to get exactly six miles in—north to the Lake Street Bridge and back across the river to Minneapolis.

One of his zigs took him around the corner from Lucas's house. As he approached the Lexus, in the early-morning light, he noticed a splash on the back window that looked curiously like blood in a thriller movie. As he passed the car, he glanced into the backseat and saw the white face and open mouth of a dead fat man, with a rifle lying across his belly.

"Freaked me out when I looked in there," Lucas admitted. "Last thing in the world that I expected. Leslie Widdler."

"Better him than you," Rose Marie said. "What kind of rifle? If he'd taken a shot at you?"

"A .300 Mag," Lucas said. "Good for elk, caribou, moose. If he'd shot me with that thing, my ass'd have to take the train back from Ohio."

"Nice that you can joke about it," Rose Marie said.

"I'm not laughing," Lucas said. They walked up to a cop who was keeping a sharp eye on the yellow crime-scene tape. Lucas pointed at Rose Marie and said, "Rose Marie Roux. Department of Public Safety."

The cop lifted the tape, and asked her, "Can I have a job?"

She patted him once on the cheek. "I'm sure you're too nice a boy to work for me."

"Hey, I'm not," the cop said to her back. "I'm a jerk. Really." To Lucas, as Lucas ducked under the tape, "Seriously. I'm an asshole."

"I'll tell her," Lucas said.

ROSE MARIE HAD briefly been a street cop before she moved into administration, law school, politics, and power. She walked carefully down the route suggested by one of the crime-scene cops, cocked an eye in the window, looked at Widdler, backed away, and said, "That made a mark."

"Yeah."

"He killed Bucher? For sure?" she asked.

"He and his wife, I think. I don't know what all of *this* is about— except . . . You've been briefed on the Jesse Barth kidnapping attempt, and the firebombing."

She nodded: "Screw the pooch."

"The Screw thing and bomb, might have been an . . . effort, attempt, something . . . to distract me," Lucas said. "To get me looking at something else, while the Bucher thing went away. Might have worked, too, except for the white van, and then Gabriella." He scratched his head. "Man, is this a mess, or what?"

"Then he decided on direct action, shooting you with a moose gun, but chickened out and shot himself instead?" She was dubious.

"That's what I got," Lucas said. "Doesn't make me happy."

"What about the wife?"

"As soon as the crime-scene guys get finished with the basics, we're going to lift up Leslie's pant legs," Lucas said. "See if he's got Screw holes. If he does, we go have an unpleasant talk with Jane."

"If he doesn't?"

"We'll still have an unpleasant conversation with Jane. Then everybody'll talk to lawyers and we go back into the weeds to figure out what to do next," Lucas said.

"How much of this would have happened if Burt Kline hadn't been banging a teenager?"

Lucas had to think about it, finally sighed: "Maybe . . . there'd be one or two more people alive, but we wouldn't solve the Bucher case."

THEY WERE STANDING, talking, when John Smith showed up, looking sleepy, said, "Really?"—looked into the car, said, "Holy shit."

"You want to come along and talk to Jane?" Lucas asked.

"Yeah," Smith said. "This whole thing is . . ." He waved a hand in the air; couldn't think of a phrase for it.

"Screwed up?" Rose Marie offered.

———————

EVENTUALLY FOUR GUYS from the Medical Examiner's Office carefully lifted, pulled, and rolled Leslie Widdler's body out of the Lexus and onto a ground-level gurney. "Guy shoulda worn a wide-load sign," one of them said. When they got him flat, one of the ME investigators asked Lucas, "Which leg?"

"Both," Lucas said.

They only needed the first one. Widdler's left leg was riddled with what looked like small-caliber gunshot wounds, surrounded by half-dollar-sized bruises going yellow at the edges. There were a few oohs and aahs from the crowd. Though they didn't really need it, they pulled up the other pant leg and found more bites.

"Good enough for me," Smith said. "DNA will confirm it, but that, my friends, is what happens when you fuck with a pit bull."

"Half pit bull," Lucas said.

"What was the other half?" Rose Marie asked.

"Nobody knows," Lucas said. "Probably a rat terrier."

ON THE WAY to Widdler's, Lucas and Smith talked about an arrest. They believed that Leslie had been bitten by a dog, but had no proof that Screw had done the biting. That was yet to come, with the DNA tests. But DNA tests take a while. They knew there had been a second person involved, a driver. They knew that Jane Widdler had probably profited from at least three killings, in the looting of the Donaldson, Bucher, and Toms mansions, but they didn't have a single piece of evidence that would prove it.

"We push her," Smith said. "We read her rights to her, we push, see if she says anything. We make the call."

"We take her over to look at Leslie, put some stress on her," Lucas said. "I've got a warrant coming, both for her house and the shop.

I'll have my guys sit on both places . . . look for physical evidence, records. We'll let her know that, maybe crack her on the way to see Leslie."

"If she doesn't crack?"

"We do the research. We'll get her sooner or later," Lucas said. "There's no way Leslie Widdler pulled these killings off on his own. No way."

THE THING ABOUT BOTOX, Lucas thought later, was that when you'd had too much, as Jane Widdler had, you then had to fake reactions just to look human—and it's impossible to distinguish real fake reactions from fake fake reactions.

Widdler was at her shop, working the telephone, her back to the door, when Lucas and Smith trailed in, the bell tinkling overhead. Widdler was alone, and turned, saw them, sat up, made a fake look of puzzlement, and said into the phone, "I've got to go. I've got visitors."

She hung up, then stood, tense, vibrating, gripped the back of the chair, and said, "What?"

"You seem . . . Do you know?" Lucas asked, tilting his head.

"Where's my husband?" The question wasn't tentative; it came out as a demand.

Lucas looked at Smith, who said, "Well, Mrs. Widdler, there's been a tragedy . . ."

A series of tiny muscular twitches crossed her face: "Oh, God," she said. "I knew it. Where is he? What happened to him?"

Lucas said, "Mrs. Widdler, he apparently took his own life."

"Oh, no!" she shouted. Again, Lucas couldn't tell if it was real or faked. It looked fake . . . but then, it would. "He wouldn't do that, would he?" she cried. "Leslie wouldn't . . . Did he jump? Did he jump?"

"I'm afraid he shot himself," Smith said.

"Oh, no. No. That's not Leslie," Widdler said. She half turned and dropped into the chair, and made a weeping look, and might have produced a tear. "Leslie would never . . . his face wasn't . . . was he hurt?"

Lucas thought, *If she's faking it, she's good.* Her questions were crazy in pretty much the right way.

"I'm afraid you'll have to come with us, to make a technical identification of the body, but there's really no doubt," Smith said. "Both Lucas and I know him, of course . . . Where did you think he was last night? Was he here? Did he go out early?"

Widdler looked away, her voice hesitant, breaking. "He . . . never came home."

"Had he ever done that before?"

"Only . . . yes. I don't think . . . well, he wouldn't have done it again, under the same circumstances . . ." Her face was turned up at them, eyes wide, asking for an explanation. "But why? Why would he hurt himself? He had everything to live for . . ."

She made the weeping face again, and Lucas thought, *Jeez.*

Smith said, "There are some other problems associated with his death, Mrs. Widdler. Some illegal activity has turned up, and we think you know about it. We have to inform you that you have the right to remain silent, that anything you say can and will be used against you in a court of law. You have the right to speak to an attorney . . ."

"Oh, God!" She was horrified by the ritual words. "You can't think *I* did anything?"

THEY WERE IN Lucas's truck, but Smith drove. Lucas sat in the back with Widdler. Lucas asked, "How well did you know Claire Donaldson?"

"Donaldson? From Chippewa Falls?"

"Yes."

Widdler made a frownie look: "Well, I knew *of* her, but I never met her personally. We bought some antiques from her estate sale, of course, it was a big event for this area. Why?"

"Your husband murdered her," Lucas said.

"You shut up," Jane Widdler shouted. "You shut up. Leslie wouldn't hurt anybody . . ."

"And Mrs. Bucher and a man named Toms in Des Moines. Did you know Mrs. Bucher or Mr. Toms?"

She had covered her head with her arms; hadn't simply buried her face in her hands, but had wrapped her arms around her skull, her face slumped almost into her lap, and she said, "I'm not listening. I'm not listening."

S H E   S N U F F L E D and wept and groaned and wept some more and dug in her purse for the crumpled Kleenex that all women are apparently required to carry, and rubbed her nostrils raw with it, and Lucas stuck her again.

"Do you know a woman named Amity Anderson?"

The snuffling stopped, and Widdler uncoiled, her eyes rimmed with red, her voice thick with mucus, and she asked, "What does that bitch have to do with this?"

"You know her?" Getting somewhere.

She looked down in her purse, took out the crumpled Kleenex, wiped her nose again, looked out the window at the houses along Randolph Street, and said, "I know her."

"How long?" Looking for a lie.

"Since college," Widdler said. "She . . . knew Leslie before I did."

"Knew him? Had a relationship with him?" Smith asked, eyes in the rearview mirror.

Snuffle: "Yes."

Lucas asked, "Did, uh . . . were there ever any indications that a relationship continued?"

She leaned her head against the side window, staring at the back of Smith's head; the morning light through the glass was harsh on her face, making her look older and paler and tougher and German, like a fifteenth-century portrait by Hans Memling or a twentieth-century farm woman by Grant Wood. "Yes."

"When you say yes . . . ?"

"When he stayed out all night . . . that's where he was," she said.

"With Amity Anderson," Lucas said.

"Yes. She had some kind of hold on him. Some kind of emotional hold on him. Goddamn her." Turning to Lucas, teeth bared: "Why are you asking about her? How is she involved in this?"

Lucas looked back at her, and saw a puzzle of Botox tics and hair spray, expensive jewelry and ruined makeup. "I don't know," he said.

WHEN LESLIE WIDDLER was in the car, he looked somewhat dead. There might have been other possibilities, that he was drunk or drugged, sprawled uncomfortably in the backseat of the car, at least until you saw the hole in his temple.

At the ME's, they had peeled him out of the body bag and placed him on a steel table, ready to do a rush autopsy. There, under the harsh white lights, he looked totally dead, pale as a slab of Crisco. His expensive black alligator driving shoes pointed almost sideways, his tongue was visible at the side of his mouth, his eyes were still open. He looked surprised, in a dead way.

Jane blinked and walked away. "Yes," she said as she went, and outside the examining room, she crumbled into a chair.

Lucas said, "We'll ask you to wait here. Detective Smith and I have to discuss the situation."

They walked just far enough down the hall to be out of earshot, and Lucas asked, "What do you think?"

"I don't think we've got an arrest," Smith said. "What about the warrants?"

"We got crime scene both at her house and the business. If you want to send along a couple guys . . ."

"I'll do that," Smith said. He looked down the hall at Jane Widdler. "Cut her loose?"

Lucas looked at her, turned back to Smith, and nodded, but reluctantly. "I agree that we don't have an arrest. Yet. We tell her to get a lawyer, and we talk to the lawyer: keep her in town, don't start moving money, or she goes inside. We can always find something . . . possession of stolen property."

"If we find any."

Lucas grinned. "Okay. Suspected possession of stolen property. Or how about, conspiracy to commit murder? We can always apologize later."

"Tell that to her attorney."

THEY WALKED BACK down the hall, Widdler watching nervously, twisting her Kleenex. Lucas said, "Mrs. Widdler. You need to get an attorney, somebody we can talk to. We believe that you may be involved in the illegal activities surrounding Leslie's death . . ."

"You're going to arrest me?" She looked frightened; fake-frightened, but who could tell?

"We're searching your home and your business right now," Lucas said. "We're not going to arrest you at the moment, but that could change as we work through the day. You need to be represented. You can get your own attorney, or we can get one for you . . ."

"I'll get my own . . ."

Lucas was looking in her eyes when he told her that she wouldn't be arrested; she blinked once, and something cleared from her gaze, almost like a nictitating membrane on a lizard. "You can call from here, we can get you privacy if you want it," Lucas said, "or you can wait until you get home."

"I don't care about privacy," she said. "I do want to make some calls, get an attorney." Her chin trembled, and she made a dismayed look. "This is all so incomprehensibly dreadful."

THEY OFFERED to drive her home, since they were going there anyway. This time, she sat in the backseat by herself, calling on her cell phone. She talked first to her personal attorney, took down a number, and called that: "Joe Wyzinsky, please? Jane Widdler: Mr. Wyzinsky was recommended by my personal attorney, Laymon Haycraft. I'm with police officers right now. They are threatening to arrest me. Charges? I don't know exactly. Thank you."

When Wyzinsky's name came up, Lucas and Smith looked at each other and simultaneously grimaced.

Widdler, in the backseat, said, "Mr. Wyzinsky? Jane Widdler, of Widdler Antiques and Objets d'Art. My husband was shot to death this morning, apparently suicide. The police say that he was involved in murder and theft, and I believe they are talking about the Bucher case. They suspect me of being involved, but I'm not."

She listened for a moment, then said, "Yes, yes, of course, I'm very capable . . . With two police officers, they're driving me home. They say my home and business are being searched. No, I'm not under arrest, but they say they might arrest me later this afternoon, depending on the search."

She sounded, Lucas thought, like she was making a deal on an overpriced antique tea table. Too cool.

". . . Yes. Lucas Davenport, who is an agent of the state, and John Smith, who is on the St. Paul police force. What? Yes. Hang on." She handed the phone to Lucas. "He wants to talk to you."

Lucas took the phone and said, "What's happening, big guy?"

Wyzinsky asked, "You Miranda her?"

"Absolutely. John Smith did it, I witnessed. Then we insisted that she get representation, so there'd be no problem. Glad she got a pro." Lucas wiggled his eyebrows at Smith.

"You're taking her to her house?" Wyzinsky asked.

"Yup."

"She says you might arrest her. For what?"

"Murder, kidnapping, conspiracy to murder, attempted murder, arson, theft, possession and sale of stolen goods," Lucas said.

"Cruelty to animals," Smith added.

"And cruelty to animals," Lucas said. "We believe she took part in the killing of a dog named Screw, after which Screw's body was thrown out on the streets of St. Paul. Make that, cruelty to animals and littering."

"Anything else?"

"Probably a few federal charges," Lucas said. "We believe she may have been involved in murders in Chippewa Falls and Des Moines, as well as here in St. Paul, so that would be interstate flight, transportation of stolen goods, some firearms charges, et cetera."

"Huh. Sounds like you don't have much of a case, all that bullshit and no arrest," Wyzinsky said.

"We're nailing down the finer points," Lucas said.

"Yeah, I got a nail for you right here," Wyzinsky said. "How's Weather?"

"She's fine."

"You guys going to Midsummer Ball?"

"If Weather makes me," Lucas said. "I do look great in a tux."

"So do I," Wyzinsky said. "We ought to stand next to each other, and radiate on the women."

"I could do that," Lucas said.

"So—let me talk to her again," Wyzinsky said. "Is it Widdler? And, Lucas—don't ask her any more questions, okay?"

WIDDLER TOOK the phone, listened, said, "See you there, then." She rang off and said to Lucas, "You two seemed pretty friendly."

"We've known each other for a while," Lucas said. "He's a good attorney."

"He won't let friendship stand in the way of defending me?"

"He'd tear my ass off if he thought it'd help his case," Lucas said. "Joe doesn't believe people should go to jail."

"Especially when they're innocent," she said. "By the way, he told me not to answer any more questions."

FOUR COPS were working through Widdler's house. Lucas suggested that she pack a suitcase, under the supervision of one of the crime-scene people, and move to a motel.

"We're not going to leave you alone in here, until we're finished. We can't take the chance that you might destroy something, or try to."

"Can I use the bathroom?" she asked.

"If they're done with a bathroom," Lucas said. "And Mrs. Widdler: don't try to leave the area. We're right on the edge of arresting you. If you go outside the 494–694 loop, we probably will."

WYZINSKY SHOWED UP while Widdler was packing. He was short, stocky, and balding, with olive skin, black eyes, and big hands, and women liked him a lot. He was bullshitting a cop at the front driveway when Lucas saw him. Lucas stepped on the porch, whistled, and waved Wyzinsky in. The lawyer came up, grinning, rubbed his hands together. "This is gonna be good. Where is she?"

"Upstairs packing," Lucas said. He led the way into the house. "Try not to destroy any evidence."

"I'll be careful."

Smith came over: "We thought she'd be happier if she moved out while we tear the place apart."

Wyzinsky nodded: "You finished with any of the rooms yet? Something private?"

"The den." Lucas pointed. Two big chairs and a wide-screen TV, with French doors.

"I'll take her in there," Wyzinsky said. To Smith, he said, "Jesus, John, you ought to eat the occasional pizza. What do you weigh, one-twenty?"

"Glad to know you care," Smith said.

"Of course I care, you're nearly human," the lawyer said. He looked around, doing an appraisal on the house; its value, not the architecture. He made no effort to hide his glee. "Man, this is gonna be good. A dog named Screw? Can you say, 'Hello, Fox News,' 'Hello, Court TV'? Who's that blond chick on CNN who does the court stuff? The one with the glitter lipstick? Hel-lo, blondie."

"In your dreams," Smith said, but he was laughing, and he went to get Widdler.

WYZINSKY AND WIDDLER were talking in the den when a cop came out of the home office: "You guys should come and look at this," he said.

Smith: "What?"

"Looks like we have a suicide note. Or two. Or three."

Eventually, they decided that there were either three or four suicide notes, depending on how you counted them. One was simply a note to Jane, telling her the status of investment accounts at U.S. Bank, Wells Fargo, and Vanguard, and noting that the second-quarter income-tax payments had all been made. Whether that was a suicide note, or not, depended on context.

The other three notes were more clearly about suicide: about depression, about growing trouble, about the unfairness of the world, about the sense of being hunted, about trying to find a solution that would work. One said, to Jane, "If I don't get back to you, I really loved you."

WYZINSKY AND WIDDLER talked for more than an hour, then Wyzinsky emerged from the den and said, "Mrs. Widdler has some information that she wants to volunteer. She says that she has to do it now, or it might not be useful. If any of this ever comes to a trial, I want it noted that she cooperated on this. That she was helping the investigation. I would like to make the point that she is not opening herself to a general interrogation, but is making a limited statement."

"That's fine with me. We'll record it, if that's okay," Lucas said.

"That's okay, though we don't really need it," Wyzinsky said. "This isn't definitive evidentiary testimony, it's simply a point that she wishes to make, a suggestion."

"Better to record," Lucas said. "Just take a minute."

THEY GOT a recorder from one of the crime-scene guys, and a fresh cassette, and set up in the den. Lucas turned it on, checked that it worked, started over, said his name, the date, time, and place of the recording, the names of the witnesses, and turned the show over to Widdler.

Jane Widdler said, "I understand that I'm suspected of being an accomplice to my husband in illegal activities. I deny all of that. However, to help the investigation, I believe that the police must watch Amity Anderson, who has had a romantic attachment to my husband since we were in college, and which I thought was finished. However, I was told by Agent Davenport today that Amity Anderson figures in this investigation. I know Amity and I believe now that she is involved, and now that Leslie is . . . gone . . . she will try to run away. That is her response to crisis, and always has been. She wouldn't even fight with me over Leslie's affections. Once she is gone, she will be very hard to find, because she is quite familiar with Europe, both eastern and western. If she has money, from these supposed illegal activities, it could take years to find her. That's all I have to say."

Lucas said, "You think she was involved?"

Wyzinsky made a face, tilted his head, thought it over, then nodded at Widdler.

"I don't know," Widdler said. "I can't believe my husband was involved in anything illegal. Why should he be? Everything is going wonderfully in the business. We are the top antique and objets d'art destination in the Twin Cities. But I can't explain how he was found this morning, where he was found, and I can't explain the rifle. Agent

Davenport said that he must have had an accomplice, and accused me of being the accomplice. I am not and never have been an accomplice. I'm a storekeeper. But Amity Anderson . . . I don't know if she did anything wrong, but I think she must be watched, or she will run away."

"That's pretty much it," Wyzinsky said.

Lucas peered at Jane Widdler for a moment, then reached out and turned off the recorder. "All right. Do not leave the Twin Cities, Mrs. Widdler."

"Are you going to watch Amity?"

"We're working on all aspects of the case. I don't want to compromise the case by talking about it with a suspect," Lucas said.

"He'll watch her," Wyzinsky grunted. "Not much gets past Agent Davenport."

WIDDLER LEFT with Wyzinsky, and the crime-scene people continued to pull the house apart. Lucas got bored, went over to the Widdler shop, talked to the crime-scene guy in charge, who said, "More shit than you can believe, but none of it says 'Bucher' on the bottom. Haven't found any relevant names in the files . . ."

"Keep looking," Lucas said.

THE ME, done with the autopsy late in the day, said that it could be suicide, or it could be murder. "Given the circumstances, we just can't tell," he said. "The gun was pointed slightly upward and straight into the temple, two inches above the cheekbone, and judging from the burns and powder content inside the wound, the end of the barrel was probably touching the skin. There was almost no dispersion of powder outside the wound, very little tattooing on the skin, so the barrel was close. I could see a murder being done that way . . . but it'd be rare, especially since the victim doesn't appear to have been restrained in any way."

AS THE SUN was going down, Lucas stood in his office, calling the members of his crew; and he called Rose Marie, and borrowed an investigator named Jerrold from the Highway Patrol.

"We're taking Widdler's word for it," he told them all. "We're gonna stake out Anderson."

24

THEY GOT TOGETHER in Lucas's family room: Del, Jenkins, Flowers, Jerrold, Smith, and Lucas, Letty sitting in, the four state agents gently bullshitting her, Letty giving it back. Shrake was already on Anderson, picking her up in St. Paul, tagging her back home.

Smith was uneasy with state cops he didn't know well, although he and Del went way back. Lucas passed around bottles of Leinie's, except for Letty, who wanted a Leinie's but took a Coke. Smith and Lucas, who'd be talking to Amity Anderson, also took Cokes.

"I think it would be perfectly all right for me to drink one beer in the house," Letty said.

"If I gave it to you, I'd have to arrest myself," Lucas said.

"And probably beat the shit out of himself, too," Del said, winking at Letty.

LUCAS BRIEFED THEM on Amity Anderson. Jenkins, who'd worked the casual surveillance, suggested good spots to sit, "as long as we don't get rousted by St. Paul."

"I talked to the watch commander, he'll pass it along to patrol, so you're okay on that," Smith said.

With six people, they could track her in four-hour shifts, four on and eight off. That would wear them down after a while, but Lucas planned to put pressure on Amity, to see if he could make her run, see what she took with her.

Lucas and Flowers would take the first shift, from eight to midnight. Shrake and Jenkins would take midnight to four, Del and Jerrold from four to eight, and then Lucas and Flowers would be back.

Tonight, after the meeting, Flowers would be set up, on the street and watching, and then Lucas and Smith would call on Anderson and rattle her cage.

LUCAS AND SMITH drove to Anderson's house separately, and Lucas left his truck at the end of an alley that looked at the back of the house. Then he got into Smith's Ford, and they drove around the corner and pulled into Anderson's driveway. Smith said, "I oughta take a shift."

"No need to," Lucas said. "The rest of us have all worked together . . . no problem."

"Yeah, but you know," Smith said. He didn't want to, but it was only polite to offer.

"I know—but no problem."

THEY WENT UP the walk, saw the curtains move and a shape behind them, and then Lucas knocked on the door and a second later, Anderson opened it, looking at Lucas over a chain. She was holding a stick of wet celery smeared with orange cheese. "Lucas Davenport, I spoke to you once before," Lucas said. "This is Detective John Smith from the St. Paul police. We need to speak to you."

"What about?" Didn't move the chain.

Lucas got formal, putting some asshole in his voice: "A friend of yours, Leslie Widdler, was found dead in a car a few blocks from here this morning. Shot to death. We have questioned his wife, Jane, and she has hired an attorney. But our investigation, along with statements made by Jane Widdler, suggests that you could help us in the investigation. Please open the door."

"Do you have a warrant?"

"No, but we could get one in a couple of minutes," Lucas said, talking tougher, his voice dropping into a growl. "You can either talk to us here, or we'll get a warrant, come in and get you and take you downtown. It's your call."

"Do I get an attorney?" Anderson asked.

"Anytime you want one," Lucas said. "If you can't get one to come tonight, we'll take you downtown, put you in a cell, and we can wait until one gets here tomorrow."

"But I haven't done anything," Anderson said.

"That's what we need to talk about," Lucas said.

IN THE END, she let them in, then called an attorney friend, who agreed to come over. While they waited, they watched *American Volcanoes* for forty-five minutes, a TV story of how Yellowstone could blow up at any minute and turn the entire United States into a hellhole of ash and lava; Anderson drank two glasses of red wine, and then the attorney arrived.

Lucas knew her, as it happened, Annabelle Ramford, a woman who did a lot of pro bono work for the homeless, but not a lot of criminal law.

"We meet again," she said, with a thin smile, shaking his hand.

"I hope you can help us," Lucas said. "Miz Anderson needs some advice."

Anderson admitted knowing the Widdlers. She looked shocked when Lucas suggested that she'd had a sexual relationship with Leslie Widdler, but admitted it. "You told me you're gay," Lucas said.

"I am. When I had my relationship with Leslie, I didn't know it," she said.

"But your relationship with Leslie continued, didn't it?"

She looked at Ramford, who said, "You don't have to say anything at all, if you don't wish to."

They all looked at Anderson, who said, "What happens if I don't?"

"I'll make a note," Lucas said. "But we will find out, either from you, with your cooperation, or from other people."

"You don't have to take threats, either," Ramford said to Anderson.

"That really wasn't a threat," Lucas said, his voice going mild. "It's the real situation, Annabelle. If we're not happy when we leave here, we'll be taking Miz Anderson with us. You could then recommend a criminal attorney and we can all talk tomorrow, at the jail."

"No-no-no," Anderson said. "Look, my relationship with Leslie . . . continued . . . to some extent."

"To some extent?" Smith asked. "What does that mean?"

"I was . . ." She bit her lip, looked away from them, then said, "I was actually more interested in Jane."

"In Jane? Did you have a physical relationship with Jane?" Lucas asked.

"Well . . . yes. Why would I want to fuck a great big huge fat guy?"

Lucas had no answer for that; but he had more questions for Jane Widdler.

HE TURNED to the quilts, taking notes as Anderson answered the questions. She believed the quilts were genuine. They'd been spotted by Marilyn Coombs, she said, who took them to the Widdlers for confirmation and evaluation.

The Widdlers, in turn, had sent them away for laboratory tests, and confirmed with the tests, and other biographical information about Armstrong, that the quilts were genuine. The Widdlers then put together an investment package in which the quilts would be sold to private investors who would donate them to museums, getting both a tax write-off and a reputation for generosity.

"We have reason to believe that the quilts are faked—that the curses were, in any case. That the primary buyers paid only a fraction of what they said they paid, and took an illegal tax write-off after the donations," Lucas said.

"I don't know about any of that," Anderson said. "I was the contact between the Widdlers and Mrs. Donaldson. I brought her attention to the quilts, but she made her own decisions and her own deals. I never handled money."

"You told me that you didn't know Mrs. Bucher," Lucas said.

She shrugged. "I didn't. I knew who she was, but I didn't know her."

"And you still . . . maintain that position?"

"It's the truth," she said.

"You didn't go there with Leslie Widdler and kill Mrs. Bucher and her maid?"

"Of course not! That's crazy!"

He asked her about Toms: never heard of him, she said. She'd never been to Des Moines in her life, not even passing through.

"Were you with Leslie Widdler last night?" Smith asked.

"No. I was out until about eight, then I was here," she said.

"You didn't speak to him, didn't ride around with him . . ."

"No. No. I didn't speak to him or see him or anything."

THEY PUSHED ALL the other points, but Anderson wouldn't budge. She hadn't dealt in antiques with either Leslie or Jane Widdler. She had no knowledge of what happened with the Armstrong quilts, after Donaldson, other than the usual art-world reports, gossip, and hearsay. She could prove, she thought, that on the Friday night that the Buchers were killed, she'd been out late with three other women friends, at a restaurant in downtown Minneapolis, where she'd not only drunk a little too much, but remembered that there'd been a birthday party in an upper loft area of the restaurant that had turned raucous, and that she was sure people would remember.

WHEN THEY were done, Anderson said, "Now I have a question. I have the feeling that Jane Widdler has been telling you things that aren't true. I mean, if Jane and Leslie were killing these people, I don't know why Jane would try to drag me into it. Is she trying to do that?"

"Maybe," Lucas said.

"Do you think they could kill people?" Smith asked.

Anderson turned her face down, thinking, glanced sideways at Ramford, then said, "You know, Jane . . . has always struck me as greedy. Not really a bad person, but terribly greedy. She wants all this stuff. Diamonds, watches, cars, Hermès this and Tiffany that and Manolo Blahnik something else. She might kill for money—it'd have to be money—but . . . I don't know."

Her mouth moved some more, without words, and they all sat and waited, and she went on:

"Leslie, I think Leslie might kill. For the pleasure in it. And money. In college, we had this small-college football team. Football didn't mean anything, really. You'd go and wave your little pennant or wear your mum and nobody cared if you won or lost. A lot of people made fun of football players . . . but Leslie liked to hurt people. He'd talk about stepping on people's hands with his cleats. Like, if one of the runner-guys did too well, they'd get him down and then Leslie would 'accidentally' step on his hand and break it. He claimed he did it several times. Word got around that he could be dangerous."

Smith said, "Huh," and Lucas asked, "Anything heavier than that? That you heard of? Did you get any bad vibrations from Leslie when Mrs. Donaldson was killed?"

She shook her head, looking spooked: "No. Not at all. But now that you mention it . . . I mean, jeez, their store really came up out of nowhere." She looked at Lucas, Smith, and Ramford. "You know what I mean? Most antique people wind up in these little holes-in-the-wall, and the Widdlers are suddenly rich."

"Makes you think," Smith said, looking up at Lucas.

There was more, but the returns were diminishing. Lucas finally stood up, sighed, said to Ramford, "You might want to give her a couple of names, just in case," and he and Smith took off.

"LET'S DRIVE AROUND for a while, before you drop me off. Get Ramford out of there," Lucas said to Smith. "I don't know where she parked, I wouldn't want her to pick me up." He got on his radio and called Flowers as they walked to the car.

"I'm looking right at you," Flowers said.

"There should be a lawyer coming out in a few minutes. Stay out of sight, and call when she's gone."

Smith drove them up to Grand Avenue, and they both got double-dip ice cream cones, and leaned on the hood of Smith's car and watched the college girls go by; blondes and short shirts and remarkably little laughter, intense brooding looks, like they'd been bit on the ass by Sartre or Derrida or some other Frenchman.

Lucas was getting down to cone level on his chocolate pecan fudge when his radio beeped. Flowers said, "The lawyer is getting in her car."

"I'll be in place in five minutes," Lucas said.

SURVEILLANCE COULD be exciting, but hardly ever was. This night was one of the hardly-evers, four long hours of nothing. Couldn't even read, sitting in the dark. He talked to Flowers twice on the radio, had a long phone chat with Weather—God bless cell phones—and at midnight, Jenkins eased up behind him.

"You good?" Lucas asked, on the radio.

"Got my video game, got my iPod. Got two sacks of pork rinds and a pound of barbeque ribs, and a quart of Diet Coke for propellant. All set."

"Glad I'm not in the car with you," Lucas said. "Those goddamn pork rinds."

"Ah, you open the door every half hour or so, and you're fine," Jenkins said. "You might not want to light a cigarette."

WEATHER WAS CUTTING again in the morning, and was asleep when Lucas tiptoed into the bedroom at twelve-fifteen. He took an Ambien to knock himself down, a Xanax to smooth out the ride, thought about a martini, decided against it, set the alarm clock, and slipped into bed.

The alarm went off exactly seven hours and forty minutes later. Weather was gone; that happened when he was working hard on a case, staying up late. They missed each other, though they were lying side by side . . .

He cleaned up quickly, looking at his watch, got a Ziploc bag with four pieces of cornbread from the housekeeper, a couple of Diet Cokes from the refrigerator, the newspaper off the front porch, and was on his way. Hated to be late on a stakeout; they were so boring that being even a minute late was considered bad form.

As it was, he pulled up on the side street at two minutes to eight, got the hand-off from Jerrold, called Del, who'd just been pushed by Flowers, and who said that a light had come on ten minutes earlier. "She's up, but she's boring," Del said.

The newspapers had the Widdler story, and tied it to Bucher, Donaldson, and Toms. Rose Marie said that more arrests were imminent, but the *Star Tribune* reporter spelled it "eminent" and the *Pioneer Press* guy went with "immanent."

You should never, Lucas thought, trust a spell-checker.

ANDERSON STEPPED OUT of her house at 8:10, picked up the newspaper, and went back inside. At 8:20, carrying a bag and the newspaper, she walked down to the bus stop, apparently a daily routine, because the bus arrived two minutes later.

They tagged her downtown and to her office, parked their cars in no-parking zones, with police IDs on the dashes, and Lucas took the Skyway exit while Flowers took the street. There was a back stairs, but Lucas didn't think the risk was enough to worry about . . .

As he waited, doing nothing, he had the feeling he might be wrong about that, and worried about it, but not too much: he *always* had that feeling on stakeouts. A few years earlier, he'd had a killer slip away from a stakeout, planning to use the stakeout itself as his alibi for another murder . . .

A few minutes before noon, Shrake showed up for the next shift, and Lucas passed off to him, and walked away, headed back to the office. He'd gone fifty feet when his cell phone rang: Shrake. "She's moving," and he was gone. Lucas looked back. Shrake was ambling along the Skyway, away from Lucas, on the phone. Talking to somebody else on the cell, probably to Jenkins, probably afraid to use the radio because he was too close to the target; she had practically walked over him.

Seventy-five feet ahead of Shrake, Lucas could see the narrow figure of Amity Anderson speed-walking through the crowd.

Going to lunch? His radio chirped: Flowers. "You want to hang in,
until we figure out where she's going?"

"Yeah."

Shrake took her to a coffee shop, where she bought a cup of coffee to go, and an orange scone, and then headed down to the street,
where Jenkins picked her up. "Catching a bus," Jenkins said.

They took her all the way back to her house. Off the bus, she
paused to throw the coffee-shop sack into a corner trash barrel, then
headed up to her house, walking quickly, in a hurry. She went
straight to the mailbox and took out a few letters, shuffled them
quickly, picked one, tore the end off as she went through the door.

"What do you think?" Flowers asked, on the radio.

"Let's give her an hour," Lucas said.

"That's what I think," Flowers said. Shrake and Jenkins agreed.

Half an hour later, Anderson walked out of her house wearing a
long-sleeved shirt and jeans and what looked like practical shoes or
hiking boots. She had a one-car detached garage, with a manual lift.
She pushed the door up, backed carefully out, pulled the door down
again, pointed the car up the hill, and took off.

"We're rolling," Jenkins said. "We're gone."

25

LUCAS GOT ON THE RADIO: "This could be something, guys. Stack it up behind her, and take turns cutting off, but don't lose her."

Shrake: "Probably going to the grocery store."

Lucas: "She turned the wrong way. There's one just down the hill."

They had four cars tagging her, but no air. As long as they stayed in the city, they were good—they'd each tag her for a couple of blocks, then turn away, while the next one in line caught up. They tracked her easily along Ford to Snelling, where she took a right, down the bluff toward Seventh. Snelling was a chute; if she stopped there, they'd all be sacked right on top of her. Flowers followed her down while Lucas, Jenkins, and Shrake waited at the top of the hill.

"I got her," Flowers said. "She took a left on Seventh, come on through."

They moved fast down the hill, through the intersection, Flowers peeling away as Lucas came up behind him. They got caught at a stoplight just before I-35, and Lucas hooked away, into a store parking lot, afraid she'd pick up his face if he got bumper-to-bumper. "Jenkins?"

"Got her. Heading south on Thirty-five E."

Lucas pulled out of the parking lot, now last in line, and followed the others down the ramp onto I-35. Lucas got on the radio, looking for a highway-patrol plane, but was told that with one thing or another, nobody could get airborne for probably an hour. "Well, get him going, for Christ's sake. This chick may be headed for Des Moines, or something."

The problem with a four-car tag was that Anderson wasn't a fast driver, and they had to hold back, which meant they'd either loom in her rearview mirror, or they'd have to hold so far back that they might lose her to a sudden move. If she hooked into a shopping center, and several were coming up, they'd be out of luck.

"Jenkins, move up on her slow," Lucas said. "Get off at Yankee Doodle, even if she doesn't."

"Got it."

She didn't get off; Jenkins went up the off-ramp, ran the lights at the top, and came down the on-ramp, falling in behind Lucas.

They played with her down the interstate, the speed picking up. She didn't get off at the Burnsville Mall, a regional shopping center that Lucas had thought would be a possibility. Instead, she pushed out of the metro area, heading south into the countryside.

Lucas could see the possible off-ramps coming on his nav system, and called them out; one of them would fall off at each, then reenter. She didn't get off, but stayed resolutely in the slow lane, poking along at the speed limit.

South, and more south, thirty miles gone before she clicked on her turn signal and carefully rolled up the ramp at Rice County 1, two cars behind Flowers. Flowers had to guess, and Lucas shouted into the radio, "She went to Carleton. Go left. Go east."

Flowers turned left, the next car went right, and Anderson turned left behind Flowers. Carleton was off to the east in Northfield, but they'd already gone past the Northfield exit; still, she might be familiar with the countryside around it, Lucas thought, and that had been a better bet than the open countryside to the west.

Now they had a close tag on her, but from the front. Flowers slowly pulled away, leading her into the small town of Dundas; but just before the town, she turned south on County 8, and Flowers was yelling, "I'm coming back around," and Shrake said, "I got her, I got her."

Well back, now. Not many cars out, and all but Lucas had been close to her, and she might pick one of them out. They kept south, onto smaller and narrower roads, Shrake breaking away, Jenkins moving up, until she disappeared into a cornfield.

"Whoa. Man, she turned," Jenkins said. "She's, uh, off the road, hang back guys, I'm gonna go on past . . ."

Hadn't rained in a few days, and when Jenkins went past the point where she'd disappeared, he looked down a dirt track, weeds growing up in the middle, and called back, "She looks like she's going into a field. I don't know, man . . . you can probably track her by the dust coming up."

"That's not a road," Lucas said, peering at his atlas. "Doesn't even show up here; I think it must go down to the river."

"Maybe she's going canoeing," Flowers said. "This is a big canoe river."

Lucas said into a live radio, "Ah, holy shit."

"What?"

"It's the Cannon River, man."

"Yeah?"

"The money that got laundered in Las Vegas, on the quilts—it went to Cannon, Inc., or Cannon Associates, or something like that."

Shrake came back: "Dust cloud stopped. I think she's out of her car; or lost. What do you want to do?"

"Watch for a minute," Lucas said. "Flowers, you're wearing boots?"

"Yup."

"I got my gators," Shrake said. "I didn't think we were gonna be creeping around in a cornfield."

"Gators for me," Jenkins said.

"You guys get a truckload deal?" Flowers asked.

"Shut up," Lucas said. "Okay, Flowers and I are gonna walk in there. Jenkins and Shrake get down the opposite ends of the road. If she comes out, you'll be tracking her."

"How do we hide the cars?" Flowers asked.

"Follow me," Lucas said. He went on south, a hundred yards, a hundred and fifty, found an access point, and plowed thirty feet into the cornfield. The corn didn't quite hide the truck, but it wouldn't be obvious what kind it was, unless you rode right up to it. Flowers followed him in and got out of his state car shaking his head. "Gonna be one pissed-off farmer."

"Bullshit. He'll get about a hundred dollars a bushel from us," Lucas said. "Let's go."

Flowers said, "I got two bottles of water in the car."

"Get them. And get your gun," Lucas said.

"The gun? You think?"

"No. I just like to see you wearing the fuckin' gun for a change," Lucas said. "C'mon, let's get moving."

HOT DAY. Flowers pulled his shoulder rig on as they jogged along the rows of shoulder-high corn, ready to take a dive if Anderson suddenly turned up in the car.

"Looks like she's down by the water," Flowers said. They could see only the crowns of the box elders and scrub cedar along the river, so she was lower than they were, and they should be able to get close. At the track, they turned toward the river, panting a bit now, hot, big men in suits carrying guns and a pound of water each, no hats; the track was probably 440 yards long, Lucas thought, one chunk of a forty-acre plot; but since it was adjacent to the river, there might be some variance.

"Sand burrs," Flowers grunted. Their feet were kicking up little puffs of dust.

———

THEY RAN the four-forty in about four minutes, Lucas thought, and at the end of it, he decided he needed to start jogging again; the rowing machine wasn't cutting it. When the field started to look thin, and the terrain started to drop, they cut left into the cornfield and slowed to a walk, then a stooped-over creep. The corn smelled sweet and hot and dusty, and Lucas knew he'd have a couple of sweaty corn cuts on his neck before he got out of it.

AT THE EDGE of the field, they looked down a slope at a muddy stream lined on both sides with scrubby trees, and a patch of trees surrounding a shack and a much newer steel building. The access door on the front of the building was standing open; the garage door was down. Anderson's car was backed up to the garage door. The building had no windows at all, and Lucas said, "Cut around back."

They went off again, running, stooping, watching the building. They were down the side of it when they heard the garage door going up, and they eased back in the cornfield, squatting next to each other, watching.

Anderson came out of the building. She'd taken off the long-sleeve shirt, and was now wearing a green T-shirt; she was carrying two paintings.

"Got her," he muttered to Flowers.

"So now what?"

"Well, we can watch her, and see what she does with the stuff, or we can go ahead and bust her," Lucas said.

"Make the call," Flowers said.

"She's probably moving it somewhere out-of-state. Dumping it. Cashing it in. Getting ready to run." He sat thinking about it for another thirty seconds, then said, "Fuck it. Let's bust her."

ANDERSON HAD GONE back inside the garage and they eased down right next to it, heard her rattling around inside, then stepped around the corner of the open door, inside. The place was half full of furniture, arranged more or less in a U, down the sides and along the back of the building. The middle of the U was taken up by an old white Chevy van, which had been backed in, and was pointing out toward the door.

Lucas felt something snap when he saw it, a little surge of pleasure: Anderson had her back to them and he said, "How you doing, Amity?"

She literally jumped, turned, took them in, then took three or four running steps toward them and screamed "No," and dashed down the far side of the van.

Flowers yelled, "Cut her off," and went around the back of the van, while Lucas ran around the nose. Anderson was fifteen feet away and coming fast when Lucas crossed the front of the van and she screamed, "No," again, and then he saw something in her hand and she was throwing it, and he almost had time to get out of the way before the hand-grenade-sized vase whacked him in the forehead and dropped him like a sack of kitty litter.

He groped at her as she swerved around him out into the sunlight, then Flowers jumped over him. Lucas struggled back to his feet and saw her first run toward her car, and then, as Flowers closed in, swerve into the shack, the door slamming behind her.

Lucas was moving again, forehead burning like fire—the woman had an arm like A-Rod.

Flowers yelled, "Back door," as he kicked in the front, and Lucas ran down the side of the house in time to see Anderson burst onto the deck on the river side of the house. She saw him, looked back once, then ran, arms flapping wildly, down toward the river. Lucas shouted, "Don't!"

He was five steps away when she hurled herself in.

FLOWERS RAN DOWN to the bank, stopped beside Lucas, and said, "Jesus. She's gonna stink."

The river was narrow, murky, and, in front of the shack, shallow. Anderson had thrown herself into four inches of water and a foot of muck, and sat up, groaning, covered with mud. "You got boots on," Lucas said to Flowers. "Reach in there and get her."

"You got longer arms," Flowers said.

"You're up for a step increase and I'm your boss," Lucas said.

"Goddamnit, I was hoping for a little drama," Flowers said. Anderson had turned over now, on her hands and knees. Flowers stepped one foot into the muck, caught one of her hands, and pried her out of the stuff.

Lucas said to her, "Amity, you are under arrest. You have the right to remain silent . . ."

FLOWERS SAID, "Cuffs?" Lucas said, "Hell, yes, she's probably killed about six people. Or helped, anyway."

"I did not," Anderson wailed. "I didn't . . ."

Lucas ignored her, walked up the bank toward the steel building, turned the radio back up and called Jenkins and Shrake. "Come on in. We grabbed her; and we got a building full of loot."

Flowers checked Anderson for obvious weapons, removed a

switchblade from her side pocket, put her on the ground at the front of the car, and cuffed her to the bumper. She started to cry, and didn't stop.

L U C A S P U T the switchblade on top of Flowers's car, where they wouldn't forget it, and walked around to the trunk. Inside were three plastic-wrapped paintings and an elaborate china clock. Small, high-value stuff, he thought. He looked at the backs of all three paintings, found one old label from Greener Gallery, Chicago, and nothing else.

Flowers had gone inside the steel building, and Lucas followed. "Hell of a lot of furniture," Flowers said. "I could use a couple pieces for my apartment."

"Couple pieces would probably buy you a house," Lucas said. "See any more paintings? Or swoopy chairs?"

"There're a couple of swoopy chairs . . ."

Sure enough: there was no other way to describe them. They were looking at the chairs when Shrake and Jenkins came in, and Flowers waved at them, and Lucas saw a wooden rack with more plastic-wrapped paintings. He pulled them down, one-two-three, and ripped loose the plastic on the back. One and three were bare.

The back of two had a single word, written in oil paint with a painter's brush, a long time ago: *Reckless.*

26

AMITY ANDERSON WENT to jail in St. Paul, held without bail on suspicion of first-degree murder in the deaths of Constance Bucher and Sugar-Rayette Peebles. Flowers said she cried uncontrollably all the way back and tried to shift the blame to Jane Widdler.

Everybody thought about that, and on the afternoon of Anderson's arrest, two officers and a technician went to Widdler's store with a search warrant, and, after she'd spoken to her attorney, spent some time using sterile Q-tips to scrub cells from the lining of her cheeks.

DNA samples were also taken from Anderson, and from the body of Leslie Widdler, and were packed off to the lab. At the same time, five crime-scene techs from the BSA and the St. Paul Police Department began working over the white van, the steel building, and the shack.

Ownership of the land, shack, and building was held by the Lorna C. Widdler Trust. Lorna was Leslie's mother, who'd died fourteen years earlier; Leslie was the surviving trustee. No mention of Jane. The land surrounding the shack, the cornfield, was owned by a town-farmer in Dundas, who said he'd seen Leslie—"A big guy?

Dresses like a fairy?"—only twice in ten years. He'd had a woman with him, the farmer said, but he couldn't say for certain whether it was Jane Widdler or Amity Anderson. They paid the farmer $225 for damage to his cornfield.

Smith called Lucas the evening of the arrest and said, "We found a pill bottle under the front seat of the van. It's a prescription for Amity Anderson."

"There you go," Lucas said.

"Yeah, and we got some hair, long brown hair. Doesn't look like Widdler's. It does look like Anderson's."

"Anything on Leslie?"

"Well, there's some discoloration on the back of the passenger seat, might be blood. One of the techs says it is, so we've got some DNA work to do."

"If it's either a dog or Leslie . . ."

"Then we're good."

THE RECKLESS PAINTING and the swoopy chairs were confirmed by the Lash kid, a painting was found on an old inventory list held by the Toms family in Des Moines, and two pieces of furniture were found on purchase receipts in Donaldson's files.

St. Paul police, making phone checks, found a call from Leslie Widdler's phone to Anderson's house on the night Widdler killed himself.

The quilts were defended by their museum owners as genuine.

SO THE REPORTERS came and went, and the attorneys; the day after the arrest, Lucas was chatting with Del when Smith came by. Smith had been spending time with Anderson and her court-appointed attorney. They shuffled chairs around Lucas's office and Carol brought a coffee for Smith, and Smith sighed and said, "Gotta tell you, Lucas. I think there's an outside possibility that we got the wrong woman."

"Talk to me."

"The hair's gonna be Anderson's—or maybe, somebody we just don't know. But I looked at her hair really close, and it's the same. I mean, the same. Color, texture, split ends . . . We gotta wait for the DNA, but it's hers."

"What does she say?" Lucas asked.

"She says she was never in the van," Smith said.

"Well, shit, you caught her right there," Del said. "What more do you want?"

"We asked her about the phone call from Leslie, the night Leslie killed himself. Know what she says?"

"Is this gonna hurt?" Lucas asked.

Smith nodded. "She says that Jane Widdler called her, not Leslie. She said that Jane told her that her car had broken down, and since Anderson was only a few blocks away, asked her to come over and pick her up, give her a ride home. Anderson said she did. She said Widdler told her she had to pee, so they stopped at Anderson's house, and Widdler went in the bathroom. That's when Widdler picked up the prescription bottle and the hair, Anderson says."

"She's saying that Jane Widdler murdered Leslie," Lucas said.

"Yep."

"Anderson never saw a body?"

"She never saw the car, she says," Smith said. "She says Widdler told her that she was afraid to wait in a dark area, and walked out to Cretin. She said she picked up Widdler on Cretin, took her back to her house to pee, and then took her home."

"How long was the phone call?" Lucas asked.

"About twenty-three seconds."

"Doesn't sound like a call between a guy about to commit suicide, and his lover," Lucas said to Del.

"I don't know," Del said. "Never having been in the position."

"SHE'S GOT THIS STORY, and she admits it sounds stupid, but she's sticking to it. And she does it like . . ." Smith hesitated, then said it: ". . . like she's innocent. You know those people who never stop screaming, and then it turns out they didn't do it? Like that."

"Hmm," Lucas said.

"Another thing," Del said. "Even if we find some proof that Widdler was involved, how do we ever convict? A defense attorney would put Anderson on trial and shred the case."

"So you're saying we ought to convict Anderson because we can?" Lucas asked.

"No," Del said. "Though it's tempting."

"You oughta go over and talk to her—Anderson," Smith said to Lucas.

"Maybe I will," Lucas said. "All right if I take a noncop with me?"

"Who'd that be?"

"A bartender," Lucas said.

AMITY ANDERSON had never been big, and now she looked like a Manga cartoon character when the crime boss fetches her out of the dungeon. She'd lost any sparkle she'd ever had; her hair hung lank, her nails were chewed to her fingertips.

"This is all off the record," Lucas said.

Anderson's lawyer nodded. "For your information: no court use, no matter what is said."

Lucas introduced Sloan, who'd put on his best brown suit for the occasion. "Mr. Sloan is an old friend and a former police officer who has always had a special facility in . . . conversations with persons suspected of crimes," Lucas said carefully. "I asked him to come along as a consultant."

Everybody nodded and Anderson said, "I didn't know about any killings. But I knew Leslie and Jane, and when Mrs. Donaldson was killed, I worried. But that's all. I didn't have any proof, I didn't have any knowledge. With Mrs. Bucher, it never crossed my mind . . . then, when I read about Marilyn Coombs being killed, I thought about it again. But I pushed it away. Just away—I didn't *want* to think about it."

Sloan took her back through the whole thing, with a gentle voice and thin teacher's smile, working more like a therapist than a cop, listening to the history: about how Anderson and the Widdlers had become involved in college, and then drifted apart. How the surprise call came years later, about the quilts. About her move to the Cities, occasional contacts with the Widdlers, including a sporadic sexual relationship with Jane Widdler.

"And then you drove down to a barn full of stolen antiques and began stealing them a second time—with a key you had in your pocket," Lucas said.

"That's because Jane set me up," Anderson said through her teeth, showing the first bit of steel in the interrogation. "I couldn't believe it—I couldn't believe how she must have worked it. She knew I was friends with Don Harvey. He's a very prominent museum person from Chicago, he used to be here. She said he was coming to town, and if he authenticated some paintings for them, that they would give me fifteen percent of the sale price, above their purchase price. She thought I had some influence with Don because we'd dated once, and were friends. If he okayed the paintings—I mean, if he'd okayed that Reckless painting, I could have gotten seventy-five thousand dollars in fees for that one painting."

She shook her head again, a disbelieving smile flickering across her face: "She gave me a key and said she'd send me a map in the mail. I got it out of my mailbox when you were watching me."

Lucas nodded. They'd seen her get home, go straight to the mailbox, and then out to the car.

"John Smith found the map . . ." Anderson began.

"He said it was a really old map, Xeroxed, with your fingerprints all over it."

"And the envelope . . ." Anderson said.

"Just an envelope . . ."

"Well, can't you do some science stuff that shows the key was inside? Or the map? I see all this stuff on *Nova*, where is it?"

"On *Nova*," Lucas said.

Her eyes drifted away: "My God, she completely tangled me up . . ."

THEY TALKED TO her for another half hour, Sloan watching her face, backtracking, poking her with apparently nonrelevant questions that knitted back toward possible conflicts in what she was saying.

When he was done, he nodded to Lucas, and Lucas said, "It's been fun. We'll get back to you."

"Do you believe me?" she asked Lucas.

"I believe evidence," Lucas said. "I don't know about Sloan."

Sloan said, "I gotta think about it."

As they were leaving, Anderson said, with a wan, humorless smile, "You know the last mean thing that Botox bitch did? She stole my alprazolam to put in the van, just when I needed it most. I could really use some stress meds right now."

OUT IN the hallway, Sloan looked at Lucas. Lucas was leaning against the concrete-block wall, rubbing his temples, and Sloan said, "What?"

Lucas pushed away from the wall and asked, "What do you think?"

"She was bullshitting us some, but not entirely," Sloan said. "I'd probably convict her if I were on a jury, based on the evidence, but I don't think she killed anyone."

"Okay."

"What happened with you?" Sloan asked. "You look like you've seen a ghost."

LUCAS CALLED the evidence guys at St. Paul, then the supervisor of the crime-scene crew who'd gone over Anderson's house. Then he went down to Del's desk and said, "Let's take a walk around the block."

Outside, summer day, hot again, puffy white fair-weather clouds; flower beds showing a little wilt from the lack of rain. Del asked, "What's happening?"

"Remember all that shit Smith said? About the evidence coming in?"

"Yeah." Del nodded.

"So one of the clinchers was an amber plastic prescription bottle," Lucas said. "You know the kind, with the click-off white tops?"

"Uh-huh. I know about the bottle."

"When I was looking into Anderson, when I first tripped over her, I didn't have anything to go on," Lucas continued. "I thought I might take an uninvited look around her house."

"Ah." They'd both done it before, breaking-and-entering, a dozen times between the two of them. Life in the big city.

"In the bathroom, I found a bottle of alprazolam and a bottle of Ambien," Lucas said. "I noticed them because I use them myself. The thing is, there wasn't any alprazolam in Anderson's house when St. Paul went through the place last night. And the stuff in the van was only three weeks old—it was a new prescription. Unless they used the van some other time, that we don't know about, and that seems unlikely, because they'd had some problems the last two times out . . . how did the alprazolam get in the van?"

"That's awkward," Del said.

"No shit."

"Hey. Don't get all honorable about it," Del said. "I can think of ways that bottle got there—like maybe she went down to take some other pictures out, or maybe she went down to clean out the van, and lost the bottle. Won't do any good for you to start issuing affidavits about breaking-and-entering."

Lucas grinned. "I wasn't going to do that. But . . ."

"We need to think about this," Del said.

THEY FINISHED WALKING down the block, and back, and nothing had occurred to them. At the door, as they were going back in the BCA building, Del asked, "Did anybody ever ask Anderson about Gabriella?"

"No . . . Gabriella. She's just gone."

BUT THAT EVENING, sitting in the den listening to the soundtrack from *Everything Is Illuminated*, Lucas began to think about Gabriella, and where she might have gone. Assuming that she'd been killed by Leslie Widdler, where would he put her? Because of the "Don't Mow Ditches" campaign, it was possible that he'd just heaved her out the van door, the way he'd heaved Screw, and she was lying in two feet of weeds off some back highway. On the other hand, he had, not far away, an obscure wooded tract where he had to take the van anyway, assuming he'd used the van when he killed Gabriella. And if he had a body in it . . .

He got on the phone to Del, then to Flowers: "Can you come back up here?"

"I'm not doing much good here," Flowers said. He'd gone back south, still pecking away at the case of the girl found on the river-bank. "My suspect's about to join the Navy to see the world. Which means he won't be around to talk to."

"All right. Listen, meet Del and me tomorrow at the Widdlers' shack. Wear old clothes."

THEY HOOKED UP at eleven o'clock in the morning, out at the Widdlers' place, the highway in throwing up heat mirages, the cornfield rustling in the spare dry wind, the sun pounding down. They unloaded in front of the shack, which had been sealed by the crime-scene crew. Flowers was towing a boat, and inside the boat, had a cooler full of Diet Coke and bottles of water.

Lucas and Del were in Lucas's truck, and unloaded three rods of round quarter-inch steel, six feet long; Lucas had ground the tips to sharp points.

He pointed downstream. "We'll start down there. It's thicker. Look at any space big enough to be a grave. Just poke it; it hasn't rained, so if it's been turned over, you should be able to tell."

Flowers was wearing a straw cowboy hat and aviator glasses. He looked downstream and said, "It's gonna be back in the woods, I think. Probably on the slope down toward the river. If he thought about it, he wouldn't want to put her anyplace that might be farmed someday."

"But not too close to the river," Lucas said. "He wouldn't want it to wash out."

They were probing, complaining to each other about the stupidity of it, for an hour, and were a hundred yards south of the house when Flowers said, "Hey." He was just under the edge of the crown of a box elder, thirty feet from the river.

"Find something?"

"Something," Flowers said. They gathered around with their rods, probing. The earth beneath them had been disturbed at some time— squatting, they could see a depression a couple of feet across, maybe four feet long. The feel of the dirt changed across the line. But there was also an aspen tree, with a trunk the size of a man's ankle, just off the depression, with one visible root growing across it.

"I don't know. The tree . . ."

"But feel this . . ." Flowers gave his rod to Lucas. "You can feel how easy it went down, how it got softer the lower you go . . . and then, doesn't that feel like a plastic sack or something? You can *feel* it . . ."

"Feel something," Lucas admitted.

They passed the rod to Del, who said he could feel it, too. Lucas wiped his lower lip with the back of his hand: sweaty and getting dirty. "What do you think? Get crime scene down here, or go get a shovel?"

They all looked up at the shack, and the cars, and then Del said, "Would you feel like a bigger asshole if you got a crew down here and there was nothing? Or if you dug a hole yourself and it was something?"

Lucas and Flowers looked at each other and they shrugged simultaneously and Flowers said, "I'll get the shovel."

While Flowers went for the shovel, Del probed some more with the rod, scratched it with the tip of a pocketknife, pulled it out and looked at the scratch. "Three feet," he said. "Or damn close to it."

They decided to cut a narrow hole, straight down, one shovel wide, two feet long. The ground was soft all the way, river-bottom silt; grass roots, one tree root, then sandy stuff, and at the bottom of the hole, a glimpse of green.

"Garbage bag," Flowers grunted. He lay down, reached in the hole and began pulling dirt out with one hand. When they'd cleared a six-inch square of plastic, Del handed him his knife, and Flowers cut the plastic. Didn't smell much of anything; Flowers pulled the sliced plastic apart, then said to Lucas, "You're standing in the light, man."

Lucas moved to the other side of the hole, still peering in, and Flowers got farther down into the hole, poked for a moment, then pushed himself out and rolled onto his butt, dusting his hands. "I can see some jeans," he said.

THE CRIME-SCENE SUPERVISOR gave them an endless amount of shit about digging out the hole, until Lucas told him to go fuck himself and didn't smile.

The guy was about to try for the last word when Flowers, his shirt still soaked with sweat and grime, added, "If you'd done the crime-scene work right, we wouldn't have had to come down and do it for you, dick-weed."

"Hey. You didn't say anything about a fuckin' graveyard."

"It's all a crime scene," Flowers said. He wasn't smiling, either. "You shoulda found it."

THEY TOOK two hours getting the bag out of the hole. Lucas didn't want to look at it. He and Flowers and Del gathered around the back of Flowers's boat and drank Diet Cokes and Flowers pulled out a fishing rod and reel and rigged a slip sinker on it, talking about going down to the river and trying for some catfish.

"Got a shovel, we'll find some worms somewhere . . ."

The crime-scene guy came over and said, "It's out. Whoever it is had a short black haircut and wore thirty-six/thirty-four Wrangler jeans, Jockey shorts, and size-eleven Adidas."

Lucas was bewildered. "Size eleven? Jockey shorts?"

AND, one of the crime-scene guys said a few minutes later, whoever it was still carried his wallet. Inside the wallet was an Illinois driver's license issued eight years earlier in the name of Theodore Lane.

"What the fuck is going on here?" Del asked.

THE CRIME-SCENE guy called for a bigger crew with ground-penetrating radar and a gas sniffer. Two dozen people milled around, talking about secret graveyards, but there was no real graveyard.

At three o'clock they found the only other grave that they would find. It was fifty yards south of the first one, in an area that Lucas, Del, and Flowers had walked right over. The top of the grave was occupied by a driftwood stump, which was why they missed it. The bottom was occupied by Gabriella Coombs, curled into a knot in a green plastic garbage bag, wasted and shot through with maggots, almost gone now . . .

AT HOME THAT NIGHT, after taking a twenty-minute shower, trying to get the stink of death off him, Lucas went down to dinner and grumped at everyone. Coombs was going to haunt him for a while; chip a chunk off the granite of his ass.

The other thing that bothered him a bit was that he knew, from experience, that he'd forget her, that in a year or so, he'd have put her away, and would hardly think of her again.

He'd gotten down a beer and was watching a Cubs game, when Weather came with the phone, and handed it to him. The medical examiner said, "I took a look and can tell you only one thing: it's gonna be tough. Nothing obvious on the body, nothing under her fingernails. We'll process anything we find, but if there wasn't much to start with, and it's been days since she went into the ground . . ."

"Goddamnit," Lucas said. "There's gotta be something."

There was; but it took him a while to think of it.

27

LUCY COOMBS CAME to the door barefoot and when she saw Lucas standing there, hands in his pockets, asked through the screen door, "Why didn't you come and tell me?"

Coombs had gone to look at her daughter at the medical examiner's. Lucas had avoided all of it: had sent Jerry Wilson, the original St. Paul investigator in the Marilyn Coombs murder, to tell Lucy that her daughter's body had been found.

Now, standing on her porch, he said, "I couldn't bear to do it."

She looked at him for a few seconds, then pushed the screen door open. "You better come in."

SHE HAD a plastic jug of iced tea in the refrigerator and they went out back and sat on the patio, and she told him how she, a man that she thought may have been Gabriella's father, and another couple, had traveled around the Canadian Rockies in a converted old Molson's beer truck, smoking dope and listening to all the furthest-out rock tapes, going to summer festivals and living in provincial parks . . . and nailing a couple of other good-looking guys along the way. "I always had this thing for hot-looking blond guys, no offense."

"None taken."

"Summer of my life. Good time, good dope, good friends, and

knocked up big-time," she said, sitting sideways on a redwood picnic-table bench. "God, I loved the kid. But I wasn't a good mother. We used to fight . . . we started fighting when she was twelve and didn't quit until she was twenty-two. I think we both had to grow up."

She rambled on for a while, and then asked the question that had been out there, in the papers and everywhere else. "Are you sure Amity Anderson did it?"

"No," Lucas said. "In fact, I don't think she did. She might have, but there are some problems . . ."

HE'D GONE BACK to Eau Claire, he told her, and talked to Frazier, the sheriff's deputy, and all the other investigators they could reach. Amity Anderson had no boyfriend, they said. Just didn't have one. They accounted for her nights, they looked at phone records, at gasoline credit-card receipts, they checked her mail. She had no boyfriend . . .

And she had that alibi for the night Donaldson was killed. The alibi was solid. Would Leslie Widdler have gone into the house on his own? Wouldn't he have wanted a backup? The night Gabriella disappeared, there were two phone calls from Anderson's house, one early, one fairly late. The recipients of the phone calls agreed that they'd spoken to her.

"That doesn't mean she couldn't have done it, but it's pretty thin," Lucas said.

"You think Widdler's wife, I saw her name in the newspaper . . ."

"Jane."

"You think she was involved?" Coombs asked.

"I think so," Lucas said. "Anderson insists that she was—and to some of us, she sounds like she's telling the truth."

"So it would be Jane Widdler who killed Gabriella."

"Probably helped her husband," Lucas said. "Yes. They worked as a team."

Coombs took a sip of lemonade, sucked on an ice cube for a moment. "Are you going to get her?"

"I don't know," Lucas said. "I see a possibility—but we'd need your help."

"My help?"

"Yes. Because of your mother, and the Armstrong quilts, you're in . . . sort of a unique position to help us," Lucas said.

She looked him over for a minute, sucking on the ice cube, then let it slip back into the glass, and leaned toward him. "I'll help, if I can. But you know what I'd really like? Because of Mom and Gabriella?"

"What?"

Her voice came out as a snarl: "I'd like a nice cold slice of revenge. That's what I'd like."

JANE WIDDLER was sitting on the floor in a pool of light, working the books and boxes and shipping tape. The cops had photographed everything, with measurement scales, and were looking at lists of stolen antiques. But Widdler knew that the store stock was all legitimate; she had receipts for it all.

Leslie's suicide and implication in the Bucher, Donaldson, and Toms murders had flashed out over the Internet antique forums, so everybody who was anybody knew about it. She'd had tentative calls from other dealers, sniffing around for deals.

At first, she'd been angry about it, the goddamn vultures. Then she realized she could move quite a bit of stuff, at cost or even a small profit, and pile up some serious dollars. She was doing that—took Visa, MasterCard, or American Express, shipping the next day . . .

Her clerk had walked out. Left a note saying that she couldn't deal with the pressure, asked that her last paycheck be mailed to her apartment. Good luck on that, Widdler thought, pouring plastic peanuts around a bubble-wrapped nineteenth-century Tiffany-style French-made china clock, set in a shipping box. Eight hundred dollars, four hundred less than the in-store price, but cash was cash.

There was a knock on the front door, on the glass. The CLOSED sign was on the door, and she ignored it. Knock again, louder this time. Maybe the police? Or the lawyer?

She made a frown look and got to her feet, spanked her hands together to get rid of the Styrofoam dust, and walked to the door. Outside, a woman with huge bushy blond hair, dressed in a shapeless green muumuu and sandals, had cupped her hands around her eyes and was peering through the window in the door.

Irritated, Widdler walked toward the door, shaking her head, jabbing her finger at the CLOSED sign. The woman held up a file folder, then pressed it to the glass and jabbed her own finger at it. Making an even deeper frown look, Widdler put her nose next to the glass and peered at the tab on the file folder. It said, in a spidery hand, "Armstrong quilts."

The woman on the other side shouted, loud enough to be heard through the door, "I'm Lucy Coombs. I'm Marilyn Coombs's daughter. Open the door."

Widdler thought, "Shit," then thought, "Elegance." What is this? She threw the lock, opened the door a crack.

"I'm closed."

"Are you Jane Widdler?"

Widdler thought about it for a second, then nodded. "Yes."

The words came tumbling out of the woman's mouth, a rehearsed spiel: "My mother's house has been attached by the Walker and now by the Milwaukee museum. They say the Armstrong quilts are fakes and they want their money back and that it was all a big tax fraud. I have her file. There's a letter in it and there's a note that says you and your husband were Cannon Associates and that you got most of the money. Mom's house was worth two hundred thousand dollars and I'm supposed to be the heir and now I'm not going to get anything. I'll sell you the original file for two hundred thousand dollars, or I'm going to take it to the police. The museums can get the money back from you, not from me."

The woman sounded crazy-angry, but the part about Cannon and the Armstrongs wasn't crazy.

"Wait-wait-wait," said Widdler, opening the door another inch.

"I'm not going to talk to you here. I'm afraid of you and I'm afraid the police are tapping your telephones. They tap everything now, everything, the National Security Agency, the CIA, the FBI. I brought this copy of the file and the letter and inside there's a telephone number where you can call me at eleven o'clock tomorrow morning. It's at a Wal-Mart and if you don't call me, you won't be able to find me and I'll go to the police."

The woman thrust the file through the door and Widdler took it, as much to keep it from falling to the floor, as anything, and Widdler said, "Wait-wait-wait" but the woman went running off through the parking lot, vaulted into the junkiest car that had ever been parked at the store, a battered Chevy that looked as though it had been painted yellow with a brush, with rust holes in the back fender. The woman started it, a throaty rumble, and sped away.

Jane looked at the file. "What?"

AT TEN O'CLOCK the next morning, Jane Widdler got self-consciously into her Audi and drove slowly away from her house, watching everything. Looking for other cars, for the same cars, for cars that were driving too slow, for parked cars with men in them. She would be headed, eventually, for the Wal-Mart.

The night before, given the phone number by Coombs, she'd found the Wal-Mart in a cross-reference website. She'd also found Coombs's address. She'd sat and thought about it for a while, and then she'd driven slowly, carefully, watchfully out to scout the Wal-Mart, where she found a block of three pay phones on the wall inside the entrance. One showed the number given her by Coombs. She'd noted the number of all three, then had driven another circuitous route out to the interstate, and then across town to Coombs's house.

She considered the possibility of shooting the woman at her own door; but then, what about the file? Would she have time to find it? Were there other people in the house?

Too much uncertainty. She'd gone home—the police had finished their search—and had drunk most of a bottle of wine.

In the morning, at ten o'clock, she started out, a feeling of climax sitting on her shoulders.

She drove six blocks, watching her back, then hooked into the jumble of narrow streets to the north, on backstreets, long narrow lanes, into dead ends, where she turned and came back out, looking at her tail. In ten minutes, she'd seen precisely nothing . . .

LUCAS WAS in his car three blocks away, Flowers bringing up the rear, Jenkins and Shrake on the flanks. Overhead—way overhead—Jerrod was in a Highway Patrol helicopter, tracking Widdler with glasses. Del was with Coombs.

They tracked her for a half mile, out to the interstate, away from the Wal-Mart, into a Best Buy. She disappeared into the store.

"What do we do?" Flowers called.

"Shrake? Jenkins?" Lucas called. "Can one of you go in?"

"Got it," Shrake said.

BUT SHRAKE had been a block away and almost got clipped by a cell-phone user when he tried to make an illegal turn. The parking lot was jammed and he didn't want to dump the car at the door; she might spot it. By the time he got parked, and got out and crossed the lot without running, and got through the front door, he was too late. She was walking directly toward him, toward the exit. He continued toward the new-release movie rack, and when she'd gone out, he called, "She's out, she's out . . ."

"Got her," Lucas said, watching from across the street. "What'd she do in there?"

"Don't know. Want me to ask around?"

Lucas thought, then said, "Ah . . . fuck it. Catch up with us. She's back in her car."

"She's heading for the Wal-Mart," Jerrold called five minutes later. "Tell Del to put Coombs in the store."

LUCAS AND HIS GROUP tracked her right into the Wal-Mart parking lot, past the main entrance, to the Garden Shop. "She's going in the back side, through the Garden Shop," Lucas called to Del.

"I'm heading that way . . . I'm heading that way," Del called back. Then "I got her," and "Lucy is headed for the phones."

WIDDLER WATCHED COOMBS from halfway across the store. Watched her for three or four minutes, looking for anybody who might be a cop. Coombs was wearing another muumuu, a blue one this time. She was a heavy woman, big gut, chunky around the hips, a potato-eating prole, a leftover hippie. She stood just inside the entrance, looking at the bank of three yellow pay phones.

Widdler, in Women's Clothing, watched for another minute. Nothing moving. She saw Coombs looking at her watch. If Davenport was behind this, Widdler thought, he could have tapped the phone, but they wouldn't have let Coombs come in her by herself, would they?

Widdler took the cell phone out of her pocket and dialed. She watched Coombs pick up the pay phone. Coombs said, "Hello," and Widdler said, "Hang up, and go two phones down. I'll call you on that one in two seconds."

Coombs hung up the phone, moved down two. Stared at the phone—didn't call anyone, didn't look at anyone. Widdler punched in the number. Coombs answered and Widdler said, "I don't have two hundred thousand dollars. I could get eighty thousand now and pay you the rest later, but I want the original of the letter."

"Why would you pay me the rest later?" Coombs asked. "If I didn't have the letter?"

"Because you could cause me a lot of trouble by talking to the police, even without the original," Widdler said. "You'd be in trouble yourself, for destroying evidence, but I don't know how crazy you are. I'd pay you, all right, but I don't have the cash now."

"I don't know," Coombs said.

Widdler: "You don't have any time to think about it. Say yes or say no, or I'll hang up."

"Ah, God. You'd pay me?"

Coombs sounded exactly like a stoned-out hippie, hoping against all expectation that something good might happen to her. "Yes. Of course. I've already started getting the money together."

"All right," Coombs said. "But I'll go to the cops if you don't pay me the rest . . ."

"*Just tell me what you want to do.*"

"Here's what I've worked out," Coombs said. "I don't trust you and I want to look at the money. So I want to do it in a semipublic place where I can scream for help if you try to hurt me, but where we'll have a little privacy. I'll scream, I really will."

"Where?"

"There's a farmers' market today in St. Paul, downtown, across from Macy's . . ."

"No. That's too open," Widdler said. "The ladies' room at Macy's, there'd still be people around . . ."

"But we couldn't say a word, I couldn't look at the money . . ." Coombs whined.

"The Macy's parking ramp in St. Paul?" Widdler suggested.

"That's too scary . . . Do you know where Mears Park is? Where the art studios are?"

"That'll be good, that'd be perfect," Widdler said. "One o'clock?"

"I'll scream if you do anything," Coombs said.

"Then I go to trial and you won't get a penny," Widdler said.

Another long pause. Then, "Okay."

"Bring the originals. I'm not bargaining anymore. Bring the originals or I'm gone," Jane Widdler said.

WITH JERROLD in the air, and Flowers, Shrake, and Jenkins on the ground escorting Widdler back to her shop, Lucas and Del helped Coombs out of the muumuu and then out of the ballistic vest and the wire. "Jeez, that thing is hot," she said. She'd told them about the phone conversation on the way out of the store. "She was behind me?"

"Yeah. And I was behind her," Del grunted. "We were cool."

"Think she'll come?" Coombs asked.

"I hope," Lucas said.

"What happened with the phone?" Del asked.

"We don't know, but she didn't use her own and she switched phones inside," Lucas said. "I think she bought a phone at Best Buy."

"She's no dummy," Del said.

"But we sold her," Lucas said, grinning at the other two. "Lucy, you were great. You could be a cop."

She shook her head. "No, I couldn't. Cops pretend to be friends with people, and then they turn them in. I couldn't do that."

THE KEY, Lucas told Coombs, was to get Widdler on tape acknowledging the quilt fraud, that she knew of the Donaldson killing . . . anything that would get her into the slipstream of the killings. Once they had her there, circumstantial evidence would do the rest.

"Get her talking," Del said. "Get her rolling . . ."

MEARS PARK WAS a leafy square, one block on each edge. The buildings on three sides were rehabbed warehouses, combinations of apartments, studios, offices, and retail, including the studio of Ron Stack, the artist that Gabriella had dated. The fourth side was newer, offices, a food court, and apartments in brick-and-glass towers.

"As soon as she's in the park, we'll have you come around the block in the car, since she's seen the car," Lucas told Coombs. "Shrake will pull away from the curb, and that'll leave a parking space open for you."

Del pointed at an unmarked cop car, already in the parking slot. Lucas pointed out the route: "Pull in, then walk down the sidewalk over here. Del's gonna be on the other side of the park, back through the trees, closing in, as soon as we know where she's at. Flowers and

I will be behind the doors in Parkside Lofts. We'll be invisible, but as long as you're on the sidewalk, we'll be right across the street from you. Sit on this bench . . ." He pointed. "There's gonna be a guy on the bench eating his lunch."

"Pretty obvious," Coombs said.

Lucas shook his head: "Not really. When people are suspicious, they look for a bum pushing a shopping cart or a woman with a baby carriage, but a guy in a suit eating a peanut-butter sandwich and talking on a cell phone . . . Won't look at him twice. Besides, as soon as you show up, he's gonna walk away. That gives you the bench. Talk to her on the bench."

"What if she doesn't want to talk there?" Coombs asked.

"Go with the flow—but as soon as you feel the slightest bit uncomfortable about *anything*, break it off," Lucas said. "Anything, I'm serious. If you feel uncomfortable, you're probably right, something's screwed up. Get out. Scream, run, whatever. Get away from her."

Coombs nodded, and started to tear up. "It'd be a shame if she got all three of us."

"Don't even think that," Lucas said.

Del said to Lucas, "Man, I'm getting the shakes. Bringing a civilian in . . ."

Lucas looked at Coombs. "What do you think, Lucy? We can call it off, try to get her to talk by phone."

Coombs shook her head, wiped her eyes with her knuckles. "I'm a big chicken—if she looks at me cross-eyed, I'm runnin'."

JANE WIDDLER GOT to the park at noon, an hour early. She'd parked in the Galtier Plaza parking ramp, had taken the elevator to the Skyway level, had scouted the Skyways and then the approaches to the park, tagged by three female cops borrowed from St. Paul. Finally, she walked all four sides of the park, and walked in and out of the buildings on all four sides.

"She's figuring out where she can run," Flowers said. They were on the second floor of the Parkside Lofts, looking out a window.

Lucas nodded. "Yup. We haven't seen her in anything but high heels. Now she's wearing sneaks."

When she'd finished scouting, Widdler walked across the street to Galtier Plaza, went to the Subway in the food court, got a roasted chicken sandwich, and sat in a window looking out at the park.

Jenkins was at the opposite end of the food court with three slices of pizza and a Diet Coke. "She's cool," he told Lucas, talking on his cell phone, sitting sideways to Widdler, watching her with peripheral vision.

At two minutes to one, Lucas called Del and said, "Put her in."

SHRAKE HAD BEEN HIDING in a condo lobby. Now he ambled up to the corner, waited for a car to pass, jaywalked to his car, got in, watched in his rearview mirror until he saw Coombs turn the corner. He pulled out, turned the corner, and was out of sight . . .

Coombs saw him leave, pulled up to the parallel-parking spot, and spent three minutes getting straight, carefully plugged the meter, and then started walking around the perimeter of the park, looking down into it.

Jenkins, on the cell phone, said, "She's moving."

Lucas and Flowers had moved to the glass doors of the building across the street from the bench. Coombs was walking slowly on the sidewalk, peering into the park. She was still wearing the blue muumuu and was carrying a Macy's bag, looking fat and slow.

Widdler stepped out of Galtier into the sunshine, slipping on sunglasses. She was carrying an oversized Coach bag, black leather, big enough to hold eighty thousand. She crossed the street, walking casually. She was forty yards behind Coombs, and closing.

"Lucy doesn't see her," Flowers said.

"We're okay, we're okay," Lucas said.

A guy eating his lunch got off the park bench, tossed the brown bag in a trash container, and started across the street, talking on a cell phone, not looking back. A St. Paul vice cop. Del called: "I'm coming in."

"We're in," Shrake said. He and Jenkins were moving down the east side of the park, where they could cut Widdler off, if she made a run for it.

From Lucas's point of view, everything seemed to slow down.

Coombs plodding toward the bench, sitting down in slow motion, looking tired, the Macy's bag flapping on the bench . . .

Widdler closing in on her, from behind, twenty yards, ten, five, her hand going in her purse, back out.

LUCAS: "Shit. She's got a gun."

He and Flowers hit the door simultaneously, Flowers screaming, "Lucy, Lucy, watch out, gun . . ."

Widdler never heard them or saw them. Her world had narrowed to the target on the bench, the big fat hippie with the bushy hair and the Macy's bag, and there was nobody around and she was moving in fast, the woman might never see her . . .

Widdler had the gun in her hand, a four-inch double-trigger, double-barreled derringer that Leslie had given her to keep in her car. He'd said, "It's not accurate at more than two feet, so you pretty much got to push it right against the guy . . ." He'd been talking about a rapist, but there was no reason that Coombs should be any different.

The gun was coming up and somewhere, in the corner of her

mind, she realized that there was a commotion but she was committed and then Coombs was half standing and turning to meet her and the gun was going and she heard somebody shout and then she shot Coombs in the heart. The blast was terrific, and her hand kicked back, and there was a man in the street and car brakes screeching and she never thought, just reacted, and she turned and the gun was still up . . .

And suddenly she was swatted on the ankle and a screaming pain arced through her body and she hit the ground and she registered a shot; she got a mouthful of concrete dust and her glasses came off and she rolled and Lucas Davenport was looking down at her . . .

LUCAS NEARLY RAN through a car. The car screeched and he was knocked forward and registered the face of a screaming woman behind the windshield, and he saw Coombs get shot and he was rolling and then he heard a shot from behind him, saw Flowers with a gun and saw Widdler go down, then he was up and running and looking down at Widdler.

Coombs was on her hands and knees, looking up at him, and she said, "I'm okay, I'm okay."

And Lucas turned to Flowers, as he straddled Widdler, his heart thumping, Flowers pale as an Irish nun, and Lucas asked, "Why'd you shoot her in the foot?"

Then Widdler screamed, the pain flooding her, hit in the ankle, her foot half gone. "No, no, no . . ."

Lucas said, "Get an ambulance rolling," and he turned to Coombs, who'd gone back to her hands and knees.

"You sure you're . . . ?"

Coombs was right there with Widdler's derringer. She pointed the tiny gun at Widdler's eye from one inch away and pulled both triggers.

The second blast was as big as the first one, and Widdler's head rocked back as though she'd been kicked by a horse.

Lucas dropped on Coombs and twisted the gun out of her hand, but before he got that done, Coombs had just enough time to look into Widdler's single remaining dead eye and say, "Fuck you."

28

THE ST. PAUL COPS closed off the park and the street where the shooting took place, stringing tape and blocking access with squad cars. Local television stations put cameras in the surrounding condos, and got some brutal shots of Widdler's dead body, faceup and crumbled like a ball of paper, crime-scene guys in golf shirts standing around like death clerks.

Coombs went to jail for three days. In the immediate confusion over the shooting, Ramsay County attorney Jack Wentz showed up for the cameras and announced that he would charge Coombs with murder; and that he would further investigate the regrettable actions by state investigative officers, which led to an unnecessary killing on his turf.

Lucas, talking behind the scenes, argued that the shooting was part of a continuing violent action—that the killing of Widdler was an unfortunate but understandable reaction of a woman who'd been shot and hit, and the fact that she was wearing a ballistic vest did not lessen the shock. The close-range shooting, he said, combined with the real shooting of Widdler by Flowers, the fact that Coombs had seen Lucas knocked down by a car, that people had been screaming at her, that Widdler had been thrashing around on the ground next to her, had so confused Coombs that she'd picked up the loose gun and fired it without understanding the situation.

Wentz, replying off the record, said Lucas was trying to protect himself and the other incompetents who'd set up the sting.

THE NEXT DAY, the local newspaper columnists unanimously landed on the county attorney's back, and the television commentators followed on the noon, evening, and late-night news.

The *Star Tribune* columnist said, "Mrs. Coombs's mother and daughter were killed by this witch, and she'd just been shot in the chest herself—thank God she was wearing a bulletproof vest, or the whole family would have been wiped out by one serial killer. That Wentz would even consider bringing charges suggests that he needs some quiet time in a corner, on a stool, with a pointy hat to focus his thoughts, if he has any . . ."

The police federation said it would revisit its endorsement of Wentz for anything, and the governor said off-the-record that the county attorney was full of shit, which was promptly reported, of course, then disavowed by Neil Mitford, but the message had been sent.

The county attorney said that what he'd really meant to say was that he'd investigate, and the issue would be taken to the grand jury.

Coombs was released after three days in jail, with her house as bond. She never went back—the election was coming, and the grand jury, which did what Wentz told them to do, decided not to indict.

ROSE MARIE ROUX told Lucas, "You got lucky. About six ways. If Coombs had wound up dead, you might be looking for a job—this being an election year."

"I know. The thought never crossed my mind that Widdler'd yank out a gun and try to shoot her in broad daylight on a main street," Lucas said. "And you know what? If it'd been real, if it hadn't been a setup, she'd have gotten away with it. She'd have walked across the street and gone upstairs to the Skyway and then over to Galtier and down in the parking garage, and that would have been it."

Mitford, who had come over to listen in, said, to Rose Marie, "We pay him to be lucky. Lucky is even better than good. Everybody is happy." And to Lucas: "Don't get unlucky."

THE PUBLIC ARGUMENT would have gone on, and could have gotten nastier, except that Ruffe Ignace published an exclusive interview with the teenage victim of Burt Kline's sexual attentions.

Ignace did a masterly job of combining jiggle-text with writing-around, and everybody over fourteen understood that Kline had semicolon-shaped freckles where many people wouldn't have looked, and that the comely teenager had been asked (and agreed) to model white cotton thongs and a half-shell bra in a casino hotel in Mille Lacs. Ignace did not actually say that little pink nipples were peeking out, but you got the idea.

Coombs moved to page seven.

AMITY ANDERSON was charged with receiving stolen goods, but in Wentz's opinion, nothing would hold up. "We don't have any witnesses," he complained. "They're all dead."

THE DES MOINES prosecutor who had gotten a conviction in the Toms' case said, "I'm still convinced that Mr. Child was involved in the murder," but the tide was going out, and the state attorney general said the case would be revisited. Sandy spent a week in Iowa leading a staff attorney through the paper accumulated in Minnesota.

THE ESTATES of Claire Donaldson, Jacob Toms, and Constance Bucher sued the estates of Leslie and Jane Widdler for recovery of stolen antiques, for wrongful death, and for a laundry list of other offenses that guaranteed that all the Widdler assets would wind up in the hands of the heirs of Donaldson, Toms, and Bucher, et al., and an assortment of lawyers. The Widdler house on Minnehaha Creek was put up for sale, under the supervision of the Hennepin County District Court, as part of the consolidation of Widdler assets.

LUCAS ASKED Flowers again, "Why in the hell did you shoot her in the foot?"

Flowers shook his head. "I was aiming for center-of-mass."

"Jesus Christ, man, you gotta spend some time on the range," Lucas said, his temper working up.

"I don't want to shoot anyone," Flowers said. "If you manage things right, you shouldn't have to."

"You believe in management?" Lucas asked, getting hot. "Fuckhead? You believe in management?"

"I didn't get my ass run over by a car," Flowers snapped. "I managed that."

Del, who was there, said, "Let's back this off."

Lucas, that night, said to Weather, "That fuckin' Flowers."

She said, "Yeah, but you gotta admit, he's got a nice ass."

AFTER A brief professional discussion, the museums that owned the Armstrong quilts decided that the sewing basket had probably been Armstrong's and that the quilts were genuine.

Coombs said, "They know that's wrong."

Lucas said, "Shhh . . ." He was visiting, on the quiet, two weeks after the shooting of Widdler; they were sitting on the back patio, drinking rum lemonades with maraschino cherries.

She said, "You know, I had time not to shoot her. I did it on purpose."

Lucas: "Even if I'd heard you say that, I'd ask, 'Would you do it again if you thought you'd spend thirty years in prison?'"

Coombs considered, then said, "I don't know. Sitting there in jail, the . . . practicalities sort of set in. But the way it worked out, I'm not sorry I did it."

"You should go down to the cathedral and light a couple of candles," Lucas said. "If there wasn't an election coming, Wentz might have told everybody to go fuck themselves and you'd have a hard road to go."

"I'd have been convicted?"

"Oh . . . probably not," Lucas said, taking a sip of lemonade. "With Flowers and me testifying for you, you'd have skated it, I think. Probably would have had to give your house to an attorney, though."

She looked around her house, a pleasant place, mellow, redolent of the scent of candles and flowers and herbs of the smokable kind, and said, "I was hoping to leave it to Gabriella, when I was ninety and she was seventy."

"I'm sorry," Lucas said. And he was, right down in his heart. "I'm so sorry."

AT THE END of the summer, a man named Porfirio Quique Ramírez, an illegal immigrant late of Piedras Negras, was cutting a new border around the lilac hedge on the Widdlers' side yard, in preparation for the sale of the house. The tip of his spade clanged off something metallic a few inches below the surface. He brushed away the dirt and found a green metal cashbox.

Porfirio, no fool, turned his back to the house as he lifted it out of the ground, popped open the top, looked inside for five seconds, slammed the lid, stuffed the box under his shirt, pinned it there with his elbow, and walked quickly out to his boss's truck. All the way out, he was thinking, "Let them be real."

They were. Two weeks later, he crossed the Rio Grande again, headed south. All but three of the gold coins were hidden in the roof of the trunk of his new car, which was used, but had only twenty-five thousand on the clock.

The Mexican border guard waved him through, touched the front fender of the silver SL500—the very car the Widdlers had dreamed of—for good luck, and called, smiling, to the mustachioed, sharp-dressed hometown boy behind the wheel,

"Hey, man! Mercedes-Benz!"

Author's Note

There are two people mentioned in this book who are *not* fictional.

Mentioned in passing is Harrington, the St. Paul chief of police. His full name is John Harrington, he *is* the chief, and years ago, when he was a street cop, he used to beat the bejesus out of me at a local karate club. One time back then, I was walking past a gun shop near the dojo, and saw in the window a shotgun with a minimum-length barrel and a pistol grip. I bumped into Harrington going in the door of the dojo—he was dressed in winter street clothes—and I mentioned the shotgun to him. He said, "Let's go look." So we walked back to the shop, big guys, unshaven, in jeans and parkas and watch caps, and maybe a little beat-up, and went inside, and John said, "My friend here saw a shotgun . . ." The clerk got it out and delivered his deathless line as he handed it over the counter to Sergeant Harrington: "Just what you need for going into a 7-Eleven, huh?" In any case, my wife and I were delighted when John was named St. Paul chief. He's the kind of guy you want in a job like that.

Karen Palm, mentioned early in the book as the owner of the Minnesota Music Café, is a longtime supporter of the St. Paul Police Federation and hosts some of the more interesting music to come through town; along with a lot of cops. Sloan's bar, Shooters, is modeled on the Minnesota Music Café.

Nancy Nicholson (who is not mentioned by name as a character) took a good chunk of time out of her busy day to show me around the most spectacular private mansion in St. Paul, and introduced me to such subjects as torchieres and butlers' pantries, the existence of which I hadn't even suspected, much less known how to spell. Thank you, Nancy.

Lucas used *The Antiques Price Guide,* by Judith Miller, when he was researching antiques. That's a real guide, published by Dorling Kindersley (DK), and I used it to get a hold on the values mentioned in the book.

—J.S.

ABERDEEN
CITY
LIBRARIES